State v. Claus

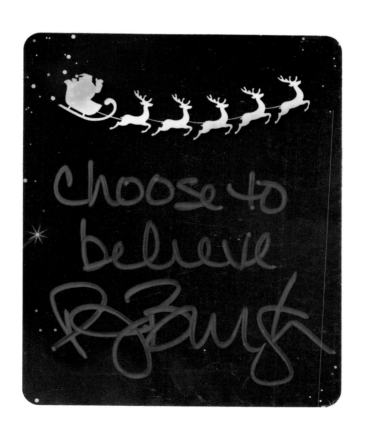

STATE
V.
CLAUS

~~~~~~

P. Jo Anne Burgh

TUXEDO CAT PRESS
Glastonbury, Connecticut

Published by:
Tuxedo Cat Press
http://tuxedocatpress.com

ISBN: 978-1-7357157-0-4 (paperback)
ISBN: 978-1-7357157-1-1 (ebook)
Library of Congress Control Number 2020917740

Cover design by Design for Writers
Interior formatting by Polgarus Studios
Author photograph by Christine Penney

To Mom and Dad, with love

CONTENTS

Tonight

When I was a little girl, I loved Christmas Eve, because it meant the best day of the year was almost here. Candy canes, cocoa with marshmallows, gingerbread men with buttercream faces. Santa Claus and his reindeer and the list he checked twice. My brother and me hanging empty stockings with our names embroidered across the tops, and then bounding down the stairs Christmas morning to find those stockings bulging with gifts. Ripping off colorful wrappings amid shrieks of excitement, because Santa always, always brought what we asked for. That jolly old guy never let us down, not once.

This year, the best thing about Christmas Eve is that I'm finally old news. My home rings with silence. The reporters who lurked outside my townhouse, my office, my life, have decamped in favor of a more interesting disaster. Yesterday's news is lining today's garbage cans, or so people said before everything went digital.

Around noon, I called my mother in Phoenix to wish her a merry Christmas. It was a calculated decision. My stepfather has dozens of grandchildren, and on Christmas Eve, they descend en masse on Mom and Phil's condo. If I didn't reach Mom first, she'd call in the evening so the kids could wish Auntie Meg in Connecticut a merry Christmas. The prospect of all these semi-relatives chirping with holiday cheer was more than I could stomach.

Mom doesn't follow Hartford news anymore. Still, I found myself asking, "What did the kids ask Santa for?"

"Oh, they know better than that," my mother said. "They're too grown up to believe in Santa Claus."

Too grown up. Maybe that's my problem. I need to grow up.

I've only spoken with two other humans today: the girl who answered the phone at Hunan Gardens, and the pudgy kid who delivered my food. If he recognized me from the news, he didn't let on. He wished me a merry Christmas. I told him I'm Jewish (even though I'm not), because only non-Christians or pathetic losers would spend Christmas Eve alone with Kung Pao chicken.

I plunk the bags on the kitchen table. Two of my cats, Harry and David, gallumph down the stairs, summoned by the aroma of sesame shrimp. Lulu, who lived in my office when I had one, used to stand on my desk demanding a share of my lunch. Now, she huddles under the bed in the guest room while Harry and David sniff and scratch outside her door.

The boys wind around my legs as I unpack my order. With all this food, I won't need to shop until New Year's. A waxed paper packet contains a dozen fortune cookies. Whoever assembled the order must have assumed I was having a party.

I pour the last of the pinot grigio, upending the bottle to get every drop. "To folly," I say; my voice cracks. I hold up my glass, but there's no one to clink with.

The cats stand on their hind legs, sniffing the plastic containers. Egg rolls and fried dumplings sounded appetizing an hour ago, but nothing appeals now. I'll eat it anyway. I didn't get to be size fourteen by accident. Unless. . . .

Before my nerve fails, I pick up the phone. My heart pounds as I punch the buttons.

"Hello?" Holly says as if she doesn't have Caller ID.

"It's me."

"Hi." Her voice is cool.

I should have planned an opener. Instead, I say the first thing that comes into my head: "Just wanted to wish you a merry Christmas."

"Go ahead." She's not giving an inch, and I'm tempted to hang up. I'm not the only one who was wrong.

But I miss my friend. At long last, the dust is settling. I push on: "Merry Christmas."

"Okay." Not welcoming, but not slamming the phone down, either.

With all the casualness I can muster, as if we just talked this morning, I toss out the invitation: "Listen, I was wondering if you ate yet. I ordered Chinese, and I guess I got carried away, because I've got a boatload of food here and I'll never finish it all, and I thought maybe if you weren't doing anything, you might want to come over." *If you're not doing anything. It's Christmas Eve, moron.* I continue, "The kids, too. I've got enough for an army." Amy should be home from college by now. As far as I know, Jack still lives at home.

"They're not here," she says.

"They're not coming for Christmas?" The news startles me out of my discomfort.

"They'll be here tomorrow," Holly says. "Amy's down in Stamford at her boyfriend's, and Jack and his fiancée are at her parents'."

His fiancée. "I didn't know he was engaged." Five months ago, I'd have been her first call for news like that.

"Last weekend," she says, mollifying me slightly.

"Congratulations," I say. "Mother of the groom. All the fun, none of the hassles." Even I can hear the forced jollity in my words. One more shot. If that doesn't work, I'm out of here. "So. Any interest in an egg roll?"

"Is that really why you called?" She's never had much patience for bullshit.

"No," I say. "I'm out of wine."

"Life's a bitch." I can almost hear her unspoken thought: *And so are you.*

I brace myself against the counter. "And I'm sorry." Silence. "I acted like a complete idiot. I was wrong. About everything." Everything she knows, and a lot she doesn't.

More silence. Then— "I was going to call you. I saw the news." The words are a slap: she knew what was happening, and all I got from her was one lousy text, months ago. If the tables had been turned, I'd have called her.

"I should have called you," she says as if reading my mind. "I'm sorry. I was—oh, I don't know. It doesn't matter. I'm just sorry."

"Thanks," I whisper. It's a start.

"Are you okay?"

Hot tears well up, spill over. "I don't know what's going to happen. It's all up to the grievance committee." I scrub away the tears with a paper napkin.

I can feel her casting around for something encouraging. "What does Michael say?"

"He's sure it'll work out, everything'll be okay. The usual crap."

"What about the others? Doesn't Eckert have any connections?"

"—That's all over."

"What do you mean?" But she knows. The squeak on "mean" gives her away.

"I disgraced the firm. They voted me out."

"What the—can they—oh God, Meg. I'm so sorry."

"Yeah, well—I can't say I'm surprised." The signs were there, but I refused to believe them.

Treading lightly now: "Have you decided what you're going to do?"

"Dunno. Assuming I can still practice, I guess I'll open my own firm. It's not like anybody's banging down my door." Funny how things turn out. All I ever wanted a simple, normal life. Nice guy, interesting job. Respectability. Security. Peace.

Too bad nobody in Hartford delivers booze. A distant memory surfaces, and I yank open the freezer. Behind ancient chicken breasts and a frost-covered container of mixed-berry sherbet lurks a bottle of citrus-flavored vodka I once bought for cosmopolitans. "Hey, what goes with vodka?"

"Borscht," Holly says. "What are you doing?"

I pour an inch of vodka into my wineglass. "Making do." I take a sip. "God, that's nasty." One more sip, and I dump it out.

"Cut it out," she says. "You made a mistake. It happens."

Except she doesn't know the half of it. I trudge into the living room and plop down in the oversized rocker-recliner. Harry jumps into my lap, rocking the chair harder.

"What's next?" Holly asks.

"Nobody knows. The state's attorney's talking about charging me with aiding and abetting. Geoff says that's what this professional discipline crap is really about."

"—Geoff—"

"—my lawyer. He thinks they're trying to intimidate me, but it could be—I don't know. If they decide I violated some big-time rule of professional conduct, I could get reprimanded, or have my license suspended, or—" I can't say it.

"You're not going to get disbarred," Holly says. It's her mommy voice, gentle and reassuring. Too bad she doesn't have a clue.

"It's not impossible." The admission sticks in my throat. "The hearing officer already thinks I'm nuts."

Her voice turns hesitant. "Have you heard from Ralph?"

"Not lately." Intentionally vague, but she doesn't know enough to press.

"What if you called him?"

"He wouldn't be there. It's Christmas Eve."

A long silence. I'm about to hang up when she says, "What did you order?"

Tears well up again. I recite the contents of the containers on my table. "Any interest?"

"In the food, not really. But the company. . . ."

I smile even as I wipe away tears. "You don't have to." It's enough that she offered. That she's back in my world, on my side. Not completely fixed, but we're heading in the right direction.

"I know." I can hear in her voice that she's smiling, too. At last. "You going up to Derek's tomorrow?"

My brother lives just outside of Albany. "They're spending the holiday with Cindy's aunt in Boston. They asked me, but I couldn't stand the thought of three days with that crowd." Or their questions.

"You can come here." It's her mommy voice again.

"Thanks, sweetie, but I don't think so." Dressing up, making conversation, sitting through a cheery holiday meal. Just the thought exhausts me.

"I've got a merlot from Chile. Nice stuff." It's the same lilting tone she used to get the kids to eat their carrots.

"Tempting, but I'll pass. You hang out with your daughter-in-law-to-be. Talk about bridesmaid gowns." I stretch my legs. Harry raises his head, eyes half-open. I should put the Chinese in the refrigerator. The last thing I need is now food poisoning.

"Can I wish you a merry Christmas?" she asks.

"You can try, but I don't think it's going to work." I hate how self-pitying I sound. "Sorry. I just—" I can't come up with an excuse.

"Don't worry about it," she says, and I know she means it. "Merry Christmas anyway. And the offer for tomorrow stands. We'll be eating around three."

"You're the best," I say. "And I really am sorry."

"So am I," she says. "Good night."

"Good night." I punch the lighted button labeled *end* and hoist Harry to my shoulder. "Come on, buddy, let's wrap this up." We lumber into the kitchen to find David on the table with his nose buried in a dumpling. "What do you think you're doing?" I demand.

I wipe his face, shoo him off the table, dispose of his prize, and put the remaining food away.

The house is so silent I can practically hear the snow falling. I yawn to try to convince myself I'm tired. Nobody is fooled. "Bedtime," I announce. Good creatures of habit, the boys race up the stairs. I stop in the guest room to cuddle Lulu, but she squirms away from the scent of the other cats on me. Her whiskers tremble; her eyes are round and nervous. I need a new office, if only so she can have her own domain.

I don't expect to fall asleep, but I must have, because something jerks me awake. I sit bolt upright in the darkness, senses prickling. David lifts his head; Harry sleeps on. For a second, possibilities swirl. Then realization drops over me like a fisherman's net. My heart thuds, because I know.

Moving silently, I pull on my robe and find my slippers. The green light of the upstairs alarm panel declares all windows and doors secure. There is only one explanation. A year ago, I'd have written it off as impossible.

A year ago, I had no idea what was possible.

Halfway down the stairs, I step onto the one that creaks. Instantly I freeze. A faint rustling from the living room ceases. Cursing silently, I remain motionless, waiting it out. After what seems like several minutes, another rustle. Part of me wants to run the rest of the way down and burst into the living room shouting. Instead, as quietly as I can manage, I creep down the stairs and across the cold slate floor of the foyer.

The streetlight penetrates the draperies, giving a faint glow to the living room. Squinting into the darkness, I see no one. I stand motionless. Maybe it was my imagination after all.

Someone sneezes.

My stomach drops like I'm in a falling elevator. My heart pounds. I flick the light switch.

Squatting beside the fireplace is a man. He wears black pants, black turtleneck, black gloves. Even his hair is near-black. He is so wiry that for a second, all I can think of is a black-garbed grasshopper. He makes no move, no sound when the light comes on, as if he thinks remaining still and silent will render him invisible. I clear my throat. Only then does he rise to face me, a sheepish smile playing on his lips.

A thousand thoughts rush through my mind, none coherent. Finally, I force words out.

"What the hell are you doing here?"

Book One

The Client

One

One year earlier

It was the Monday after the long Christmas weekend, and all through downtown Hartford, computer monitors sat dark at empty desks. In our office, I was the only lawyer present, the others having elected to enjoy the lull after a blizzard of holiday events. Eckert, our managing partner, believed that the firm's success depended on its reputation in the community, and so the Lundstrom Law Firm attended every possible function. As the firm's litigators, Michael and I went to events involving judges, prosecutors, defense counsel, bar associations, or anybody else we'd want remembering us warmly when it was time to refer a case. Eckert, our probate guru, and Elsa, who handled corporate matters, appeared at parties thrown by or on behalf of wealthy people, business leaders, and high-ranking politicians. Roy, our numbers expert—tax, bankruptcy, real estate— hated social affairs, but he did his part, handing out business cards at functions attended by CPAs, realtors, and members of zoning boards.

Basking in the prospect of an uninterrupted morning, I settled in with a mug of Irish breakfast tea, a blueberry muffin, and my to-do list. Working when other people weren't meant I could scatter emails and voicemail messages all over town, checking those tasks off my list because they just became my opponent's problem. If the morning remained as quiet as I expected, I'd dispose of half a dozen matters before lunch.

At 8:42 a.m., our receptionist, Marilyn, buzzed me. "Belinda on line two."

"Cripes," I muttered through a mouthful of muffin. Belinda was the caseflow coordinator at the criminal court. I swallowed and punched the button. "Good morning, Belinda. Did you have a nice holiday?"

"Yes." Belinda didn't chat. New lawyers would try to engage her in conversation, only to be met with a perplexed stare: *Why are you speaking to me?* "Judge Pearce asked me to call you. They've got someone in lockup who needs representation for an arraignment."

So much for my quiet morning. If a judge asked personally for you to represent someone, "no" was not an acceptable response. Not that I'd turn down this judge anyway; I'd known the Honorable Ethan Harrison Pearce for nearly twenty years, since our first year of law school when everybody called him Spike. "Of course. What's the charge?"

"Burglary. Criminal trespass."

"No problem." But it was a curious request. Public defenders always handled arraignments. Afterward, the PDs might send the case to a "special public defender"—a private lawyer who covered criminal defense matters for the state—but not until the plea was in. Still, it wasn't a big deal. Most likely it was a staffing issue: on the first court day after the long Christmas weekend, there was probably a shortage of PDs and a plethora of defendants. "When was the arrest?"

"Thursday night. The twenty-fourth."

What a dirtbag. "Who breaks into somebody's house on Christmas Eve?"

Then I heard a sound I'd never heard from Belinda: a laugh. Not just a snort or a giggle. An honest-to-God laugh. "Arraignment is at ten."

"Hang on—what's the defendant's name?"

More laughter. "Claus. C-L-A-U-S. First name, Ralph."

"*Ralph* Claus?"

"The state thanks you."

Two

The marshal escorted me into the small windowless room. "Here's your lawyer," he said to the man seated at the metal table which was bolted to the floor. The marshal withdrew, closing the heavy door with a clank.

My new client rose. He was tall and lanky, with dark hair and four days' worth of whiskers. His eyes were a surprisingly light green, and his nose had a high, prominent bridge. His city-issued orange jumpsuit clashed with his olive-toned skin. He reached out his hand. "Thank you for doing this, Ms.—"

"Riley. Megan Riley." I took his hand. His grip was firm and sure.

But it was his smile that stopped me. Full lips and strong-looking white teeth bespoke years of good nutrition and probably a mother who made him brush after meals. A slight dimple in his right cheek showed beneath the whiskers. And a curious familiarity, as though he was greeting a friend, not meeting a stranger.

"Please sit down, Mr. Claus." I draped my coat over one of the chairs on my side of the table and dug in my briefcase for my pen, the firm's representation agreement, and the intake sheet from the bail commissioner. My impossible-to-control curls—nearly as dark as his, except for a few silver threads—fell forward, hiding my face from his scrutiny. I took my seat and took charge. "Your full name, please?"

"Ralph Henry Claus. C-L-A-U-S."

"Address?" The space on the intake sheet was blank.

His smile faded. "This is confidential, right?"

The question was encouraging. Regulars in criminal court knew all about the attorney-client privilege. If this one wasn't a frequent flier, the judge might be a bit more lenient. "I've been appointed to represent you this morning. Assuming you agree to that, yes. Do you agree?" When he nodded, I handed him the representation agreement and my pen. He skimmed the document, scrawled his name, and passed it back across the table. I tucked the form away. "Now, whatever you tell me about your case is privileged. So, as I was saying—what's your address?"

"I don't exactly have one."

"Are you homeless?" Ordinarily, I tried to be sensitive about such matters, but we were due upstairs in a few minutes.

"I live at the family compound. There's no street address."

The family compound. A far cry from indigent, and yet Spike Pearce had appointed counsel. Something wasn't adding up. Maybe the bail commissioner had suspected mental illness. I tried a different angle. "How do you get your mail?"

"Most of it's electronic. The snail mail gets picked up and brought home."

"Picked up from where? What post office?" He didn't answer, and I didn't have time to play twenty questions. "Mr. Claus, please tell me where you live."

"Why? You're not going to believe me." The smile was back.

"You tell me, and I'll decide what I believe." I glanced at my watch. "One more time: where do you live?"

He met my eyes squarely. "The North Pole." Before I could respond, he added, "I told you you wouldn't believe me."

Whatever. "What were you doing at the—" I scanned the document known in criminal proceedings as the "information." "—Leopolds'? Why were you there?"

"To deliver Christmas presents."

Okay, I should have seen that one coming. "So, you're not just Ralph Claus—you're *Santa* Claus."

"Not quite."

Spike Pearce owed me big-time. "We've got—" I checked my watch "—three minutes. Explain."

"My father is Santa Claus. When he retires, I'll inherit the job. For now, I help out."

"Like the Santas at the mall?" That had always been my mother's explanation when I asked how there could be so many Santas all over town.

"Not exactly. Delivering all those gifts in one night—nobody could do that. It's always been a team effort."

I scanned the paperwork. No mention of an accomplice. "What happened with the Leopolds? Didn't they like their presents?"

"I don't know," said Ralph. "I was just putting them down when Trevor Leopold came into the room. He's only six, but he's got a set of lungs that would stop a train. Next thing I knew, Victoria—that's his mom—was screaming into the phone that there was a cat burglar in her house."

"A cat burglar?" Granted, he was a lot younger and skinnier than the traditional Santa pictures, but the red suit should have been a clue.

"Probably because of the clothes," he said. My confusion must have shown, because he explained, "We wear all black—even boots and gloves. Soot doesn't show, and it's harder to see us in the dark."

"What about the red suit with the white fur?"

"Are you kidding? The laundry crew would kill us. You ever try to get soot out of fur? The red and white is strictly the dress uniform. It's only used for very special appearances. You wouldn't expect soldiers or cops to run around in their dress blues all the time, would you?"

I couldn't deny the logic. Still, if I found a stranger dressed in black in my house in the middle of the night, my first thought would definitely not be about the gifts he'd brought.

"What happened to the presents?" He looked away, saying nothing. I leaned forward. "Mr. Claus. Ralph. What happened to the presents you were supposed to be delivering?"

"The gifts for the Leopolds were delivered, and the rest were picked up." He sounded detached, as if he was talking about someone else's crime.

"They 'were delivered'? By whom? And who picked up 'the rest', whatever those are, and when? And how? Was somebody else with you?" I texted my paralegal to check with caseflow immediately to see if anybody else had been picked up on similar-sounding charges. All I needed was another defendant with a conflicting story, and Ralph Henry Claus was screwed.

"Does it matter? This case is just about whether I broke into the Leopolds' house, right? What does it matter what happened to the rest of the gifts?" For the first time, he sounded edgy.

A sharp rap on the metal door interrupted us. The door opened, and a slight sandy-haired young woman with freckles poked her head in. "Sorry to interrupt, counselor, but we need to get the defendant upstairs."

"Thank you, marshal. One more minute, please." I waited until the door closed behind her before I asked my client, "Do I assume correctly that you're pleading guilty?"

"That depends," he said. "What exactly would I be pleading guilty to?"

I consulted the information. "Burglary in the second degree. It means you unlawfully entered the Leopolds' home at night with the intent to commit a crime. Criminal trespass. It means you went in when you knew you weren't allowed to, and you didn't leave when somebody told you to."

"I never intended to commit a crime, and I wasn't there unlawfully."

"Victoria Leopold says you were."

"She's wrong. Trevor invited me. He wrote a letter to Santa and asked us to bring him a catcher's mitt. Left-handed. I did. Ask him. We left it."

Fine. I wasn't about to get into the question of who "we" might be. Enough that I could argue he was there by invitation. That would suffice for purposes of a good-faith plea of "not guilty" at the arraignment.

Which, as it turned out, was the easy part.

Three

I'd just found a seat in the packed courtroom when the marshal brought in my client to join the other defendants in the locked area, separated from the rest of the room by bulletproof plexiglass. He searched the gallery until he saw me, and he smiled.

The lawyers next to me were absorbed in their conversation. "You know where he's going?" asked the plump one. His faded blond combover was shellacked in place.

The gray-haired, gray-suited lawyer beside him shook his head. "Probably gonna open his own firm. I can't imagine anybody'd hire him. Would you?"

"Not a chance. I've got enough hassles. Last thing I need is a partner who can't keep his fly zipped." His tone shifted: "Anybody know what he did with the money?"

"They found it in one of his operating accounts. Swears it was an accounting mistake, that he meant to put it in the escrow account and the girl had nothing to do with it." Gray Suit lowered his voice; I had to strain to hear him. "Between you and me, I'm not sure he did anything criminal. I think he was just stupid."

Combover shrugged. "What an idiot. Losing your whole practice over a piece of ass—"

A knock from the other side of the door behind the bench interrupted him, and we all rose. The judge entered, and the marshal opened court. "Case number CR 2488739, State versus Claus," intoned the clerk.

Talk about a stroke of luck. Considering the number of miscreants in the locked area, we could have waited for hours. Instead, we'd be out before lunch.

I edged past Gray Suit and Combover. By the time I reached the front, the marshal had already escorted my client to the counsel table. She stood directly behind him throughout the proceedings, a stern presence intended to discourage disruptions.

As I plunked my briefcase by the table and my coat on the chair, Judge Marcos raised his eyebrows slightly. *Eyebrows* may be overstating it: what should have been two separate brows looked like a furry gray caterpillar perched on top of his dark-rimmed glasses. The mustache that tracked his upper lip was an exact match. He inquired, "Claus?"

"Yes, Your Honor," I said. "Megan Riley for the defendant, Ralph Henry Claus." I hoped that providing his first and middle names might distract the judge from the surname.

"Looks a little young to be Santa Claus," said the judge. The lawyers in the gallery snickered obediently.

"Well—" Ralph began.

"Of course, Your Honor," I interrupted. "I know there's a full docket, so I won't take up the court's time with details." As if I would have otherwise.

"Very well. On the count of burglary in the second degree, how does the defendant plead?"

"Not guilty, Your Honor."

"On criminal trespass in the first degree?"

"Not guilty, Your Honor."

He turned to the prosecutor, a squat young man with heavily-gelled black hair and the unfortunate name of Antonio Antonio. "Does the state wish to be heard on bail?"

"The state asks that bail be set at five hundred thousand dollars," said Antonio.

Any sympathy I might have had for A. A. and his absurd name vanished. "Your Honor, there's no call for that kind of bail," I said. "The charges are minimal, and there's no claim that he poses a danger to society. In fact, I have every reason to believe that if the court were to release him on a promise to appear, Mr. Claus would honor that promise." A promise to appear—which was exactly that, with no bail—was reserved for the most innocuous cases.

The fuzzy unibrow went higher. "A promise to appear?"

"Your Honor, Mr. Claus has already spent several days in jail over what is, in actuality, nothing more than a misunderstanding. He was in the Leopold home at the invitation of one of the family members. I'm certain this case can be disposed of very quickly, and if it becomes necessary to pursue the issue of bail, that will simply complicate matters."

The judge peered at Ralph. I could tell he was itching to find out what was going on, but dozens of defendants were waiting. He turned to Antonio. "Counsel?"

"We don't have a local address on him," Antonio said. "He's a flight risk."

"Hmmm. Mr. Claus, where do you live?"

The worst possible question. Before Ralph could speak, I said, "Mr. Claus isn't local. He was just in town for the holidays." It was true enough. *Don't ask more*, I begged whatever powers watched out for Santa Claus wannabees.

"How do I know he won't return to the North Pole and never come back?" Judge Marcos chuckled at his own wit. "Mr. Claus, if I let you out, whether it's a promise to appear or I set bail, you can't leave the state until the charges against you are resolved. Is there someplace you can stay in Connecticut? Maybe with the people you were visiting?"

"That isn't an option, Your Honor, but I see no reason why suitable accommodations can't be made for Mr. Claus to remain in-state for the necessary time," I said before Ralph could speak. "As Your Honor is aware, Mr. Claus has no prior record. There's no claim of violence or disorderly conduct. There's no allegation that any property is missing or damaged. No one's saying that he behaved inappropriately or that he caused any harm. The sum total of the charges against my client is that he was in the house without invitation."

Antonio was on his feet. "But Your Honor, some kind of bond is necessary to make sure he doesn't skip town."

Before I could respond, Judge Marcos said, "I'm setting bail at five thousand dollars. Consider it a Christmas present, Mr. Claus." He banged the gavel. "Next case."

"One more thing, Your Honor," said Antonio. "Since there's a child involved, the state requests a no-contact order." No-contact orders were standard fare in kid cases.

Judge Marcos turned to me. "Any objection?"

"I don't think it's necessary, Your Honor. There's no claim that Mr. Claus engaged in any improper conduct regarding the child."

The judge grunted. "Well, it may not be absolutely necessary, but better safe than sorry," he said. "Mr. Claus, you're to have no contact with any of the victims. No phone calls, no correspondence, no in-person visitation. Stay at least three hundred feet away at all times. Any problem with that?"

"No, Your Honor," I said.

The gavel banged again. "Next case."

"Thank you, Your Honor," Antonio and I chorused automatically.

"Thank you, Your Honor," Ralph added, sounding sincere. He turned to me. "What happens now?"

"I'll see you downstairs," I said. Antonio was flipping through his next file, and a balding lawyer in a well-worn suit was waiting none too patiently for me to move away from the table so that he could plop his battered briefcase on it.

Four

By the time I got down to the client consultation room, Kat Williams from KW Bail Bonds was sitting with Ralph. Kat had been bonding out my clients ever since I started practice fifteen years ago. All Ralph had to do now was to come up with five hundred dollars—ten percent of the bail—and he'd be out of jail until I got his case pled out.

Except Ralph was shaking his head with a rueful smile. "I don't have any money," he said as I came in. "Just the ten bucks I had when they arrested me."

"Do you have access to any other funds? Anybody y'all can borrow from? Friends, family, boss?" Twenty years in New England, and her Georgia drawl was still as thick as honey.

"I could ask my family," Ralph said. "It might take a little time to get it, though. They're not from around here."

"That's okay," Kat said. "Be sure to tell them you're lucky it's so little. Five thou is really low, especially from Judge Marcos. He must have liked you."

"I'm sure that's it," I said. "Kat, can I talk to you outside?"

"Sure," she said. To Ralph, she added, "If you want to give me a number, I can call somebody for you."

"We'll be right back," I said before he could take her up on it. We went out into the hall, and I closed the door.

"What's up?" she asked.

"What has he told you?"

"His name and his bail amount. Why? What should he have told me?" She didn't sound concerned. After thousands of bonds, there was practically nothing Kat hadn't heard.

"Look, I can't breach client confidentiality, but—well, this guy may have a screw loose." I had absolute faith in Kat's discretion, but Ralph Claus had made a point of not disclosing his North Pole affiliation until I assured him of confidentiality, so it was clear this was what the law called *a communication in furtherance of the representation*. In other words, his claimed address was privileged information, which meant my lawyer-lips were sealed.

"Let me guess," she said. "He's got an internet startup that'll be worth millions if we all give him twenty bucks?"

"I can't say anything. Just—be careful." I tried to invest my words with heavy-duty meaning.

"You're the one who needs to be careful," she said. "I heard some of the guys talking before y'all came back down. Victoria Leopold has *friends*." Her emphasis on the word made it clear she wasn't talking about workout buddies or a Mommy-and-Me group.

"Politicians or mob?"

"Politicians. Her cousin is a legislative assistant to Senator Zenkman. She might be related to him, too. The guys weren't sure."

"Oh, jeez." Hal Zenkman was a Greenwich millionaire whose primary qualification for public office was the number of companies he'd taken over, dismembered, and sold for parts at enormous personal profit. Unions had fought his election, citing his well-documented position that collective bargaining undermined the free market. Teachers' organizations had banded with parents' groups against his stated intention to preserve tax loopholes for high-end estates by cutting school-funded meals and after-school programs for children of working parents. When challenged on this particular legislation, he'd once been heard to say, "You dance with the one that brought you."

"Any chance your boy's a rich Republican?" Kat asked.

"Doubt it." This was a guy who gave away free stuff without making anybody take a drug test.

"Then he needs a bond," she said. "'Cause if he doesn't have influence someplace, you're gonna have a tough time getting Antonio to agree to anything, and Mr. Santa there is going to be going over next year's naughty-and-nice list in jail."

"Mr. Claus," I corrected her. We went back into the room to see Ralph Claus looking as relaxed as someone sitting in a coffee shop with a latte. "Here's the thing," I said without preamble. "You need to come up with five hundred dollars, or you'll be sitting in jail until we dispose of your case."

Ralph frowned slightly. "I really need to get back home. Post-holiday clean-up is a bear."

I met his eyes hard, then glanced meaningfully at Kat and shook my head slightly. "You're not going anywhere. If you make bail, you still have to stay in the state until your case is over. If you don't make bail, you're definitely not going any place. Those are the only options, Mr. Claus."

Ralph's mouth pursed with mild irritation. "I need to make a call." Kat mumbled something about checking in with her office and slipped out of the room. Once the door closed, I handed him the phone I kept exclusively for client use. "It's an international call," he warned. I gestured for him to proceed, and he punched in what seemed like a very long string of numbers, even for an international call. "Hey, Ivy, it's me. . . . Don't worry, I'm fine. . . . I know. But everything got delivered all right? . . . Good. . . . Listen, is Phil around? . . . I really don't have time to talk to her right now. . . . No, I really don't—hi, Mom. . . . Yes, I'm fine. . . . It's just a misunderstanding. I've got a lawyer, and I'm getting out on bail, but I'm not allowed to leave the state. . . . Connecticut, remember? . . . I know. Maybe next time. . . . Look, I'm in kind of a hurry. Can you transfer me to Phil? . . . Because I need money for a few things. . . . It's Hartford. I figured I'd buy some insurance while I'm here—I'm kidding. Bail, for one. Can I just talk to Phil? . . . Yeah, well, time zones are like that. What are you doing up at this hour, anyway? . . . Mom, I'm fine. Everybody's been terrific. Let me talk to Phil. . . . Hey, buddy. . . . Okay, but I need cash. . . . Bail, lawyer, living expenses. . . . Hang on." To me, he said, "Any idea how long I'll be here?"

"Could be a few days, could be months. Depends on the prosecutor." I'd explain about Zenkman later.

He repeated my words into the phone. "Uh-huh. . . . Yeah, that's what I was thinking. . . . I know, I know. Next time, someplace warm. . . . How about Aruba? . . . Fine. Next time I get arrested, I'll make sure I'm in Aruba. . . . Oh, for the love of—Philip, take twenty bucks and buy yourself a sense of humor, okay? 'Cause I don't think there's anybody in the workshop who can make something that small. . . . Look, I've gotta go. My extremely patient lawyer is waiting, and we're running up her phone bill. . . . Don't be stupid. Of course, we're paying for it. . . . Hang on." He turned to me again. "How much should I have him send for legal fees?"

"I was appointed." Which was another discussion we needed to have since it appeared that he did have funds to pay for counsel.

He waved his hand impatiently. "We're paying you. Just tell me how much." A rare statement, to be sure. I could practically hear my partners shouting "Hallelujah!"

"Tell him to send the bail money, plus a retainer of five thousand. If the case goes fast, that should do it."

"And if it doesn't?"

"We can deal with that later." My partner, Roy, was probably clutching his chest in sudden agony. Any lawyer knows that if a client offers to pay, you take the money before they decide they'd rather put it toward a month on the Cape or a new roof.

"Ten thousand for the lawyer," he said into the phone. I held up my hand, five fingers spread, but he shook his head. "Hey, what can I say? Lawyers are expensive down here. . . . No, I can't use Kristofer. . . . All he does are contracts and websites. . . . I don't know. Reykjavik? Why are you asking me this? . . . Philip, I'm sitting in the basement of an American courthouse running up my lawyer's cellphone bill—which reminds me, I need a new phone. . . . One of the reindeer stepped on it. Now, can we wrap this up? Who's bringing everything down? . . . No. Absolutely not. . . . Because she'll never leave. . . . I don't care. Tell her you're using carrier pigeons. . . . I swear to you, if she shows up down here, I'm jumping bail, and I'm coming home and I'm going to beat the crap out of you *and* your computer, and you can have Kristofer sue me if he can find a courthouse. . . . You know what? Transfer me to Charles. . . . Thanks, buddy. . . . Hey, Chaz. Sorry to wake you. I need a favor. Very quiet. . . . Yup. . . . No, nothing like that." He glanced at me. "Phil's putting together some stuff for me, and I need somebody to bring it down to Connecticut. . . . Exactly. . . . Double-check with Ted, but I'd use Chloe and Blitzen. . . . Huh-uh. Check his hoof. He was landing rough the last few houses. . . . Whatever. Just move fast, because she already knows I called, and she's going to be trying to organize this. . . . Hang on." He turned back to me. "What's your address?" I handed him my card, and he read it into the phone. "What's the ETA?" He listened, then said to me, "They might not get here by five. Is that okay?"

"Somebody'll be there." For ten thousand dollars, somebody would definitely be there.

He ended the call and handed the phone back. "Be sure to put that on my bill." I was looking forward to that phone bill myself.

I dropped the phone into my briefcase and headed out into the hall where Kat was still waiting. "He says the money's on its way, but it might not be here by five."

She picked up her bag. "I'll go through the paperwork with him now, and tomorrow morning, we'll get him out."

A thought began to form. "Why don't you get started, but don't fill in the release date yet. I'll be right back." I headed down the hall to the locked double doors. A marshal waved me through, and I entered a much nicer corridor with tightly-looped dark red carpet and chalky paint that looked as if it had been applied more recently than the Reagan administration. At the gray steel door to the lawyers' lounge, I punched the code on the door lock and slipped into the least-dingy public room in the courthouse. Luckily, no one else was there. I closed the door firmly behind me, took out the phone, and punched "redial."

The beeping of the dial took much longer than a typical international call. I didn't recognize the country code. One ring, and I heard, "North Pole, this is Ivy. How may I direct your call?"

"Sorry, wrong number." I disconnected. Aloud, I said, "He's good." He must have known I'd do this, so he set it up—but how? Unless he planned it before he went to the Leopolds'. Maybe this was a much more elaborate scheme than a simple break-in. Maybe that charming "I'm Santa" bit was a mask for something bigger, darker.

Except that after years being lied to, my bullshit detector was first-rate, and I wasn't getting the con vibe from this client. For better or worse, he meant what he was saying.

On the way back to lockup, it occurred to me that I might have a bigger problem than Ralph Claus making bond. If he'd mentioned this North Pole nonsense to anyone else, we could have a media situation. If Judge Marcos and Kat were any indication, the jokes were already starting. All we needed was somebody posting about Santa breaking and entering, and we'd be lucky if it didn't go viral—in which case, Senator Zenkman was liable to take up the cause of his friend or relative or whatever she was, especially if he could get some air time out of it. The most dangerous place in Connecticut was between Hal Zenkman and a television camera.

I rapped once on the metal door to the miniscule client consultation room, then opened it without waiting to be invited. "Kat, can I talk to my client for a second?"

"Sure. Give me a call whenever you're ready." She gathered up the documents.

"No, don't go anywhere. He may not be done." Kat pursed her rosy lips in confusion, but she went outside and closed the door.

"Everything okay?" Ralph asked.

"I'm not sure."

He broke into a wide grin. "You hit redial, didn't you?"

"That doesn't matter. Listen, have you mentioned this North Pole thing to anyone other than me?" He shook his head, and I persisted, "What about when you were being booked? What did you say when the police asked for your address?"

"That I don't have one. Which is true. The North Pole isn't an address. I mean, Connecticut isn't your address, right? It's just the place where you live."

His logic wasn't sterling, but as long as he hadn't been having North Pole conversations, I didn't care. "So you haven't told anybody except me that you're Santa Claus."

"I'm not Santa. I'm his son."

Fine. "You haven't told anybody you were at the Leopolds' on Santa's behalf, right?"

"Well—not exactly."

Shit. "What do you mean? Exactly."

"You know how it is. Everybody's sitting around, and when somebody new comes in, they ask what you're in for. I said trespassing. They asked where, and I said I was in somebody's house. Right then, the cop called my name, and when those guys heard 'Claus,' they started calling me Santa Claus and ragging on how I must have come down the chimney, all that stuff. I told them I wasn't Santa, but that was what they called me the rest of the time I was there."

"The cops, or the other people in jail?"

"At first, it was just the other guys, but the cops started to pick it up."

I thought fast. Cops, criminals, the judge, and Kat. By tomorrow, everybody in the Hartford defense bar. The best way to shut down this Santa thing was to get Ralph out of there. Out of sight, out of mind. But the money wasn't arriving until this evening, which meant at least another twenty-four hours until he could be bonded out.

I should have left right then. Called it a day, packed up my bag, gotten out into the brisk December air, and returned the next day with the bail money in hand. Much later, when I was asked why I hadn't done precisely that, I said I was concerned that if he stayed in jail, this Santa Claus story would gain traction and garner publicity, and it would be that much harder to cut a deal. I said I'd been assessing client credibility for a long time, and I believed him when he said the money was coming. I said that advancing client costs wasn't unheard-of, and having him out of jail would make it easier for me to get to the bottom of everything. I denied vehemently that I was attracted to him at that point or that this attraction was the real reason I fronted the bond money. I told them I wrote the check on my personal account because I didn't have an office check with me and I never carried that much cash, especially in the vicinity of the criminal court.

Most of what I said was true.

I didn't mention how Kat told me flat out that I was crazy, or how I retorted that if she didn't want to write the bond, I'd find someone who would. And I didn't tell them that later, when it all fell apart, Kat sent me a text that said simply, *Anything I can do?* I texted back, *No, thanks.*

Because by then, there was nothing anybody could do.

Five

An hour later, I was walking the three blocks to my office alongside my newest client. Our breath made little clouds in the frosty air. He had no coat, but he'd brushed off my offer to fetch my car and pick him up. "Compared to home, this is nothing," he assured me.

After a block of companionable silence, I decided to test his claim. "Do you really make toys at the North Pole?"

"Not me specifically," he said. "Mainly the elves."

"What about video games and tablets?" The Christmas movies of my childhood depicted short people with pointy ears hammering on wooden toys.

"We have an electronics department. They can do anything the kids ask for. A couple of them work with my brother, Phil, on the office computer system."

"Your naughty-and-nice list is on a computer?" So much for romantic images of Santa poring over long sheets of foolscap.

"That, and everything else." My sudden trepidation must have shown, because he added, "Names, addresses, gift requests. What did you think we had on our hard drives? Creepy pictures of little kids?"

"Of course not!" *Of course not, please, God.*

"You wouldn't be the first," he sighed. "We see it all over the internet. Santa-porn. Makes me sick. I probably shouldn't tell you this, but my little brother is really good at crashing those sites."

Our office was halfway down South Pine Street. If you stood in front of the building and looked to the north, you'd see the sun gleaming off the gold dome of the capitol. Like a dozen other law firms on South Pine, we occupied a converted Victorian with a tasteful sign and a handkerchief-sized parcel of grass on either side of the slate walk leading to our front door; at this time of year, the grass was dull and soggy with half-melted snow. The backyard was paved, fenced, and marked with signs proclaiming that parking was for staff and visitors of the Lundstrom Law Firm only. It was a prime location, but we'd been spared the exorbitant rent some of our neighbors paid because Eckert had bought the house for an excellent price from the widow of his law school classmate, Judge Oliver.

The judge hadn't been much for decorating, but Elsa's girlfriend Desirée was an interior designer who understood the kind of décor a house like ours needed. The framed artwork included pieces she'd found at high-end galleries, regional antique shops, and local juried art shows, giving the place an air that was polished yet unconventional. The oak floors gleamed where they weren't covered with Oriental-style rugs. Not a smudge marred the freshly-painted plaster walls. The glossy table in our large conference room began its life in a private gentlemen's club, and the receptionist's desk originally belonged to a bootlegger who had been forced to sell off his holdings when the repeal of Prohibition made him redundant. Most of the other furnishings boasted similar origins, and nearly nothing matched, but we liked it that way. Eckert wouldn't have traded his nineteenth-century British umbrella stand for a dozen matching secretarial stations.

In Eckert's office on the main floor, Judge Oliver's mahogany desk graced the far end; a pine conference table from His Honor's chambers, flanked with four armchairs, occupied the near end. On the second floor, Elsa's office blended vintage molding with contemporary furnishings. The fabrics were sumptuous, the lines were elegant, and the artwork proclaimed that someone had superb taste and a significant budget.

To no one's surprise, Roy had resisted authorizing unnecessary expenditures on his workspace—*unnecessary* meaning anything more than inexpensive, basic, and functional. Michael bet me a hundred bucks that Roy would furnish his entire office at IKEA. He hadn't, but only because he was even less comfortable with a screwdriver than he was at social functions. As a result, his furniture came from a discount office supply catalogue. The only decoration was his fifteen-year-old wedding portrait, framed in ceramic pastel roses and placed by the bride on the gray metal bookcase.

Michael didn't notice his surroundings as long as they were

reasonably comfortable, which meant Desirée had free rein until the day she presented him with the bill for an antique conference table that cost half his annual draw. The table went back, and Michael's wife Ruby took over decorating his office.

For my solitary space on the top floor, Holly and I spent weekends searching estate sales and consignment shops. Our efforts produced a honey-colored Shaker desk and matching side table, a pair of wingback chairs in front of the desk and a club chair in the corner, draped with a blanket to protect it from Lulu's shedding. My favorite of Holly's watercolors—a tilted umbrella, beach blanket, and blue-striped towels, waves breaking on the sand and sailboats barely visible in the distance—hung on the wall opposite my desk; she said it was to remind me that there was more to life than work.

Ralph and I entered the office to find Marilyn at the reception desk, sorting mail with her customary frown. Tight marigold-colored curls bore witness to her traditional holiday perm and color job. "Hey, Meg," she said, barely looking up. Then, she caught sight of Ralph, and she straightened. "Can I help you, sir?"

"He's with me," I said. "We're going up to my office. Ralph, would you like coffee?"

Ralph smiled at Marilyn. "I'd love some."

Just like that, her frown softened. "I'll bring it up," she said, an event that was practically unprecedented.

I took Ralph up the wide staircase leading from the first floor to the second, and then up the narrower carpeted one to the third floor. The payoff for this hike was space and privacy. My legal assistant Robin occupied the smaller office on the other side of the bathroom, and the remainder of the third floor contained eight years' worth of closed files.

The conference table in the middle of the room was topped with white ceramic tile. I loved it because Lulu could jump on and off without leaving scratches. I invited Ralph to sit, but he'd already caught sight of my girl in her club chair. "Who's that?"

"Lulu." One triangular black ear flicked at the sound of her name, but she gave no other hint that she knew she was under discussion.

"Is she yours?"

"She's my office kitty. I found her in the parking lot last summer. I tried taking her home, but she and my other cats didn't get along." To put it mildly: every time I tried to effect a rapprochement, one of the boys hissed or swatted, and petite Lulu dove under the bed. After three stressful weeks, I told myself we'd have more time together if she lived at the office. Now, she reigned over the third floor.

"Does she like to be petted?"

"Go ahead." Lulu was very picky about who was allowed to touch her. She was one of the best barometers for character I'd ever known.

Ralph squatted beside the chair. Normally, this kind of familiarity from a stranger would be enough to send her leaping to the floor and out the door. But she didn't move as he stroked her silky back. Across the room, I could hear her purring.

Lulu approved.

Marilyn appeared with a tray. "Cream and sugar?" she asked in a breathy tone that nearly made my jaw drop. "Or milk? Or fake sweetener?"

Ralph straightened, smiling at her. "Black is fine, thanks." He accepted the cup, and I thought she was going to melt into a puddle of adoration. The woman was a grandmother, for crying out loud, and she was acting like a groupie meeting her favorite rock star.

And she didn't even know who this guy claimed to be.

As soon as she left the room, I handed Ralph a pad and pen. "I want you to write down everything you remember about that night at the Leopolds'. Every detail, no matter how insignificant. You never know what could be useful."

"I thought you and the prosecutor were going to work this out," Ralph said.

"There's a possible complication. The Leopolds have connections to a state senator. He shouldn't be a huge problem, but there may be some delays if he decides to get involved. The best thing is to write down everything now, while it's still fresh."

"Sure. Do you want the letter, too?"

"The letter?"

"Trevor's letter to Santa—well, his email. That's how most kids do it now. I'll have it forwarded to you."

"A six-year-old wrote an email?" Six years old meant first grade. *Dear Santa, bring me a catcher's mitt* sounded pretty sophisticated for someone who was just meeting Dick and Jane.

"Kids almost never write their own letters," he said. "Usually it's Mom or Dad. Most kids who are old enough to write for themselves have already stopped believing."

"Can you tell whose computer it came from?" If Victoria Leopold sent the email asking Santa to come to her house, she could hardly object when he accepted the invitation.

His responsive laugh wasn't quite *ho-ho-ho*, but it was close. "I'm afraid you've got me confused with somebody who knows tech. Maybe my brother can track it. Can I have your phone?" I fished the phone out of my bag and tossed it to him. He caught it easily. "You're a better pitcher than my brother, Phil," he said.

"You play baseball at the North Pole?

"Sure. One of the elves has been the home-run champion for twenty-seven years."

He made it all sound so plausible. "The letter," I reminded him.

"Oh, okay." He punched redial, just as I'd done a short time earlier. "Hey, Ivy, me again. Is Til around? . . . Thanks. . . . Hey, Tillie, it's me. . . . No big deal. I'll be down here for a little while, but we should wrap it up pretty fast. Listen, I need you to do me a favor. . . . My lawyer needs the letter from Trevor Leopold. West Hartford, Connecticut, U.S. . . . Catcher's mitt. . . . Lefty. . . . Because I'm that good. . . . See if Mitch can figure out who sent it. . . . You know you're my favorite, right? . . . Let me ask." He turned to me. "Where should she send it?"

"Use this address." I handed him a sheet of office stationery.

He read the email address into the phone. "How long? . . . Terrific. Tillie, you're the best. . . . I love you, too, sweetheart. I'll see you soon. Bye." He pressed the "end" button and handed the phone back to me. "You should have it in a few minutes."

"Was that your wife?" I felt my cheeks getting hot as soon as the words were out of my mouth. Hastily, I turned to look for something, anything, in the file cabinet.

"Who, Tillie?" He laughed—a rich, happy laugh. "Tillie's my father's cousin. In some ways, she's been more of a mother to me than my own mother."

"What do you mean?" It wasn't even close to being an appropriate question, but somehow, I knew it was all right to ask.

Ralph leaned back and sipped his coffee. "Mom is the CEO of the organization. She's got the heart and soul of a CEO, and thank God she does. Somebody needs to oversee this conglomerate. Someday, I'll tell you all about it. Suffice to say that she married Pop, moved north, and when my grandparents retired a few years later, Mom stepped into the job at the ripe old age of about twenty-four. Don't get me wrong—she's amazing. It's just—well, she's a little tough to take sometimes. She likes to run things."

"Like what?"

"Like everything. Like if Charles doesn't sneak that delivery out of there before she realizes it's gone, she's going to be on your doorstep come nightfall. She gets obsessed with details, and she's definitely not about to take chances with the next in line."

"With what?"

"Me. I'm the eldest, so when Pop steps down, the job is mine. From what I've heard, she hasn't lost sight of that since the minute she figured out she was pregnant."

I jotted a note. Maybe the pressure of parental expectations—even imaginary ones—could cause some sort of psychotic break.

"She does a great job managing everything," he continued. "Back in August, we were having a problem with supplies, and she was on the phone around the clock."

"How do you get supplies?" I asked as casually as I could manage.

"We have a handful of suppliers," he said. "They all have strict confidentiality agreements, of course."

Of course. "And they ship to the North Pole?"

"We have a site in Iceland for business. All our deliveries are sent there, and then our people pick them up and get them up to the Pole."

It was so logical. Too logical. "Is that where you run your finances through, too?"

He looked at me sharply, but I didn't back off. I wanted to see how far he'd worked out his story.

"Phil handles the finances," he said, but he was dodging the question and we both knew it.

I sat down at the table across from him. "You need to level with me. What were you doing in the Leopold house on December 24?"

"Delivering Trevor's gifts. I told you that." His voice had a slight edge now. "Look, I know you think I'm either a nutcase or a liar, but just for one minute, could you maybe consider the possibility that I am who I say I am?"

"I don't mean to insult you," I said. "The thing is, I need to be able to sell the prosecutor on an account of the facts, and if I start with the notion that you're Santa Claus—"

"—I'm not Santa, I'm his son—"

I held up my hand. "Okay, you're Santa's helper or whatever. In any case, if I try to tell the prosecutor that, not only will he not cut a deal, but we'll have to go to trial with that story. I don't know what you've heard, but real life isn't like *Miracle on 34th Street*. In real life, it doesn't matter how well-meaning the guy is who's claiming to be Santa. In real life, when somebody with political connections finds an intruder in her living room in the middle of the night, that intruder is going to jail unless there's a credible explanation, and Santa's helper delivering the presents isn't a credible explanation. Now, did somebody hire you to play Santa? Do you know Trevor, and maybe you were doing this as a surprise for him? Is there something else you can give me?"

Ralph regarded me for a long minute. "No," he said at last. "I was delivering Trevor's gifts from Santa. That's all I can tell you. If it means I'm going to jail, then I guess I'm going to jail."

Obviously, I'd handled this badly. "Let me look at the letter when it comes in. Maybe we can get somewhere with that. In the meantime, we need to find you a place to stay." I buzzed for Robin, who appeared in the doorway almost instantly. Her blue-black hair shone in the lamplight, and her brown eyes were impenetrable behind her dark-rimmed glasses. A tiny silver ring pierced one nostril. Robin was a single mother with a four-year-old son, and she was the best assistant I'd ever had. Nothing was asking too much. If I was unavailable on a Saturday or Sunday, she came in to feed Lulu, and she routinely took my girl home over holiday weekends. When she finally left for law school—and I knew she'd make it someday—Lulu and I would both miss her like crazy.

I introduced them. "Robin, Ralph is out on bond, but he's from out of state. He needs in-state accommodations."

"Sure thing." She was out of the room before he could respond.

"She can do that?" He sounded impressed.

"You're not the first client who's needed temporary housing while he's out on bail. We know a few people who rent out rooms short-term."

"What kind of information are they going to want?"

"They don't care what you're charged with," I reassured him.

"That's not what I mean," he said. "I don't advertise who I am to just anybody. I told you because it was confidential, but I'd rather not have everybody in Hartford talking about how Santa Claus has really come to town."

"Like you said, you're not Santa, so that shouldn't be an issue," I said. "These places are used to getting referrals from me. Mainly, they want to know you'll be quiet and well-behaved and pay the rent on time."

Ten minutes later, Robin came back. "Carla and Sergio have space." To Ralph, she added, "You'll like them. Really nice, and the house is immaculate. You don't smoke, do you?" He shook his head. "Good. The house is on the bus line, so you can get around. Rent's reasonable." She quoted a figure.

"That sounds great, thanks," he said.

"I'll tell them you'll be over shortly," she said, already on her way back to her office.

Ralph smiled at me, little crinkles appearing at the corners of his eyes. "This is above and beyond the call of duty. I really appreciate it."

"You're welcome," was all I said, but I could have added that I had a vested interest in making sure he didn't leave town. If he ran out on me, not only would it cost me money, but it would damage my credibility the next time I argued for a low bail. I'd learned early in my practice was that no case was so completely isolated that it wasn't going to affect another one. As Marilyn liked to say when another lawyer did something dirty, "Karma's a bitch."

Much later, when everything fell apart, I would wonder whether karma was to blame, and if so, what terrible thing I'd done.

Six

The phone beeped. "Ed's on one." Marilyn's voice was flat, as it always was when announcing Ed's calls.

"Thanks." I picked up the receiver and punched the button. "Hi." If my client hadn't been sitting less five feet away, I might have said, "Hi, honey." Not that Ralph would have noticed. He was busily writing something—hopefully, a more credible account of his activities on December 24.

Ed didn't notice, either. "Listen, I'm not going to be able to make it for dinner tonight. Pete Gerlin has an extra ticket to the UConn game. His brother can't go."

"Oh." I knew Ed loved basketball, but we hadn't seen each other since before Christmas. On the twenty-third, he drove up to Vermont to stay in his usual cut-rate motel half a mile from the home occupied by his ex-wife, the plumber for whom she'd dumped Ed three years earlier, and Ed's three hostile children. The first time I'd met the kids, the eldest, fifteen-year-old Nicole, informed me bluntly that she wished I would get out of her father's life so he would come back home. It took real effort to keep from pointing out that my presence was irrelevant. The plumber was twenty-six with a perpetual two-day beard, and tight jeans over a tighter ass. No way in hell was her mother going to shove him out of bed in favor of a middle-aged actuary with thinning hair.

Ed hadn't invited me to join him in Vermont for Christmas. That was fine with me. Christmas might be all about children for some people, but I was happy to spend it with good wine, sashimi, and a few amiable adults. If that was sacrilege, then call me a heretic.

The truth was that I'd never found kids all that interesting. I oohed and aahed when cuddling a friend's newborn, but it never bothered me to hand the baby back. I loved Holly's kids from the moment I met them, but that was because they were Holly's. Auntie Meg was present for all the important occasions—birthdays, prom, graduations. When Don left and Holly was struggling to get through the day, I spent countless hours with the kids, taking them to the beach, playing in the snow, and even hosting overnights and weekends. But as much as I loved Jack and Amy, and as happy as I was to be a part of their lives, I never felt a need to make a Jack or Amy of my own.

One downside of dating at forty was that most men had at least one ex-wife with whom they shared custody of the kids. Sometimes these extraneous people were pleasant. Other times, the remnants from Family #1 were such an intrusion that the man simply wasn't worth it. I'd once ended a promising relationship with a lovely, intelligent man because I couldn't tolerate his eight-year-old daughter. In addition to lying, whining, and ignoring my instructions to not to take her juice into the living room, she chased my cats around the house, stomping and screeching after them. Her father knew all this, but he kept bringing her with him anyway, sheepishly explaining that he'd forgotten it was his custody weekend, or Alexis had begged to come along because she had so much fun at my house. Then came the day when my cellphone vanished from my purse, and it turned up in his daughter's backpack. He returned the phone and made Lexie apologize, but we both knew it was over. The cats watched from the bedroom window as they drove away.

Ed's kids didn't steal my things or harass my cats, but they were obnoxious, rude, and spoiled. I tried to convince myself they were screwed up because of their broken home, but that was a hard sell since as far as I could tell, neither of the parents had ever disciplined them. Once, I sat in Ed's living room for an hour past our dinner reservation because he was on the phone trying to explain to ten-year-old Lawton why he couldn't have a dirt bike. Lawton screamed so loudly that Ed had to hold the phone away from his ear, but Ed kept addressing the little monster as if they were having a reasonable discussion. By the time Lawton hung up on him, Ed was so drained that we stayed in and ordered pizza.

I'd expected that when Ed returned from Vermont, we'd have our own belated Christmas. But to have even that canceled. . . . No matter. I wasn't having that conversation now, especially in front of a client. Instead, I turned toward the window and, with my back to Ralph, I murmured, "What about tomorrow night? I still have your Christmas presents."

"I can't tomorrow," Ed said. "Year-end reports are due. Probably an all-nighter."

"Wednesday, then." Casual. No big fuss.

"I'm going back up Wednesday. The kids want me to come back to spend New Year's with them." I could almost hear him grinning at the notion of his children desiring his presence.

"What about—" I broke off. No way would I be one of the whiny *What about me?* contingent. I shifted gears. "I was hoping to spend New Year's with you, too. I had some . . . plans." I drew the word out seductively.

"Meg!" He sounded shocked. "The kids want to see me! You can't mean I should tell them 'no'!"

You never do, I was tempted to retort. "You just spent Christmas weekend with them," I said instead. "It's not fair of them to expect you to drive back up there again." Never let it be said that this lawyer couldn't spin an argument. As long as he didn't think I meant—

"I could bring them down here for the weekend," he said as if he'd read my mind. "Then we could all be together."

"No!" escaped my lips before I could stop it. Memories of last New Year's Eve still lingered like the pain from a broken leg. Edie had spent the evening bawling for some unspecified reason, Lawton tried to sneak a swig of champagne whenever he thought we weren't looking, and Nicole remained glued to her phone, casting dark looks in our direction and heaving heavy, theatrical sighs every time she told her boyfriend how terrible it was to be stuck in Connecticut. "Isn't she supposed to be texting?" I whispered to Ed at one point. "I didn't think kids actually spoke on phones anymore."

He shrugged. "If I couldn't hear her, how would she let me know I'm the worst father on the planet?" It boggled my mind that he understood this and still let it go on.

Before he could take offense at my rejection, I amended hastily, "Maybe you should let Kimberly have some time alone with them."

"She gets them all the time. She'll probably be glad for the break." An understatement, no doubt. "I'll go up Wednesday and bring them down Thursday, and we can all spend the weekend together. You want to drive up with me?"

If I'd had any sense, I'd have broken off the relationship then and there, but I'd never had any sense where Ed was concerned. Not from the first day I met him, when I couldn't resist the sandy hair that flopped onto his forehead or the crisp, slightly British inflection in his voice (even after I discovered it was a put-on and he was really from Ohio). He was stocky and muscular and excelled at practically any sport he tried. I'd spent many hours watching him playing touch football, golf, basketball, and softball. He could also row crew and climb rocks, two pastimes I'd gamely tried to enjoy with him. As I told myself while the doctor set the arm I broke falling from a crumbling ledge, there was no need for us to do everything together. Having separate hobbies and interests would just make us more interesting to each other. So I tried not to let it bother me when Ed came over and spent the evening watching ESPN while I worked on a brief. This was adult companionship, I told myself. Besides, our truly adult companionship was so delicious that it more than made up for any deficiencies that might have come before.

Behind me, Ralph coughed. A small sound, but enough to bring me back to sanity. "Actually, I need to work this weekend," I lied. "I figured we'd spend New Year's Eve together, but other than that, I'll be in the office. So maybe you should go back up to Vermont for the weekend, and I'll see you when you get back." I waited for him to protest, to say he missed me and that he could go to Vermont on New Year's Day instead.

"Really? Meg, you're the greatest. Hey, I've gotta go. I'll call you later. Bye!"

"I lo—" But he'd hung up.

Ralph was still writing. It was impossible to tell from his posture what he'd pieced together from that brief conversation. But the corner of his mouth quirked upward just a bit, as if he was trying to hide a smile.

Seven

A quick tap on the door, and Michael stuck his head in. "Hey, Riley, you eaten? Wanna get a late sandwich?" Then, he saw Ralph. "Sorry. Didn't know you were with somebody."

"Don't mind me," said Ralph. "I've got plenty to do here."

"We're just gonna bring back," said Michael. "You want anything?"

"Don't worry, I've got it," I said when Ralph hesitated. With ten grand coming, I could spring for a sandwich. "What would you like?"

"Roast beef and Swiss on a hard roll," he said. "Thanks."

"Be right back." I snatched my coat off the rack and headed out behind Michael. I waited until we were walking down South Pine to ask, "So, what do you think of that guy?"

"You dumping Ed?" He sounded almost hopeful. Michael never thought any man was good enough for me.

"Don't be ridiculous. He thinks he's Santa Claus." I pushed open the door to the South Pine Deli. The string of bells clanged against the scratched glass. Even though it was a holiday week, the place was crowded.

"Hey! Mr. and Mrs. Law!" called Sergio from behind the counter. When Michael and I first started coming in, Sergio said we bickered like an old married couple, and he assigned us nicknames that had never gone away. "Robin talked to Carla," he added when we reached the counter. "Bring your guy over whenever."

"Thanks, Sergio." I placed my order and Ralph's, and Michael added his. I couldn't help smiling at Sergio's frown when I took out my wallet. Michael and I bought each other lunch all the time, but in Sergio's world, there were rules, and one was that women don't pay.

A few minutes later, we were back on the sidewalk. I pulled my scarf tighter against the frigid air. "Santa Claus?" Michael shrugged. "I'm not worried. You've brought home weirder dudes than that. At least this one isn't wearing a foil hat to keep aliens from stealing his thoughts."

"It was Mylar, and he thought the aliens were going to melt his brain with a laser." I'd definitely had some odd people in my office over the years. "But there's something different about this one," I added, careful not to mention the bond money. "Lulu likes him."

Michael glanced at me. "What about you?"

"What about me?" I kept my voice casual.

"What do you think of him?"

I gave him my best *are you kidding* smirk. "He's a con artist. Anybody can see that." Which was probably true, but it irked me anyway. I'd take a sincere crazy over a charming liar every time.

The third floor was empty save for sleeping Lulu. I dropped the bags on the table and called downstairs to Marilyn. "Where's my client? I've got his sandwich."

"Robin took him over to Carla and Sergio's," Marilyn said. "He said he'd be back later."

I hung my coat on the antique coat rack behind my door. The table was bare except for the food bags. Ralph had taken his papers with him. Too bad. I'd love to have seen what his story looked like so far.

I pulled both phones out of my bag. The personal one showed seven new calls, which made me glad I'd placed it on "silent" at court. I scrolled through them quickly: two prosecutors (but not Antonio Antonio), Kat, three clients, and the family court. As always, I called the court first, but it was just caseflow wanting to reschedule tomorrow's status conference. I noted the change on the firm-wide calendar, as was our mandatory practice ever since the day that Michael and I each thought that the other was covering an appellate argument, and I returned from a meeting to find Robin in a panic because the court had called looking for us. The next morning, I gathered the entire firm in the conference room and informed them all, partners and staff alike, that everyone—with *no* exceptions—was to post on the office calendar every appointment, hearing, or other event which would require them to be anywhere other than at their desks. Eckert bridled at this since it meant acknowledging his frequent out-of-office activities, including golf with his prep school buddies and liaisons with his long-time mistress.

Fortunately, he believed partners should present a united front, and so he refrained from objecting in front of the staff—which was precisely why I'd required their presence. In the following weeks, Eckert's schedule suddenly included large blocks of time labeled, "Client Development—Out of Office." No new clients were developed, but at least we knew when not to expect him.

The message light on the client cellphone was blinking. I dialed into voicemail. A woman's voice said, "This is Tillie Hansen. I'm calling for Ralph Claus. Ralph, I tried to send that letter, but the email kept bouncing back. I assume it's something about their security levels. In any case, I'm sending a copy down with Charles. If the person getting this message isn't Ralph, please ask him to call me. He knows the number. Thank you."

Before I could decide what to make of that message, the desk phone beeped. "Mrs. Lane is here," Marilyn announced.

"Thanks. I'll be down in a minute." I'd been so caught up with the Claus matter that I nearly forgot about my other clients. Hastily, I sorted through the folders on my desk until I came to Janine and Gary Lane's file.

Theirs was a straightforward divorce—no messy affairs or hidden assets. Just two people who'd grown apart. They met in college, married a week after graduation, and set out into the world thinking their paths were clear.

The problem came when Gary realized that he wasn't cut out for a career in engineering. He tried to soldier on, but marital counseling revealed that his anger and hostility at home had their roots in his misery at work. To save the marriage, Janine and Gary agreed to swap roles. He stayed home with the twins, and she found a job in a small graphic design company. They were a modern, progressive family.

Except that while their arrangement was progressive, Janine and Gary weren't. Neither could forsake their deeply-entrenched beliefs about spousal roles. In the end, mutual resentment smothered everything else. Tears rolled down Janine's face as she admitted at our first meeting that when Gary finally moved out, her primary reaction was overwhelming relief.

I was working with Janine and Gary on a collaborative divorce, a fairly new concept designed to preserve whatever relationship the couple had left. The twins were only six, which meant Janine and Gary had at least twelve years of co-parenting ahead of them. At our initial meeting, they agreed that it would be best to manage the divorce in the least acrimonious way.

Only now, the good will and cooperation were breaking down. First, Gary announced that he wouldn't waive alimony since "you never know." Janine informed him that she'd supported his lazy ass long enough and if he wanted money, he could get a job. I had to send them out of the room to calm down. When they returned, the calm lasted for nearly two minutes before they started bickering about who would get the twins for school vacations. I'd practiced family law long enough to know the difference between a regular dispute and one that masks a deeper issue. So, when Janine called last week and asked to see me alone, I figured the amicability was over.

"I can't do this," she announced. "I can't collaborate with that man."

That man. Never a good sign.

"This whole business of dividing up the holidays—it's not working." She favored me with the same wide-eyed sad look she utilized to entice Gary into surrendering a point.

"Janine, one of the problems with breaking up a marriage is that your holidays will never be exactly the way you want," I reminded her. "You agreed that you would have the twins on Christmas Eve, and Gary would have them on Christmas Day so he could take them up to Boston to his family. They'll be back Wednesday, and you'll have them for the rest of their break."

"But it didn't feel like Christmas without them."

"I understand, but you did agree to it." Sometimes, I felt as though I spent half my life reminding people what they'd agreed to.

"I'll bet the judge would understand," she said. "I'm their mother. I should have custody." I fought the urge to grimace. Judges liked parties who could work out agreements, and they disliked parties who wasted the court's time because they'd changed their minds. If Janine reneged on the current plan, it was highly unlikely she'd be rewarded with the custody arrangement she wanted.

An hour later, I'd accomplished nothing except growing an hour older. Janine had apparently spent Christmas listening to happily married friends tell her how unfair her situation was. Finally, I said, "If you want to walk away from the collaborative divorce, that's your decision, but remember that if you do, I can't represent you anymore. You'll have to start fresh with a new lawyer. That's going to cost you a lot of money." Once Janine assumed the role of breadwinner, she tightened the household purse strings, insisting that Gary spend hours online comparing prices before making even minor purchases. "She's just plain cheap," Gary said. I made noncommittal murmuring noises, but privately, I agreed.

"Oh, I don't *know!*" She dropped her head into her hands as if she was bursting into tears. When I didn't respond, she looked up again, eyes conspicuously not reddened.

"Why you don't go home and think about it some more?" I suggested. "Don't forget—the kids will be back day after tomorrow, and you'll have practically an entire week with just the three of you." Madison and Bryant were typical high-energy six-year-olds. Having them for five solid days might cause her to rethink her new custody demand.

Ralph was perusing the newspaper in the waiting area as I ushered Janine out of the room. "Let me know what you want to do," I said to her. She grumbled something that might have been "okay" as she retrieved her coat from the closet.

With that matter resolved, I turned to Ralph. Freshly showered and shaved, with clean clothes that might have been borrowed from Sergio, he was the picture of respectability. "Did you need to see me?"

"If you've got some time." He seemed distracted by Janine.

"Can you give me a few minutes?" I liked to write up notes of a meeting immediately afterward. It was a practice that served me well, especially when emotional clients misremembered conversations.

I closeted myself in the library and recorded the gist of my meeting with Janine. When I emerged, Ralph had vanished. "Where did he go?" I asked Marilyn. She gestured toward the conference room. The door was closed. I knocked once before going in and stopping stock-still.

Ralph was sitting almost knee-to-knee with Janine, and she was crying—for real, this time. "What's going on?" I asked. To Janine, I said, "Are you all right?"

She nodded, sniffling. "I just—he said—oh, Meg, I'm such a fool!" Ralph slid the tissue box to her, and she dabbed her eyes. "I don't know who you are or how you know what you know, but you're so right about everything. I never even thought—it never occurred to me—oh, I can't believe it! I'm going to call Gary and tell him that if they want to stay up in Boston another day or two, that's fine."

I couldn't have been more stunned if she'd thrown her purse at me. "That's wonderful, Janine. I'm glad to hear you're thinking about what we discussed."

She waved her hand dismissively. "It's not that. It's what *he* said." To Ralph, she added, "Are you one of those Buddhist monks?"

Ralph chuckled. "Not even close."

"You could be the Dalai Lama as far as I'm concerned, because you're the wisest person I ever met." She wiped her nose and stood up. "I've got to get home. Meg, Gary and I will be in next week to finalize everything. And you—"

"—Ralph—" he supplied.

"—Ralph, you're amazing. Thank you so much!" She kissed his cheek and practically danced out of the office.

I stared at him. "What did you say to her?"

"Don't worry about it," he said. "The important thing is that she's seeing reason."

"What do you mean, don't worry about it? You can't tell my clients what to do. You're not a lawyer. You're not even a counselor. You're—you're just—"

"Santa Claus? More specifically, some deranged lunatic who thinks he's Santa Claus?"

"'Deranged lunatic' is redundant," I snapped.

"You don't say." He leaned back in his chair, the smile widening. The arrogant son of a bitch was laughing at me.

"I need to get back to work," I said. "Was there a reason you came back?"

"You have my lunch," he said. "Besides, I don't have anything else to do until the delivery gets here, so I thought I'd see if I could help. Need any copying or filing? Or I could do deliveries. I've got some experience at that." His grin widened.

"The office is fully staffed, thank you." I didn't care whether my tone was frosty. "Your sandwich is upstairs. You're welcome to take it with you."

"Okay," he said, apparently unoffended. "But if you think of anything I can do for you, let me know."

"There's nothing," I said. "Now, if you'll excuse me—" I went back up to my office without finishing the sentence.

Eight

The rest of the afternoon passed in a blur of phone calls and emails. A surprising number of people were working today after all. Either they remembered the Christmas bills that would come due, or they were escaping the chaos of noisy kids and visiting relatives.

Or maybe they had nothing else to do. The solitary might be invited for meals on major holidays, but the next day was life as usual.

By the time I hung up the phone for the last time, the streets had gone quiet. Snow was falling lightly. Everybody else was probably at home in flannel pjs or enjoying a candlelight dinner with an attractive partner. I deposited a scoop of Super Salmon Supper in Lulu's dish. Her munching rang in the stillness.

A knock on my open door made me jump. Lulu darted down the hall to Robin's dark office as Ralph stuck his head in. "The delivery arrived," he said.

"I didn't know you were still here." The wall clock showed it was nearly six-thirty.

"I waited downstairs. I didn't want to disturb you." He handed me a manila envelope. "Everything's in there."

"Who else is still here?" Surely my colleagues wouldn't have left a client unattended.

"Charles. He just got here."

I dumped the contents of the envelope on the desk. Ten—no, fifteen—bundles of fifty-dollar bills. With forced casualness, I picked one up and flipped through it. Twenty bills. One thousand dollars. I was alone with a strange man—make that *two* strange men—and fifteen thousand dollars in cash.

"Ten is yours," Ralph said. "Except—you covered the bail bond, didn't you?" I managed a nod. "Then this is yours, too." He moved ten bundles off to one side, then opened another and counted out five hundred dollars, adding it to my stack. "I told Carla I'd bring them the rent money tonight, but she said tomorrow was fine. Nice people. Listen, do you have a safe here? I'm not nuts about carrying this kind of cash around."

"Sure, fine." I knew I sounded distracted even before his brow crinkled. *Focus*, I told myself. "Let me give you a receipt," I said when the lawyer part of my brain came to life. For a few minutes, there was no sound except the clicking of my keyboard. I sent the documents to print, and the normally quiet hum of my small printer buzzed like a swarm of angry yellow jackets.

"Hey, Ralph, if you don't need me, I'm going to head back." The deep voice couldn't have startled me more if it had been a gunshot. A very short man of indeterminate age stood in my doorway. Dark-rimmed glasses perched on his bulbous nose. His pale scalp shone in the gleam of the energy-saver lights. A gingery beard began where sideburns would normally have ended, as if somebody had put his hair on upside down.

He wore a black jumpsuit and clunky black boots that were clearly designed for much more severe weather than we ever saw in Connecticut. He held black gloves and a black hat in one hand. What looked like ski goggles hung around his neck.

"Come in and meet my lawyer," said Ralph. "Meg, this is Charles. Charles, this is Attorney Riley."

"Meg," I corrected him. "How do you do?"

"Nice to meet you," said Charles. He strode across the room, his hand extended. The top of his shiny head barely cleared Ralph's belt. His ears were as pointy as Lulu's. His grip was firm and hearty.

Pleasantries completed, he said to Ralph, "You good?"

Ralph nodded. "Thanks again, Chaz. Appreciate it."

"Just don't break this phone," Charles said. "It's not like there's boxes of them sitting around."

"I know, I know," said Ralph amiably. To me, he said, "One of the reindeer stepped on my phone outside of Vancouver. That's why I didn't have one before."

"You don't have any reindeer this time, so this shouldn't be a problem," Charles said.

"Unless I fall down the stairs and break my neck and land on the phone," Ralph said.

"Funny," said Charles. "That's what we all need. A funny Santa."

"You haven't seen Pop in action," Ralph said.

Charles snorted. "I was seeing your old man in action before you got your first candy cane," he said. "Believe me, I know how to take care of Santa."

"I know," was all Ralph said, but a look passed between them as if a great deal more was being said than just those few words.

Charles turned to me. "You have any trouble with him, call me. The number's in there." He pointed to the non-cash papers that had fallen out of the envelope. "And make them put you through to me personally. Don't take any crap from anybody."

"Watch your language," said Ralph.

"Sorry, ma'am," Charles said. "I'm just saying. Ivy tries to put you through to the missus, you tell her no. Hang up if you have to."

"—the missus—"

"My mother," Ralph clarified.

"Whatever it is, you call me," said Charles. "Not her."

"Thank you." I shuffled through the papers; a small yellow sheet, no bigger than an index card, bore a number and the word "Charles." I tucked it into the side pocket of my purse. Then, because I couldn't resist, I asked, "Are you going back to the North Pole tonight?"

"Of course," said Charles. "I got work to do." He shook my hand. "Nice to meet you, counselor. And you—" he poked a finger at Ralph's chest. "Behave yourself."

"Why start now?" Ralph winked at me.

"Clauses," Charles muttered. He waved goodnight, and Ralph followed him out of the room. I stuffed the cash back into its envelope. It needed to get into the safe, pronto. I moved to the window to close the blinds, and—well, I couldn't have said for certain since the lights in my office made it hard to see outside, but for an instant, I thought I saw something down on the street the size of a small vehicle, with creatures in front that might have been Shetland ponies. I squinted, and it was gone.

I was still standing at the window when Ralph returned, his head and shoulders dusted with snow. I didn't know what to say, what to think. Finally, I said, "Is he—" I couldn't finish.

"—an elf?" His voice was gentle. "Yep. Been with the family his whole life." I must have looked skeptical, because he said, "Tell you what. You let me take you out to dinner with some of that cash, and you can ask me anything you want about elves." He reached into the envelope and extracted one of the bundles of fifties, peeling off several bills. "Put this stuff away, and take me to the one restaurant where you've always wanted to go. We'll have Christmas dinner a few nights late. Deal?"

"Deal." I knew I sounded dazed, but I didn't care. I adjusted the receipts, he signed them, and I made copies for him. "Wait for me by the back door," I said. When I heard him reach the bottom of the stairs, I went to Eckert's office to stash the original receipts and the cash in the fireproof safe in his closet where we kept original wills and other irreplaceable documents. Then I headed down to the first floor where Ralph was waiting, holding my coat. As his hands brushed my shoulders, I closed my eyes, savoring the brief contact. Then, I picked up my purse, and led the way out of the office, locking the door and resetting the alarm.

I turned around to see him watching me. In the light of the parking lot, softened by the snow, he almost looked sad. Our eyes met, his smile returned, and he offered me his arm.

"Let's go," he said, and I knew again the feeling I had watching him with Charles, that a great deal more was being said than just those few words.

The question was: *what?*

Nine

As we opened the door to Oishii, the tiny Asian woman behind the counter beamed at me. "Meg! So good to see you!"

I felt Ralph glancing at me. "Hello, Akira," I said. "Did you have a good holiday?"

"Oh, yes!" Her smile widened at the sight of Ralph. "How about you?"

"Very nice, thank you." She led us past the sushi bar to my usual booth. Once we were seated, Ralph commented, "So this is the place where you've always wanted to go."

I couldn't help smiling. "No," I admitted. "But it's my favorite."

"Someplace familiar and reliable," he grinned. "Because having dinner with the future Santa Claus is anything but."

I ignored his comment. A female lawyer learns early not to let arrogant men rattle her. Not that Ralph Claus was arrogant exactly, but he certainly seemed convinced of his own charm.

He flipped open the menu, nodding as he read. "Interesting selection."

"I should have asked you if sushi was all right." It wouldn't be quite fair to say that I'd chosen this restaurant in the hope of catching him off balance, but I did like the notion of a home field advantage.

"It's great," he said. "I don't get it often. Mainly when I'm in Japan."

So much for the home field advantage. "Do you travel a lot?"

"More lately," he said. "I'm still learning the geography. It's a big world."

"Can't you use GPS like everybody else?" His story was so outrageous that it was difficult to refrain from the occasional jab.

"I don't like it," he said. "My brother put it in all the sleighs, but it feels like cheating. My grandfather used stars and maps, and he managed fine."

"There's nothing wrong with technology if it makes the job easier." It was a ludicrous conversation.

"Maybe, but I'm old-school about some things," he said. "Do you like gyoza?"

"Gyoza are old-school?"

"I thought we'd order appetizers and drinks first, and then we could decide about the meal. What do you drink? Saki?"

"Wine for me, but you go ahead."

"I'm not a huge saki fan," he said. "Let's get a bottle of wine. Whatever you like." Ed would have spent the next twenty minutes bent over his phone, comparing vintages and prices.

By the time our appetizers and wine arrived, we'd decided on an assortment of sashimi and two of my favorite rolls—a spicy scallop handroll and the restaurant's signature roll with tuna, salmon, yellowtail and avocado inside and shrimp and kani salad on top. "Why do they call this a 'Bye, Bye, Birdie' roll?" Ralph asked after the waiter left. "There's no poultry in it."

"No idea. Maybe the chef liked the movie. Have you ever seen it?"

He shook his head. "I only know about it because my aunt used to call out, 'Bye, bye, birdy!' whenever Pop and the sleigh took off. Are you a fan of old movies?"

"My parents were. We were the first on our street to have a VCR. I knew the classics better than any of the new stuff." A memory nudged me like a cat wanting treats.

"What? You can't smile like that and not tell me." His grin was impish.

"When I was right out of college, a group of us got together one night to play Trivial Pursuit. We played girls against guys. The couple who was hosting had two different versions of the game, the regular and the movie version. We used all the cards, so when you landed on a color, you could pick from either set. I was kicking ass with the movie questions, and my girlfriends thought this was great. I didn't notice the guys getting quieter until I drew the question, 'Who played Nathan Detroit in the film version of *Guys and Dolls*?' I said, 'Frank Sinatra.' One of the guys said, 'How did you know that?' Totally without thinking, I said, 'Everybody knows that.' Then, I looked around the table, and all these men were glaring at me. It was the first time it occurred to me that maybe *not* everybody knew that. I thought of trying to play dumb after that so they'd feel better, but that ship had sailed."

"For what it's worth, I like having a smart lawyer," Ralph said. As his chopsticks hovered over the gyoza, he asked oh-so-casually, "What about your husband? Is he smart, too?"

"I'm not married." As he well knew since he'd been sitting in my office when Ed called. "What about you?"

He shook his head. "Came close a couple times, but let's face it— it's a lot to ask of somebody, changing their whole life like that. Do you have any kids?"

I was tempted to point out that this was information Santa would have known. "Nope—never married, no kids, but three cats. Your basic spinster."

"Hardly." Our eyes met, and my stomach flipped. We talked until I realized that we were the last people in the restaurant. I beckoned to our waiter, who trotted over with the check.

I reached for my purse, but Ralph said, "No, I've got this, remember?" He picked up the check and peeled off some bills from the wad in his pocket. "We don't need change," he said to the waiter. "Thanks very much."

"Thank you, sir, ma'am," said the waiter. He glanced ever so discreetly at the bills, and his expression shifted a fraction toward a smile.

Outside, flurries drifted as we crossed the near-empty parking lot. I unlocked the car, and something occurred to me. "We never got to talk about you," I said. Which showed how good a con artist he was, because I never noticed when I lost control of the conversation.

"I'm not all that interesting. You, on the other hand. . . ." He let the words fade. Before I could react, he rested his hands on my shoulders, leaned down, and kissed me. His lips were soft, his breath slightly tinged with wasabi. But as his hands began to move from my shoulders to my back, pulling me closer, I opened my eyes.

"No," I said with as much firmness as I could muster.

"No?"

"I'm your lawyer." *I'm his lawyer,* I repeated silently. *His lawyer.* "We can't get involved. It would violate my professional ethics." The rule forbade a sexual relationship, not a social one, but it didn't take a genius to connect these dots.

He studied me for a long minute. Then, he released me and stepped back, leaving me shivering without his warmth. "All right," he said, his voice heavy. "I guess I'm glad those rules mean something to you." He didn't sound glad. No matter. I'd been in practice long enough to know there was never a good enough reason to violate ethics for a client.

When we reached Sergio and Carla's, I was careful not to turn off the engine. I thanked him for dinner, adding, "Next time, we need to talk about you and your case."

Even in the dimness of the dash lights, I could see his smile. "Next time," he said. For a second, I thought he was going to try to kiss me again, but he bade me good night and got out of the car. The snow was picking up, but he didn't seem to notice. He strode up the walk, unlocked the door, and let himself in. As he closed the door, he waved, like he knew I was watching.

Ten

When I arrived at the office the next morning, Lulu was waiting for me at the top of the stairs, meowing disapproval at the lateness of her breakfast. "Sorry, girlfriend," I said as I caressed her head. I collected her dishes and my electric tea kettle and carried them into the third-floor bathroom to be rinsed and refilled. The little cat wove around my ankles as I opened a can of Fabulous Tuna Feast, and she practically danced as I carried her pungent meal to the fish-shaped placemat next to her club chair.

The most important task finished, I set the kettle to boil and spooned English Breakfast tea into the teapot filter. A British client gave me the teapot after I successfully defended her son against a bogus paternity claim. The vibrant red peonies on the ceramic pot were a welcome spot of color on a gray winter day.

As the tea steeped, I emailed Lucy Jane, our office manager, to let her know about the retainer in the safe. I fired off a second email to lawyers and staff, reminding them of our end-of-day protocols, such as double-checking conference rooms and rest rooms for clients before locking up and setting the alarm. Within minutes, I received a response from Marilyn:

> *Before I left at 5:10, I checked everywhere. You were the only person here, and you were on the phone. I locked up and set the alarm.*

Yet Ralph and Charles were in my office at six-thirty.

Maybe Ralph was in the rest room when she left, and then he let

Charles in. That would explain it.

Except that if Ralph had opened the door, the alarm would have sounded.

So both of them were here, and Marilyn missed them. Or else the alarm wasn't working, or she hadn't set it properly. I sent another email to Lucy Jane:

When did we last have the alarm serviced?

A second later, my intercom beeped. "What's going on?" Lucy Jane asked without preamble.

"A client got left behind here last night. He came upstairs around six-thirty." Silence. "Nothing's been disturbed, has it?"

"I'll check," she said. "The system was serviced right before Thanksgiving, but I'm going to call anyway." Minutes later, she reported that the alarm people were coming out this afternoon. Nobody had noticed anything missing or out of order, but she was going to meet with the staff about security protocols anyway. "I'll do a memo and send it around to everybody," she concluded. Lucy Jane was nothing if not thorough.

Marilyn beeped to let me know my next appointment was here. Just as well. The idea of Ralph Claus getting into our locked and alarmed office was unsettling.

Alyssa Jenson was a potential client who wanted to sue her condo association over a slip-and-fall outside the fitness center. The case sounded promising until she mentioned that she could hardly see where she was walking because the snow was falling so hard. A few more questions revealed that prior to the storm, the pavement had been absolutely clear of any snow or ice. The association's contractor was plowing the parking lot when Alyssa went for her daily Pilates workout. "I'm positively addicted," she said. "That's how I got this body." She pulled up her sweater to reveal a perfectly toned abdomen.

I could feel the roll of flab pushing at my waistband. "The thing is, under the law, a property owner isn't required to clear snow from a sidewalk until the storm is over."

She dropped the sweater. "That's absurd! What was I supposed to do—stay home? What if it snowed all day? I have a *life!*"

And a sprained ankle, I nearly reminded her. When she admitted that her only claim of monetary damage was missing two weeks of Pilates—

not prepaid—I laid down my pen. "I'm sorry, but you don't have a case," I said with as much regret as I could manufacture. "There's no liability, and your damages are—well, minimal." A fair chunk of my practice involved entitled pains in the ass, but those people were usually one of my partners' cherished clients. For instance, Elsa had long represented the owner of a local chain of popular mid-level restaurants. She advised him on his business dealings, Roy took care of his tax issues, Eckert wrote his will, and I handled his divorce and his teenage son's periodic motor vehicle infractions. Michael referred to this approach to practice as "cross-pollination."

"Anything good?" Marilyn asked after the door closed firmly behind Ms. Jenson. I shook my head and trudged up the stairs to find fourteen voicemail messages—had I done this, when would I finish that, over and over. My email showed forty-seven new messages, including one from Elsa that was marked "URGENT." Concerned, I clicked on it, but it was just a referral. One of her corporate clients, Cyril Walker, had been sued by a former employee. My other partners would have relayed such information by phone or in person, but Elsa believed in documenting everything. In the same spirit, I emailed back that I needed to see the file before I spoke with him.

At four-thirty, Robin poked her head in the door. "I'm out of here," she said. I must have looked startled, because she said, "Nate's dropping Jordy off at five-thirty. He has a rehearsal." She and her ex-boyfriend had a custody schedule I could never quite keep track of. Luckily, Nate, a heavily-tattooed drummer who taught world literature at a nearby community college, was blessedly flexible about taking the child when Robin had to work.

Muffled "good nights" drifted up the stairs. Finally, the building was quiet. Lulu hopped onto my desk, which was my cue to prepare her supper. As she gobbled the evening's smelly offering, I relished the peace. At moments like this, when it was quiet enough to think, I remembered that I loved my job.

I finished drafting a demand letter and turned to a motion to dismiss that had arrived in today's e-filing. At first pass, it looked like a slam dunk for the defendant, but most motions looked good on their faces. It was only when the reader began to dig that the flaws appeared. I logged into our legal research database and started searching for ways to distinguish our case from the decisions the defendant had cited.

Just as I was teasing out a fine-line distinction, the phone rang. The clock revealed that it was 6:53 p.m. "Forget it," I said aloud. I logged off and kissed Lulu, who purred softly as she slept.

I was buttoning my coat when I heard the distinctive ring of my client phone. The caller ID display showed the number as blocked. I told myself to decline the call, that it was probably a robo-call. But I pressed the "talk" button anyway.

"Hi, Meg, it's Ralph." He sounded relaxed, even jaunty.

"Hi, Ralph. What can I do for you?" Dumb question. I should have told him I was leaving the office. Keep things strictly professional.

"I was calling to see if you wanted to grab some dinner."

"I have to work tonight." Not that the file in my briefcase was urgent, but it would be useful to pick up with the objection while my thoughts were still fresh.

"You have to eat, too."

"What makes you think I didn't?"

"Because I'm standing in your parking lot. Your car is still here, and the light in your office is on. So, unless you ordered in, you haven't eaten."

A shiver ran down my neck. "Are you spying on me?"

"Nothing like that. I just thought you might like to join me for dinner. I had a good time last night," he added, his voice softening.

It's just dinner, I rationalized. It would help the case to find out more about him. Last night might have been a date of sorts, but tonight, we would talk business.

"I'll be right out," I said before my nerve could falter. I clicked off the phone, shoved a legal pad into my briefcase, and switched off the desk lamp. The streetlight cast oblong blocks of light on the rug. In the doorway, I hesitated on the precipice of something I couldn't identify. My fingers tightened around the handle of my briefcase, and I plunged down the stairs toward whatever lay ahead.

*****

Twenty minutes later, we were seated in a booth at a local twenty-four-hour Greek diner, perusing a menu only slightly thinner than *War and Peace*. I'd purposely picked the least romantic restaurant I could think of, but Ralph didn't seem to mind. To the contrary, a smile played at the corners of his mouth as he scanned page after page of breakfast offerings, sandwiches, and dinners ranging from beef stew to broiled cod to spaghetti with meat sauce.

"The desserts here are amazing," he said when he finally closed the menu. "I recommend the strawberry layer cake. The frosting is real whipped cream."

"You've been here before?" The diner wasn't on the same bus line as Carla and Sergio's house. He must have spent the day exploring. Either that, or he was really a local and this place was his high school hangout.

He shook his head, the dimple showing in his right cheek. "Not everybody leaves cookies and milk. Spiro's kids make sure Santa's well fed. Sometimes Pop brings home some of the best stuff, and last year, he brought that cake."

I wouldn't say I slammed the menu shut, but I definitely closed it firmly. "We need to talk about this whole Santa thing."

"I had a feeling you'd say that," said Ralph, unperturbed. "But let's order first. What do you recommend?"

"I haven't been here in ages. I used to come on weekends for breakfast. The French toast is wonderful. They make their own bread."

Ralph closed his menu. "You sold me. French toast it is."

"For dinner?"

"I love breakfast food for dinner," Ralph said. "Did you know the notion of breakfast food or dinner food is a western one? If you go to someplace like Thailand, there's no such thing. You get rice and vegetables at all three meals."

I imagined facing a hamburger for breakfast. "Sorry, can't do it."

"You haven't traveled very much, have you?" he asked.

His tone didn't suggest criticism, but I bristled anyway. "I'm busy. Practicing law isn't the kind of job you can walk away from for weeks at a time. I have commitments to my clients, and they expect me to make good on it."

"At what cost?" His voice was unexpectedly gentle. "What if you blocked out a couple weeks, or even a month, and traveled? Would your practice come to a screeching halt?"

"I couldn't leave Michael with everything. He's the only other litigator in the firm. Besides, even if I could afford the time, I can't afford the money. It's one of the downsides of being self-employed— no paid time off. If I don't work, money doesn't come in the door, and that affects the entire firm."

"Don't any of your partners take vacations?"

I sipped my water to avoid answering. Eckert routinely spent

August in New Hampshire at his family's lake house, but he usually worked at least some of the time; I suspected it was his way of escaping his wife's sisters and their hordes of children and grandchildren. Elsa and Desirée traveled to exotic locales and returned with tales of going backstage at the Russian ballet, traveling down the river through a South American jungle, or scoring an incredible bargain on a chandelier at an Italian glass factory. Roy and Camille visited their families in Pittsburgh between tax deadlines. Michael and Ruby did what I thought of as American Tourist vacations, renting RVs to drive to the Grand Canyon or Yellowstone.

My infrequent vacations usually involved visiting friends who lived in interesting places like San Francisco or Vancouver or, less often, my mother and stepfather in Phoenix. Once, I went alone to Sanibel Island and spent four days in February sitting on the beach with Jane Austen and fried grouper sandwiches from the takeout shop next to my motel. I vowed to go back every winter—it would be my cherished break from New England snowdrifts, my mental health retreat—but when February rolled around the next year, my schedule was packed with back-to-back trials. The year after that, Michael and Ruby went to Vegas for their Valentine's Day anniversary, and we couldn't both be gone. And the following year, it was something else, until the glow of those Gulf sunsets faded.

Not that any of this was Ralph Claus's business. "Some people can get away with the whole vacation thing. Teachers who don't have classes for the summer, or people who work shifts, but not lawyers. It's so much work to get everything taken care of before you leave, and when you come back, you have the stuff that was already scheduled, plus whatever piled up while you were gone. Or you pay for a fancy vacation, and you end up sitting in a hotel room with a laptop, trying to manage some crisis back at the office. Frankly, it's more hassle than it's worth."

"Sounds like it," Ralph said.

His ready agreement startled me. "Don't you have the same thing? I mean, you're self-employed, right?" At least, Santa was.

"Not the same way you are," he said. "The organization's big enough that one person taking some time off—the way I'm doing now, for example—isn't enough to throw everything off kilter. I've got people who can cover until I get back as long as I'm not gone too long. How long do you think this whole thing will last, anyway?"

For an insane moment, I thought he meant us, but he was talking about his case. "No idea," I admitted. "Depends on the prosecutor. That's one reason I wanted to talk to you. I need to offer him a credible explanation for why you were at the Leopolds' that night."

"You could try telling him the truth," he said with a hint of reproach.

"The Santa thing? Look, you may know toys, but I know prosecutors. If I tell this guy you're Santa-in-training, not only will he not agree to any kind of a plea, but we'll have to sell that story to a jury, and he's going to have a psych expert talking about your delusions."

"Sounds like *Miracle on 34th Street*," Ralph mused.

"Do you watch all the Santa Claus movies?" I envisioned him sitting in front of the television, taking notes.

"Oh, jeez, no," he said. "There's a limit to how much of that stuff I can stomach. Most of it's straight out of the poem, which is about ninety-eight percent wrong."

"What about the other two percent?"

"Even a blind reindeer can find a carrot once in a while."

The waitress came over. She was short and plump, her dark hair streaked with gray. Gold-rimmed glasses perched at the end of her nose. "You know what you want?"

Ralph gestured to me to go first, so I said, "I'll have the French toast with crisp bacon, orange juice, and hot tea with lemon, please."

"Make that two," said Ralph. He smiled, and almost unwillingly, she smiled back. As she walked away, he said in a low voice, "She had a tough Christmas this year. Her oldest boy's in basic training—Seattle area, I think—and he couldn't get home for Christmas. His wife and little girl are living with her until he gets back. First time they weren't all together."

I studied him, not even bothering to pretend otherwise. Neither of us spoke until the waitress had brought our juice, a pot of tea, and two thick white mugs. As she walked away, I said, "I can't figure out what to make of you. You say these things, and you sound completely convincing, but they're so . . . outrageous. I can't make up my mind."

He regarded me. "It's actually pretty simple. You have to decide whether I'm the most amazing liar you've ever met, or I'm completely deluded, or—"

"Or?"

"Or I am who I say I am."

I ripped open two packets of sweetener as I framed a careful, diplomatic response. "As lovely as that notion is, you know and I know that there's no such thing as Santa Claus." I focused on pouring the tea to avoid his eyes. "Don't get me wrong. I wish it were true. Spending your life making people happy, making children happy—I think that would be wonderful. I would love to live in a world where Santa was real. But this isn't that world."

"Who says it's not?" His eyes were intense, his voice quiet. "Look, I know this is hard to believe. I probably wouldn't believe me, either. But I'm telling the truth. Really. I mean, think about what you've seen so far. You checked your phone. You saw the number. Have you ever seen that country code before? No, because nobody else has it. It's ours."

"You've got your own country code?"

"We've got our own country, in a manner of speaking. Not that we have land—it's mainly ice—but it's ours. Back when people started coming there on expeditions, there was talk about moving the whole operation onto a ship—kind of like those aircraft carriers your military uses—but there were too many logistical problems. Besides, reindeer like the tundra."

"Gotta keep the reindeer happy," I said, slightly dazed. The waitress set down our plates. If she'd heard us, she didn't let on.

"Well, you know those reindeer unions. They're pretty tough." I must have looked startled, because he burst out laughing. "Kidding!" he chortled. "It's animal control that gets after us. Kidding again!" It was like having dinner with a nine-year-old.

"But what about—" I began, but Ralph was already groaning with delight over his first bite of French toast.

"Oh, that's good," he said. "I've got to get that recipe."

I drizzled syrup over my toast. "Chefs don't give out their recipes."

"Betcha she'll give it to me."

"Oh, really? What's the bet? If you win, I ride a reindeer?" I took a bite, savoring the spices swirled through the bread.

He pondered the question as he chewed. "If I win—you go to the prosecutor with the Santa explanation."

Plunk. Back to reality. "I can't compromise my representation of you on a bet."

"It's not compromise—it's the truth. Besides, don't you have to do whatever the client says?"

That nine-year-old grew up fast. "No," I said pointedly.

"That's not what I meant," he said. My cheeks grew warm. "I meant, you have to follow my directions about how to represent me."

"Not if I don't think it's in your best interests. I can't take a position that opposes yours, but I'm not obligated to do something if I believe it's going to harm your case."

"That's only because you don't think Antonio Antonio will buy it." He seemed unperturbed by the prospect.

"I know he won't," I retorted. "That's a fact, not an opinion."

Ralph slathered butter on another slice. "Have you considered the possibility that maybe I know things about this guy that you don't?" He reached for the syrup pitcher, as casual as milk. I studied his face for some sign that he wasn't implying what I suspected, but he blithely poured out maple sweetness and sliced off another bite. As he began to chew, I said, "You can't blackmail a prosecutor."

You'd have thought I punched him in the gut. He coughed and wheezed and gasped for breath until half-chewed bread flew out of his mouth, landing on his plate with a soggy plop. "Are you okay?" I asked as he tried to catch his breath. I pushed his water glass into his hand, and he managed a sip.

"Jeez," he said finally. "You lawyers really have your own way of seeing the world, don't you?" His voice was still raspy. "I was talking about—well, what he was like when he was a kid. What he liked. What he wanted for Christmas. Stuff that can give you a real picture of a person."

A disconcerting thought occurred to me. "Do you know those things about everybody?"

"You mean, do I know stuff about you?" I blushed, and he reached across the table to rest his hand on mine. "I could get it," he admitted. "But I haven't."

"It's not fair." I slid my hand out from beneath his. "I don't have any way to find out about you except from you." Robin had run the standard searches, but the internet was silent.

This time, his smile was gentle. "Fair's fair. Here's my promise: I won't use any of the organization's resources to find out about you. We'll be like two regular people who happened to meet. We'll find out about each other the way normal people do. You know—we'll Google each other, check Facebook pages, hire investigators. I'm kidding," he laughed as I started to protest. "One thing I've learned—you're very easy to tease." He winked. "Do you have room for strawberry layer cake?"

"Didn't you have that the other night?"

"I never got home," he reminded me. "Besides, if I'm going to ask Ella for her French toast recipe, it doesn't hurt to butter her up a little first."

I'd forgotten about the recipe. "Okay, go for it. I want to see this."

"And if I get it, you'll talk Santa with Antonio?"

"I'll *think* about talking Santa with Antonio," I said. "You can't ask for more than that." *Hey, Antonio, my client thinks he's Santa Claus, and he was at the Leopolds' on Christmas Eve to deliver presents. What do you think of that?* He'd laugh so hard that even his industrial-strength gel wouldn't keep his coiffure in place.

"Fair enough." We both scanned the room for our waitress. Finally, we caught sight of her near the door. Ralph raised his hand. She strode over, her round face somber.

"Ella, this French toast was incredible," he said. "Best I've ever had."

"Do you want anything else?" She didn't quite snap, but she came close.

"Now that you mention it, there is one thing," Ralph said. "My friend says there's nutmeg in the French toast, but I think it was cloves. Who's right?"

She ripped the check off her pad and slapped it down on the table. "Have a good night." She turned on her heel and stalked out of the room.

"You lose," I said, reaching for the check.

He put his hand on mine to stop me from taking it, but he was still watching the waitress. His brow furrowed. "I'll be right back," he said, sliding out of the booth.

Nearly ten minutes passed before he returned. "Is everything okay?" I asked.

He shook his head. "Her son was hurt in a training accident," he said. "Jeep overturned. The kid's okay—just a broken leg. She's pretty upset, though. She wants to go see him, but they don't have the money."

"That's awful," I said. "She seemed okay when we came in."

"She got the call while we were eating," he said.

"Poor thing," I said. "That must be hard."

"That's why I was gone so long. I had to make some calls." His casual tone belied the meaning of his words.

"What are you talking about? Christmas is over."

He gave me a wry smile. "It is if you view it as just a day," he said. "But at the Pole, it's a state of mind, and that lasts all year."

"What does that mean?" I asked.

"It means she has a flight to the coast at 8:30 tomorrow morning," he said.

Right then, we heard a shriek from the kitchen, and Ralph grinned. "She just checked her email and found the ticket."

"What? You bought her an airline ticket?" That couldn't be true. Not with all the security hoops you had to jump through.

"Not me specifically. I just passed on the information." There was a glow about him so intense, so luminous that while I couldn't see a halo of light, I could feel it.

No. This was ridiculous. Just because he was a nice guy—maybe even a philanthropist—it didn't make him Santa. I seized on the most obvious flaw in his story: "You can't buy an airline ticket without a credit card and ID."

"Phil handles that kind of thing. I don't know who he talked to."

Either Ralph wasn't very bright, or he was a whole lot smarter than I was giving him credit for. The notion that somebody at the North Pole had arranged for a waitress in Rocky Hill to fly to Seattle was preposterous. I was about to tell him so when our waitress came running out of the kitchen and embraced the older man behind the cash register. A dark-haired young man and a woman who could have been his sister rushed over to the register, all four talking in rapid, excited voices, cutting each other off, gesturing wildly.

I drank the last of my juice to tamp down a flare of anger. It was the power of suggestion, nothing more. There had to be a rational explanation. Ralph probably overheard something and decided to engraft it onto his story to make the whole Santa fantasy more plausible. Except instead of believing him, I was furious. How gullible did he think I was?

"Since you're such good friends with our waitress, maybe you can get her to bring us the check." My tone was nastier than I'd intended. I dug in my purse to avoid his eyes.

The words were barely out of my mouth when our waitress came to the table. Her eyes were reddened as if she'd been crying, but her smile was radiant.

"May we have the check, please?" I asked, trying to sound reasonably pleasant. It wasn't her fault my client was a con artist.

She moved my cup and saucer to reveal the check she'd left us earlier. "This?"

"I'm sorry," I said. "I forgot we had it."

She smiled. "Everybody forgets sometime."

As she began to walk away, Ralph said, "Excuse me, Ella." She turned back, and he said, "I wonder if you could do me a favor. My mother's French toast—well, Mom's great, but cooking isn't her gift. Yours was really good. Can you tell me what you did?"

"Must use homemade bread, two days old," Ella said. "Fresh bread soaks up too much liquid, gets soggy. Mix egg and milk and nutmeg—must be fresh, not from can. Melt butter in skillet, dip bread and fry. Only real maple syrup and real butter. And then. . . ." She waved her hand at our empty plates.

"Thanks so much, Ella," said Ralph. "I'm sure my mother will appreciate it."

Ella beamed at him. "A good son," she said. "Good sons take care of their mothers." She picked up our dishes and carried them to the kitchen.

"So it was nutmeg," he said. "I thought so."

"Let me guess. You're a gourmet chef on top of being Santa Claus." Next, he'd say he was a reindeer in disguise.

"Hardly," he said. "But I like to eat. And I wasn't kidding about Mom. If it weren't for Annaliese, we'd all have starved to death a long time ago."

"Who's Annaliese?"

"Head chef," he said, reaching for the check. "I've got this," he added. "I'm the one who asked you out, remember?"

"This isn't a date, it's a meeting," I reminded him. "You're supposed to be telling me about your Santa defense."

"I guess that's better than calling it the 'Santa thing'," he conceded. He took out his wallet as the waitress came back with a bag.

"You take this to your mother," she instructed Ralph. "Two days, it will be perfect for French toast."

"Thanks, Ella," Ralph said. He turned his wonderful smile on her, and I thought she might melt right there. "Would you mind taking this?" he added as he held out the check and some cash. "We don't need change."

"Of course," she said. "Thank you, have a good night." As she turned to go, I noticed for the first time that she wasn't wearing a nametag.

Once we were in the car, Ralph held out the bag. "You can have this," he said. "It's not like I'm going to be making French toast anytime soon."

"Use it for sandwiches. Do you want to stop at the supermarket?"

"I don't want to take up too much of your evening," he said.

"How long can it take to buy peanut butter? You could even get teabags."

"I'm not that much of a tea drinker," he said.

That surprised me. "You drank it tonight."

"It sounded good with the French toast, but usually I drink coffee. What about you?"

"Tea all the way. Guess that means we're not compatible."

"Let's not jump to conclusions," he said. "Coffee drinkers and tea drinkers can live happily ever after."

I didn't answer as I made the turn into Sergio and Carla's neighborhood. I didn't know what it would mean to be compatible with someone who thought he was Santa Claus, but I had a suspicion it involved a lot more than resolving a coffee-tea debate.

Eleven

The next morning found me bleary-eyed at the conference room table, guzzling my third mug of tea. The year-end partnership meeting was usually held on the thirty-first, but Elsa had asked to move it up so she and Desirée could get a head start on their trip to New York, presumably for an extra-long weekend of fabulous shopping and glamorous parties.

I fought a yawn as Eckert reviewed the year's accomplishments. On the whole, we'd had an excellent year. As he congratulated us, Elsa nodded like a queen being afforded appropriate reverence, a dignified smile playing on her perfectly-glossed lips. I fumbled in my pocket for a strawberry Chapstick.

Next to me, Roy fidgeted. He hated the year-end meeting. He spent days assembling data and projections, and inevitably, someone would have a question that required him to investigate and—horror of horrors—make a correction. Few things caused him more anguish than discovery of an error. I once reminded him that if it weren't for mistakes, none of us would have jobs. He replied, "Clients make mistakes. Not us."

"We're human," I said, but he remained unconvinced.

Once the year-end wrap-up was complete, the focus shifted to existing and potential business. Eckert inquired about my new case. "Anything we should know?"

"Judge Pearce asked me to take it," I said. Eckert beamed approvingly. "Turns out the appointment was in error. The client has money. He's already delivered the retainer. Cash." Roy brightened considerably. "There's only one concern, and it's minor. Apparently, the victim's mother has some political connections."

"Who?" asked Eckert.

"Senator Zenkman," I said. "He's a family friend of some sort."

A slight frown furrowed Elsa's flawless brow. "A number of our clients support Hal."

Hal. No surprise they'd be on a first-name basis.

"That's why I mentioned it," I said. "It's not a conflict of interest as such, but I figured you all should know in case anyone asked."

"This isn't going to make Cyril Walker happy," said Elsa. "He was a major contributor to Hal's campaign. You got those materials, right? The wrongful termination case?"

"Is that what it is? I haven't had a chance to review it."

Her frown became more pronounced. "Please do. He's already emailed me to say he hasn't heard from you."

"Did you tell him I didn't receive the materials until last night?" I kept my tone even.

Elsa waved her hand. "Just get back to him as soon as you can. I don't have to tell you how important a client Walker Industries is."

And yet you did. I could feel Michael holding back a smirk. Walker Industries led the client list for billings in the calendar year now ending. None of my clients had even made the top half of the list.

By mid-afternoon, everyone was trickling out of the office. Every year, holiday weekends started earlier and earlier. Far be it from me to buck the new tradition: at 4:30, I put on my coat and flicked off the lights.

The supermarket was crowded, the liquor store more so, but finally, I closed my garage door behind me. Harry and David napped as I put the groceries away. All was calm, all was bright. In the quiet of my living room, with a glass of wine in hand, partners and politics neatly tucked away, the question that had been rattling at my consciousness finally surfaced: did I–could I—actually believe, in some part of my mind, that Ralph Claus was who he said he was? Was it possible that Santa Claus existed? Not as a lovely myth or a children's story, but as a human who walked and talked, lived and breathed, ate and drank, laughed and cried like everybody else? A real person who snored and belched, whose feet stank after hours of wearing winter boots? Somebody who might curse if a reindeer stepped on his foot or his bag split and presents tumbled off a roof and into the snow? Somebody with sexual urges? The popular image of Santa with his round belly and white beard took on a new and startling dimension as my mind removed his red suit and pictured his dimpled butt as he gave Mrs. Claus the ultimate present.

I gulped my wine. It seemed wrong to think about Santa Claus this way. Sacrilegious, even. And yet, if Ralph Claus was telling the truth, Santa was definitely that kind of man. That kiss the other night was not merely polite. It was intended to lead to more kisses, and then deeper ones, and then hands roaming and buttons being undone and—

"Enough!" I said aloud. *This* was what was turning my brain into the proverbial bowl full of jelly. Periodic crash diets might keep my waistline from looking like Santa's, but small comfort that would be if my mind had all the analytical capabilities of the average spider plant.

I grabbed the phone and punched in Ed's cell number. With any luck, he hadn't yet crossed from Massachusetts into the dead zone at the southern edge of Vermont. Moments later, his crisp, assured voice informed me that he was unable to take my call at this time, but if I would kindly leave a message, he would return my call at his earliest opportunity. I said, "Hi, it's me. Just calling to say I miss you. Talk to you soon."

Except I didn't miss him. I'd been so busy with the whole Santa matter that I'd barely thought of him since he called to cancel New Year's.

The phone in my hand rang. I must have caught him as he emerged from the dead zone. Before the talking caller ID could announce him, I punched *talk* and said, "Hi, honey."

Silence on the other end. Then Ralph said, "Hello, sweetheart."

My stomach did a major elevator-drop-style lurch. "I'm sorry," I said when I'd regained control of my voice. "I thought you were somebody else." I waited for him to state his business. When he didn't, I asked, "What can I do for you?"

"We still need to talk about my defense. I thought we could do it over dinner."

"I'm sorry, but we can't," I said as firmly as I could. The rich velvet of his voice was tickling my ear and causing other sensations elsewhere. "The office shouldn't have given out this number."

"Don't blame them," he said. "I got it from Tillie."

"You *what*?" Harry lifted his head at my tone. "You promised you weren't going to use your—special resources, or whatever they are, to find out about me."

"I didn't," he said with infuriating calmness. "Since you're representing me, my people checked you out—strictly as a lawyer, mind you. Just the regular stuff—your education, where you're admitted, what kind of law you practice, things like that."

"And my *unlisted* home phone number." A quick scan of the room confirmed that the drapes were closed, but I still felt as if someone was watching me.

"I don't know how they got that. They were only supposed to check the regular stuff." When I didn't reassure him, he said, "Look, I'm sorry if I overstepped. I had the impression that you and I—that there was something happening between us. I was hoping, anyway. If I was wrong—well, I'm sorry about that, too."

Shit, shit, shit. "You weren't wrong," I admitted. "But I told you on Monday—I can't get involved with a client. If I screw up because I'm distracted by our personal relationship, you could end up in jail. So you have to leave me alone. Let me do my job."

Another silence. "I understand," he said. "But here's the thing. If you handle this like it was any other case, you're not going to see what's really there."

"What are you talking about?"

"The Santa thing, as you call it. If you don't believe me, there's no way you're going to convince anybody else."

"That's not how legal representation works," I said. "Whether I personally believe in your position doesn't matter. What matters is what the jury believes."

"How are you going to convince them if you're not convinced?"

Clients were so naïve. "The prosecutor has to prove you were there without permission. All I need to do is create a reasonable doubt about that lack of permission."

"But if you want to be technical about it, I'm not the one who had permission. Trevor invited Santa. So the only way it works is if I'm Santa's representative, and that only makes sense if Santa really exists."

A fair point, but I was ready for it. "What I'm thinking is this. We'll argue that you sincerely believe you're Santa's son. That way, the issue isn't whether Santa exists—it's whether the jury believes that you believe he does."

"In other words, you want to tell them I'm nutty as a fruitcake, but they shouldn't worry because I really mean it." Coming from him, my clever defense sounded harsh and cynical. I was about to wrap up the conversation when he said, "You need to see the place for yourself."

"Okay. Email me the pictures or whatever you have." I drained my wineglass, imaging what sort of photoshopping he'd do.

"No, I mean really see it. Go there. Then, you'll understand."

"*What?*"

"I want you to go up to the Pole. See the place for yourself."

"I don't understand," I said very, very slowly.

"Don't worry, we'll handle everything—all the transportation and such. And of course, we'll pay you for your time." He sounded determined now. A man with a plan.

"You want me to go the North Pole so I can argue that the reason you believe you're Santa Claus is that you really are?" Talk about upping the ante.

"Santa's son," he said impatiently. "I think that would be the perfect way for you to finally understand that I'm not nuts and I'm not conning you. This is a holiday weekend. We can go up tomorrow and be back on Sunday. Nobody will even know we were gone."

"'We'? *You're* not allowed to leave the state. If you do, they're going to revoke your bail, and you'll be sitting in a cell until trial which, if you're lucky, will be sometime next summer."

"So you'll go without me. I'll set it up. One of the guys'll come down and get you, and you can fly up and see what's there."

"Do you have your own pilot? A private plane, maybe?"

"Of course not. You'll go by sleigh, just like the rest of us." His tone wasn't quite *everybody knows that*, but it was close. Apparently, I wasn't the only one who'd been drinking. He was gaining steam now: "You'll see everything, and then you'll have all the evidence you need. Plus, you'll get to meet my mother. She wants to meet you."

Something in the way he said it made me pause in the act of reaching for the wine bottle. "Why?" I asked, my tone ominous.

"You're my lawyer." His voice was bright and innocent. "Hang on, I'll conference in Charles, and we can set everything up. You can go up tonight. You're off tomorrow, right?"

"Wait a minute! Don't be ridiculous! I'm not going anywhere, tonight or any other night!" My escalating volume woke David, who lifted his head and blinked.

"Don't worry, you won't be gone that long. Besides, your boyfriend's out of town, right? Who's going to know?"

Who, indeed? The thought induced both a thrill of excitement and a shiver of fear. If I were to dash out of town on a secret junket to—wherever—indeed, who would know?

But on the flip side: if I never came back, who would know what had happened to me?

Ralph Claus was charming, attractive, and clearly off his rocker. "This is insane," I half-muttered. "You want me to head off to—God only knows where—to investigate whether you're Santa Claus. I can't even—there aren't even words to describe how completely insane this is."

"You've said it was insane twice in three sentences, so obviously there's one word." He was positively chipper now. "I'm going to conference in Charles. Right back." The line clicked, and for a long minute, I heard nothing.

To this day, I don't know why I didn't hang up. My wacko client was allegedly conferencing in the North Pole because he wanted me to interview Santa Claus. It should have been enough to make me unplug the phone and hide under the covers.

And yet. . . .

In the months to come, when the world came crashing down around me, I would try a thousand times to put words to it. Why did I listen to him? Why didn't I pull back into my safe little lawyer shell? Why didn't I write him off as crazy and go back to my nice sanitary motion to dismiss? Why did I think this case—this client—was different, special, worthy of more than just excellent representation? Was it the undeniable attraction? Or something more?

The best answer I ever managed was this. For years, I'd read books and watched movies in which lawyers, real and fictional, made grand gestures and took breathtaking chances to prove to an unbelieving world that their clients were truly innocent. Clarence Darrow. Atticus Finch. Perry Mason. Deep in my heart, I wanted to be one of them. I wanted to defend my client brilliantly, with daring and zeal. I wanted to be legendary, memorable, larger than life. After fifteen years of slip-and-falls and custody disputes, this was my chance. Maybe it was the wine. Maybe the kisses. Maybe the French toast and the waitress and the things he seemed to know. All I knew at that instant was that I wanted his story to be sane and honest and true. *Miracle on 34th*

Street be damned: Santa was real, and I was the lawyer who would prove it to an unbelieving world. If that meant climbing into a sleigh and flying to the North Pole, so be it.

But as the violins swelled and the trumpets blared and a grand blazing passion for justice surged through me, the rational corner of my brain woke up from its long winter's nap: *Are you crazy? There's no Santa Claus! There's no Santa's workshop! There's nobody at the North Pole but polar bears and penguins! And not for nothing, dumbass, but reindeer can't fly! You're not going anywhere, because there's nowhere to go! Santa doesn't exist!* It wasn't thrilling or heartwarming, but the truth seldom was. Visions of legal immortality faded like a dream upon waking. There would be no drama, no magnificence, no proof of the impossible. I gathered up the tattered shreds of my common sense and trudged back to reality.

A click, and Ralph said, "Meg? Are you still there?"

"Yeah. I'm still here." And I needed a refill. Or maybe I'd already had too much. I poured out the last drops and tucked my glass into the dishwasher before I could change my mind.

"Okay, I've got Charles on the line."

"Hi, Charles." Polished and polite.

"Hey, counselor," Charles said.

"You can call me Meg." I heard a responsive grunt, but he never did call me anything but "counselor."

"Listen, Chaz, I need for you to set something up," Ralph said. "Meg needs to come up and see the place and talk to some people. Since it's a holiday weekend down here, I want to send her up tonight or tomorrow. She has to be home by Sunday."

"You want to do *what*? Are you *insane*?" The gravelly voice nearly screeched.

"Funny you should put it that way," said Ralph. "She's got questions about my defense. I can explain it all until I'm blue in the face, but that's not the same as if she actually sees the operation first-hand."

"Ain't gonna happen," Charles said. "You know the rules."

"This is a special case," said Ralph. "If we lose, I could be stuck here for a long time."

"What's the matter, counselor? Don't you believe him?" Charles's voice took on a hint of menace. "Clauses don't lie."

"I'm not saying he's lying," I said. "But it's a tough sell." *To put it mildly.*

"I think it'll be easier for her to explain everything to the jury if she sees it," said Ralph.

"You do." Charles's voice was flat and skeptical. "Look, you know as well as I do that even if she went up, she couldn't come back and talk about it. The missus would never allow it."

"I couldn't talk about it anyway," I said. "I'm the lawyer, not a witness. I wouldn't be able to testify." *Brilliant!* How had I not thought of this before? There was no point in going if I couldn't tell the court about it. I fetched a fresh wineglass for a celebratory sip.

No one spoke while Ralph contemplated this wrinkle. "Is there somebody you could take with you? A friend, maybe? Brother? Sister?"

"What're you, nuts?" Charles exploded. "Why not take her whole family, and maybe a few of her neighbors?"

A thought began to form. "I'd have to make a call," I said.

"Who do you have in mind?" Ralph asked.

"My friend Holly." Holly was always up for an adventure. Whatever Ralph came up with, she'd be fun to have along.

"No, no, and no!" Charles was clearly losing patience with both of us. "This ain't happening. The missus will never allow it."

"I'll talk to her," said Ralph. "Meg, I'll call you right back." And they were gone.

While I waited for Ralph to call back, I rummaged in the kitchen for supper. I found an egg, a few damp mushrooms, two limp stalks of asparagus, and a slice of deli ham. By the time the phone rang, I'd finished my omelet and was trying to talk myself out of a brownie.

"We're all set," he said. "A few ground rules, though. First, you can't take pictures."

"Okay." I wouldn't need to. Holly could make sketches as accurate as any photograph.

"Second, no tape recorders or anything like that."

"No problem."

"And no posting about anything on Facebook or whatever."

"I don't use Facebook or whatever."

"Perfect."

I decided to needle him a bit. "Can I take notes?"

Pause. "I guess it's okay as long as you keep them to yourself. No showing them to anybody."

"Deal. Anything else?"

"I think that's it. Have you talked to your friend? Is she in?"

"Um, I didn't want to call her until I knew it was all right on your end." In other words, I didn't want to look like a complete jackass without cause.

"Let me know when you've got everything set up," Ralph said.

After we hung up, I contemplated my folly. Obviously, we wouldn't end up at the North Pole. Still, traveling anywhere at the behest of a client was pretty stupid. Michael would have told me to make up an excuse. Stomach flu, maybe.

But I was curious. If Ralph was going to this much trouble, there had to be *something* to see. It would help my argument that he was sincere in his belief if it turned out that he lived in some homemade Santa wonderland. On the other hand, if he was a sociopath who wanted to get us alone to kill us. . . . My bullshit detector was usually set pretty high, but this guy was throwing it way off.

I felt like I was in one of those horror movies where the woman is alone in the house and there's a power failure during a thunderstorm. As the driving rains lash against the windows, she hears a suspicious noise from down in the basement, the kind that would make any marginally intelligent person lock herself in the bathroom with the phone. Except instead of calling 911, Our Heroine opens the basement door. She descends the creaky, cobwebby stairs, shrieks as a mouse runs over her foot, and—just in case she hasn't advertised her presence quite enough—she calls out, "Who's there?"

At which point the psychopath lunges, she screams, and he slashes her throat.

"But that won't happen to us," I said aloud. Ralph had no reason to harm me. Not that lunatics were noted for their fine analytical skills, but one thing I knew from representing other crazies: they have their own peculiar logic. Their actions make perfect sense to them. When a wacko ties a bath towel around his neck and jumps off a roof, it's because he truly believes he can fly.

I recited all this as I paced through the house, arguing my case as though Holly walked beside me. "Wherever we end up, if there really is something useful, I'll need a witness. We do this with investigators all the time." Not that I'd consider taking a regular investigator, because I hated the prospect of looking stupid in front of a colleague when we ended up in somebody's backyard amid six-foot plastic candy canes, sparkly fake snow, and a life-sized plastic Rudolph with a red light bulb nose. At least with Holly, I could laugh about it.

I could still feel imaginary-Holly's reluctance, so I assured her, "I'm sure it's nothing dangerous." No. Not *dangerous*. If the word wasn't already in her head, I didn't want to plant it. I rephrased it: "If we're not comfortable, we can always say we changed our minds, or one of us is feeling sick. Not even a sociopath wants to get puked on." That was better. I could sell that. Just leave out *sociopath*.

If all else failed, I had the silver bullet: "Remember Graceland?" Back when Amy was in high school, Holly talked me into co-chaperoning a class trip to Graceland. She'd promised that the kids would be well-behaved and the trip would be a blast. A blast it was, assuming *blast* can be stretched to include bailing out the bus driver after his arrest on a drunk-and-disorderly, camping in the hall all night to keep the boys from sneaking into the girls' rooms (and vice versa), confiscating a bag full of little bottles of liquor swiped from the maid's cart (at our request, the hotel had emptied the mini-bars in the kids' rooms), and the bout of food poisoning that prevented us from leaving for home as scheduled since the single microscopic bathroom on the bus was completely inadequate for eighteen adolescents with the runs. Once we were safely back in Connecticut, pale and shaky, standing by the bus as the last greenish teenager stumbled off, Holly met my eyes for the first time in a hundred miles and said, "I owe you. Big."

Time to pay up.

Twelve

"Are you out of your mind?" Holly demanded when I'd finished my pitch.

"I promise not to subpoena you or put you on the stand. Just come along to help me figure it all out."

She wasn't buying it. "Listen to me. This is weird. Why can't you defend this guy without heading off to the wilds of wherever?"

"Okay, I admit it. I'm curious. I want to see what he's going to come up with. Besides, the more I see, the more evidence I have that he truly believes he's Santa.

"You really think we'd go somewhere? Not like, 'Oh, shucks, my reindeer has a flat tire, guess the trip's off'?"

"I have no idea." The truest words I'd said all day.

Long silence. Very long. "You realize this completely pays for Graceland."

"I figured you'd say that."

"I'm meeting this guy before we go anywhere. And I'm leaving a note. If we don't get back on time, my kids are going to call the police, and your client will be toast."

Fifteen minutes later, I opened the door to the most disapproving glare I'd seen in years. "I can't believe we're doing this," Holly said instead of "hello."

Neither could I, but I couldn't think of anybody I'd rather do it with. "Come on in. He hasn't called back yet."

Just then, the phone rang. The talking Caller ID intoned, "Call from Unidentified Caller."

Holly tossed me the handset. "It's show time."

I punched the "talk" button. "Hi," I said, ignoring her raised eyebrow. Did she expect me to pretend I didn't know who was calling?

"How did it go?" Ralph asked. "Did you get everything set up with your friend?"

"She's here now. In fact, we were thinking we could meet you down at the office and we could sort out the details there." Holly shook her head and mouthed *public place*, but I mouthed back, *it's okay.*

"Sounds good to me. Listen, have you two had dinner?"

"Um—no." A one-egg omelet didn't count.

"Me neither. How about I bring pizza?"

"That's sweet, but you don't have to." I avoided meeting Holly's eyes.

"Actually, I do," he said. "Because I'm hungry, and if I don't get something to eat soon, I'm going to get really grumpy, and that would be bad for Santa's image. What do you ladies like?"

"Mushrooms, roasted garlic, ricotta, and sweet sausage, but only if it's the crumbled type. If it's sliced, skip it." Behind me, Holly murmured something to one of the cats about "your crazy mother."

"Done," he said. "I'll make them crumble the sausage myself. I'll even threaten to take back their Christmas presents if they get it wrong."

I chuckled. "Can you do that?"

"No, but they won't know that." His laugh was rich and full. He probably did an amazing *ho ho ho*.

I shook my head to rid myself of that particular thought. "See you at the office in half an hour." I disconnected and turned to find Holly staring at me. "What?"

"You were flirting with him." Her tone was halfway between revelation and scorn. "So that's what this is all about."

"I was not!"

"Yes, Megan, you were. You were flirting with your client, the potential con man, nutcase, or whatever he is. I've heard that giggle enough times."

"I didn't giggle!" Forty-year-old lawyers did not giggle.

"You most certainly did. When you were talking about the sausage. He said something, and you giggled."

My mind raced over the conversation. "It was an appreciative chuckle. He said something amusing. It would have been rude not to acknowledge that. Now, let's go." I pulled on my jacket and opened the door to the frigid December night.

"Wait a minute." Holly doubled back to the kitchen. I heard her rummaging in a drawer. Moments later, she returned with a bottle of wine and a corkscrew. At my raised eyebrow, she shrugged. "We're having dinner with Santa Claus. I think a drink is in order."

Thirteen

When we arrived at the office, Ralph was standing on the back step holding two pizza boxes. "How many people are coming?" Holly asked in a low voice as we got out of the car.

"Just us," I said. Gesturing to the boxes, I called, "Are we having a party?"

"I didn't know how hungry you'd be," he said. "Hi, I'm Ralph Claus," he added to Holly.

"Nice to meet you," said Holly. "I'd shake your hand, but it seems to be occupied."

I unlocked the door, disabled the alarm and flipped the light switches. "Come on in," I said. "It may be a little chilly." The thermostat was programmed to go down to 60 at night. One of Roy's cost-cutting ideas.

"It's fine for me," said Ralph. He went ahead into the conference room, which meant that he didn't see Holly roll her eyes.

"Of course, it's fine for him," she whispered. "He lives at the North Pole."

"Sssh!" I didn't want things to get off to a bad start. "I'll get the plates. You go make small talk." I collected plates, glasses, a handful of knives and forks, and a wad of napkins from the kitchen. On the way back to the conference room, I walked as soundlessly as possible, but if Holly and Ralph were talking, they were doing it quietly.

The white cardboard boxes lay open on the long table, displaying the crumbled sausage. Both pizzas were the same, which surprised me. If Ed had been getting the pizzas, he'd have gotten one the way I said and the other the way he liked it, with green peppers, caramelized onions and anchovies, a revolting combination of three of my most despised foods.

I must have been staring, because Ralph asked, "Everything okay?"

"Oh, sure. I just wondered—I thought you might want something else."

"This sounded good. My brother Ted likes those Hawaiian pizzas—you know, the ones with ham and pineapple—but I like something more traditional."

"How many brothers do you have?" Holly asked with what could have been casual interest.

"Four," he said. "I'm the oldest. Phil's next in line, then the twins, Ted and Fred, and the youngest is Mitch. Here, I'll get that," he added as I fitted the corkscrew onto the bottle.

"Don't worry," said Holly. "She's had plenty of practice." As I poured and Ralph distributed glasses, she asked, "So, all brothers? No sisters?" She laid a slice of pizza on a plate and handed it to Ralph, who promptly passed it to me. Her eyes flicked at me: *nice manners.*

"Just the five boys. My mother should probably be canonized."

"I'm sure it wasn't that bad," I said.

"Ignore her," said Holly. "She's never had a son."

"Have you?" asked Ralph.

"Just one, and that's plenty," she said. "One son and one daughter." Ralph turned to me. "And you have cats."

"I do," I said. "You've met Lulu. The boys are Harry and David."

"You mean the mail-order people? With the fruit?"

"Harry for Houdini, because when he was a kitten, he could get out of any room I closed him in. David for Copperfield."

"'Chapter One: I Am Born,'" he intoned, quoting the first words of Dickens's classic.

"Not the book. The magician," said Holly. "She had the biggest crush on him. Instead of going to the prom, she made her boyfriend take her to see David Copperfield live."

"It was an amazing show," I retorted. "Besides, what would you rather see? The same people you've seen every day for twelve years, or an artist who makes an elephant disappear?"

"So, you like magic. Do you know much about it?" His tone was carefully neutral, but he might have been preoccupied with separating another piece of pizza from the rest of the pie.

"Not compared to David Copperfield." I passed him a napkin. "I still can't figure out how he does what he does. I mean, the guy made a jet disappear. He made the Statue of Liberty disappear. And they say it's not camera tricks, either."

"Do you think it's really magic?" Ralph poured wine into my glass and Holly's.

"Copperfield's a genius, but it all has a rational explanation. Sleight of hand, visual illusions, mind games." I sipped my wine. "You can't make an elephant or a jet disappear into thin air. Think about your physics classes. Matter doesn't cease to exist. It has to go somewhere."

"I was never much for physics," said Ralph. "Magic, on the other hand—that's fun."

"Can you pull a rabbit out of a hat?" Holly asked.

"We don't have rabbits where I'm from," he said. "I assume Meg's told you all about my situation."

Holly shook her head. "Practically nothing. Just that you want us to go on a trip."

"I'll tell you whatever you want to know," he said. "More pizza?" Each of us accepted another slice. "Where should I start?"

"Hold on." I waited until I had their attention before continuing. "Holly, for purposes of this meeting and—whatever—you are my assistant." She and Ralph exchanged puzzled looks, so I clarified, "It means that whatever Ralph says about his case—including any possible defenses—is still privileged."

"Fine by me," said Ralph. To Holly, he said, "Here's the deal. I'm Santa's oldest son. I live at the North Pole. I was arrested on Christmas Eve. I was delivering presents. Meg's my lawyer. She's going to go and see where I live so she can defend me. What else do you want to know?"

"Do you really build toys?" asked Holly. I couldn't tell if she was buying his story.

"Me personally? Not anymore, but that was part of my training. We all spend time in the workshop. Fred's the foreman now. He oversees production and coordinates all the requests. It's a massive job, and there's no break. I guarantee you, he's already started working on next year. At least the delivery team gets a little breathing room after Christmas." He selected another wedge of pizza. "Of course, I'm getting a whole lot more of a break now than anybody wants. There's only so much you can do from three thousand miles away."

"Three thousand miles? That's all?" Holly topped off her wine.

"Give or take," he said. Later, when I Googled it, I learned that the North Pole was a mere 3,341 miles from Hartford. Closer than London, and a little over half the distance to Honolulu. It seemed as if it should be much farther.

"What exactly do you do?" I asked.

"It's hard to describe. I'm the next in line for the job, so what I need to be most concerned about is the essence of Santa Claus."

Holly and I exchanged a quick look. "I don't understand," I said for both of us.

"Who Santa is. What he does. His philosophy." We must have looked as blank as I felt, because he said, "Okay, here's an example. This year, there was a little girl in Atlanta who wrote and asked for an American Sweetheart doll. Normally, this wouldn't be a problem, but in this case, there was a catch. This little girl was originally from Korea. She'd been adopted by her American parents when she was very little, so she was completely American in her tastes and opinions. She wanted one of those dolls, but she wanted it to look like her. Well, American Sweetheart doesn't make Asian-American dolls. So, Fred came back to me and said, 'What do you want to do?' If we made it, it wouldn't be authentic, but if it wasn't Korean, it wouldn't be what the little girl wanted." His gaze was intent, probing to see if we understood. When neither of us spoke, he spelled it out: "Santa doesn't do second-best."

"What did you do?" Holly was leaning forward, her pizza clearly forgotten.

"Made some calls, pulled some strings. Did what we had to. She got the doll she wanted, and it had all the certificates and everything else from American Sweetheart. She has the only Asian-American Sweetheart doll in existence, at least for the time being. Apparently, the company's thinking about adding an official one."

"What do you mean, you pulled some strings?" I asked.

"We make dolls," he said. "Doll makers can talk to doll makers." He pointed to the pizza boxes. "Anybody for more?"

"I want to hear about the doll makers." If I was learning anything, it was that Ralph was a master of misdirection when he wanted to avoid answering a question.

He slid another slice onto his plate. "One of the things you need to understand about toy companies is this: somewhere in every company, there's somebody who actually cares about the kids who are going to play with their products. They tend to be hidden behind all the corporate types, but if you can get to that one person—and sometimes there really is just one—then you've got somebody you can work with to make sure that a child gets what she wants for Christmas."

"What happens if you can't find that person?" Holly challenged.

"That's when it helps to be with us. We've got information on all these places. We've also got people on the inside in a lot of them."

"You have elves working in regular toy companies?" Just what I needed: a simple unlawful entry case turning into a corporate espionage ring.

"Elves only work at the Pole. These are regular people who happen to have connections to somebody in our organization. Like Fred's wife's cousin, Heather. She and a bunch of computer geeks have a company where they take old-fashioned board games and update them for today's kids. Game companies hire Heather's people to analyze their products and figure out how to upgrade them. So, if we needed to contact somebody in the game industry, we'd go through Heather. It's like any other kind of networking. We're not trying to recruit people or steal secrets. We just want to make the kids happy."

"Do they know who you are?" Holly poured out the last drops of wine. "Is there any more?"

"I'll be right back." I pointed unsteadily at Ralph. "Don't answer any more questions until I get back."

"I'm your assistant," Holly protested.

"It's not that," I said. "I don't want to miss anything."

"Okay, I'll come with you. Right back, Ralph." She followed me out of the room and up the stairs to my office, where she started giggling.

"What?" Robin had taken Lulu home for the holiday weekend, and the room felt empty.

"He's cute," she said. "I can see why you were flirting with him. He's very sweet, and he's funny, and he's cute."

"And you're tipsy," I said.

"I bet Santa Boy will make a good witness," Holly mused. "The women on your jury are gonna love him."

"They won't get the chance. Defendants don't testify." Rule #1 for criminal lawyers: *Keep the client off the stand.*

"Too bad," said Holly. "If I was on the jury, I'd believe him."

I contemplated this as I retrieved a bottle of pinot noir from the case I'd received as a thank-you gift from a wine merchant after defending his teenage son on a DUI. When we got back to the conference room, Ralph smiled as if he knew exactly what we'd been saying upstairs. "My turn," he said, reaching for the bottle as he picked up the corkscrew. I knew Holly's estimate of him had just risen again. It probably shouldn't have mattered, but every woman wants her best friend to approve of the guy she likes. We're like that in fourth grade, and we're like that three decades later. It's the way we're wired.

"The question before the break was whether these toy companies you work with know who you are," said Holly. She shot me a smug look. "I watch *Law and Order*." Definitely tipsy.

"Not exactly," Ralph said. "Heather might say she's got a relative in the toy business. Santa is never mentioned."

"Do they suspect?" I asked.

"In order to suspect, they'd have to believe," he pointed out. "Not that many do."

"Are you saying some people do?" Holly asked.

"You'd be surprised," said Ralph. "Believers are everywhere, but it's like believing in Bigfoot or the Loch Ness monster. Most people are reluctant to admit it." He looked from me to Holly. "What about you two? Do you believe?"

Holly and I exchanged a long look. "The jury's still out," I said finally. "You've made a strong presentation, but let's face it—this is an idea most adults discarded long ago."

"But you're not completely ruling it out," Ralph said. When I didn't contradict him, the grin widened. "In that case—are you ready to go for the ride of your life?"

"What are you talking about?" Holly drained her glass.

"Didn't Meg tell you? You'll be traveling by sleigh."

"You mean, jingle bells? A one-horse open sleigh? Over the river and through the woods?" As she tried to process this notion, I corked the bottle.

"More like Rudolph." Ralph transferred what was left of the first pizza into the second box and closed it.

"What—you mean like *flying* sleigh?" Holly yanked her hand off her wineglass as though it were on fire.

"I told you that," I said. I wasn't certain whose memory was more wine-fogged at that point, but I set down my glass anyway. "I'm sure we'll be fine. I mean, they do this all the time, right?" I smiled brightly. *Your move, Santa.*

"All the time," said Ralph. "And we're here to tell the tale."

Holly studied the two of us with wine-bleary eyes. "When do we leave?"

"I'll call now," Ralph said. The mantel clock on the bookcase showed nearly nine-thirty. "Can you be ready to go by two?"

"Sure," I said. "Earlier, if you want. I need to get a couple things taken care of in the morning, but I can be ready by lunchtime."

"I meant a.m.," he said. "It's better if we get in and out at night. Less traffic than in daytime. Less chance of being seen."

"Charles came down during the day," I said, suspicions simmering again.

"We have ways of managing when it's just one person," Ralph said. "But that wouldn't work with three of you. It has to be the sleigh."

Holly shrugged. "If it has to be the sleigh, it has to be the sleigh."

"You're smashed," I said. "Come on. We have to pack."

She began to sing, "Jingle bells, jingle bells, jingle all the way. . . ."

"That's it. I'm getting an Uber." I probably wasn't within the legal blood alcohol limits, and I was positive Holly wasn't.

Holly slammed her palm on the table. I waited for a major pronouncement. Instead, she stared intently for a minute before flopping back in her chair. "Call Jack," she said. "He and Jill should be at the house. Unless they went up the hill to fetch a pail of water." She snickered. "Wouldn't it be a hoot if it turned out that all those nursery rhyme folks existed, too?"

I didn't bother answering. Instead, I busied myself with cleaning up the dishes while Ralph stashed the pizza in the refrigerator. Then, I stole into the library. I found a pad and pen and tried to compose a note for Michael. Nothing I wrote made any sense, but I couldn't blame the wine. The whole thing was just too bizarre. In three days, I'd gone from a perfectly normal, calm, quiet life to—*this*. I was at my office with my drunken best friend while my client, the successor to Santa Claus, was arranging for a flying sleigh to transport us to the North Pole. I crumpled the note and tossed it into the trash.

"It's all set," said Ralph when I returned. "Mitch will be here at two."

"Mitch? What about Charles?" Too many names.

"My brother," he reminded me. "He's a good kid. You'll like him."

"Kid? How old is he?" I had visions of placing my life in the hands of a thirteen-year-old.

"Nineteen, but he's an excellent driver. He's been driving the sleigh every chance he could get since he was about eight."

"Do you all know how to fly?" I asked.

"Of course," said Ralph. "We all do deliveries. Which reminds me—dress warm. It gets cold at those altitudes."

Holly roused herself. "What altitudes?"

"The ones that get you over rooftops," said Ralph. "Sure you don't want me to drive you home?"

"You've been drinking as much as we have," I said although he wasn't showing it. "Holly's son will pick us up. He can give you a ride."

"I'll walk." His eyes met mine. "But you can see me to the door."

Warmth spread through me that had nothing to do with wine. "Let me call Jack." I made the call, and he promised to come right over. "He'll be here in a few minutes."

"So we don't have much time." Ralph glanced meaningfully toward the door, and I followed him out to the waiting area. Whether it was the wine or just the faint intoxicating biscuity smell of his skin, I'll never know, but when he reached for me, I didn't hesitate. We kissed until we heard a knock at the back door.

"Jack's here," I whispered.

"Jack's here!" Holly called from the conference room.

"Then I guess this is good night," Ralph said. We met Holly in the hall, and as soon as Ralph's back was turned, she raised her eyebrows.

Jack was either polite enough or uninterested enough not to ask why we were at my office drinking on a weeknight. By the time we got to my house, the frigid night air had cleared our brains a bit.

"I'll be right back," Holly told him, climbing out of his pickup after me. Without speaking, we went up my front walk. At the door, my best friend asked, "Are you okay?"

Stars sparkled in the cold, clear sky. Darkness lit by diamonds. An exquisite night to fly. I faced her squarely. "Tell me the truth. Is this the stupidest thing I could ever do?"

Her eyes searched my face. At last, she said, "Did you ever see *National Velvet*?"

"We're talking reindeer, not horses." Whatever Ralph came up with, there would have to be reindeer.

She waved her hand impatiently. "That's not what I mean.

Remember how Velvet wants to ride her horse in the Grand National, and Mickey Rooney keeps saying it's folly? Then her mother says something I've been thinking about all night."

"What?" I prodded.

"I don't remember her exact words. Something about everybody being entitled to one breathtaking piece of folly, but you have to choose well, because it'll need to last you your entire life." She rubbed her gloved hands together. "Let's go have some folly."

"But—what if it's a disaster?" Because it could be, in twenty different ways.

"The mother doesn't say anything about that. Maybe it isn't the result that matters." She kissed my cheek. "Now, go take a nap. I'll see you later."

I stood on the front step, waving as she and Jack drove away. Then, I put my key in the frosty lock and went inside. I closed the door and stood with my hand resting on the knob. In just a few hours, I would be on my way to—somewhere—to investigate one of the most remarkable tales anyone had ever explored.

A breathtaking piece of folly, indeed.

Book Two

The Pole

Fourteen

Icy air slapped my face as I climbed out of the Uber. "It's freezing!" Holly muttered behind me. I refrained from reminding her that any weather Connecticut could dish up would pale compared to the biting cold at the Pole. What would the wind chill be in a place like that? Minus a hundred and thirty-seven?

Beyond folly.

Ralph lounged against the parking lot fence as if it were a balmy summer evening. His breath made little clouds when he asked, "You ready?"

"Oh, sure." My neighbor Rodrigo would feed Harry and David. As casually as I could manage, I added, "You're not going to leave town, right?"

"I thought the limit was on leaving the state," Ralph said.

"Well—technically, but under the circumstances, it would be better if you stuck right around here." *The circumstances* being that if we actually went somewhere and didn't return on schedule, I wanted him to be easy for the police to find. "How cold is it up there, anyway?"

"You won't even notice it," he assured me.

Because it's not real, the voice in my head taunted. *Because there's no "there" there.* I hushed the voice. Inexplicably, it made me sad.

"Heads up!" Ralph called out. A loud whoosh, like hurricane force winds, and an instant later, a sleigh—an honest-to-God sleigh—was in my parking lot, with four antlered creatures harnessed to it that could only be—

"Holy shit!" Holly breathed.

It's an illusion, I told myself. *It's not real.* But one of the reindeer turned its head toward me, its dark eye glinting in the light: *You sure about that?*

"All aboard for the North Pole!" the driver sang out. "With an arrival rate of nearly fifty percent!" The driver jumped out of the sleigh without opening the door. He was dressed all in black from his head to his foot—ski suit, ski mask, gloves, hat, and goggles. Not much taller than I—five-nine, maybe—but with a trim, youthful physique. He pulled up the goggles and mask, revealing dancing green eyes and a wide, white smile. "Everybody ready for the flight into the night?"

"Keep it down" said Ralph. To us, he added, "He's just kidding."

"He only says that because he doesn't know about the ones I've lost," said the young man. "Except for an old girlfriend he told me to dump. What was her name again, Big Brother?"

"Can it, Mitch." For the first time since I'd known him, Ralph sounded irritated. Standard brotherly fare, I suspected. "This is my brother, Mitch."

"Greetings, ladies," said Mitch. "And you are. . . ."

"Meg Riley." I stepped forward to shake his hand. "This is my assistant, Holly Beardsley."

"Pleased to meet you, ladies. What do you think of your chariot?"

This sleigh wasn't Santa-red. In the light of the parking lot, it gleamed, black with hints of violet. Instead of storybook gold trim, the runners looked like chrome. Doors closed in the passengers, unlike the open sides I'd seen in countless Christmas specials. The reindeer looked around, curious but unfazed.

"Nice reindeer," I said as casually as I could manage.

The corners of Ralph's mouth quirked. "You can pet them if you like. They're very comfortable with people." *Of course they were.* Several local Christmas tree farms rented reindeer for the holidays. This crew had probably spent the past month being adored by schoolchildren.

The reindeer were harnessed in pairs, one in front of the other. They were no bigger than ponies, their backs not even as high as my chest, but the antlers extended well over my head. I took off one glove. Gingerly, I laid my hand on the shoulder of the closest reindeer. Its hair was thick and coarse. A tuft of white hung from the creature's throat like a misplaced beard. The reindeer turned its head slightly, and I narrowly missed being poked in the eye by an antler tip.

"That's Polly," said Mitch. "She's an old hand at this. Don't worry, you're in good hooves. Where's your faucet?" He reached into the back of the sleigh, extracting several plastic buckets.

"What?"

"Faucet. You know, for water?"

"Oh, sorry—I didn't even think. Do you want something to drink? I can open the office." At two in the morning, my hostess skills were not at their sharpest.

"It's for the reindeer," Mitch said. "It was a long flight down. They need to rest and have a drink before we head back."

"Oh, right." *A long flight down.* More likely, they'd gotten off a trailer half a block away. Even so, I wouldn't begrudge them a pail of water. I unlocked the back door, disarmed the alarm, and led Mitch down the hall to the impeccably designed powder room. He lined up the buckets on the tiled floor and attached a rubber hose to the oil-rubbed bronze faucet. I tried to imagine Elsa's face if she knew Desirée's high-end fixtures were being used to give reindeer a drink.

Mitch and I hauled the buckets outside to find Ralph loosening harnesses. "So they can rest better," he explained. He scratched one reindeer between the ears as we positioned buckets on the ground in front of each. Eagerly, they pushed their noses into the buckets, and for a minute, the only sound was water being slurped.

"Who put the team together?" Ralph asked in a low voice.

"Ted," said Mitch. "Why?"

"Just didn't expect to see Leggo." Displeasure masquerading as casual.

"Oh, for God's sake. He was perfect the entire way down. Besides, Ted said to use him." There was a shadow of *so, there!* in that last statement.

"Is everything okay?" I asked brightly from across the team.

"Sure, it's fine," said Ralph. As if aware his response lacked general Santa jollity, he asked, "What do you think? Can David Copperfield do this?"

"How come that one doesn't have antlers?" I pointed to the one closest to the sleigh on the left. "Is it a baby or something?"

"He's male," said Ralph. "The females keep their antlers in the winter, but the males lose theirs around late November."

"But they always have antlers in the pictures," said Holly. "Aren't Dasher and Dancer males? I know Rudolph is."

"The guys who draw those pictures probably never saw a reindeer in their lives," said Mitch.

Granted, the setup was very good so far, but the reindeer still had to fly. Which meant that any minute now, Ralph or Mitch would "discover" a problem requiring cancellation of the trip—an issue with the antlerless reindeer, or something wrong with the harness. But there would be something, I knew, and we'd all go home with assurances that it would happen for real tomorrow night. Tomorrow night would come and the problem wouldn't be resolved, and on and on until Ralph announced regretfully it just wasn't going to work out and we should try a different approach. Still, I couldn't help being impressed by the elaborate lengths he'd gone to. It was downright Copperfieldesque.

Although I'd bet DC could have gotten those reindeer off the ground.

"I figured they'd be a lot smaller," Holly said. "You know—'a miniature sleigh and eight tiny reindeer.'"

Mitch snorted. "You know that poem was made up, right?"

"I'm warning you." Ralph fixed him with a steely glare.

Mitch flashed us a dazzling grin. "You ladies ready to go?"

"Last chance," I said. My words were directed to Holly, but I meant them for Ralph, too. A frisson of sadness went through my heart at the prospect of his imminent unmasking.

Holly regarded the sleigh, the reindeer, and the black-clad young man. "Oh, what the hell. Can we get a picture before we go?"

"Sure," said Mitch as Ralph started to speak. "Everybody crowd in." Mitch took my phone, we crowded in, and the flash went off.

"You didn't get the reindeer," Holly protested. Since we'd been facing the sleigh, it was just a photograph of four people in a parking lot. She reached for my phone, but Mitch dropped it into my pocket. When I started to retrieve it, he laid his hand on mine.

"Next time," he said. For an instant, the joking dropped away, and I saw something intent in his gaze. I relented, and he released my hand. I probably wasn't supposed to see him wink at Ralph. "This everything?" he asked as he tossed our overnight bags into the back of the sleigh.

"Sure. We're just going for a couple days, right?" It couldn't hurt to pretend a little longer. The end was almost here.

"This time." Mitch reached into the sleigh for straps and fastened them around the luggage.

"What do you mean?" I asked.

"Nothing," said Ralph with a meaningful look at Mitch.

"Just making conversation," the younger Claus said. From the back seat he retrieved a duffle bag from which he pulled two outfits like his. "Put these on. It gets cold up there."

I took one and held up the pants. The elastic at the ankles stretched over my boots, and the pants fit nicely over my jeans. Too nicely, as if somebody knew what size I wore. Holly's were a bit baggier, but she didn't seem concerned. We pulled the tops over our heads, zipped them up, and put our jackets over them.

"Masks and hats," said Mitch, tossing them to us. I pulled the ski mask over my head and then the hat, thoroughly smashing down my curls. Holly's sudden frown let me know that she was thinking about hat-hair, too. We were such *girls*.

Ralph tightened the harnesses while Mitch tossed the remaining water and secured the buckets in the sleigh. The reindeer lifted their heads as if they were eager to get going.

Ralph wasn't stopping this show. We were really doing— something. Going somewhere.

Folly of the highest order.

No, I told myself firmly. *It's an illusion. You'll see. There's no such thing as flying reindeer. Get in the sleigh—it's not going anywhere. Even David Copperfield can't make reindeer fly. So just do it.* We were playing chicken: who would back down first?

"Okay, let's hit the road," said Mitch, tugging his mask back down. In all that black, we looked as though we were about to pull off a heist. "Kiss everybody good-bye."

"She's my lawyer," Ralph said, not looking at me.

"Uh-huh." Mitch opened the sleigh door. "Who wants to ride shotgun?"

"I'll take the back," said Holly. She clambered over the front seat and settled herself in next to the luggage. Mitch busied himself checking the already-checked harnesses.

I looked up at Ralph. "See you in a few days," I said lightly, because in that moment, it all seemed possible.

Get away from this guy, my mind hissed. Every time I got too close, I started to buy into his outrageous story. I needed to keep my distance, to remember that everything I was seeing was illusion, fabrication, sleight of hand. Not magic. Definitely not truth.

"I'll be here," he said. In a lower voice, he added, "I really appreciate what you're doing. And don't worry. Mitch is a cowboy, but you couldn't be in better hands." His hand rested on my shoulder. "You can call me from there if you want," he added as he helped me into the sleigh and closed the door firmly. "Have fun!"

"Shoulder belts," Mitch said. We buckled in, and he pushed a button on the dash. "GPS," he said in response to my questioning look. He tossed a pair of goggles over the back seat and handed another set to me. "You'll want these." He adjusted his goggles, and I did the same. He slapped the reins and yelled, "Geeyap!"

The sleigh bolted forward, slamming me back against the seat. I don't know what I expected—a little taxiing down the road, maybe—but instead, with one deafening whoosh, we were far above the rooftops. When I peeked over the side, I could see the lights of the parking lot, but if Ralph was there, waving, I couldn't see him.

Oh, my God. It's really happening. They're flying. We're flying.

In the backseat, Holly swore. "It's freezing!"

"Just wait!" Mitch shouted over what sounded like either ferocious wind or engine noise. "We'll be above it in a few minutes."

"Above it?" My voice squeaked. What in hell was he talking about? Unless I was very much mistaken, going up only made things colder. A person didn't need to see a lot of snow-capped mountains to know that.

See. It took a second to realize it. Even though it was the middle of the night, I could see Mitch, and the sleigh, and the reindeer. The goggles must have been for night vision. Funny, but none of those pictures of Santa included that kind of thing. "How long have you guys been using these?" I shouted, gesturing to the goggles.

"About thirty years," Mitch shouted back. "Our tech guys are good. You warm enough? There are blankets in the back if you want."

Remarkably, I was fairly comfortable. The air didn't feel any different than when I'd been standing in the parking lot.

Then I understood. These weren't night vision goggles. They were virtual reality glasses, the kind that let you tour the Louvre or stand on the Great Wall of China from the comfort of your recliner. *Thank God.* "I'm okay," I said, and for the first time since I saw the sleigh, I meant it.

Mitch slapped the reins again. It felt as if we rose sharply. I didn't even want to think about how high we were—or would have been, if this were real. Since I had nothing to lose—I was sitting in my own parking lot—I leaned over the side to see what was visible "below."

"Get back here, you idiot!" Holly grabbed the back of my hat and yanked me upright.

"Relax. There's nothing to worry about." I wanted to clue her in, but I wasn't ready to let Mitch know I'd caught on.

We banked to the left, and Mitch clucked as he slapped the reins once more. This time, when we leveled off, I realized that the loud wind or whatever it had been was much quieter, the temperature milder. I was no expert, but I knew this wouldn't be so if we were actually flying. Some of those gadgets on the dashboard must have been for climate control. I tried to twist in my seat to look at Holly, but I was strapped in tightly.

"Where are we?" I asked.

Mitch checked one of the lighted gauges on his dashboard. The sleigh's dashboard boasted more lighted dials and gauges and digital readouts than I'd ever seen on any instrument panel, except maybe in movies involving space travel. "We're over New York. Herkimer County."

"What's that?" I asked.

"Pretty much dead center in New York state." His tone wasn't quite *everybody knows that*, but it was close. I had to hand it to him: he was an excellent actor.

"Already?" Holly sounded skeptical. "We just left."

"We travel a little faster up here than you do down on the roads," Mitch said.

"How fast?" Holly asked. "How many miles per hour?"

"It's complicated. Let's just say there are a lot of variables, so the measurements aren't exactly the same as on the ground."

It was the kind of no-answer answer an official might give the public about some confidential matter. I was itching to take notes.

"How high are we?" I asked, just to see what he'd come up with.

"About one-point-five."

"One-point-five what? Thousand feet?"

"One-point-five aerostrata," he said. Before I could ask, he explained, "It's a way of measuring. Sort of like—you know those rocks with the different layers? The atmosphere is like that, too. Some layers have heavier, colder air, and others are more like a slipstream. Not exactly, because usually, with a slipstream, you're following something, and we're not, but it's the same idea where you get into a place where you get the benefit of—well, lighter air, for lack of a better term, and it doesn't take as much effort to fly there. Sort of like being the geese at the back of the V, where it's a lot easier than for the guy at the point. That's why it's milder here. We're going to stay here, but when we go down, it'll be colder for a while."

It still wasn't clear, but I was impressed at Mitch's grasp of aeronautics—or at least, by how well he'd learned his lines. "Don't planes fly in these slipstreams?"

"Too big. Some of the smallest planes might be able to squeeze in, but they don't usually travel fast enough to break through."

"But reindeer do?" came Holly's voice from the backseat.

"You'd be surprised at what reindeer can do," he said. "I probably could have done this trip with just two, but Ted—he's in charge of the stables—he said to use four. Since you two aren't real big and you don't have much luggage, we might just use two on the way back. Depends how many are available."

"What else would they be doing?" Rental season was over. Nobody would need them again until next Christmas.

"Training, breeding, resting. We'll probably use four. It'll be up to Ted."

"How many of you are up there?" Holly asked. "People, not reindeer."

"Five brothers," said Mitch. "Ralph's the oldest. I'm the youngest."

"And in between are Phil, Ted and Fred," I recalled. "Is it just you guys and your parents up there with the elves, or are there other—" I wasn't certain what to call non-elves.

"Clauses? A few. Phil, Ted, and Fred are all married. Ted has two boys, Fred has a little girl. Cute kids."

I was surprised. "How did—I mean, where do you guys meet women?"

"The usual ways."

"Like Match or Tindr?"

"Yep," he said to my surprise. "Used to be that the Claus men were only supposed to meet women through introductions with a few approved folks from down below, but these days, we meet people online like everybody else. That's how Fred met his wife. It gets complicated because of security, but there are a few sites we can visit."

"Are you seeing anybody?" Holly asked.

Mitch flashed a smile that could only be described as devilish. "Nobody special. What about you?" I couldn't see his eyes behind his goggles, but I'd have bet anything he winked.

"Honey, I'm old enough to be your mother," said Holly.

"So?" His grin widened.

I asked, "What do you tell women about who you are and where you live?"

"I say I'm from up north. They usually think that means Canada. When they ask what I do, I tell them tech work in the family business. If they ask more about the business, I say we make toys. That usually gets them remembering some toy they had when they were little, and we're off to the next topic." It sounded as if Mitch was as skilled at diversion as Ralph.

"What about Ralph? Why isn't he married?" Holly asked.

Mitch turned slightly as if he was glancing at me from behind his goggles. "My big brother's very picky."

"Is he gay?" Holly asked. If I hadn't been strapped in, I'd have shot her a glare that would have melted her goggles.

Mitch guffawed. "Um—no," he managed. "Is he?" he added, elbowing me.

"Tell me more about these flying sleighs," I said deliberately.

"They're pretty easy," he said, still chuckling. "You want to drive?"

"Sure." Anything to change the subject.

"Just hold the reins like this." He held up his hands to show me how the reins were threaded between his fingers. "Pull back with your right hand to turn right and with your left to turn left. It's easy."

"How do I know when to turn?" In the vast star-spangled sky, anything seemed possible.

"Don't worry, I'm not going anywhere." He shifted his hands over, and I took the reins. There was just enough jiggling to feel as if the reins were indeed connected to something moving. I lifted my right hand, and the rein attached to the right-hand reindeer moved. There must have been something in the gloves that tied into the images projected in the goggles. Impressive. Even though I knew the whole thing was a fake, it was still fun to play that I was driving Santa's sleigh. I slapped the reins and called, "Let's go!"

The sleigh rocked, and the wind increased. "What are you doing? Slow down!" Mitch snapped. He reached over and tugged slightly at the reins, and the wind lessened. "It's a long trip. You've got to pace them."

"Aye, aye, captain." I transferred all the reins to one hand and gave a snappy salute.

"If you crash this thing, I'm never going to forgive you," Holly warned.

"Oh, be quiet." When we got home, I'd hire an electronics expert to figure out how this worked. Oblivious to my plans for exposing them, the reindeer continued on through the darkness as if nothing extraordinary was happening—which, of course, it wasn't since we were still in the parking lot.

Except that didn't account for why I could see their legs moving. Even if we were just driving down the street, I should have heard hoof striking pavement. There must have been some sound-deadening software involved.

Mitch sat back, his arm stretched out along the back of the seat, his hand barely touching my shoulder for support. "Relax, you're doing fine," he said. "It's not like they're going to run off the road." The illusion was brilliant. If I hadn't known better, I'd have thought I was really driving a team of reindeer.

Suddenly, the sleigh jolted as though we'd hit a huge pothole. The buckets in the back clattered. Without the shoulder belt, I'd have gone flying out of the sleigh. "What the—!" I started as Holly yelled, "Hey!" and Mitch grabbed the reins.

One of the reindeer—the one without antlers—was tossing his head and jerking about as if he wanted to get free of the harness. The one next to him was looking over at him instead of straight ahead, and the two in front had their ears perked up.

"Easy, guys." Mitch's voice was soothing, steady. "You're okay, Leggo. Calm down, buddy. You're fine."

"What's going on?" Holly asked.

"What happened? What did I do?" He must have pushed a button somewhere. Apparently, there were sensors in the suits so we could feel things like fake bumps in the non-existent road. Mitch wasn't kidding—their tech guys were top-notch.

"Ssssh, you're okay," Mitch said, ignoring us. The antlerless reindeer began to thrash in his harness. Mitch cursed softly and transferred all the reins to one hand, releasing his shoulder belt with the other. Still speaking in quiet, soothing tones, he reached beneath the seat and brought up a long strap with a clip on the end, wrapping it around his waist and clipping it to a metal ring on his jumpsuit, and he stood up.

"Where are you going?" I asked.

He stepped up onto the seat. The reindeer were all agitated now; Leggo was frantic. The sleigh jerked again and again. Holly reached forward to grab my shoulder. Mitch stepped up onto the dashboard.

Another jerk nearly sent him backward, but he regained his balance. From there, he swung one leg over the front of the sleigh. "Here," he barked, handing the reins back to me. "Hold steady. Don't try to steer. Whatever you do, don't let go." He swung the other leg over and maneuvered until he was astride Leggo.

"What the—" Without thinking, I lifted up my goggles.

All about me was darkness. The only thing visible was the lights on the dashboard. No parking lot, no street lights. No buildings. No headlights driving past. No trees. No mounds of dirty snow on the ground.

No ground.

I could hear Mitch talking, but I couldn't have answered if my life had depended on it. If this was an illusion, it was beyond anything DC had ever imagined. I could feel the sleigh bucking, like it was all real. Like we were really flying through the night, miles above the earth, in an open sleigh pulled by panicky reindeer.

"Oh, my God," I breathed. I reached up with one hand to put my goggles back on, and from the darkness Mitch snapped, "Steady!"

I'd forgotten about the reins. I bent my head down so I could replace my goggles without lifting my hands. When I sat up, I could see Mitch and the reindeer again. He leaned forward, adjusting something on the reindeer's harness. Leggo threw his head back, soundly clonking Mitch's head. My stomach lurched as I pictured Mitch falling off and down, down, down into the night, but remarkably, he kept his seat, reaching out with one groping hand to steady himself on the other reindeer.

"Are you okay?" If he heard me, he didn't answer. My heart pounded as he leaned down again. I couldn't see what was happening. Acid rose in my throat. What if he was unconscious? What if the reindeer went crazy? What would happen? Would we fall to our deaths?

Finally, he straightened up. Leggo was still tossing his head, but he seemed to be calming down. Mitch stayed astride for a few more minutes before he slid back, reaching over the front of the sleigh to find a handhold and swing back over. He seated himself, removed the waist strap and fastened his shoulder belt. "I'll take those," he said, relieving me of the reins.

"What just happened?" Holly demanded. Good thing she could speak: my mouth was desert-dry, a bitter taste lingering.

"Leggo got spooked, that's all. He's fine now." He sounded casual enough, but he gripped the reins more tightly than before.

"Mitch? Everything okay?" came a male voice over a speaker.

Mitch pressed a button. "We're fine. Tell Helena she needs to look at Leggo's harness when we get back."

"Okay. The women still with you?"

"Haven't dumped them yet."

A chuckle. "Ralphie'd kill you."

"Let him try. How does the weather look up ahead?"

"Nothing special. You sure everything's okay?"

"Yeah."

Pause. "Go down to one."

"I don't need to. We're fine."

"Mitch. Go down to one." The voice didn't allow for dispute.

With an exasperated snort, Mitch said, "Hang on." I'd barely grabbed the dashboard when he eased the reindeer into a downward track. For a few minutes, frigid winds blasted as I braced my feet against the front of the sleigh to keep from sliding off the seat. Then, we leveled off, and the winds diminished and the chill softened.

"What was that?" Holly asked once we leveled out.

"Flight instructions." Our pilot was terse.

"How much longer do we have to go?" I asked.

"A while." He glanced in my direction. "You might as well take a nap." *Fat chance.*

But the journey went along smoothly after that. In the backseat, Holly snored. Mitch was alert, his flight suit not quite touching the seat back. Every so often, he had a brief innocuous exchange with the voice over the speaker.

I tried to convince myself it was an illusion, that what I'd seen without the goggles was just a visual disturbance, the way you see the ghost of a light bulb after looking straight at it, but it was no use. Seeing nothing, I'd seen too much. One bite from the apple, and there was no going back to Eden.

Wind rustled my jumpsuit. Frost glistened on the edge of the sleigh door.

A reindeer ear twitched.

No. It can't be.

There was no such thing as magic. Or flying reindeer. Or Santa Claus.

Except no technical genius, no sleight of hand could have created this illusion. Even David Copperfield couldn't make reindeer fly.

Nothing could lift a sleigh full of people—and four reindeer—off the ground and send them soaring into the night sky.

In the real world—my world—logic and evidence reigned. There was no room for the incredible, the fantastic. For anything that couldn't be scientifically proven, like the lighted gauges before me on a sleigh's dashboard. Or the young man sitting beside me, holding reins attached to reindeer harnesses. Reins I'd held in my own hands, heavy leather conveying the movement of the four living creatures pulling a sleigh.

Barely more than arm's-length away, a reindeer tail fluttered in the chilly wind.

A shiver of near-panic raced up my spine. I squinched my eyes closed, shutting out the evidence that contradicted everything my rational mind recognized as true. My gloved hands gripped each other. My boots pressed the floor of the sleigh, a futile attempt to ground myself.

High above the darkened earth, a fragment of possibility tapped the shell of my certainty, as light as an eyelash, as insistent as a woodpecker, until the slightest crack granted admittance to a single terrifying word.

Maybe.

Oblivious, Mitch broke the silence. "Get ready for descent."

Behind us, Holly stirred. Over an enormous yawn, she inquired, "Are we there yet?"

"Almost. Hold on." He slapped the reins and called out, "Going home!" All four reindeer heads perked up. An abrupt increase in speed jolted me against the seat back. Icy wind pummeled us. As we dipped below the clouds, snow swirled, stinging like a thousand tiny bees.

"Damn, it's cold!" Holly shouted.

"It's the North Pole!" I shouted back. Maybe it was the slap of the wind waking me up, but a sudden flush of folly-infused determination surged through me. I would ride this crazy roller coaster right to the end. Why not? For all I knew, this might really be the place. Wouldn't that be a kick?

The sleigh trembled. Mitch was pulling back hard. "Easy, guys!" he shouted. "Easy!" His feet were braced against the front of the sleigh. "Whoa! Whoa, Polly! Whoa, Chloe!" Lights began to show below amid an expanse of white. Mitch half-stood, still shouting to the reindeer. I grabbed for anything to secure myself against a crash landing.

And then, with a single bump, we were on the ground. Dimly, I became aware of cheering. I opened my eyes—I hadn't even realized I'd closed them again—to see what looked like hundreds of small people applauding.

"Nice landing!" called one of them.

I pulled off my goggles as a tall parka-clad man hustled out from what looked like a barn. "Welcome to the North Pole, ladies," he said. "I'm Ted Claus."

Toto, we're not in Connecticut anymore.

My heart pounded as I rose on shaky legs and tried to take it all in—the people, the barn, the light, and reindeer ambling toward us from the edges of nowhere.

Ted helped me out of the sleigh as Mitch hopped out the other side. When Ted smiled, I could see the resemblance to Ralph.

"Is this how your visitors always travel?" Holly was still plastered to the back seat.

"Pretty much," said Ted. He extended his hand to Holly as she managed to stand. "And you must be Holly."

"Almost the late Holly," she retorted, gripping the side of the sleigh. Ted must have noticed, because he said, "Please, let me." Before she could respond, he had helped her over the front seat and out of the sleigh, steadying her as she reached the ground. "This is my wife, Claire, and my sister-in-law, Isabella," he said as two women approached. "They'll take you inside."

"Pleased to meet you," said Claire. To Ted, she said, "Mom said they're to have the east guest suite. Can you have somebody bring up their bags?" He relinquished us to her care. As we walked away, I heard Ted say to Mitch, "I want to take a look at Leggo."

Fifteen

The walk to the east guest suite felt interminable. I couldn't even muster up the energy to make small talk. "Sorry we can't use the cart," said Isabella. "It only fits elves."

As if on cue, we heard a high-pitched *beep-beep-beep*. A motorized cart appeared from a side hallway. It looked like a golf cart for eight-year-olds. Four elves filled it—the driver, the front-seat passenger, and two on a seat facing backward. They waved as they left us behind.

The corridor was barely wide enough for the four of us to walk abreast. The ceilings—relatively low by modern standards, more like the 1950s ranch-style house in which I'd grown up—added to the feeling of being in a tunnel. Traffic, foot and cart, had worn the red woven carpet paler in the center. Simple brass rings in the ceiling framed inset lighting fixtures. The light was soft, but all-encompassing, as though we'd simply gone outside during the day. Probably they used those light bulbs that simulated natural daylight. In a place with long dark winters, I could understand a thirst for sunlight.

Clusters of framed photographs dotted the walls. Deserts, fields of corn, oak trees, beaches. "Where's that?" I pointed at a photo of lush greenery around a pedestrian bridge high above a stream.

To my immense relief, the others stopped walking. Claire plucked the photo off the wall and turned it over. "Vancouver, British Columbia. The Capilano suspension bridge," she read. She rehung the photo, taking a moment to straighten it.

Every so often, we passed a closed door. A low thrum of activity was audible, but the sounds were so muffled that I couldn't pick out any particular kind or source. "What's in there?" I asked as we passed one of the doors.

"That's part of the workshop," Claire said. "You'll get the tour after you've had a chance to freshen up."

By the time she said, "Here we are," I felt as though we'd walked halfway back to Connecticut. She opened the door and flipped a switch. Three wall sconces emitted the same kind of daylight I'd noticed in the hall; I couldn't tell whether it was the light or the paint that gave the walls just a hint of blush. The hallway's serviceable red carpet gave way to deep green cut-pile as soft and lush as a bed of pine needles. A love seat and matching armchairs were covered in tightly-woven fabric printed with wildflowers. A ceramic vase of silk flowers sat on the glass-topped coffee table. On the wall to our left, dark green ceramic tiles surrounded a fireplace with a beautiful slate hearth. More framed photographs graced the walls—an Asian couple beaming from behind their stall in a bustling street market, a little girl with a Dutch-boy bob and a red coat eating an ice cream cone, a young man dressed in camouflage holding out a scrap to a dog. The pictures were so entrancing that only later did I realize the room had no windows.

The cozy bedroom contained two single beds covered in handmade quilts and piled with pillows that echoed the quilt colors. Pocket closet doors slid back to reveal rods bearing padded hangers and a chest of drawers. Between the beds sat a small chest of drawers with a lamp and a brass clock. The photographs in this room were of quieter tones and subjects—a sunset over a river, a trio of speckled eggs in a nest, a cat sleeping beneath a lilac bush. The clock's narrow black hands showed that it was nearly eight, but since I had no idea whether it was morning or night, this scrap of information did nothing to orient me.

Every inch of the bathroom was pure white, right down to the thick towels. Glass doors enclosed the shower stall. On the compact vanity surrounding the sink sat a small woven basket bearing any toiletries a visitor might need. The drawers beneath the vanity held those necessary items not deemed fit for public display. I lifted the lid on a cylindrical basket in the corner, revealing three rolls of toilet paper.

The entire suite could probably have fit into my living room, but nothing about it felt cramped or stingy. Just the opposite: it provided exactly what one might require, with no surplus space to tempt the extraneous.

"If you need anything, just dial O," said Isabella. When I looked at her, perplexed, she said, "The phone is on the desk in the sitting room." Which showed how tired I was, because I hadn't even noticed the desk, much less the phone.

A knock on the door drew our attention. "That must be the bags," said Claire. "Would you like them in the bedroom?" Anticipating our response, an elf placed our bags next to the closet. Far from seeming like anybody's private house, this felt like a four-star hotel.

They all departed, leaving Holly and me to stare at each other. I slumped onto one of the beds. "Are we really here?"

"We're somewhere," she said. "Somewhere with a lot of short people. I've never felt so tall."

"That flight was real?"

"We sure didn't take an Uber."

I flopped back. "What in God's name have we done?"

"Now you ask?" Holly looked around the room. "On the other hand—the people seem nice enough, the room's comfortable—assuming the food's good and nobody kidnaps us into white slavery, there are worse ways to spend a weekend." She plopped her bag on the other bed. "Might as well unpack."

A ringing phone pulled me back to reality, if that was what it could be called. I stumbled into the sitting room where the desk phone summoned. "Hello?"

"Welcome to the North Pole!" Ralph sounded almost too hearty. "Everything okay?"

"Sure," I said. "Why wouldn't it be?" Holly was watching me from the doorway.

"I heard you had a little excitement on the way up," he said.

"We're fine. It was nothing." When he didn't respond, I said, "Seriously, I don't even know what happened, but whatever it was, Mitch fixed it and everything was fine."

"As long as you're all right."

"We're fine," I said again. I was tempted to tell him not to yell at Mitch, but his family issues weren't my problem. Instead, I said, "This house is incredible. Who decorated it?"

"My mother. Have you met her yet?"

"Not yet. We've met Ted and Claire and Isabella."

"You'll meet the rest of the family soon enough," Ralph assured me.

"Ask him if there's a map of the buildings," called Holly.

"You don't need one," said Ralph before I could repeat her request. "There'll be somebody to take you wherever you want to go."

"But I like maps. I like to see where I'm going." When he didn't respond, I said, "Let me guess. It's top secret?" So much for unfettered access.

"It probably would be if it existed, but nobody's ever made one. We don't need it."

"But this place is enormous. What do you give the new elves?"

"What new elves? They're born here, they grow up here. They don't need maps."

"Well, I didn't grow up here, and I'm very visual. If I don't see it, I don't understand it."

"Seeing is believing? Does that mean that since you've seen the place, you believe now?"

"I haven't seen anything yet, except a few hallways and a lovely guest suite."

"You saw reindeer fly," he pointed out.

A knock at the door saved me from having to answer. "I've got to go. Somebody's here."

"Tell Mom I said hi," said Ralph.

"What makes you think it's your mother?"

He chuckled. "I'll talk to you later."

I hung up as Holly opened the door to admit an elegant gentleman who was barely three feet tall. He had pointed ears and the most perfectly tailored suit I'd ever seen, made of exquisite navy wool. His red bowtie bore a small pattern I couldn't quite make out. "Greetings, ladies," he said in a surprisingly deep voice. "My name is Owen. Mrs. C. would like to see you when you're ready. Would you care to meet with her now, or would you prefer to rest first?"

I wasn't sure whether I'd ever be ready to meet the woman who ran Christmas for children all over the world, but this was why we'd come. Owen ushered us out into the corridor and led us back the way we came, then down another hallway. Eventually, we stopped before a mahogany panel. He pressed a button in the small brass plate by the panel. The panel slid soundlessly aside to reveal an elevator barely large enough for the three of us. He ushered us in, and as the door slid closed, he pressed a button next to the letter "C".

Within moments, the door slid open to reveal a tiny foyer. We stepped from the elevator onto a plush beige carpet. Side by side in the creamy walls were two forest green doors with brass handles. Neither bore a nameplate or label.

"What are those?" I asked.

Owen glanced at me. "This is Mrs. C.'s office," he said, gesturing to the right-hand door.

"What's the other one?"

"Mrs. C. is waiting." Before I could press about the left-hand door, he had knocked once.

"Come in," came a voice with a slight accent that I couldn't place.

Owen opened the door to reveal a woman walking toward us with a welcoming smile. She was smaller than I'd pictured—barely my height, and much slimmer. Her silver hair was pinned into a loose knot. She had the same light-green eyes as her sons, the rays emanating from the corners suggesting a lifetime of laughter. It was impossible to know whether her makeup was so artfully applied as to appear utterly natural or whether she wasn't wearing any. She reached out a graceful hand; her fingers were long and elegant, the nails unpolished and filed short.

"How do you do," she said. "I'm Meredith Claus. Welcome to the North Pole." Her voice was low-pitched and crisp. She took Holly's hand, then gestured for us to sit in the wingback chairs in front of the desk. Had it not been for the fabric—jewel-toned paisley—they might have come straight from my own office. "Ralph tells me you're a tea drinker. Would you like some?" A tea service sat on a small side table, ivory cups decorated with rich pine accents. The swirled handles and graceful curves suggested that the pieces were very old. To Holly, she said, "He didn't know whether you prefer coffee, so we have that as well."

"Tea's fine," said Holly. We started to rise to serve ourselves, but Mrs. Claus said, "Allow me. You must be tired after your trip. Sugar? Milk?" She handed us delicate teacups on saucers. "Please, help yourself," she added as she set a plate of cookies on the desk in front of us.

Up close, the pattern revealed itself as holly leaves joined by tiny crimson berries. The rims bore the merest tinge of gold. "This set is lovely," I said.

"Thank you." Mrs. Claus seated herself behind the desk. "It belonged to my mother-in-law, who inherited it from her mother-in-law." She stopped there, but it wouldn't have surprised me if she could recite the complete history of the tea service, back to its humble origins as clay on a river bank.

"I'm impressed that you've kept it intact," Holly said. "I mean, with all those boys."

Ralph's mother smiled. "We've lost a few pieces along the way, but by and large, it has survived." I wondered how often five rambunctious boys had been permitted to grace the inner sanctum of their mother's office. "I'm so sorry about the disturbance in your flight. I hope it wasn't too difficult for you."

"Thank you," I began as Holly asked, "Exactly what did happen?"

Mrs. Claus glanced at her. Somehow I knew that she'd seen more in that glance than most people would have noticed if they'd stared for an hour. "One of the reindeer is still training," she said. "The sleigh hit an air pocket, and it startled him."

"Something happened with the harness," I said.

"When Leggo spooked, he pulled a piece loose. It started to flap around, and that spooked him even more. He's still fairly young."

"Mitch did an amazing job fixing everything," I volunteered.

"I'll tell him you said so," she said, neither agreeing nor disagreeing with my assessment.

"If Leggo is so young and untrained, why did you send him to pick us up?" Like a child, Holly got cranky when she was overtired.

"Leggo was one of four," said Mrs. Claus. "The other three are experienced. You were in no danger."

I didn't want start off by arguing with Ralph's mother, but she hadn't watched Mitch straddling Leggo, secured to the sleigh by a single strap, trying to fix the harness as I held the reins. "What would have happened if Mitch had been alone in the sleigh when Leggo spooked?"

"My sons are well-trained. If there had been any danger, Mitch would have landed the sleigh." She sounded like a CEO speaking of a competent subordinate.

"What if we'd been over water?" Holly asked.

"One might ask the same about a jet crossing the ocean," Mrs. Claus replied. Before I could point out that jets came with many more safety features than an open sleigh, she continued, "Any worthwhile endeavor involves a certain amount of risk. The greater the value of the endeavor, the greater the risk. Take you ladies, for instance. Attorney Riley could have stayed safely in her office in Connecticut and handled Ralph's case the way she would any other, but she's here. She's taken a risk." *Attorney Riley.* Lest anyone wonder, this was a business meeting.

Or an audience with a monarch. The Queen of the North Pole.

Mrs. Claus—not Meredith or, God forbid, Merry—continued, "And you, Ms. Beardsley—you could have wished your friend a safe journey and gone back to bed. Instead, you rose in the middle of the night and climbed into a sleigh. That certainly counts as risk. Some might even call it folly." Out of the corner of my eye, I saw Holly startle.

"What do you see as the value of this particular endeavor?" I asked.

"That is an assessment you'll need to make for yourself." The three of us regarded one another. Just as the silence bordered on uncomfortable, she smiled again. "Tell me what you wish to accomplish here," she said. An invitation or a command. It was hard to know.

"I'm planning Ralph's defense." I was back on familiar ground. Her office, but my territory. "He says he was in the house by invitation because the boy had written to Santa. We're debating whether to argue that defense. As I'm sure you can appreciate, it would be a very tough sell. Ralph thinks that by coming up here, I can gather enough information to persuade a judge and a jury that all this—" I swept my arm to indicate the entire experience "—is real." I wasn't about to tell Ralph's mother about my plan to present her firstborn as a charming lunatic with delusions of Santa-ness.

She considered my words. At last, she said, "That's not going to happen."

"What do you mean?" Damn Ralph. He promised his family would cooperate. "I need information. Otherwise, there's no point to our being here."

"Isn't there?" She sipped her tea. She was clearly quite comfortable with the kind of attenuated pauses that make people blurt out truths. Luckily, so was I. Holly glanced from one of us to the other, but she followed my lead and remained silent.

The corner of Mrs. Claus's mouth tipped ever so slightly. "No matter how much you see or who you talk to, you'll never persuade a judge that the North Pole is real. Those who believe don't need to be persuaded, and the rest . . . you're not going to change their minds."

"I earn my living changing people's minds," I said evenly. Our eyes locked: *Your turn.*

"So you're saying it's hopeless," Holly interjected.

"Not at all," said Mrs. Claus. "I'm simply saying that you're not going to achieve the goal you've articulated. Even if you could, I can't allow you to use what you learn here." Her words had the finality of a prison cell clanging shut.

I didn't move, but inside, a flush of anger rose. "That will be up to Ralph," I informed her. Only my client could tell me what defenses I could or could not use. This woman might be the checkbook, but she wasn't the client.

"Ralph has a duty that goes beyond his case." Her voice was a degree cooler. "He knows that. He will not do anything to compromise this place or our mission."

"I recognize that you have certain priorities," I said, matching her tone. I would not lose my temper in front of the ice queen. "But my priority is representing my client. He, and he alone, will tell me what defenses I can or cannot use." The gauntlet was down.

A gentle chime sounded. "Excuse me," Ralph's mother said, reaching for the phone. "Yes. . . . Yes. . . . I have every intention of it. . . Perhaps you should leave that to me. . . . I understand. As I said. . . . Of course. Now, if you'll excuse me. . . . Goodbye." She hung up the phone. "I apologize for the interruption. Do I assume correctly that you ladies might enjoy a chance to rest and have something to eat before beginning your tour?" Clearly, the question-and-answer part of the meeting was over.

"Yes," said Holly before I could respond.

"Very well," said Mrs. Claus. She pushed a button on her phone, and an instant later, Owen opened the door. "Owen, please take these ladies back to their room. They will be resting. Let Annaliese know that they will be calling for their meal at some point."

"Thank you," Holly said. I forced myself to echo the sentiment. We all rose, and Mrs. Claus smiled as though we'd had a charming chat.

"I trust you will find your time here interesting," she said. "Owen, please give the ladies your contact information in case they need anything."

"Yes, ma'am." It almost appeared that he bowed slightly, as though acknowledging royalty. He waited by the forest-green door as we made our farewells, pulling it closed behind us and ushering us into the waiting elevator.

"Where's Santa?" I asked as the elevator door closed.

Owen glanced up at me. "Why do you ask?"

"We're at the North Pole. We came to see Santa."

"You'll need to talk to Mrs. C. about that." He handed each of us a small card. The elf carried business cards. "When you're ready, call me on the house phone, and I'll arrange for your meal. After that, you'll have a tour of the facility."

"But where's Santa?" I persisted.

"Once you've rested, there will be plenty of opportunities to have your questions answered." The elevator doors opened, and he exited the elevator. When we didn't follow, he turned back, his brow creasing ever so slightly.

"I need to see Santa," I said. "I'm sure the rest of the place is very nice, but if I don't see Santa, I won't be able to make the argument I need to." Ralph's mother might think she could buy us off with tea and Christmas cookies, but Ralph had *two* parents in this bizarre place. Queen Meredith, Ruler of Elves and Underlings, wasn't the court of last resort. That was Santa Claus, a/k/a my client's father. If Pop was anything like his firstborn, he'd help me.

"Please come with me now," Owen said. "I will tell Mrs. C. of your concerns."

"And?" Holly was plainly prepared to stay in the elevator all day.

Owen didn't flinch. His eyes, as rich as dark chocolate, remained fixed on hers. He stood only as high as my armpit, but he exuded the authority of a soldier and the polished dignity of a European attaché. "Please follow me," was all he said. I glanced at Holly and shook my head slightly. It was too soon to draw a line in the snow.

With no real choice, we followed him to our room. Another bow, and he drew the door closed behind him, leaving us to stare blearily at each other.

"Food or sleep?" I asked as if I didn't know the answer.

"Sleep," Holly said. "We've been up all night."

"Have we? I don't know even what time it is." I checked the clock on the bedside table. "Nine in the morning. Or at night. I can't tell. Hell, I don't even know what time zone we're in."

"Assuming we're even in one." Holly peeled off her sweater. "Don't forget, everything converges at the poles. We probably walked across three time zones getting from the sleigh to here." She yanked off her boots and slid down her jeans. "Right now, I don't care. I just want to go to sleep and wake up in a world that makes sense."

"What world is that?" I muttered as I tossed my clothes at my suitcase. Clad in silk long johns, I crawled under a comforter as light and soft as cashmere. Holly was still talking, but her words faded as if she were riding in a reindeer-drawn sleigh that had taken off in a swirl of snow and was moving farther and farther away.

Sixteen

I sat bolt upright in the darkness. Cripes, what a dream. Flying sleighs. Reindeer. Elves. Mrs. Claus. The North Pole. I shook my head to rid myself of the remnants of sleep and groped on the bed for the cats, but they weren't there. The covering didn't feel like my comforter. I moved my leg and nearly fell off a bed that was much narrower than my own.

In an instant, I was awake, my mind clear and frantic as memory supplanted the fog of sleep.

It wasn't a dream.

Muted voices filtered into my consciousness. I scrambled toward the floor-level sliver of light and yanked open the door.

"Shit!" I slammed the door, but not before everybody in the sitting room had gotten an eyeful of my underwear. I stumbled back to the bed and jammed my bare toes against the base of the bedpost. Swearing under my breath, I groped along the bed until I reached the night table. A moment later, I'd located the lamp switch, and the darkness was dispelled in favor of light and some semblance of normalcy.

I debated throwing on clothes and resuming my investigation, but all at once, a *what the hell* attitude came over me. Whoever had decided to drop by could cool their heels while I freshened up. I donned the plush terry robe at the foot of the bed and sauntered into the sparkling white bathroom. A long, hot shower, followed by careful grooming and wardrobe selection, and I was ready for Round #2.

My hand rested on the doorknob as I considered who our visitors might be. We'd already had our audience with Mrs. Claus. Unless

Santa himself sat on the loveseat, these visitors didn't have authority to override her mandates, so it was unlikely they'd be much help. On the other hand, maybe they could sway her, in which case there was no point in alienating them. I straightened my shoulders, assumed a charming smile, and opened the door.

"Hello, Meg," said Claire. "I'm sorry if we startled you."

"No problem," I said breezily. "I didn't expect anybody to be here."

"Claire and Anya brought up some food," said Holly. "We've been having a very nice chat." Her eyes met mine: *Don't ask now.* The investigator had done some good work.

"Holly's been asking how the Pole functions," said Anya. The lilt in her voice suggested that English wasn't her first language. She had dark eyes, long dark hair, and skin the color of milky tea. "It's challenging for an outsider to understand. I've been here for six years, and I still don't know everything."

"I don't think we've met." I extended my hand. "I'm Meg Riley."

"This is Anya," said Holly. "She's Fred's wife."

"Your husband is in charge of the animals?" I tried to scope out the women and the food at the same time.

"No, that's Ted," said Holly. "He's Claire's husband. Anya's husband is Fred. He's responsible for the workshop."

"Holly's a fast learner," said Claire, her pale blue eyes glinting with amusement. With her blond bob and Icelandic sweater, she looked like an ad for a Norwegian vacation.

"Is there an organizational chart of this place?" I asked.

"No need," said Claire. "If there's a major function, there's a Claus at the head of it."

I sank into one of the deep, soft armchairs. "Does it have to be a Claus by blood, or do you wives head things up?"

Claire and Anya exchanged a glance. "Mrs. C. married in," Anya reminded me, sliding a plate of sandwiches toward me.

"What are your jobs?" I asked. "How did you get stuck with the outsiders?" I bit into a sausage grinder, savoring the tang of what might have been goat cheese.

"It's a treat to see new people," Claire said. "We don't get a lot of visitors. Would you like some tea?" Without waiting for an answer, she removed an embroidered tea cozy from the pot it insulated, pouring just as Mrs. C. had. The golden brew shimmered in the bone china. "Darjeeling," she said before I could guess.

"The champagne of teas." I wasn't about to be one-upped. "What do you do here?"

"I'm responsible for the operations of the facility," Claire said.

"What does that mean?" I licked a bit of tomato sauce from my finger.

Claire waved her hand. "All of this," she said. "Meals, housekeeping, maintenance, décor, you name it. I'm the North Pole's housewife."

"I'm sorry," I began, but she waved me off.

"Don't worry about it," she said. "Believe me, I resisted at first. I thought I was being relegated to women's work. It took a while before I understood that we all have the same job."

"Which is?" Holly reached for a cookie.

"Helping Santa to do his work," she said. "It's such an honor to be involved in any tiny corner of something so incredible. Even if I spent my days polishing the sleigh runners—if that made it a teensy bit easier for Santa to get out there on Christmas Eve, it would be huge." I must have looked skeptical, because she added, "It's a lot more than most people do."

I munched my sandwich as I tried to frame my next question in the least offensive manner. "If you don't mind my asking, did you come here because you were in love with your husband or because you wanted to work for Santa?"

"Yes," Anya piped up. At my bemused expression, she explained, "I came here because I fell in love with Fred, but I couldn't have changed my life this way if I hadn't also believed in his work. Marrying a Claus means uprooting your entire existence."

"Plus, you kind of have to go undercover," Claire added. "It's not like you'd go on Twitter and post about how you're moving to the North Pole, hashtag 'Santa's daughter-in-law'."

"Is that forbidden?" Visions of Meredith Claus handing down a list of *thou shalt nots* flashed through my mind.

Claire favored me with the kind of indulgent smile you give when a small child asks a question to which the answer is obvious. "More like disrespectful."

Now I was really out of my depth. Holly said it for me: "Disrespectful how?"

"Maybe 'disrespectful' isn't exactly the right word," Anya said. "But the legend depends on the mystique. It's like the Wizard of Oz. You pull back the curtain, and we're just normal people. That would ruin it for a lot of children. I mean, you've seen Ralph. Does he look like the typical picture of Santa Claus? He's not going to gain fifty pounds and grow a white beard overnight when he steps into the job. He'll still be Ralph."

"What if you got here and decided it wasn't for you?" Holly asked. "Like my husband. We had a regular life in Connecticut, but one day, he decided he wanted to be a cowboy."

"What was his job up to then?" Claire asked.

"He was an HR manager at an insurance company," Holly said. "We were married for fifteen years, and suddenly he decided he wanted out of everything—his job, our marriage, the whole ball of wax. He ditched it all and headed off to the wild west."

"Your husband's a cowboy?" Anya said, impressed.

"For about ten minutes," Holly said. "Until he figured out it wasn't like the movies. Now, he works for an insurance company in Montana." She focused her attention on her teacup.

"The point is, what if you didn't want to stay here?" I asked.

Claire and Anya exchanged glances. Claire said, "Nobody here would try to force someone to stay against their will. On the other hand, we consider marriage to be a lifelong commitment." She rose. "On that note, I need to leave you. Anya will take care of your schedule. Have fun!" The North Pole's housewife was out the door before I could respond.

I finished my tea and set down the cup. "Just so we're clear—I'm here to gather information about how best to defend Ralph. I'm not looking to move in."

"Of course not." Anya held out a sheet of paper. "Here's your itinerary. Since the workshop is the heart of this operation, you'll start there. After that, if you want to see the stables, Ted can arrange to show you around. You've already seen Mrs. C.'s office, and you'll see the cafeteria at supper. There's really not much else."

"Will we get to meet any elves?" Holly asked.

"In this place? You'd be hard-pressed to miss them," Anya said. "I don't remember the exact numbers, but there are probably a couple dozen elves for every Claus." I tried to do some quick math, but Anya was still talking. "I know Meg met Charles when he went down below, and you've met Owen. Is there anybody in particular you'd like to talk to?"

"Well—" I thought fast. "What about Tillie? Is she an elf?"

"Tillie's a Claus—Santa's cousin. She moved up here when her husband died. Everybody here is either family or an elf." She stood up. For the first time, I noticed her baby bump. "If you're ready to go, I'll let Owen know we're heading down to the workshop."

"Why Owen? Is he going with us?" I snagged one last cookie off the tray.

"Oh, no," she said. "He's far too busy for that." She took out a cellphone and sent a quick text before handing it to me. "This is for you to use while you're here."

"You have cell service up here?" Relief flooded through me, but Anya's musical laughter cut it short.

"It's strictly internal." She punched a couple of buttons. "This is the list of people you can reach with this phone. See, I'm right here—" she scrolled down. "And here's Owen. You won't need anybody else."

"What if I want to talk to Ralph?" I asked.

"You can use the house phone for that," she said. "Dial O and ask Ivy to connect you."

"What if I want to call home?" Holly asked.

Anya shook her head. "Not from here. Ready?"

"Wait a minute. I can't call my kids and tell them I'm alive?" Holly was on her feet.

"Not from here," Anya met Holly's gaze squarely. "If that's a problem, let me know."

"What will you do about it?" Holly demanded.

"I'll tell Ted to get the sleigh ready so you can go home." Anya was probably four inches shorter than Holly and at least twelve years younger, but she had a quiet self-possession that I envied. "You can either stay here or talk to your children. What would you like to do?"

"Holly." My voice was quiet, but urgent. I wasn't ready to go. We'd seen so little of this place. I still didn't know whether it was real or just the world's most elaborate theme park. And we still hadn't met Santa Claus.

"All right," said Holly grudgingly. I stifled a sigh of relief. As Anya opened the door, Holly said, "By the way, we never got a room key."

"That's because there aren't any," Anya said. "Nothing locks here. Don't worry, though. Your stuff is fine." She led us to a small foyer with corridors radiating in all directions. "This is where you came through before," she said. "It's called the Star, because you see how there are all those hallways? It's like Paris, where the Arc de Triomphe is, with all those avenues radiating out. Same design." We were trotting along at a pretty good clip, but she wasn't even slightly out of breath. As she pointed and explained like a tour guide, I couldn't help thinking that bombarding a person with information is an excellent way to distract from what you're *not* telling them.

"Can I ask you something?" I asked. "What is your job here?"

She smiled broadly. "Public relations."

A curious job for a place so conscientiously hidden from the world. "What dealings with the public do you have?"

She looked at me as if I were a tad slow. "Same as any other business. Communications, social media, image management—the usual stuff." She pushed open the door, and I forgot all about public relations, because we were in Santa's workshop.

Seventeen

Forget the pictures. Forget the old-fashioned illustrations, the adorable movie sets, the cutesy television specials, the kitschy displays in department stores and malls. Forget the cherry red and kelly green, the gilt and fur. Forget the little people with pointy caps and pointy shoes tapping on wooden trains with miniature hammers. Because none of that can hold a candle to the real thing.

The world outside might be snowy-white, but inside the workshop danced a riotous, joyous festival of every imaginable hue. Throughout the vast room—as long and wide as a gymnasium, but with half the height—three-foot barriers cordoned the space into work stations that fairly vibrated with color, from brilliant work mats to jewel-toned elf worksuits. The ceiling was painted with shining stars dotting a deep blue sky, the underside of a dark-green sleigh, the dark hooves and creamy tan bellies of reindeer, and a trail of sparkles in their wake.

Joyous laughter and chatter rang through the room, but make no mistake—these elves were here to work. Dozens of shelves bore everything from unfinished toys to binders to tools whose use I couldn't begin to fathom. As Fred led us through a maze of aisles separating work areas, elves debated and evaluated, drawing and notating and trying out combinations. On a whiteboard, a cluster of elves sketched out a diagram of some sort of go-kart. In the near corner, the hum of sewing machines heralded the creation of doll clothes. At another station, a team fashioned the dolls who would wear those clothes. Across the room, a group of elves worked under high-intensity lamps, tracing details on toy vehicles—details which would be filled in later in the finishing room.

Anywhere from four to twenty elves might be working in a given station. Knitting machines, jigsaws, potters' wheels, vises, drills, glue guns, and anything else you might find on your father's workbench, in your mother's sewing room, or in the art rooms and woodshops at your school. In the midst of it all, a bevy of elves in bright orange vests ferried trash cans and brooms through the aisles, removing scraps and shavings with the same delight as the elves who were creating the toys.

Later, with the glow of the workshop lingering like the warmth of a hug, I asked Fred about the low ceilings. There were two reasons for this, he explained. First, the pragmatic: heat rises, and at the Pole, conserving heat was a major concern. Second, the emotional: elves were small, and the higher the ceiling, the smaller they felt. Since the elves meant so much to Santa's mission, it was important that they felt valued, not minimized. Hence, the lower ceilings.

"Why not make the ceilings even lower?" I asked. "You could bring them down to seven feet and still not bump your head."

"When ceilings are too low, the noise is amplified. We've experimented with different ceiling heights over the years, and eight feet gives us the best balance."

"Why don't you soundproof?" Holly suggested.

"The elves like to hear each other working," Fred said. "It reminds them that they're part of a bigger operation."

The floors were a material that I couldn't quite identify, because it wasn't carpet and yet it didn't cause the sound to bounce the way tile or hardwood would have.

"Bamboo over cork," Fred said when I asked. "Softer underfoot than tile or concrete, but just as easy to clean." He led us down the hall to another room. "The metal workers are in a separate room because of the noise," he said as he opened a heavy door. At once, we clapped our hands to our ears to shut out the screech of metal sheets being cut. "You'll need sound protection gear if you want to go in there," he said directly into my ear.

"No need," I yelled before Holly could pipe up.

It would take days to describe everything we saw, heard, smelled, touched. As simple as wooden blocks in bold colors, as complex as a child-safe tablet ("It can be dropped from thirty feet. We tested it by throwing it out of the sleigh."). Dolls of every skin tone and hair color and type, dressed in princess-pink gowns, golden saris, gingham dresses with muslin aprons, blue jeans, raincoats with matching umbrellas. Fashion dolls in silvery sequin-look evening dresses ("We don't use real sequins. Choking hazard."), and even dolls in riding clothes with their own ponies—not to mention the baby dolls in pink and blue onesies and the classic Raggedy Ann and Andy ("With the hearts!"). Stuffed animals of every size and species and color, from purple elephants with googly eyes to startlingly realistic puppies and kittens. An entire room devoted to bikes, trikes, scooters, wagons, and anything else with wheels, including a track around the perimeter where several elves were test-driving their wares. Action figures of firefighters, police officers, soldiers in camouflage, sports figurines, movie characters ("Star Wars is going to live forever!"), and every superhero I'd ever heard of (and plenty I hadn't), with accessories ranging from vehicles to light sabers. Another room filled with sketches for playhouses and large flat boxes ("The parents assemble those—otherwise, we'd never get them on the sleigh."). Games of every type, from classic board games to some I couldn't figure out whose pieces glowed in the dark. Puzzles with four large wooden pieces or a thousand cardboard ones. Arts and crafts supplies for projects from finger-painting to beadwork to papier maché. Baseballs and bats, basketballs, footballs, soccer balls. Toy guitars and xylophones and one-octave keyboards with all the keys in different colors.

Everything you could possibly have wanted to play with was there. It was kid heaven. Forget kids: I wanted to play with it all. I wanted to grab a scooter and race the elves around the track, make a tea party for a doll in a princess dress, assemble a playhouse and play board games inside, cuddle a plush teddy bear. I wanted to turn the calendar back thirty-five years and write to Santa so he could bring me these beautiful presents. "It's wonderful," I breathed.

Fred beamed. "It's the North Pole."

The plastics department was in its own space because of the fumes, but Fred pointed out the circulation system designed to filter the air. We peered through the window in the door to see elves wearing protective eyewear as they poured viscous-looking liquid into molds.

"You make your own plastic?" I asked.

"Most of it," Fred said. "There are some things we don't have molds for. That stuff we import. The rest we do here."

"Because it's cheaper?" I asked as an elf whisked away a mold and set it into a rack.

"That's one reason. The main one is quality." He indicated a trio of 3-D printers. "When the technology improves, we'll print instead of pour, but right now, printing's too slow."

Another door led into a small airlock. "What's this?" Holly asked.

"Electronics," he said. "We have to make sure there's no dust. They have a separate entrance on the other side. You can go in as far as the interior door, but that's it unless you want to change and put on a hairnet." He opened the exterior door, and we peeked through the window in the interior door. The elves inside looked like a gaggle of scientists working on some highly contagious disease process. The walls were a jumble of colors, but the work stations were white, and the elves were dressed in white jumpsuits. "They're working with tiny parts," Fred said. "It's easier to see them against white."

The elves all wore hairnets, and some wore masks. "What's with those guys? Do they have allergies?" I asked, imagining a sneeze sending tiny electronic parts flying.

Fred grinned. "Beards."

In one room, elves threw balls, carts wove around obstacles, trains ran on track a foot below the ceiling. Dolls and doll houses on one table, yipping toy dogs turning backflips on another. Elves walked around with tablets, jabbing screens and asking questions of the ones whose job seemed to be playing with the toys. "What that?" I asked. "Break time?"

"Research and development," said Fred. "Kids' preferences change. We have to keep up."

By the time we reached the cafeteria, I felt as though we'd been walking for miles. A luscious aroma filled the air. "It's spaghetti night," Fred said. "Annaliese uses her great-grandmother's recipe for the sauce."

"One person cooks for all of you?" Holly seemed astounded.

"Oh, no," Fred chuckled. "Annaliese is the head chef, but there are about a dozen elves in her crew. One group does all the baking— bread, cookies, the works."

"Where do you get your—well, everything?" I asked when we sat down at a long table. A handful of elves occupied other tables. Some were chatting; at one table, two elves were reading. An elf family sat nearby, the parents smiling as the kids enjoyed cookies and cocoa.

"We have suppliers," said Fred. "Do you want something to eat? Are you thirsty?"

"I'd love coffee," said Holly. Her eyes had that faraway expression I'd seen so many times. It meant she was dying to start sketching.

"Tea would be great," I said.

"Coming right up."

As soon as Fred was out of earshot, I leaned in close to Holly. "What do you think?"

"If this is a scam, it's the most elaborate one I've ever seen," she whispered. "Imagine what it would cost to fake all this. The actors alone would break any budget."

"It's like Disney World meets Frozen." All the attention to detail, carefully scripted tour leaders, characters who never broke, breathtaking illusions—it was the Magic Kingdom without Mickey Mouse. I made a mental note to investigate whether there was any connection between this place and any of the major entertainment conglomerates.

Except that wouldn't make sense. Disney, Six Flags, Universal— they made their money by bringing the public to their parks. Why would they want a secret facility? Even if people knew about it, how would they get here? Where would planes land? Where would they stay? Our little guest suite only had two single beds. Unless there were guest dormitories somewhere, they'd never be able to bring in the numbers necessary to sustain such a place. Would they come by cruise ship?

"Here we are," said Fred, cutting off my ruminations. He set down a tray bearing pots of coffee and tea, three mugs, a sugar bowl and creamer, and a plate of cookies whose aroma made my mouth water. "The bakers were just taking them out of the oven," he said.

I bit into one. It was still warm, soft enough to melt but firm enough not to crumble. A heavenly blend of spices—cinnamon, cloves, ginger—played against buttery sweetness and a hint of orange. "This is fabulous," I murmured, my eyes half-closed.

Holly laughed. "She's in love!" My eyes flew open, and she added hastily, "I mean, with the cookies!" Fred looked away, but I could see a dimple in his cheek, just like Ralph's.

I finished my cookie and poured my tea. The others chose coffee, and for a few moments, the only sounds at our table were contented purrs as we relished our snack.

When the plate was empty, I said to Fred, "Is that it?"

"You want more cookies?" He started to rise. A mannerly group, these Clauses.

"Oh, no—I meant, have we seen the entire workshop now?"

"Most of it," he said. "There's still finishing and wrapping. When you're ready, we can go over there."

"We really appreciate your time," I said. "You must have lots of other things to do besides give tours." Out of the corner of my eye, I saw Holly's hand move to her mouth to hide a smirk. "What would you be doing if we weren't here?"

"Bunch of things," he said. "We're in post-Christmas right now, so there's a whole lot of clean-up. We assess what kids wanted and what they didn't so we can adjust production for next year. Plus, we replenish the inventory. Most kids don't write their letters until pretty close to Christmas, but some toys never go out of style, so we get them ready during the slower season."

"What exactly is your job?" I asked. "Do you actually make toys, or are you the foreman or supervisor or whatever?"

"Both," Fred said. "At crunch time, everybody pitches in." He leaned in, grinning conspiratorially. "Here's something the poem doesn't tell you: elves are better at making toys than Clauses."

"Gracious me, I'm shocked and appalled," said Holly.

"Utterly scandalous," I agreed. "I'm calling the tabloids the moment we get back."

Fred's laugh was a lighter version of the classic *ho ho ho!* "Some of us are pretty good. Mitch is a whiz with the electronics, but don't tell him I said so. It's hard enough to get him to respect his elders."

"What's the age gap between you brothers?" I asked.

"Ralph's thirty-six, Phil's—let me think—thirty-three, Ted and I are turning thirty in a few months."

"And Mitch?"

"Nineteen. He was born on Christmas morning." He shook his head, remembering. "That was one crazy night. Thank God Grandpa was still alive so we could have three sleighs out. Mom went into labor on Christmas Eve, which meant she couldn't run the command center."

"What do you mean?" Visions of enormously pregnant Meredith Claus barking orders dashed through my head. "What's a command center? Is that like air traffic control?"

"It's all the logistics—who's out on which sleigh, what they have with them, what routes they're covering, what's been delivered where, what's still outstanding, any weather developments—everything. On Christmas Eve, it's the most important place in the world."

"If your mother was in labor, who took care of all that?" Holly asked.

"Phil," Fred said. "He was barely fourteen, but he ran the command center like a champ while Grandpa and Pop and Ralph did the toy deliveries and Mom did the Mitch delivery."

"What did you and Ted do?" I asked.

"We were on the sleighs. That's part of our training. There's always a second on the sleigh, an elf or a young Claus. The second keeps track of the list. Ted's older boy went out this year on Ted's sleigh." He chuckled, remembering. "You think kids are excited to get presents on Christmas morning? That's nothing compared to how excited Justin was to be giving them out." He gestured toward the tray. "What do you think? More coffee, or are you ready for the finishing room?"

"Finishing room," Holly said.

"Wait—can we see the command center?" The workshops were wonderful, but I wanted to see the most important place in the world.

"Sorry, that's classified," he said. "Besides, unless it's Christmas Eve, there's not that much to see. Computer screens, keyboards, that kind of thing. For my money, it's not nearly as interesting as watching elves make toys."

He reached for the tray, but I said, "I'll get that. Just tell me where to go."

"Leave it on the counter over there," he said, pointing to a closed red door. "I'd show you the kitchen, but they're getting ready for dinner now, and nobody—not even my mother—is allowed in during meal prep."

So the great and powerful Mrs. Claus, Queen of the Command Center, deferred to an elf. I pictured her going toe to toe with an irate elf waving a wooden spoon dripping red sauce. On the other side of the kitchen door, I could hear chatter and clanging and the hiss of boiling water. When I caught up with Holly and Fred, I asked, "How many are they cooking for?"

Fred led us into the hallway. "Pretty much everybody. Takeout's available, but most of us like to eat together."

"Will we get to eat with the elves tonight?" I asked.

"If you want. If you're tired and you'd rather eat in your room, that can be arranged."

Miss dinner with Santa's elves? Was this guy nuts? Except I knew Holly would be itching to get to her sketch pad by then, and I couldn't fault her for it. After all, that was why we were here—to gather information for Ralph's defense. Wandering through this wonderland, it was easy to forget about courts and juries and the law.

Fred led us through a labyrinth of hallways to another red door. "This is the finishing room," he said. "It's actually a suite because there's so much finishing to do." He opened the door to reveal a dozen elves sitting before large white tables with rims. "Keeps tiny parts from falling off," he explained. Each table had several long-arm lamps clamped to the side.

We paused to watch as one of the elves attached eyelashes to a baby doll. Using long pointed tweezers, he held the eyelashes over a small pad that caught any drips as he applied an infinitesimal line of adhesive to the tiny strip. Then, he picked up another pair of tweezers, and using them as surrogate hands, he placed the eyelashes on the doll's eye. He pulled down one of the lamps so that it hovered just above the doll. A fan whirred. Seven seconds under the lamp and fan, and he clicked them off. He pushed that lamp back and pulled forward another with a magnifying glass attached. He inspected his work, pushed that lamp back, and proceeded to do it all again for the doll's other eye.

"There's a lot of detail work here," Fred said as he led us through the next doorway. Several elves were painting a veritable fleet of vehicles—fire trucks, police cruisers, helicopters, tractors. I was about to ask why the room was so warm when a blast of heat heralded removal of a tray of vehicles from the kiln, freshly-baked and glossy.

Fred led us into the next room. "This is the soft room. They do the stuffed toys."

"Holly, look!" A calico cat was curled up in the middle of a work table. "May I?" I asked, but I was already reaching out to pet it.

"Of course," said the curly-haired elf working at that table. Her bright blue eyes sparkled with pride. "That's Cleo. She's one of our most popular pets."

"She's not real?" Laughter like sweet silver bells rang through the room as I bent down to look more closely.

"She's as real as your imagination says she is," the elf said. "Here, feel her fur. Isn't that nice?" She laid my hand on the cat's silky back.

"She feels like my Lulu," I said.

"Thanks!" said the elf. "She's almost done. I just have to put in her eyes and whiskers, and she'll be ready to go."

"That'll be one lucky kid who gets her," I said, giving the toy's back a final pat.

As we continued through the finishing rooms, Holly's eyes grew wider, her steps slower. Periodically, she paused to study the fine work an elf was doing. She always stood an appropriate distance back, saying nothing unless the elf invited comment—one artist respecting another. I was interested in watching the elves who wielded paintbrushes and glue guns and tools I couldn't identify, but Holly was captivated. "A painted lady," she whispered as we watched two elves painting the trim on a Victorian-style dollhouse.

At long last, we reached the final finishing room, where elves were packaging completed toys and loading them onto carts. "Is this everything?" I felt like a little kid who didn't want the magical day to end.

Fred's smile broadened. "For the workshop, yes," he said. "I can take you down to see wrapping and the warehouse, but I don't know if you're interested in that."

I turned to Holly, but she was watching the elves. Her eyes were soft and sad, as if she was seeing a beautiful land to which she could never gain access. I nudged her arm. "You want to see the wrapping place?"

"Sure." Her voice sounded far away. Fred led us out of the last finishing room, the door closing behind us with a quiet thump. Down yet another hallway—how *did* anyone find their way around?—and we entered a room filled with massive carts bearing toys, large tables spread with wrapping paper, and a variety of bizarre-looking machines.

"They're for wrapping odd-shaped presents," Fred explained. He pointed to the one on the far right. "That one's for balls." I must have looked confused, because he said, "I take it you've never tried to wrap a football?" He gestured to the ring at the top. "Anything up to a basketball can go in there." An elf dropped a soccer ball through the ring into what seemed to be a hammock of paper. He operated a lever, and mechanical arms maneuvered the ball and paper. Moments later, a perfectly-wrapped round ball dropped into the tray below.

"Amazing," I said.

We declined the offer to tour the warehouse. Fred pulled out his phone and tapped. "Anya'll be here in a few minutes to get you," he said. We thanked him profusely, but our words seemed hopelessly inadequate. For a few hours, I'd forgotten this had to be some sort of scam. It felt real, every inch of it. Even if it was simply the world's most amazing toy factory, it was magical.

And if it was what these Clauses claimed it was . . . the implications were staggering.

Eighteen

"So? What did you think?" Anya asked as she led us down the hall. Her eyes darted from me to Holly, the corners of her mouths tipped up as if she knew the answer.

But I wasn't ready to give it to her. "I think I'm exhausted. Is there time to rest before dinner?"

Anya consulted her watch. "They'll start serving in about an hour."

Along one hallway was an enormous collection of framed photographs of children and drawings and notes. "You'd be surprised how many kids write thank-you notes," Anya said. "A lot of them include pictures of themselves with the gifts, especially since everybody started taking selfies."

We stopped to peruse the display. Most pictures were of young children—maybe six or seven at the most, with gap-toothed smiles—but every now and then, we saw someone older. One cluster of photographs was especially intriguing: the same woman, with progressively graying hair, standing in front of the same fireplace. In each photo, she wore a different sweater, but each sweater bore a picture of a cat.

"Who's this?" I asked.

"That's Margrethe," Anya said. "She's one of our special ones."

"What do you mean?"

"Don't get me wrong—all the kids are special—but every year, we make some extra-special gifts. Margrethe has been writing to us for as long as anybody can remember."

I squinted. Margrethe was squat and wore glasses with round pink frames. Her eyes had the tell-tale upward slant common to people with Down syndrome. In every picture, her smile shone with perfect happiness.

"She lives in a group home in Scotland," Anya continued. "Every year, she writes to us, and she always wants the same thing—a sweater with a cat on it. Martha and Ross in the workshop make the sweater by hand. They're great knitters. Then, sometime in January, she sends us a picture of her wearing the new sweater." There were at least three dozen pictures of Margrethe in the display. The sweaters boasted long-haired cats, short-haired ones, solid colors, calicos, Siamese, and tabbies. In one picture, she was waving to the camera.

"She looks so happy." I reflected.

"She seems to be," Anya said. "When she writes to us, she tells us things that have happened to her during the past year, and even when it's sad news like somebody dying or leaving the home, she still sounds positive." She reached out and touched the glass covering one of Margrethe's pictures. "I wonder sometimes who her caregivers think she's writing to. They probably think she's throwing her letters away, but they always get to us."

"These sweaters are beautiful," Holly said. "How old is she?"

"I think she's sixty, or close to it," said Anya. "I read once that the average life expectancy for someone with Down syndrome is somewhere in the fifties. So now we all worry until her letter arrives. She usually writes in October."

"And if you don't get one. . . ." Holly's voice trailed off.

"Then we'll know." Anya sounded more philosophical than sad. "But in the meantime, we get to make sweaters for this beautiful woman." Her fingertip brushed the glass as if to stroke Margrethe's hair.

I wandered along the hall, scanning the display for pictures of other adults. I was surprised at how many I found. "Do all of these people have some sort of . . . cognitive problems? The adults, I mean."

"Some of them," Anya said. "I'd love to be there when the caregivers find our gifts under the tree. They know they didn't buy them."

"Do these caregivers ever try to contact you? I mean, to find out who you are?"

"Occasionally," Anya said. "We've even gotten a couple cease-and-desist letters accusing us of causing harm to the person by encouraging their delusions."

"What did you do?" I asked.

"Threw them away. Our job is to deliver the gifts, not get involved in legal battles. Besides, the one thing we know is that when someone believes in Santa, it's not a delusion—we're really here. So we keep doing our job, and eventually the complainers fade away."

"Do you answer any of the letters?"

She shook her head. "It's hard sometimes, because some of these letters would break your heart. It's so tempting to write back and tell the kid everything's going to be okay, but we can't. It's—what do you lawyers call it? Outside the scope of our job."

Later, when Holly and I were alone, she said, "I never would have expected that adults would write to Santa."

"Me neither," I said.

"I wonder if having their kind of difficulties makes it easier to believe," she mused. "Childlike faith and all that. Less noise coming at them from the outside world."

Something in her voice caught my attention. She sounded almost wistful. "What?"

"Nothing. Just—it would be nice if the world were simpler. If there was space to believe the improbable."

"Maybe you should move up here. I'm sure they could use another artist."

"Now that really would be folly," she said. "What about you?"

"I haven't seen a courthouse around here. I'd be completely useless."

"Not to Ralph," she said slyly. "Or you could do Mrs. C.'s job. Wouldn't that be your role anyway when Santa retired and Ralph got promoted?"

I snorted. "What have I ever done to make you think I could run an operation like this? I can barely handle a small law firm."

But Holly looked unconvinced. "I'll bet you could do it," she said. "Besides, this place is huge. I'm sure you'd find your spot."

"That would be one hell of a chance to take." Especially for someone who'd spent her entire life in the tiny state known as Land of Steady Habits.

"Maybe," she allowed. "But you'd have Ralph. That's a decent consolation prize." Her hazel eyes searched mine. "Assuming, of course, you wanted to be with him."

"You're getting way ahead of yourself. I barely know the guy. There's a world of difference between being attracted to someone and uprooting my entire life. Marriage is hard enough when both people come from the same background. I've seen enough divorce files to know that."

"Folly, every last one," Holly agreed. "But sometimes, folly works out. Now go take a nap. I need to draw before I forget what we saw." She rummaged in the bottom of her bag for her sketch pad and the soft leather packet of pencils she carried everywhere.

I couldn't imagine forgetting any of it, but I knew when I was being dismissed. I left her to her pencils and headed into the bedroom where I stretched out on the bed, cozy and warm under the handmade quilt, and closed my eyes as visions of elves danced in my head.

Nineteen

I woke to the aroma of an Italian restaurant. Blinking in the darkness, I groped for the lamp. The bedside clock read eight-thirty. "What the—?" I fought my way free of the quilt and pounded into the sitting room where a covered tray waited on the coffee table. "Why didn't you wake me?" I demanded. "You knew I wanted to have dinner with everybody in the cafeteria."

"I tried," said Holly without looking up from the sketch before her. "You were dead to the world. Mumbled something about being in command and smacked me away. I figured you were down for the count."

"Damn it all, I really wanted to eat with everybody. Talk to the elves, see Santa." I lifted the cover to see a bowl of fettucine and meatballs, a small dish of grated cheese, and a plate bearing slices of still-warm bread. "What about you? Did you go to the cafeteria?"

"I had too much to do." She gestured toward a few sheets of paper on the corner of the desk. I picked up the top one. With a few pencil strokes, she'd captured the movement, the energy, the vitality of the first workshop we'd seen. The next sketch showed the hallway with the photographs. The third depicted the elf family we'd seen in the cafeteria. I peered over her shoulder to see the curly-haired elf in the finishing room, working on Cleo.

"This is good stuff," I said. "Thanks."

"Yeah." But she didn't sound pleased.

"What?" I bit into a piece of bread.

"It feels wrong," she said. "I mean, we know they don't want this stuff to get out."

"They don't want it plastered all over the internet," I clarified. "Ralph sent me here specifically to get information to defend him. What you're doing is recording that information. Which reminds me, I should make some notes."

"Eat first. Claire said that little covered tray thing will keep the food warm for a while, but she brought it a couple hours ago."

The aroma of herbs and garlic was tantalizing. I dipped my bread in the rich red sauce. "Did she say what's on for the evening?"

"Wasn't there an itinerary?" Holly reminded me.

"Somewhere." My brain was still fogged with sleep. I twisted a few strands of pasta on the fork and maneuvered it into my mouth. It was better than anything at the dozens of Italian restaurants in Hartford. The sauce was sumptuous, redolent with oregano and garlic and other herbs I couldn't quite place. The pasta tasted homemade. The meatballs had a light, mild flavor that was more garlic and cheese than beef. A thought occurred to me. "You don't suppose—are these reindeer meatballs?"

"Probably. It's not like there are a lot of beef cattle wandering around."

The thought of eating Rudolph made the meal a bit less appealing, but when in Rome, and all that. Besides, they were delicious. I'd been subjected to several venison dinners back when my brother was going through his manly-man hunting phase, and these meatballs had none of the gaminess I'd so disliked in white-tail deer.

I savored my meal as Holly sketched. When I'd finished, I retrieved my bag from the bedroom closet and rummaged for the itinerary, to no avail. Before I could ask whether she knew where it was, the phone rang. I reached past her to lift the receiver. "Hello?"

"Hi!" said Ralph. "How's it going?"

"Pretty well," I said. "This place is amazing. I wish I could take pictures. The jury would love it." At my elbow, Holly continued to draw.

"Did you see the workshop?"

"That was pretty much the whole day. Fred took us through everything."

"And what did you think?"

"It's incredible. I've never seen anything like it."

"So. . . ?"

"So . . . what?"

"So, do you believe me now?"

This wasn't a conversation I wanted to have with Holly creating contraband six inches away. "Let's save that discussion for when I get back."

"Come on, Meg. You flew in a sleigh. You've seen Santa's workshop. You've met elves. What more do you need?"

"I want to meet Santa." The words popped out without thought.

He was silent for so long I thought we'd been cut off. At last, he said, "I'm sorry, but no."

"What do you mean?"

"I mean—no."

"I don't understand. I've seen his workshop. What's the big deal about seeing him?"

"I could ask you the same question. Why do you need to see him?"

"Because I do." Even I could hear the petulance in my voice. Holly glanced up at me. "Here's the thing," I said finally. "We've seen a lot of stuff and we've talked to a lot of people, but so far, we haven't seen Santa. It doesn't really help if we go back and talk about seeing this place, because the whole point is that you're supposed to be acting for Santa and we still can't say that we've seen him. Would you please set up a meeting?"

Long pause. "I'm sorry. I can't do that."

"What do you mean?"

"I can do practically anything else for you, but I've already talked to my mother about this. She said no way. No audience with Santa."

"No 'audience'? This is Santa Claus we're talking about. Not the pope."

He didn't chuckle. "I'm sorry," he said again. "The answer is no."

"Then we might as well just come home." Out of the corner of my eye, I saw Holly frown. "If we can't see Santa, then the whole trip has been a waste."

"Has it?" When I didn't answer, he said, "Have you tasted the cocoa?"

"What are you talking about?"

"It's pretty amazing. You really should try it."

"I'm not here to do taste-tests." I tried not to sound irritated.

"I know. I just thought—you should try the classics. Cocoa and Christmas cookies."

"We already had cookies."

"But did you try the cocoa? You have to try it. Call Owen and tell him I said to take you over to the kitchen. You can pick your own cookies to go with it."

Unbelievable. He thought this would fix everything. "Sure. Right. Thanks."

"—Meg—"

"—what?"

Another pause. "I'm sorry this trip hasn't turned out to be . . . what you were hoping for." There was a note in his voice that suggested that he, too, had found the trip to fall short.

"Don't worry about it. How do I arrange for the trip home?"

"I'll take care of it. Just—forget about being a lawyer for a little while. Go have some cocoa and cookies."

"Whatever. Let me know about the travel arrangements."

"Will do." He waited, and when I didn't say anything else, he said, "Good night."

"Good night." I hung up the receiver, carefully not looking at Holly.

"What does he want you to taste?" she asked.

"Cocoa and Christmas cookies."

Holly snorted. "Men have no sense."

"He said we should go and raid the kitchen for our favorites."

She looked slightly less irked. "You mean we get to wander around without an escort?"

"Not hardly. We're supposed to call Owen."

"What if we didn't?"

"Meaning . . . ?"

"What if we went out on our own?" She sounded downright impish.

I tried to tamp down a flicker of excitement. "They probably have an alarm system or something."

"They don't even have locks," she reminded me. "We can go anywhere. Even that command center, if we can find it."

That clinched it. I located my shoes, and Holly tucked her sketches into the drawer with a blank sheet on top. I opened the door and peeked out. Empty.

"The coast is clear," I hissed. We slipped into the hall like a pair of fugitives.

Maybe it wasn't polite to be sneaking around somebody's house in the middle of the night, but we'd been polite and well-mannered and all it had gotten us was a great big waste of time. Granted, it had been one hell of an adventure, but for what? So Ralph's family could see whether I was Mrs. Claus material? Because it didn't take an advanced degree to figure out that the Clauses were evaluating me at least as closely as I was them.

The lights in the halls were dimmer now, barely enough to keep us from bumping into walls. According to Fred, the workshop operated 24/7 from September to Christmas, but there was no sign of a night shift now.

"What do you want to find first? The kitchen or the command center?"

"Duh." We made our way down the hall to the Star. The darkened hallways radiating off the lobby offered no clue.

"Excuse me, ladies. May I help you?"

We both jumped. I whirled, expecting Owen, but the man was tall, with a craggy face and plaid flannel shirt.

"We were looking for the kitchen," I said hastily. He tilted his head, and I added, "Ralph said that we should go and have some cocoa and cookies." I assumed he knew who we were. Claire had said they didn't get a lot of visitors.

His face broke into a delighted smile. "That's just where I was going. May I accompany you?" His courtly manner was at odds with his rustic appearance; I half-expected him to offer me his arm. Instead, he led us toward one of the hallways—not the one I'd have guessed—and we set off at a brisk pace.

"What's your name?" I asked.

"I'm Julian." Despite his advanced age, he wasn't out of breath.

"Do you mind if I ask what you do here?" I inquired.

"Oh, a little bit of everything. I'm sort of a jack of all trades. I grew up here. Helped build this building, in fact." He sounded proud, and appropriately so.

"It's an incredible complex," I said. "Who designed it?"

"A fellow named Elisha. A man of vision. Long, long time ago. It took many years for it to be completed this far."

"'This far'? It's not finished?"

"A place like this will never be finished. It has to change and grow with the need. Forty years ago, nobody would have thought of having an entire separate shop for electronics, but it became necessary, and so it was built. Survival means adapting."

"How long have you been here?" Holly asked as we turned down another corridor.

"All my life," Julian said. "It's quite a place, don't you agree?"

"It certainly is," I said.

He caught my tone. "But?"

"We were hoping to meet Santa. I've been told that can't happen." As casually as I could manage, I tossed out the question: "Any chance you can get us in to see him?"

He stopped. In the low light, his eyes were impossible to read. "Would it matter?"

"Yes," I said firmly.

"Why?" His tone was unexpectedly gentle.

"Because then I could go back and tell the judge that Ralph is telling the truth, that Santa Claus really does exist. That is—assuming he does." I felt Holly tensing.

"No. You couldn't." He began walking again.

"What do you mean?" I hustled to catch up. "Listen, I'm sorry. I didn't mean—"

He held up his hand to silence me. "We could arrange for an audience, and you could see Santa in full regalia, and you would still doubt. After all, how hard would it be to put a red suit and white beard on someone and tell him to go 'ho ho ho'? It happens all over the world every Christmas season. You'd see and you'd ask questions, and in the end, there's nothing Santa could say to prove himself to you. He could tell you what you received for Christmas when you were five years old, and still you'd doubt." I wanted to deny it, but no words came. "It's nothing to be ashamed of. It's human nature. For those who believe, there is no need to see. For those who don't believe, seeing, hearing, touching—none of it will ever be enough." He opened a door with a flourish. The flick of a switch flooded the kitchen with light so bright we squinched our eyes against it.

"You may not believe in Santa, but I dare you to doubt Ralph's word about the cocoa." Julian selected three red-and-white striped mugs from a cabinet and led us to a large urn. I held my mug under it as he opened the valve. Steam rose as thick cocoa poured out. He closed the valve, opening it again when Holly's mug was in place, and he repeated the performance one more time for himself. "Whipped cream or marshmallows?" he asked. We both opted for whipped cream. With a mischievous glint in his eye, he said, "Would you like something to perk that up a bit?"

"Meaning?" Holly asked.

He beckoned with one finger, and we followed him to the corner, where he opened a cabinet to display practically every kind of liquor I could imagine. I selected creme de menthe, Holly chose Chambord, and Julian poured a bit of chocolate liqueur into his own. "You can never have too much chocolate," he pronounced as if speaking *ex cathedra*. Then, he led us to the next room and opened a large stainless steel cabinet to reveal racks and racks of beautifully decorated cookies. "We should have an assortment," he said. He filled a plate with cookies of all shapes and colors, led us into the empty dining hall, and gestured for us to sit. He raised his mug, and we all clinked.

"To lovely visitors," he said.

"To the North Pole," said Holly. "Weird and wonderful place that it is."

"To Santa Claus," I said. "Whether he exists or not, he's got some pretty amazing people working for him." I sampled my cocoa and groaned in delight. "And some incredible cocoa."

Holly sipped, and her eyes grew round. "Oh, my God, that's better than sex."

"Holly!" I was mortified, but Julian burst out laughing.

"Sex does happen here, you know," he said. "How do you think we get new Clauses?"

Just then, a soft chime sounded. "Excuse me," Julian said, taking a phone from his belt. He studied the display for a moment, then tapped a response. "I'm afraid I must bid you ladies good night," he said. "It's been a delight. Do you remember how to get back?"

"I think so," I said.

"Two lefts and a right. Then, yours is the corridor to the right of the elevator. Good night." He made a slight bow and left us to our feast.

"Damn," I muttered. "I wish he'd stuck around. I'll bet he could have told us a lot."

"Imagine growing up here," Holly said. "He must know where all the skeletons are."

"It's the North Pole," I said. "Hardly a venue for skeletons." I munched a cookie thoughtfully. Maybe not skeletons, but certainly secrets. On the other hand, Julian was quite willing to leave us alone, so maybe there weren't as many secrets as it seemed.

Or maybe he was confident that they were so well-hidden that an outsider would never discover them.

Twenty

I was deposing an enormous reindeer when a faint, but insistent, ringing interrupted my question. I groped my way out of the dream and toward the sitting room, where I fumbled for the lamp and the phone simultaneously. "Hello?" I mumbled.

"Meg! Where the hell are you!"

"Michael?" I put the phone to my other ear. "What's going on? Is everybody okay?"

"Your client's back in jail. It's bad. You better get back here."

"Which client? How did you get this number?"

"Your Santa Claus guy. I'm using his cellphone. He said the number was programmed in. Where the hell are you?"

I plopped onto the desk chair, the last wisps of sleep-fog vanishing. "I'm . . . doing some investigation into his case. What happened?"

"He met with the kid. The mother had him arrested. Claims he assaulted the boy."

"*WHAT?*"

"What are you doing?" Holly muttered sleepily from the doorway.

I waved at her to shut up. "I'm gonna kill him," I said. "I'm going to get him out of jail, and I'm going to choke him with a string of jingle bells." I tried to contain myself, and failed: "*THERE WAS A NO-CONTACT ORDER!*"

Holly's eyes grew slightly wider. I mouthed, *What time is it?* She consulted the clock on the bedside table and held up four fingers. Four o'clock. Into the phone, I demanded, "What time is it there?"

"Just past ten," said Michael.

"Morning or night?"

"What? What the hell kind of partying have you been doing?"

"Forget it. Can you get him bonded out?"

"Are you kidding? He went after the kid. They've got him in PC." *Protected custody.* Where certain inmates are kept safe from the general population. Most of the segregated prisoners were unduly violent or former law enforcement—or child molesters.

I forced myself to breathe. "Tell me about this so-called assault. What are they claiming?"

"It's kind of fuzzy. Mom says she walked into her living room and there he was with the kid, and when the kid tried to get away, your guy grabbed him."

"He was at their *house*?" Forget the jingle bells. I'd choke him with my bare hands.

"That's where the police picked him up."

I clutched for a straw, any straw. "But she's not saying anything else happened, though, right? No sexual touching, nothing like that?"

"Not so far, but it wouldn't surprise me if she starts throwing accusations around."

"Okay. Tell Ralph I'm on my way." I hung up and met Holly's bleary stare. "He went to see the kid. They're claiming he assaulted him."

"No. He wouldn't." Absolute certainty. The kind no lawyer would ever own.

Whatever. Play time in Santa's workshop was over. I punched the "O" button. "Ivy, it's Meg Riley," I said when she answered. I wondered if she ever slept. "Something's come up at home. I have to leave right away. Who do I talk to?"

"I'll take care of it," she said.

All the jolliness I'd sensed during our brief stay vanished. A somber red-haired female elf brought our breakfast and a message that Ted was working on flight arrangements and we should be ready to go in an hour. Mitch came to collect our luggage, wearing the same tight expression as when he'd handed me the reins on our trip up.

Breakfast over, we trudged through the hallways in what I thought was the direction of the stables. So much for cajoling someone into showing us the command center, for getting answers to our questions.

So much for meeting Santa.

I stopped. "Where do you suppose Julian is?"

"The guy from last night? Why do you want him?"

"Because he knew things." Maybe now I could convince him to

take me to Santa. These Clauses were a loyal bunch. With news of this latest development, Ralph's uncle—or whoever he was—might cooperate to keep Ralph safe. I was certain of it.

Except that I had no idea how to find him. I pointed to a hallway. "Down here."

"I don't think that's how you get to the stables," Holly protested.

"I don't care. This is my last chance to find Santa." I unzipped my jacket as I stormed down the hall, throwing open doors and calling, "Santa? You in there?"

"Excuse me, can I help you?" A young male elf in overalls came out of the plastics shop.

"I'm the lawyer who represents Ralph Claus. I have to go back to Connecticut because he's done something incredibly stupid, and before I go, I need to see Santa."

The elf's eyes grew round. "Ma'am, I don't know what to say—"

"Tell me where I can find Santa," I snapped.

"Easy, Meg," said Holly. To the elf she said, "We don't have a lot of time, but it would really help Meg represent Ralph if she could talk to Santa for a few minutes."

It was clear from the elf's expression that he didn't know what she meant, but he knew enough not to be telling a couple of strangers where to find Santa Claus. "Wait here." He darted back into the shop. I saw him talking excitedly to a gray-haired elf and gesturing wildly. The older elf pursed his lips and shook his head.

"That's it." I stormed into the plastics shop. Feeling like Gulliver in Lilliput, I said, "Is this or is this not Santa's workshop?"

"It's part of it." The older elf seemed completely unflapped by my size or tone.

"Then where is Santa?" I demanded.

"Meg, settle down," said Holly, to no avail.

"I absolutely will not settle down!" Every elf in the place was staring at me. Defiantly, I stared back. "I've got a hundred bucks for anybody who'll take me to Santa right now."

"Miss—" began the older elf.

"Fine, let's go." I reached for my wallet, but he said, "Miss, nobody here can help you."

"Why not?"

"Because we don't know where Santa is." All around us, elves bobbed their heads in agreement.

I crossed my arms. "Really," I drawled. Holly shot me the same glare I'd seen her direct at Jack and Amy countless times.

A flicker of annoyance passed over the older elf's face. "This is an enormous complex. Santa could be anywhere. He might not even be here. He's been known to leave the premises when it's necessary."

"Who would know where he is?" As if I didn't already know.

To the overall-clad elf, the older one said, "Homer, have Owen come down here, please."

"So we can get the runaround again? No, thanks, Homer, don't bother. I already know what I'm going to hear."

Homer looked questioningly at the older elf, who nodded ever so slightly. Homer scampered off to the desk in the corner, lifted the handset on the phone, and pressed a button.

Less than a minute later, Owen came in. He looked every bit as impeccably groomed as when we'd first seen him. "Thank you, Nigel," he said. The older elf went back to his work as Owen shepherded us back to the hall. "The sleigh is ready."

"We want to see Santa." I said, fully aware that I sounded like a petulant child.

"I'm afraid that's not possible. Now, if you'll come with me—"

"Listen, I need to talk to Santa if I'm to represent Ralph properly."

"I'm aware of your position." I'd bet he was aware of a whole lot more, too. Like precisely where Santa was. No way the old guy left home without telling the Queen of the North Pole. Before I could ask for her, he continued, "Mrs. Claus is waiting for you at the stables."

"Fine," I muttered. Holly refrained from comment as we trotted after Owen.

When we got to the stables, we were greeted by Mrs. Claus and Ralph's brothers, as well as Claire, Isabella, Anya, and three children who were identified as Fred's daughter and Ted's sons. Everyone, from Mrs. Claus to little Ryan, thanked us for coming and for all we'd done for Ralph. I half-expected them to break into a well-rehearsed farewell song.

Holly and I climbed into the flight outfits and goggles we'd worn for the trip up. Mrs. Claus took my gloved hand. "I'm sorry you didn't get everything you desired out of this trip."

"You can still make it happen," I reminded her.

"No," she said with what almost seemed to be a touch of sadness. "I can't."

"I don't understand." An understatement if ever I'd uttered one.

"That's correct," she said. "But it's not your fault. In all candor, it won't make the slightest difference anyway. I have faith that you'll do an admirable job of representing Ralph."

There was something in her eyes that I couldn't quite identify. For a wild moment, it occurred to me to wonder whether there really was a Santa Claus—at least, a *Mr.* Santa Claus. Maybe I'd been seeing Santa all along and hadn't realized it.

Maybe the elegant woman with the silver hair was the real Santa.

It was a thought so revolutionary that in that moment, I was certain it was true. If I'd been alone with Holly, I'd have tested it on her.

Ted adjusted his goggles. "You ladies ready to go?"

"You're driving us?" Involuntarily, I looked over at Mitch.

The youngest Claus brother winked at me. "I have to stay here. Software glitch. If I don't get it fixed, a whole lot of little boys will be getting baby dolls for Christmas next year."

Ted helped us both into the sleigh and fastened us in. As he buckled himself in, Claire handed each of us a small thermos. "Yours is tea," she said to me.

"Thanks." It felt like the most generous gesture of the day.

"Ready?" said Ted. We confirmed that we were, and he slapped the reins. "Geeyap!" An instant later, we were out of the barn, ascending into the frigid darkness.

Twenty-One

As we headed south, the darkness gradually gave way to light. I assumed that it was simply getting later in the morning, but Ted explained that as we got closer to the equator, there would be more sunlight. "You know what they say about how the Scandinavian countries have those really long nights and days at different times of the year while people farther south have a more normal division? That's what you're seeing. Since the Pole is the most extreme point, we get twenty-four hours of dark in the winter and twenty-four hours of light in the summer."

"Must be hard to sleep," Holly commented.

"Is that why there aren't any windows?" I hadn't thought about it before.

"Partly," he said. "Mostly, it's easier to heat the buildings when you've got solid walls. Windows would be pretty pointless."

I resisted the urge to tell him that a lot of things were pretty pointless. This entire trip, for instance. We'd all have been better off if I'd stayed home and kept tabs on my idiot client. When I told my partners where I'd been—because eventually it was going to come out—there was going to be so much hell to pay that Hell would have to open a branch office in Hartford.

It probably sounds ridiculous to suggest that I didn't pay a whole lot of attention to the trip home, but it's true. You'd have thought I was used to traveling by sleigh. I dozed on and off, but mainly, I fretted and fumed about Ralph. Or more specifically, about how I'd let Ralph con me. How many times had I seen a lawyer's judgment get clouded by his emotions? My friend Frank was a prime example:

I couldn't count the number of times he'd confessed over a beer that another client hadn't paid him despite promise after promise. Or a potential client would suck him in with the saddest of all sad stories about her horrific accident, but two weeks after Frank filed the lawsuit, opposing counsel would send him pleadings from six different jurisdictions where the client had sued other people for the exact same injuries. Whenever I told Michael a Frank story, he rolled his eyes and said, "Doesn't this guy ever learn?"

I was so engrossed in my thoughts that I barely noticed we were descending until Ted said, "Hang on." He punched some buttons on the keypad on the dash and said, "Preparing for descent." To me, he said, "Since it's daytime, I can't drop you where we picked you up. I'm going to take you to another spot we use and you can call somebody from there."

"What kind of a spot?" Holly piped up, her voice thick with sleep.

"Secluded," said Ted.

"The kind of place where people dump bodies?" She was wide awake now, probably with visions of *CSI* running through her brain.

Ted looked startled. "Nothing like that. Just a place where we won't have people gawking." He steered expertly as we descended into the cold white silence of a cloud. Then, we broke through the underside and glided to a stop in a field occupied by half a dozen horses.

"What day is it?" I climbed out of the sleigh and began to shed my flight suit.

Ted helped Holly out of the back. "Hang on, I'll find out." He retrieved his phone from his pocket and punched in a number. "Yeah, me. . . . Fine. Listen, what day is it down here? Thanks." He ended the call and said, "New Year's Day. You can watch football."

"Oh, jeez." Ed was probably having fits. If he'd tried to call to wish me a happy new year and gone to voicemail, he'd be frantic, sure that I'd been murdered, or—even worse—gone off with another guy. He felt free to leave whenever he chose, but if I wasn't available when he beckoned, it was a major catastrophe. Standing in a horse pasture, my feet freezing in the snow, it occurred to me that maybe he wasn't in love with me. Maybe he was just an ass.

"Tell him since he wasn't around, you and I took off," Holly said as she tossed her goggles into the back. When you've been friends this long, it doesn't take much to figure out what the other is thinking.

I was fumbling in my bag for my own phone. "Damn," I muttered. I couldn't have left it behind. That would be the cherry on the aggravation sundae. "Oh, who cares!" I flung the bag on the ground. The horses regarded us with the mildest of interest. "How do we get out of here? Where are we, anyway?"

"Marlborough," said Ted. Close to Hartford, but its woods and hills made it feel a million miles away from the city streets. "Is there somebody you want to call for a lift home?"

"Uber," I said. At the same time, Holly said, "I'll call my son. Tell me where to tell him to come." Ted gave her directions, and she repeated them into her phone. "Hurry up," she added. "I'm standing in a horse field, and it's cold. . . . Just get here, will you?" She punched a button to end the call. "Kids. What does it matter why I'm standing in a horse field?"

Ted handed us our bags. "See you later." He climbed back in the sleigh, and with a loud *whoosh*, it was gone.

"'See you later'?" Holly said. "As in, 'you'll be coming back to the North Pole'?"

"I'm sure he didn't mean anything," I said even though I'd had the same thought. The horses ignored us as we untied the lead ropes holding the gate closed and slipped out. We tied the ropes securely even though the horses didn't seem the least bit interested in leaving their enclosure. Then, there was nothing to do but lean against the gate and wait for Jack.

By the time his pickup came down the rutted dirt road, my feet felt half-frozen. He tossed our bags in the back, and the three of us crammed into the cab. We drove around a hill and past a pond, more paddocks, and a stand of evergreens. Ted had chosen well; we never saw a building until we were back on the main road.

Part of me wanted to call Michael and let him know I was back. Another part couldn't bear to face him. As Jack maneuvered the ruts and curves of the frozen dirt, I recalled the time I lied to my parents about going to a dance when my boyfriend's parents were away. It would have been perfect except that after several bouts of energetic adolescent sex, we fell asleep. The ringing phone at three o'clock in the morning was as sudden and terrifying as a gunshot. My heart pounded as I yelled, "Get it! Get it!" Steve groped for the receiver and managed a groggy "Hello?" When he mumbled, "Yes, sir," I knew we were done for. We stumbled through the house searching for the clothes we'd flung off in a frenzy of desire. As I pulled my sweater over my head, irate pounding on the front door announced my father's arrival.

I stood just behind Steve as he opened the door. For a second, I thought my father was going to punch him. Instead, he shoved past Steve and yanked my arm to pull me out the door, shouting, "If you ever come near my little girl again, I'll have you arrested!"

"Yes, sir," said Steve, his voice barely audible. Without a word to me, he closed the door. For an eternity, my father and I faced each other on the Whitmans' front steps. Early frost glistened on the metal railing. The only sound was the distant hum of highway traffic. With the bluish halogen light casting an eerie glow on his face, my father's mouth pursed as if he were about to spit on me.

"You lied," was all he said. He dropped my arm and turned his back, leaving me to follow or not. Hot tears blurred my vision. I ran down the steps before he could leave without me. All the way home, I tried to find the words to apologize, but there was no explanation, no excuse. I'd betrayed his trust. The honor student, debate club president, junior class secretary, cross-country team member—none of it mattered now. I was a deceitful slut. He didn't say it, but I knew.

When we arrived home, he got out of the car and walked to the house as if he were alone. As he jammed the key into the lock, I managed, "I'm sorry, Daddy. I'm so sorry."

He didn't even look at me. All he said was, "Do not lie to me again. Ever."

"I won't. I promise, Daddy. I won't. I'm so sorry, Daddy. I'm so sorry. . . ." My voice broke. I wanted him to turn around, to tell me I was forgiven, but he walked heavily through the kitchen and up the stairs without even bothering to shut the door behind us. I closed it— good girl, taking care of details. Then I sank to the floor, sobbing. The next morning, my mother yelled at me for a solid hour. I barely heard her words, because my father's silence was overpowering.

"We're here," said Jack. I hadn't even noticed him pulling into my driveway. Holly was sound asleep.

"Thanks," I said. "Tell your mom to call me when she wakes up, and wish Jill a happy new year for me."

His face lit up at the mention of his beloved's name. "Will do."

I stumbled into the house, nearly tripping over Harry and David. Traces of wet food in cat dishes showed that Rodrigo had already been in to feed them. They followed me upstairs, where I upended my bag onto the bed. The cats bounded up onto the quilt to sniff everything. Suddenly, David hissed. He began to paw at the small pile of clothes and toiletries. "What are you doing?" I asked, rescuing a sweater before he could dig at it.

Then I saw it. Beneath the sweater was a bulky package wrapped in golden tissue. A simple tag, white with a red border, read, "To Meg, From Santa."

"What the—" I picked it up, felt its lightness, and I knew.

Sure enough, when I tore away the paper, there was Cleo.

Book Three

The Trial

Twenty-Two

Harry and David galloped past me as I trudged down to the kitchen. I half-expected to see Cleo racing with them. After the last two days, it wouldn't have surprised me.

Rodrigo always left the mail and newspapers on the kitchen table. Resisting the gentle tug of an herbal blend that would allow me to drift off to sleep, I dumped a large scoop of bracing Irish breakfast tea into the teapot's mesh filter and filled the pot with boiling water. While the tea steeped, I unfolded this morning's paper to find the front page proclaiming, "SANTA CLAUS BREAKS INTO WEST HARTFORD HOME."

My gut clenched, but nobody would have seen me flinch. *Step back. Breathe. Nothing to see here, folks. Just another client, another case. Same stuff, different day.* Very deliberately, I set the filter on a saucer, poured the tea, and sprinkled fake sweetener into the mug. With all the dignity of a dowager countess, I took a sip of the scalding brew, scorching my tongue. "Shit!" I shouted; the cats darted out of the room.

Damn it all, why couldn't he have been a regular garden-variety nutcase? Nobody would have paid any attention, and I could have pled the case out in three days with no more than a quick paragraph in the "Police Action" column. Instead, this would play out in the spotlight, and it would be ugly. Nothing like a whiff of publicity to get lawyers acting like drama queens, waving the Constitution and pontificating about justice on the eleven o'clock news.

I settled on the sofa with my tea and newspaper as if I were a casual reader. The author appeared to have found the basic information, including "no determinable address," in the original arrest documents. For the rest, he relied on Victoria Leopold, who claimed she walked into the den in her own house and found Ralph with his arms around her son.

There it was, in black and white. He *touched* the kid. Laid hands on him. Engaged in physical contact. Bad enough he was in the kid's house, but why the hell couldn't he have been across the room? Instead, he *touched* him.

God Almighty, how stupid was he? It could have been the most innocent of hugs, but it didn't take a genius to see where this was leading. Any minute, somebody would claim Ralph had been getting his rocks off by rubbing up against the boy, and the original story would get lost in a firestorm of innuendo and speculation. It was the worst kind of case: a child, a beloved public figure, and claims of sexual misconduct. Santa the Pervert.

It took two more read-throughs before I spotted the hole in the story: the author never mentioned how Ralph got into the house. Victoria Leopold said she "found" him in the den, implying that she hadn't known he was there. So how did he gain access? Did he pick a lock? Break a window?

Climb down the chimney?

The article quoted her as saying that Ralph told Trevor he was Santa Claus, which made him sound like one of those sick bastards who seduces kids with promises of video games and Disney World. But that didn't make sense either. When could Ralph have said it? Not during his first visit, because he hadn't had time to tell anybody anything—the kid screamed, the mother called the police, and Ralph was hustled out of there. And now he was showing up at the Leopold house to proclaim his Santahood to Trevor even though the whole Santa mystique depended on secrecy? It wasn't adding up.

I reviewed the article once more, making notes. An online search revealed that the wire services had the identical story, and a couple newsfeeds had thirty-second videos. I wished I could believe this was all the coverage we'd have to endure, but it was New Year's. Today, most people focused on resolutions and football. By tomorrow, a story about Santa molesting a kid, complete with the picture of Ralph being led from the Leopold home in handcuffs, would spread like an ugly rash.

Even the Irish breakfast wasn't enough to combat the fatigue that suddenly smothered me. I moved the laptop to the coffee table and pulled the blue-striped fleece throw over myself. David snuggled next to me, and Harry made himself a nest between my leg and the sofa. I slid into a deep sleep where I was chased by elves, lawyers, and a little boy with a left-handed catcher's mitt.

When the phone rang, I thought it was part of the dream. The mechanical male voice of the talking caller ID intoned, "Call from Ruggiero Michael. Call from Ruggiero Michael." I fumbled for the handset on the coffee table. "Hello?"

"Riley! You're back!"

"This is a recording. Meg is on an island in the South Pacific."

"Where the hell have you been?" asked Michael, ignoring my drowsy attempt at levity.

"—It's hard to explain."

"Harder than why Santa Claus went back to the scene of the crime and manhandled the kid?"

He sounded so casual. Just another client, another case. For him, maybe. "It's complicated."

"I had a very enlightening talk with your client. You and I need to discuss some things."

"Like?"

"Like whether to try an insanity defense. Does this guy really think he's Santa?"

"He thinks his father is Santa. He's the heir apparent who's training for the job."

Michael snorted. "Yeah, that's the distinction that's going to win this thing."

"Antonio hasn't asked for a psych evaluation yet, but I'm expecting it." I stretched, and David poked his head out from under the throw. "What else did he say?" I squinted at the clock across the room. Nine-eighteen. Kind of late for a casual status update call. My heart started to pound.

"Mainly that," he said. "We didn't have much time. But I'd be careful if I were you. He also seems to think you two are involved."

My breath caught. "What do you mean?"

"He said you were at his home to do some investigation and 'meet his family.'" Heavy emphasis on the last phrase. "The way he says it, there's a ring in your future."

"He *said* that?"

"Not in so many words, but if he were free right now, who knows?

When he talks about you, he looks like a lovesick puppy. Lucky thing Eckert wasn't there. You'd have been out on the street right next to Rick."

A jolt like lightning shot through me. I hadn't thought about our former partner in years. I forced myself to sound matter-of-fact. "What's Rick up to these days, anyway?"

"Besides banging his clients' ex-wives? No idea. Last I heard, he was trying to get an adjunct position at the law school."

"Teaching what? Ethics?" My hypocrisy was screaming inside my head. Barely a year after we formed the firm, one of Rick's divorce clients barged into the office and accused Rick of screwing around with the client's not-yet-ex-wife. Eckert didn't wait for the grievance committee's conclusions: he convened a partnership meeting and confronted Rick. Rick hung his head and confessed all—including sex with three of his own clients—but his quivering chin and tear-filled eyes won him no sympathy. I had no qualms about voting him out. As Eckert said, a lawyer who was willing to compromise his professional ethics for his own self-interest was a disaster waiting to happen, and he damned well wasn't going to happen to our firm. *I haven't slept with Ralph*, my feeble conscience argued, but the memory of those kisses burned as hot as my sudden shame.

"Who knows?" I could almost hear Michael shrugging Rick off. Michael had no use for stupidity, especially in lawyers; he always said that if someone wanted to be an idiot, they'd have to pay him to listen. "Anyway, be careful with this Claus guy. He's liable to end up stalking you."

"He'd have to get out first." Even to my own ears, I sounded breathless. "Since he went back to the scene and laid hands on the kid, I'd say that's a long shot."

"Still. . . ."

"Don't worry. I know what I'm doing. I've had crazies before. Mylar dude." *Confident. Not overly concerned. This is just another wacky client.* But my disloyalty—to Ralph? To Michael?—caught in my throat like rancid peanut butter.

Oblivious to my moral dilemma, Michael came in with the zinger: "Mylar dude wasn't in love with you."

"Ralph says he's in love with me?" My voice went up half an octave. Another snort. "He didn't have to."

I swallowed hard. *Control.* "Listen, I need to see him. Any chance

Drew can get me in for an attorney visit?" Ruby's nephew Drew was a corrections officer.

"On a holiday weekend? With a client in PC?"

"What's the problem? Doesn't he like Auntie Ruby anymore? What did you guys do—get him a lousy present?" I was breathing better now. "Tell him to do it for Uncle Mikey's partner. I'll owe him."

"You'll owe *me*," he warned, but I knew it was as good as done.

"Always." Shaking my head, I hung up. My possibly insane, possibly sociopathic, possibly just perverted client was in love with me. Not only had I not discouraged Ralph's feelings, but I'd reciprocated. On top of that, I'd lied to Michael—or at least, I hadn't corrected his misconceptions.

David yawned, pink tongue curling, and snuggled up against me. He didn't care if I was stupid or deceitful. Being a cat was so simple. "Hey, Mr. Copperfield," I said, stroking him. "Work a little magic here, will you?"

Because the way my life was going, I needed all the magic I could get.

Twenty-Three

The magic kicked in the next morning. Before I'd finished my bagel, the phone rang. "I did what I could," Michael said in lieu of *hello*. "No pro visits until Monday."

"What if I visited like a normal person?" Not ideal, but we could keep our voices down. Regular visitors to the prison met with nonviolent inmates in a large room with two very long tables, well separated, with rows of chairs on either side. At these visits, known as "contact visits," the inmates and the visitors sat across from each other without any kind of barrier between them, and they were permitted a very brief hug and kiss upon greeting and leaving. "Non-contact visits" involved the kind of separation everybody saw on television, where visitors sat on one side of the bulletproof glass while the inmate sat on the other, and they conversed through a telephone.

Pro visits—visits by attorneys, evaluators, or other professionals—took place in tiny private visiting rooms. A CO—corrections officer—escorted the inmate to the room and stood immediately outside the door throughout the meeting. You could hear COs talking in the hallway, so I knew they could hear us, but the supervisor swore they never listened. *Sure, right.*

"Let me finish. Drew says since your guy's protected, the shift commander can put you in a pro visit room as long as nobody else needs it." Pro visits had to be scheduled in advance, because the prison had only three pro visit rooms and over a hundred inmates.

"Tell Drew thanks a million."

"No problem. I had to promise you'd register first thing Monday, so don't forget."

"I won't." I scribbled a note on the back of an envelope. When the COs did you a favor, you had to hold up your end. True for inmates, and just as true for the lawyers.

Half an hour later, I was on my way to Foster Correctional Institute in Granby, near the Massachusetts border. The southbound traffic on I-91 was heavy with holiday travelers returning home from the airport. Only a few of us were heading north.

Not that Granby was particularly "north." Not after where I'd been.

As I drove, I considered the past few days. There was no question that we'd been somewhere extraordinary, but there could be any number of explanations. It might have been the world's most elaborate theme park, or some billionaire's secret fantasy land, or a little-known sovereign nation. Maybe it was nothing more than a corporate entity that wanted to become the Amazon of toys. Or some sort of international toy co-operative located in an obscure part of the world to avoid taxes and tariffs. By the time I signaled for the exit ramp, I was congratulating myself for my deductive reasoning.

But what about the reindeer?

I traveled along a winding two-lane road for what felt like ten miles through an enchanted forest. One more curve, and the enchantment came to an abrupt end. The land around the enormous concrete prison facility bore winter-brown grass topped with patches of weary snow, flat and treeless for at least half a mile in every direction from the building. Chain link fencing twenty feet high declared the perimeter of the property. Atop the fencing perched three rows of sinister-looking coiled razor wire, one on top of the other, each two feet high and topped with barbed wire. What wasn't obvious was that the fencing was also electrified. This was the high-bond facility, for inmates whose bond was set at such a large sum that only the wealthiest could pay the price for pretrial freedom. These men had done serious harm to someone.

Official white-on-blue signs identified the visitor parking lot. I removed my attorney ID card from my wallet and tucked it into my pocket. Briefcase in hand, purse and phone locked in the trunk. A healthy walk in the crisp winter air to the break in the fence where the guard booth loomed.

Visiting prisons was my least-favorite part of criminal work. Too many movies where an innocent outsider arrived at the wrong moment and a riot erupted so that the facility went into lockdown, and the outsider was trapped in the chaos with no way out. Except I wasn't an outsider. I was a lawyer, a part of the system. Prosecutors worked to put men behind these massive walls, and I worked to get them out. Sometimes I won, sometimes the state did, and nobody knew from one case to the next what justice would look like.

When I opened the door to the guard booth, a huff of hot air toasted my cheeks. Bulletproof plexiglass, tinted black, its metal frames bolted to counter and ceiling, separated the invisible guard from the rest of the room. In the corner, the unblinking eye of the camera captured my image for the COs watching security monitors. "Name?" a voice said through the round metal vent instead of "hello."

"Megan Riley. Attorney." I slid my identification card into the tray under the window.

"No pro visits scheduled today." The card lay in the tray, untouched.

"One of the COs set it up with the shift commander. My client came in over the holiday. He's in PC."

"Name?" Not mine this time.

"Claus. Ralph Claus. I don't know his number." All inmates were assigned an individual identification number, the DOC equivalent of a social security number. The inmate ID number appeared on everything related to the inmate, from commissary order slips to pleadings filed by self-represented prisoners.

Well-manicured fingertips slid my card out of the tray and out of my sight. He wasn't speaking into the microphone, but I could still hear him. "Got a lawyer for a pro visit. . . . Claus. . . . She doesn't know. . . . Hang on." His voice returned to the microphone. "Who set it up?"

"Drew Ferraro. My partner talked to him earlier today. Michael Ruggiero. Lundstrom Law Firm."

The CO relayed the information. I waited for what seemed like an unduly long time. Finally, the CO grunted, "Okay. Sign in." He would keep my ID until I left. On an electronic pad on my side of the glass, I wrote my name, phone number, time in, and Ralph's name. Under the heading for his number, I wrote "unknown." It must have sufficed, because the CO said, "Through that door." The door to the right of the counter buzzed—not the one on the left, which led to the parking lot, to freedom, but the one that led to the prison. I thanked him and pushed the heavy door open, stepping back out into the cold. The door closed behind me with a solid, ominous clank.

I was outside again, but at the same time, I was inside—inside the prison grounds, within the gates. With every shred of bravado I could muster, I strode up the sidewalk to the building, head high and shoulders back, just as though cameras weren't tracking my every move. One locked door at my back, another ahead of me. Fencing and razor wire as far as the eye could see. A hulking concrete behemoth of a building before me where men were herded and corralled like so many cattle. Even outdoors, with a cold breeze blowing my hair and rolling clouds in varying shades of gray overhead, I felt trapped.

As I reached the next door, a buzzer announced that it was being unlocked to admit me. I entered a tiny overheated room. In the far corner—"far" being arm's length from the doorway—a grim older CO sat behind a larger counter and more bulletproof plexiglass. This window was untinted, but numerous scratches told stories of displeased visitors. "Name?" he asked as if someone else could have slipped in before I traveled the fifty feet from the guard shack.

"Megan Riley. Attorney."

"Through there." He gestured to the door opposite the one through which I'd entered. I crossed the room, my rubber-soled boots squeaking on the worn linoleum. A loud buzzer announced the release of the latch on the second door. I stepped through, and again, the door swung shut behind me, locking me into a miniscule foyer. Moments later, another buzzer signaled the release of the third door. I pushed through to a hallway dominated by metal detectors for people and bags. The pockmarked CO who stood behind the metal detector instructed me to put my coat and briefcase on the conveyor belt. He pressed a button, and my belongings vanished into the scanner. Next to the machine stood a tall gray metal detector that could have been Frankenstein's doorway. When the lights around its perimeter turned green, CO #4 grunted, "Step through, please." I walked slowly; moving quickly could set off the alarm. On the other side, I retrieved my coat and briefcase.

"Lockers over there," he said, gesturing to a small room behind the scanners.

"I'm an attorney. I'd like to take my briefcase in if that's all right." Courtesy to the COs was about more than human decency or good manners. I didn't want any of the COs taking a dislike to Ralph because he had an obnoxious lawyer. When CO #4 consented, I tucked my coat into an empty locker and pocketed the key.

I followed the CO to Pro Visit Room #3. Next to the doorway, a large one-way window afforded anyone in the hall a clear view of the room's occupants. The walls were pale institutional green. A small table was bolted to the linoleum floor. On each side, two molded plastic seats were attached to a metal pole anchored to the concrete block wall. Harsh light illuminated every corner of the room, but no switch graced the wall; someone outside controlled light and dark. I slid into a seat and drew my pad and pen out of my briefcase. And waited.

When the CO escorted Ralph into the room, I caught my breath. He looked like hell. It wasn't just that he was unshaven; another time, the stubble might have been sexy. But he looked . . . beaten down. After only two days in PC, that was bad.

The CO maneuvered Ralph into the other plastic chair. This furniture wasn't designed for someone as tall as he. "I'll be outside," the CO said, closing the door behind him.

"Keep your voice down," I said in a low tone as the jingle of keys evidenced another CO passing.

"Okay." His voice was glum. He wasn't agreeing to please me.

I wanted to reach over and take his hand, but I couldn't risk it. Instead, I asked, "Are you okay?" He nodded. "All right, then. What happened?"

"Trevor wrote to me," Ralph said. "He was upset. His friends were giving him a hard time about having Santa arrested. We agreed to meet at that park with the rose bushes."

"Elizabeth Park." The Hartford park was famous for its rose bushes. "So you arranged to meet the kid in Elizabeth Park. Just the two of you?"

"His name is Trevor," said Ralph with the slightest bit of heat in his voice. "It wasn't just us. His nanny was there. A blond girl. Brittany. I met them by that restaurant next to the pond."

I jotted a note: *depose Brittany.* "The paper said you were arrested at the Leopolds' house. How did you get there?"

Ralph sighed. "That's the part where maybe I wasn't so smart."

That's the part? "Let's back up. You said he wrote to you. How? Regular mail?" As far as I knew, nobody outside the firm knew he was at Carla and Sergio's.

"Email," Ralph said. "I told you before, there's a whole slew of fake Santa websites. We keep an eye on them, just to make sure there's no funny business going on in Santa's name. Some of them have email addresses or links so that kids can supposedly email Santa."

"How many Santa websites do you have?"

"Just one. TheSantaClaus.xyz. You should check it out."

Try and stop me. "Is that where Trevor emailed you?"

"I'm not sure," he said. "Mitch could tell you."

"Can he retrieve the emails sent to these other sites?" He nodded. "Even though they're not actually yours." Another nod. I shouldn't have asked, but I did: "Is there any chance you're going to tell me you have permission to do this?"

"Ask Mitch," Ralph said.

I scribbled another note. "Go on."

"After I got arrested, Mitch was keeping an eye out for anything from Connecticut. The other day, he saw an email from Trevor L. in West Hartford, so he forwarded it to me."

"When was this?"

"Wednesday, I think." He wasn't meeting my eyes. He didn't think. He knew.

"So by the time Mitch showed up to take Holly and me to the Pole, both of you knew about this. Is that why you arranged for me to go away?" Talk about a fool. I couldn't believe I'd fallen for that load of crap.

"No," he said. My skepticism must have been obvious, because he said again, "No. You really needed to go. The timing—well, it just worked out that way because of the holiday."

"Quite a little coincidence, wouldn't you say?" Ralph looked away, toward the door: *Gosh darn, you ever seen a handle like that?* "Damn it, Ralph! How am I supposed to protect you if you don't tell me what's going on?"

"I'm sorry." He didn't sound sorry. "But Trevor was upset, and you'd never have let me go near him."

"You think?" *Rein it in.* "Couldn't somebody just email back that everything was okay?"

"You don't handle children with emails. You talk to them." His words didn't say *everybody knows that,* but his tone did.

Fine. I was no expert in childrearing, but I knew the law. "I need that email."

"Somebody's supposed to send it to you. They might have already."

Now they got efficient. "What happened next? Where did you pick up the email? On your phone, or did you use a computer?"

"I read it on the phone, but I wanted to print it, so I went to that library across from the capitol building. You know it?"

I knew it. The library was in the same building as the state supreme court. The way this case was going, one of these days I'd be standing there in front of seven justices, arguing for a reversal of the conviction in *State of Connecticut v. Claus.*

Voices outside the door. The COs were switching off. Probably shift change. My allotted visiting time was trickling away. "Why did you print the email?"

"His phone number was in it." His words were rushed. He knew what was coming.

"Did you call him?" He looked away. I repeated the question: "Did. You. Call. Him."

"I tried," he admitted with appropriate sheepishness. "But nobody answered, and I didn't leave a message." Which was the first intelligent thing he'd said since he sat down.

"Where did you call from? Your cell?"

"Oh, I wouldn't do that. That's only for secure calls. I used the pay phone in their basement." Courthouses and libraries were among the few holdouts that still had pay phones.

"What did you do when you couldn't reach Trevor by phone?"

"I emailed him back. That's when I told him I could meet him at the park if he wanted."

"So meeting was your idea." *Just when you thought a client couldn't get any dumber. . . .* "How did you sign the email?"

"What?"

I knew he'd heard me. "Did you sign it 'Santa'?"

"Uh-huh." He was balancing on the knife-edge between chastened and brazen.

"Even though you're not Santa?" I tried to keep my voice even.

"As far as the kids are concerned, we're all Santa. I told you. They don't distinguish between Santa and his sons or his helpers. If Mitch was answering, he'd be Santa." I might not be an experienced parent, but I was willing to bet a six-year-old was capable of understanding the difference—and of getting pissed off if somebody who wasn't Santa showed up. Unless I was way off the mark, six was right around the time most of them stopped believing.

Any thoughts I might have entertained about Ralph testifying vanished like a snowball in an inferno. Not only had he participated in intercepting a little kid's email—which was likely a violation of federal law as well as state law—but he'd arranged to meet the kid by posing as a beloved mythical figure. It didn't matter what magical experiences I'd had over the weekend. This was my reality: a grim room in a prison with a one-way window and a client who told a small child he was Santa Claus.

I pulled my attention back to the immediate issue. "When you got to the park, was Trevor there?"

"Him and Brittany. It was cold, so I suggested we go to that restaurant over by the pond."

"Lizzie's." At least four restaurants had occupied that location in the past ten years. I only remembered this one because Elsa handled the latest purchase and Roy did the closing.

"We went in and got hot chocolate. It was pretty quiet at that time of day. At one point, Brittany got a text, and she went outside to call the person back."

"How old was this girl?"

"Eighteen, nineteen. Definitely not more than twenty."

Young enough to text instead of talk. "How long was she gone?"

"A few minutes. Not long." What kind of nanny left a child alone with a stranger? Especially one who'd been arrested for being in the child's home. I made another note: *background check on B.*

"Who was she talking to?"

"She said it was Trevor's mom. I guess they were supposed to be home by then."

"Did Mrs. Leopold know that they were meeting you?" I couldn't imagine her consenting to such a thing. "Let's back up. Tell me what you all said. From the moment you arrived."

"Like I said, when they got there, I suggested going inside for hot chocolate. After the waitress took our order—Trevor got a cookie, too—I asked him how his Christmas was. He said it was okay, but his mom wouldn't let him keep the mitt and that was what he really wanted. His mom got him a remote-control sailboat. I tried to talk up what a great present that was, but he wasn't buying it. Said none of his friends had them, so he wouldn't have anybody to play with."

"Is there a Mr. Leopold?" Ordinarily, I'd have run a background check on Victoria Leopold by now. With the holidays and the other distractions, I was behind on my due diligence.

"Doctor, and they're separated," said Ralph. "He lives with a 'friend.'" The quotation marks were practically audible. "Trevor's not taking it well. That's one of the reasons it was so important for me to see him. He needs to know not all grown-ups are going to bail on him."

I steeled myself against his empathy. "Why did Trevor want to see you? Did he want another catcher's mitt?"

For a second, I thought I saw a trace of pity in his eyes. "Nothing like that. He said his mom shouldn't have had Santa Claus arrested because it wasn't going to make his dad come home. Obviously, that's something he'd overheard. I didn't ask who said it."

The CO knocked twice, then opened the door. "Ten minutes."

"Thank you." I waited until the door was closed. In a lower voice, I asked, "How did you introduce yourself to them? Did you walk up and say, 'Hi, I'm Santa'?"

"I told them my name."

"Ralph or Santa?"

"I said my name was Ralph."

"Wait—these people expected to see Santa Claus. They weren't at all concerned about seeing somebody who wasn't round and jolly with a white beard?"

"I can be jolly," Ralph said with the first hint of a smile I'd seen all morning.

"But why were they talking to you? Why weren't they waiting for standard-issue Santa?"

"Dunno. Don't forget—Trevor saw me that night, so he already knew I didn't look like the storybooks." And then he emailed Santa, and the same guy showed up. Of course he'd think Ralph was Santa. I didn't know if this helped or hurt, so I made another note and moved on.

"Okay. You went inside, got your hot chocolate, talked about his presents. Then what?"

"He said his mom shouldn't have had me arrested, and he asked why I hadn't gone back to the North Pole. I said I had to stay around for a little while to get everything cleared up about what had happened at his house that night, but I'd be heading for the Pole real soon. He asked if he could come visit, and I said we had a top-secret organization and he'd need special clearance. He thought that sounded really cool."

"What did Brittany have to say about all this?"

"She seemed pretty bored. I tried to bring her into the conversation. I asked how long she'd been working for the Leopolds, but she just said she'd known them for ages and told Trevor to hurry up and finish his snack. That's when she got the text. While she was gone, Trevor talked about his Christmas break. His dad and his 'friend' decided to go skiing, and his mom didn't like that. Trevor said she cried a lot and he felt bad, but he really likes skiing and he wanted to go. Trevor's dad picked him up on Christmas and they went to Vermont. When Trevor got back, they sent the email." He shook his head. "What a mess. Anyway, that was when Brittany came back and said they needed to go now. I paid for everything and we got our coats and went outside. I walked them to their car, and Trevor asked where mine was. I told him I took the bus. Brittany offered me a ride, which surprised me. I said I didn't think it was a good idea—"

"—which it wasn't—"

"—but she insisted, and then Trevor asked me *pleeeeeease*, so I said okay. Poor kid." Ralph was in protected custody in a state prison and Trevor Leopold was just back from a ski trip with his father, but it was Ralph who felt sorry for Trevor. "I gave her directions to Carla and Sergio's place, but she said she needed to stop back at Trevor's house for a minute and then she'd take me home. I said I'd rather go straight to my place and asked her to let me out, but she kept driving. When we got to their house, she insisted that I come inside. I told her I needed to get home, and she said it would only be a minute and she needed to use the bathroom. Trevor grabbed my hand and pretty much dragged me inside. The whole thing was feeling really strange. I told Trevor I was going to go, but he started crying and said he didn't want me to leave. I knelt down and hugged him, and that's when his mom came in and started screaming."

The CO knocked again. "Time's up."

"Okay, thanks," I said. To Ralph, I added, "Take care of yourself. I'll be in touch." He rose so the CO could escort him back to his cell or wherever inmates in PC awaited their next contact with the outside world.

Twenty-Four

I emerged from the prison to a slick gray world. Freezing rain pelted me all the way to my ice-glazed car. Once inside, I blasted the heater, writing down every detail I could recall.

Driving in icy weather demands absolute concentration, but Ralph's strange story kept intruding as I tried to focus on the treacherous roads. Assuming his account was accurate—and I had no reason as yet to doubt it—something was definitely off. A six-year-old might know how to use email, but it seemed like a stretch to think he could craft a readable message. And why would he include his phone number? Maybe the mother wrote it. But why would Victoria Leopold facilitate her son's contact with the man who broke into her house? The nanny, then. Maybe Trevor asked her to help because he was worried about Ralph.

Except what six-year-old kid worries about a grown man? Even Santa Claus?

The whole setup smelled funny.

Oncoming headlights glared, reflecting off the slippery pavement. More than two hours after I left Granby, I finally pulled into my garage. Few units in the complex had attached garages, and I paid a premium to get one, but on nights like this, it was worth every penny.

By the time I'd hung up my coat, fed the cats, and flopped on the sofa, I was done for. I located the remote under a magazine and scrolled through the channels, searching for a brainless distraction.

This time last week, I'd never even heard of Ralph Claus, Trevor Leopold, or a host of others who had suddenly become major players in my life. I had a nice, sane practice, and if I didn't precisely adore all my partners, at least they respected me—a state of affairs that was likely to melt away like ice pellets on my windshield if they ever heard about my weekend. A few days ago, I'd never even thought about behaving inappropriately with a client. I'd been mostly content in my relationship with—

The doorbell interrupted my thoughts. Odd, especially on a night like this. Maybe Rodrigo needed sherry for his famous seafood chowder. Harry snored in the recliner, but David the Watch Cat leaped down from the sofa, growling, tail swishing, ears perked up. I followed him to the front hall and called, "Who is it?"

"Meg! It's me!"

Ed sounded irked, as if he'd expected me to fling open the door and welcome him with open arms. Not an unreasonable expectation. A week ago, I'd have done precisely that.

I mustered a smile and opened the door. David surveyed him briefly before vanishing. "I didn't expect to see you tonight," I said. A weak welcome, but honest. Seeing him hadn't even crossed my mind. He wasn't due back until tomorrow. I reached out to hug him, but he was coming in for a kiss that missed my lips and landed sloppily at the corner of my mouth. I tried to realign for a proper kiss, but he was already drawing back.

I helped him off with his soggy jacket and hung it on the iron coat rack in the foyer. I'd forgotten how short and solid Ed was. Even Mitch was taller than Ed, and wiry. Compared to the Claus brothers, Ed was as squat as a fireplug.

"I've been trying to call you." He sounded like a petulant child.

"I'm sorry, sweetie." I hadn't even checked messages since returning home. "It's been insane around here. Holly and I went—*out* for New Year's—" I caught myself before I could say we'd been away. "And I had a client who got himself re-arrested over the holiday, and I went up to the prison this afternoon to see him. Michael's nephew works up there. He pulled some strings so I wouldn't have to wait until Monday." Even though it was all true, I felt as if I was making excuses.

I still had part of a bottle of pinot noir from the night Holly and I . . . went out. There wasn't quite enough for two glasses, but I made do. When I carried them to the living room, I found Ed in the recliner. Harry was nowhere to be seen.

"Here you go." I handed him a glass and clinked mine against it before settling myself into the corner of the sofa nearest the recliner. "Happy New Year," I added.

"Happy New Year," he said, lifting his glass slightly. Then, we sat in silence.

"So, how was Vermont?" I asked finally.

"Fine," he said in a tone that made it clear it hadn't been fine at all and he was waiting for me to pull the details out of him. A week ago, I'd have done exactly that. I'd have asked, coaxed, and cajoled until he grudgingly opened up, and we'd have spent the rest of the evening dissecting every comment, every silence, every gesture. We'd have analyzed what Nicole really meant when she screamed, "I hate you!" or why Lawton had gotten so angry when Kimberly asked him—didn't *tell* him, mind you, but very politely *asked* him—to stop texting at the dinner table, or what it meant that Edie didn't seem to absolutely adore the doll that Ed bought her for Christmas.

Except tonight, I didn't feel like traveling that road for the millionth time. It wasn't that I didn't care, I told myself hastily. Because I did, honest. But I was tired from my own crazy week, and I wanted him to be warm and supportive for *me*. I wanted him to ask what I'd done, to dig for the details, even to figure out that there were things I wasn't volunteering. I wanted him to be concerned about me. I wanted him to care.

Maybe it wasn't fair to expect him to focus on my life when I was so uninterested in his. Maybe we were both monumentally self-centered prigs who deserved each other.

"Is there any more wine?" he asked suddenly.

"Sorry," I said. "I haven't had a chance to shop." *And it's not as if you brought any.*

"I guess you've been really busy," he said, not looking at me.

"Uh-huh." *Ask me one simple question. Anything. "What's going on? What's kept you so busy? How's work? Where did you and Holly go for New Year's?"* The silence lengthened. I drained my glass, wishing for more.

"I missed you." Ed finally looked at me, his eyes puppy-dog sad.

I knew the correct response was, "I missed you, too." But I hadn't, not really. After he canceled New Year's Eve, I barely thought about him. When he did cross my mind, he was more of an obligation—*I have to call Ed*—than a refuge in the midst of some very strange storms.

"Feels like forever," I said in quasi-agreement. "We haven't even exchanged Christmas presents," I added as though I hadn't noticed he'd arrived empty-handed.

"No time like the present." He smiled at his play on words. He went out to the foyer and returned with a small box. A very small box. The kind certain jewelry comes in. I could feel myself getting light-headed as he set it on the coffee table in front of me. "Merry Christmas."

I gaped. *It's not that*, I told myself. *It's not that*. The box was wrapped in silver paper and encircled with a red velvet ribbon. That meant it was just a gift. After all, nobody gift-wrapped an engagement ring. I was almost positive.

"Wait, I'll get yours." It was as good an excuse as any not to touch the box. Maybe if I left the room, it would be gone when I came back.

I practically ran out of the living room and up the stairs to the bedroom. I dumped out my purse on the bed and grabbed the phone to text Holly: *Ed's here. I think he brought a ring.* A moment later, the unmistakable *brrring!* heralded her response: *OMG!*

Pull yourself together, I told myself firmly. The box might contain earrings. Or a ring that wasn't *that* kind of a ring. Or something else entirely, like . . . I couldn't come up with anything.

The shopping bag filled with Ed's gifts had stood in the corner since Christmas. The big gift was a new parka; the littler gifts were things like insulated gloves and socks and a hat. I chose them because I knew how much he loved being outside in the winter, but now, they seemed impersonal.

"Merry Christmas!" I called out with forced jollity as I returned to the living room with the gifts. Ed was still in the recliner. *Good*. A man who was going to propose would have moved to the sofa, next to me.

I plunked the boxes in his lap. "Open away!"

"Um . . . I think you should open yours first."

Shit.

I picked up the small silver box. It was the right size. The right weight. I pulled the end of the bow, and the ribbon fell away effortlessly. Without looking at him, I turned the box over and loosened the tape. I removed the paper and lay it on the table, smoothing it out. My hands trembled slightly. I drew a deep breath and opened it, the small click resonating like a gunshot.

A diamond gleamed at me. It took me a few seconds to realize that it was a necklace. Not an engagement ring.

I exhaled. "It's lovely."

Ed leaned forward, brow furrowed. "Don't you like it?"

"Don't be silly. It's beautiful." It was the most honest reaction I'd had since he arrived. The brilliant-cut stone flashed fire from the center of a swirl of platinum nestled against deep blue velvet. The fine mesh chain disappeared behind the display pad.

"I was thinking—I thought about getting you—something else," he stammered. "But I thought you might like this better."

"Huh?" I was so eloquent.

"You're not the traditional type," Ed said. "So I figured you wouldn't want a traditional engagement ring."

"What?" My voice was much louder than I'd intended. "This is an engagement necklace?"

"Well—yes." He looked uncertain. "I mean—if you want it to be, that's what it is. Otherwise, it's just a necklace. That's okay, isn't it?"

The necklace was undeniably exquisite. Any woman would have loved it. If I'd seen it in a store, I might have tried it on, turning this way and that before the mirror. Now it was mine, courtesy of a man who seemed to want to spend his life with me. Granted, he came with baggage, but who didn't? The diamond sparkled in the lamplight. I was a fool even to hesitate.

"It's beautiful," I repeated, snapping the box shut. "Now you open yours." I pretended not to see his disappointment.

I'd never known anyone to open gifts so slowly or with such a minimal display of interest. He kept looking at me. The first time he did, I realized that I was still holding the box. As soon as he looked away, I set it down on the table, but the movement drew his eyes back to me. After that, his gaze kept darting back and forth from the table to me as if he was waiting for me to pick it up again, to take the necklace out and put it on.

He shook out the parka. "It's very nice," he said in a flat voice.

"It's good to thirty below," I said.

He shook his head slightly, as if at my ignorance. "It never gets that cold around here."

"It does in Vermont," I pointed out.

The room was silent save for the rustle of tissue paper as he opened his remaining gifts. Finally, when no distractions remained, I picked up the box. Such a beautiful necklace. I wanted to remove it from the box, to model it in front of the mirror, to admire the way the diamond reflected the light, but I couldn't. Doing so would mean taking possession, committing to something unspecified. No lawyer signed on the dotted line without knowing the terms of the contract. "So, which is it?" I asked. "An engagement necklace or just a necklace?"

"It's whichever you want it to be," he said.

At one time, that might have been the right answer. I could have told myself it meant he respected my independence. Now, his response felt wishy-washy. Indifferent, almost. Engagement/Christmas present. Marriage/dating. Whatever I wanted, he'd go along. Not because my happiness was paramount, but because it was all the same to him.

The thought startled me. *That's not fair,* I scolded myself. *Maybe he's scared.* A legitimate notion, but I couldn't sell it. To be scared, you had to care deeply about the outcome. Now, instead of watching me, gauging my reaction, his eyes flicked to the clock on the mantel. I knew in my heart that he would accept any answer without question or quarrel.

The diamond blazed against the dark blue velvet, a gorgeous fiery *whatever*. But I didn't want *whatever*. I wanted him to take a stand, to declare himself. To make a grand, unambiguous gesture. To proclaim that I was the woman he wanted to spend his life with. That he loved me. That I was The One.

Except he wasn't The One for me.

The realization slammed into my heart like an icy snowball. I studied the necklace to avoid meeting his eyes. Too much had gone on in the past few days, I told myself. I was mixed up. Overwhelmed. Exhausted. I had feelings for a man I barely knew, and I didn't know if those feelings had anything to do with these feelings. So many questions. As freezing rain pelted the windows and the diamond flashed and a decent man waited for me to decide his life, the only answer I knew was . . . no.

I closed the box and held it out to him. "It's neither," I said as gently as I could.

"What?" Of all the answers he might have been prepared for, this wasn't one of them.

"I can't keep it," I said. "It's a beautiful necklace, and you're a wonderful man, but—no."

"No what?"

"No . . . everything." He still didn't take the box, so I set it in his lap, on top of his new gloves. "I can't marry you, Ed—and I think we're at the end of the road." It wasn't anything I'd expected to say, but I didn't take it back. A vision of unshaven Ralph in prison browns flashed through my mind. I shoved him away. This wasn't about another man. It was about me.

"What do you mean? What happened?" He looked genuinely perplexed, and anger flared up in me. Was it possible he thought everything between us was fine? Spending holidays apart, going days without contact—did he think this was normal? Maybe this was why his marriage ended. I always assumed they broke up over the plumber, but suddenly I wondered. Maybe Ed had been as uninvolved with Kimberly as he was with me.

Or maybe I was too demanding, my expectations too high. Maybe Ed was as good as it gets.

But as we sat in uncomfortable silence on that icy New Year's night, I wasn't ready to settle. If it meant spending my life with my cats, my work, and a few dear friends, so be it. *Good enough* wasn't good enough.

He didn't try to change my mind. He didn't seem heartbroken, or even particularly upset at this turn of events. At most, he seemed perplexed. Since I hadn't planned to break up with him, I had no farewell speech ready. So, I thanked him and told him I'd enjoyed our time together, and I wished him well. It sounded impersonal, as if I were firing an employee who hadn't worked for me very long, but it was the best I could do. Launching a volley of criticism would be self-serving and unkind. After all, he wasn't evil or dishonest or violent. Granted, he was obsessed with his kids, but you couldn't fault someone for that.

As he walked out my door for the last time, weighed down with his gifts and the necklace—all of which I'd insisted he keep—I knew the truth. The problem wasn't that his children were a priority.

It was that I wasn't.

Twenty-Five

The next morning, the world looked surprisingly normal. The sky sparkled deep azure, accented with a few wisps of cloud. The leftover ice was already melting. David stretched out on the sofa, and Harry returned to the recliner as though no scent lingered to remind him of the presence of somebody he hadn't liked anyway. I did my best to enjoy a quiet Sunday, a task made easier when my repeated online searches confirmed that the media was merely rehashing the existing Ralph stories rather than unearthing new information.

On Monday, the office hummed with post-holiday normalcy. I arrived to find Robin and Marilyn in the conference room with a platter of bagels and cream cheese. "Eckert brought them," said Marilyn. "Want one?"

"Maybe later." I headed up the stairs, and Lulu met me at the top. "Good morning, sweet girl. Did you have fun with Robin and Jordy?" She rubbed her face against my leg. "If you'd learn how to get along with the boys, you could come home with me," I told her. She hopped on my desk and bumped her nose against my hand. Obediently, I kissed her head. "They should make a cat who looks like you. Cleo's pretty, but she has nothing on a Lulu kitty."

"Good morning."

I hadn't heard Elsa's footsteps. Her perfectly-glossed lips were set in the slightest frown. She'd never approved of Lulu's presence in a law office, but she tolerated what she referred to as my eccentricities because I was useful.

I beckoned her in. "Come on in. How was your New Year's?"

She moved across the room as gracefully as Lulu. "Lovely," she said, brushing off the seat of the wingback chair in case of lingering cat hair. "We went down to the city. Remember Frederich Bonner?"

"The one who did that sculpture in your office?" Elsa had a wrought iron piece on her bookcase that she said was an abstract representation of Dante's ninth circle of hell. Frederich Bonner had given it to her as partial payment of a substantial bill, and she claimed we'd gotten the better end of the deal.

She smiled, clearly pleased that I was becoming more culturally aware. The sculpture looked like a mangled pitchfork to me, but it was so valuable we had to put it on a separate rider to the office insurance policy, which was the only reason I remembered it. "He had a party at his gallery. You should get down there some time. He has some amazing pieces." She glanced at Holly's watercolor of the beach towels at the water's edge.

"What's up?" I asked. Elsa rarely graced the third floor with her presence.

"Cyril Walker called again." I must have looked blank, because she said, "The wrongful termination case."

"He's on my list to call as soon as I get back from court." It wasn't quite true, but it was close enough. I'd planned to call him at some point during the day.

"Please do. He's getting a bit concerned." As was Elsa, obviously. Landing Walker Industries as a client had been her major triumph two years earlier. Their IPO paid for her BMW.

Since she was here, I decided to probe. "Any idea what happened? I mean, beyond what the complaint says."

"It's all pretty cut and dried. He fired his office manager, and it turns out she was pregnant."

Something about her expression kicked my bullshit detector into high alert. "Any chance he didn't know?"

"You'll need to talk to him," she said. "Just—be diplomatic."

"I beg your pardon?"

"He's a huge client. We can't afford to alienate him."

"What do you think I'm going to do?" Lulu looked up, perplexed by my sharp tone.

The slightest crease appeared between Elsa's impeccably groomed brows. "It's just that sometimes—well, you tend to be direct."

Which was more than I could say for Elsa. "Is that a problem?"

"This one needs kid gloves. If he pulls his business, that's a huge loss for the firm."

"Maybe you should give him to Michael. Then you wouldn't have to worry about my offending him."

"Oh, don't be like that," Elsa chided. *Silly Meg, getting her feelings hurt over nothing.* "Besides, he likes dealing with women. All I'm saying is, he can be kind of a jerk sometimes, and you can't let that get to you—or at least, you can't show it."

"I've been practicing law for fifteen years. I think I know how to behave with an obnoxious client." Just to make Elsa wait, I petted Lulu for a few moments before I asked, "What time is he coming in?"

To her credit, she looked slightly abashed. "Ten-thirty."

"Can't do it. I'm in court. Pretrial, then an arraignment." A fact she'd have known if she'd checked the firm calendar before scheduling the appointment.

"There's no way you could meet with Cyril first?"

"I don't schedule these things. The court does." In fact, pretrial conferences were rescheduled all the time, and arraignments often didn't start until past noon, but a transactional lawyer wouldn't know that. "Now if you'll excuse me, I need to get going. Text me with the new time. Nothing before three. And get me the rest of the file. All I have is the complaint."

I half-expected her to bridle at my tone, but she merely said, "Dawn will give you whatever you need. Let me know if you have any questions." She was gone before I could reply.

*****

The pretrial conference resulted in a nice settlement for a slip-and-fall client, which meant an equally nice fee for our firm. From there, I went over to the criminal court to meet with Ralph in the lock-up before his arraignment. "How much longer am I going to be inside?" he asked.

"Depends. I'll argue for bail, but Antonio's going to paint you as a pedophile who was preying on this kid. If the judge buys it, you could be in until trial."

The judge bought it. I made my arguments, but Antonio had the no-contact order on his side. "It wasn't the child's responsibility to stay away from the defendant," he said, his hair glistening with a fresh coat of gel. "It was up to the defendant to stay away from the child. Even if it's true that the child initiated the contact—and all we have is the defendant's word on that—it wasn't the child's job, or the mother's, or the nanny's, to make sure the defendant complied with this court's order. That was the defendant's obligation. He stood right here when Your Honor entered the order, and he said he understood, and four days later, he was caught in the victim's house with his hands on the minor child. This is not a man who can be trusted."

"Your Honor, there's no evidence of any harm or any intent to harm," I pointed out. "Mr. Claus knows now not to respond if the child or anyone acting on the child's behalf initiates contact again. As Your Honor is aware, that was Mr. Claus's first experience with this court's orders. It wasn't unreasonable for him to assume that if he was contacted by the family, he was permitted to respond."

"If he had any questions, he should have asked his lawyer," said Antonio.

I widened my eyes as if shocked. "Surely counsel is not inquiring about any conversations Mr. Claus may or may not have had with his attorney." The attorney-client privilege was sacred, especially in the criminal arena.

"Certainly not, Your Honor," said Antonio, but the point had been made.

I continued, "If the Court feels additional supervision is appropriate, the defense requests electronic monitoring in lieu of imprisonment." Electronic monitoring, known to the public as ankle bracelets, was a reasonable and cost-effective means of keeping tabs on non-violent offenders without the hassles of imprisoning them. "Otherwise, Mr. Claus will be sitting in jail for months until trial. There's no justification for such a severe restriction on his liberty, especially in view of the presumption of innocence." The well-worn line about how a criminal defendant was innocent until proven guilty had never persuaded a judge about anything, but clients expected it.

Judge Marcos studied Ralph for what felt like a long time. "This court's role is to balance the defendant's rights against those of society," he said finally. "In this case, the member of society I'm most concerned about is that little boy. For whatever reason, the defendant was able to gain access to him. I don't care how it happened. What I care about is that even though the boy has parents and a nanny, the defendant was able to convince the child to meet with him."

"Mr. Claus was not alone with the child," I reminded him. "The nanny was present, and the meeting took place in public."

"And then they went back to the victim's home," said Antonio.

"In the nanny's car, with the nanny driving," I shot back.

The judge said, "This is all very interesting, but the fact is that the defendant was barely released from lockup when he was found engaging in physical contact with the child."

By my side, Ralph moved slightly as if he was about to stand and speak. I put out my hand to signal that he should remain seated and silent. "Your Honor, the child was upset, and Mr. Claus hugged him. It was a normal, compassionate response."

"Maybe for someone who isn't under a no-contact order, but in this case, it was inappropriate and the defendant should have known it," Antonio interjected.

The judge regarded Ralph sternly. "While the court has every interest in ensuring that a man's liberty is not unduly compromised, that concern must take a back seat to its interest in protecting an innocent child. If there had simply been an email exchange, I would be displeased, but what happened here went far beyond that. The child is too young to exercise judgment. The defendant is not. The defendant's right to liberty is important, but in this case, it is trumped by the child's right to safety. The new charges include risk of injury to a minor. I will not contribute to the increase of that risk. Bail denied. The defendant will remain in custody until trial." He banged his gavel, and it was over.

Twenty-Six

With the bitter taste of defeat lingering, I forced myself back to the office. Elsa's paralegal had texted me that Cyril Walker would be in at two-thirty. At two-fifty-three, Marilyn buzzed me. "Mr. Walker is here," she said.

"Thanks," I said. "Please get him settled in the conference room and offer him coffee." I sat back and sipped my tea. Maybe it was childish, but when a client was late, he waited.

But not too long, because if the firm lost Walker Industries, I'd probably be next out the door. I readied my smile and headed down to the conference room. The aroma of freshly-brewed coffee was rich and warm. I extended my hand to the silver-haired gentleman seated at the table. "Good afternoon, Mr. Walker, I'm Megan Riley."

He held out his hand without rising. "Hello, Attorney Riley." The faintest scent of expensive cologne highlighted his immaculate barbering.

I seated myself across from him. "I understand from Elsa Spector that you're in need of some assistance. What can I do for you?"

"Did she tell you I've been sued?" He sounded irritated, as if Elsa had fallen down on the job.

"Yes."

"Well, then, that's what I need!" He sat back, clearly satisfied that he'd won that round.

Not so fast, Sparky. "Mr. Walker, all I know is that a lawsuit has been commenced. I don't know whether you're looking for representation or just advice. The only facts I know are what's been alleged in the complaint. I don't know whether those allegations have merit. I also don't know whether you want to fight the lawsuit or settle it. So I ask you again: what can I do for you?" I held his gaze until he looked away, a small smile tipping the corners of his mouth.

"You're tough. I like that." He cocked his head, approving.

"You haven't answered my question."

"This can't become public," he said. "You need to make it go away,"

"It's a lawsuit. By definition, the minute it hits the courthouse, it'll be public."

"Then it can't hit the courthouse," he said.

"So you want to settle." I opened my file and considered the summons. The return date was two weeks from tomorrow. The summons and complaint had to be returned to court six days before the return date, a fact that always confused new lawyers who couldn't understand why the return date wasn't the date you returned the documents to court. ("That's just how it is," was my first supervisor's explanation.) "We only have a few days. That's not much time."

"You have to figure something out!" Commanding and imperious, but I detected a thread of panic.

I reviewed the complaint again. "She's named you individually in addition to the company. That's unusual in a wrongful termination action. Any idea why she's doing this?"

If I'd expected him to crumble and confess, I'd have been disappointed. Instead, his jaw hardened. "Because I'm the one who fired her," he said. "And she's a vindictive bitch."

"Does she have anything to be vindictive about?" He glared, obviously expecting me to back off. I held his gaze for a count of five before I spoke. "Mr. Walker, if I'm going to work out a deal, I need to know what ammunition she has. But first things first. If you want me to represent you, you need to hire me." I passed the fee agreement across the table. Elsa would have been outraged at my business-like conduct with her pet client, but I knew Eckert would approve—assuming he wasn't annoyed that it had taken this long for me to raise the issue.

Cyril Walker reached into the inside pocket of his exquisitely-cut suit coat and withdrew a Mont Blanc pen. He flipped to the last page and scrawled his name. He shoved the agreement across the table. I pushed it right back. "Please read that."

"I know what it says," he barked. "I already signed one."

"This agreement is for this specific lawsuit," I said. "The terms are different from corporate representation. Both the company and you as an individual are bound by this agreement." Elsa had prepared the agreement, assuring me that there was no conflict of interest because the board of directors would never disavow the company's founder and majority shareholder.

Cyril Walker skimmed through the document, thumbing the pages faster than anyone could have read and understood them, and shoved it back to me. "It's fine."

I signed on behalf of the firm with a felt-tip pen. "Now, everything you tell me is privileged. So, let's start again. Why did you fire Ms. Howley?"

"Because—I couldn't let her stay." He didn't even try to make up something about too much missed time or incompetence in her job performance. It was too early to know whether he was candid or simply unimaginative.

"She claims you fired her because she was pregnant. Is that true?"

"Not exactly," he said. I made no response. Most people abhorred silence, and they would rush to fill it with ill-advised disclosures. Cyril Walker was no exception: "She *said* she was pregnant. I don't even know if it's true. With a girl like that, who knows what the truth is? They'll say anything. I mean, screwing around with a married man—they figure it's carte blanche to do whatever they want."

As I suspected. "Were you and Ms. Howley involved in a personal relationship?"

"Define 'personal relationship.'" He smirked at his Clintonesque response.

"Were you having sexual relations with Sally Howley?" I asked. Upstairs in her elegant office, Elsa had probably just keeled over.

His jaw tightened. "One time. It only happened that one time. I'm a faithful husband, Ms. Riley. I made one tiny mistake, and this little tramp is trying to parlay it in to a fortune. I want this thing shut down. Immediately."

"When did this—indiscretion—occur?"

He backed up slightly. "Why does that matter?"

"We need to know whether she's going to claim the child is yours. If it is, you're looking at child support in addition to any other damages." I looked him straight in the eye. "Given the timing of your relationship, is there any possibility the child is yours?"

He was silent for a long minute. "It's possible."

I nodded to show I wasn't shocked. I consulted the complaint again. "She says she was two months pregnant when you terminated her employment in November, which means she's just four months pregnant now. I'll be frank, Mr. Walker: if she agrees to a settlement that doesn't include a DNA test and a guarantee of child support, she's a fool, and I don't get that impression from her behavior. If you look at the timing, it appears she walked out the door of your office and went straight to a lawyer." Which, of course, could mean they were both lying, him about it being a one-night stand and her about being pregnant.

I turned to the last page of the complaint to see if there was a chance she'd hired someone reasonable. Instead, the complaint was signed by Herman R. Jacobsen, Attorney at Law. Hermy was in my law school class. If we'd had an award for Most Likely to Become an Ambulance Chaser, Hermy would have won. His favorite self-descriptor was "colorful." He claimed he hadn't cut his wiry hair since he was twelve, a look that might have been less bizarre now if he hadn't lost every strand on top of his head. The last time I saw him, his dome was shiny from the ears up, and below that, he looked like Cousin It. He'd lost his left eye in a bar fight shortly before graduation, but rather than wearing a prosthetic like anyone else, he sported a variety of custom-made eye patches that matched his ties. Hermy touted himself as the Great Defender of the Downtrodden—a term emblazoned across the top of his website—and he routinely appeared on the news to pontificate about the persecution of the powerless.

I considered our options. On one hand, Hermy loved the limelight. On the other, he loved money more. If our offer included attorneys' fees, he might pressure his client into taking it.

"Here's what we need to do." I explained about Hermy. "I'll put together a proposal for your review. If you agree, I'll present it to Attorney Jacobsen. If it doesn't fly, we'll go from there."

Cyril Walker didn't look pleased, but he seemed to understand how few choices he had. "Fine." He handed me his business card. "Only call my cell. No other number. My wife cannot know anything about this."

"That's fine," I said. He stood, but I remained seated. "Do you want to give me a check for the retainer now, or would you prefer to make an electronic payment?"

He actually looked shocked. "Retainer?"

I tapped the fee agreement at Section 3, Compensation. He sat back down. His thin lips pursed as he reached into his inside pocket, withdrew a folded check he'd obviously brought for this purpose, and made it out to the firm. He scrawled his signature and tucked the Mont Blanc away, leaving the check on the table he rose again.

"If you'd like to wait, I can have someone make a copy of the fee agreement. Otherwise, I'll send it to you." I pretended not to notice he hadn't handed me the check. Passive aggression wasn't unusual. People needed representation, but they resented actually having to pay for it.

"Don't bother," he practically spat. Sometimes, the aggression wasn't quite so passive.

As graciously as I could manage, I said, "In that case, I'll put a settlement proposal together, and we'll go from there. It's been a pleasure meeting you, Mr. Walker." A bold-faced lie, but a necessary one.

With obvious reluctance, he shook my hand. I felt like the mommy who was making the sick boy take his nasty-tasting medicine: we both knew I was doing what was best for him, but he was going to blame me anyway.

Twenty-Seven

After Cyril left, I delivered the check to Lucy Jane. She was seventy-two years old, with iron-gray curls and violet eyes. In the fifty-year-old engagement photo on her bookcase, she was a dead ringer for Elizabeth Taylor.

Lucy Jane came from McGooley, Rose & Swarthorn, the mega-firm where we all met. Eckert began his career at MR&S, working his way up to senior partner and chair of the trusts and estates division. Everyone who gave the matter any thought figured this courtly gentleman would stay there until he died at his desk, but Eckert had a secret dream: he wanted his own firm, with his name on the door. And he wasn't just dreaming. He was making plans.

Michael, Roy, Rick, and I were sixth-year associates when Eckert approached us. None of us were destined for partnership. The partners praised our work, but we weren't well-suited to big-firm life: Roy was too reticent, Rick too flamboyant, Michael too independent, and I too headstrong. More importantly, none of us were bringing in the kind of big-money clients the partnership committee required. So, in the midst of eighty-hour workweeks, we updated our resumes and put out feelers.

Elsa was two years ahead of the rest of us. By the time Eckert was ready to make his move, she had become of counsel to the firm, which meant they wanted her to stay, but they wouldn't make her a partner. She was superb at her job—no one denied this—but she was also female, of mixed race, and a lesbian. The partners—most of whom were older, white, male, and straight—might have accepted a woman partner, and even a woman of color, but Elsa was too much diversity in one package. Nobody said it out loud, but we all knew.

Even though Eckert's corner office on the sixteenth floor seemed isolated from our areas, little escaped his notice. And so the time came when he quietly summoned us, one by one. He laid out his vision and invited us to join his new venture. Once he assembled his team, he went to Boston to meet with the other senior partners and announce the formation of the Lundstrom Law Firm which, he said, would carry on the tradition of excellence in which we'd all been so well trained at MR&S. His last maneuver, executed with the same consummate graciousness, was to engage Lucy Jane to manage the office, handle the billing, supervise the staff, and generally run the firm. In my opinion, it was the smartest thing he ever did.

I handed her Cyril Walker's check. "Good," she said. Lucy Jane approved of checks. "I'll have your draft bills this afternoon. Get them back to me by Wednesday morning."

"Come up and get them," I said. "I just replenished the Irish Breakfast."

"That wimpy stuff? No way, honey. Down here, we drink Yunnan," she retorted with a grin. Yunnan was Lucy Jane's favorite tea. Bold, black, and sumptuous, it was not for the faint of heart.

"You have Yunnan. I have Lulu," I reminded her. Lulu and Lucy Jane always exchanged Christmas presents. This year, Lulu got a pound of dried catnip, and Lucy Jane got a gift card to her favorite day spa.

"Didn't I tell you? She called while you were in your meeting. Said she wants to move down here. Better view of the bird feeder."

"How many votes do you think that would get?"

"Mine," she said firmly. "Who else matters?"

"Good point." I headed up the stairs, barely reaching my office before the phone beeped.

"Meredith Claus on three," said Marilyn. It took me a second to realize she meant Ralph's mother. I drew a deep breath and punched the appropriate line button.

"Good afternoon, Ms. Riley," said Mrs. Claus, her voice as smooth as ever. "I trust you had a pleasant trip back to Connecticut."

"It was very nice, thank you. I also want to thank you for all you did for Holly and me while we were visiting. It was quite an experience." *To put it mildly.*

"I don't want to take up your time. I'm calling to find out when Ralph will be released."

It was the kind of news I hated delivering. "He's not getting out. The judge denied bail."

"I don't understand." Her words were measured, careful.

"The judge had the option of releasing him on bond again or holding him until trial. He decided to hold Ralph."

"But why?"

I chose my next words carefully. "Mrs. Claus, Ralph has never given me consent to speak with you about his case. Unless he does so, I'm not free to discuss it with you."

There was a long silence. Just when I thought we'd been cut off, she asked, "What is the phone number for the prison?"

"Pardon?" She probably didn't plan to call the warden, but I wouldn't rule it out.

"I'd like to call Ralph directly," she said as if it should have been obvious.

"It doesn't work that way. Inmates can't receive calls. They can only call out." I didn't know whether the system allowed for international calls, especially to unknown countries.

"If I can't telephone him, how do I reach him?" She sounded as if she were talking about a delivery problem instead of her son's incarceration.

"You can write to him. Just don't include material they consider contraband, like books or magazines."

"I can't send him a book?" The queen was displeased.

"You can, but only if it comes straight from the bookseller. Same with magazines or CDs. There are instructions on the website for the Department of Corrections. I'll forward the link."

"We can find it. But he *is* allowed to receive letters, correct?"

"Letters are fine. The prison staff will open them, and as long as the content is appropriate, they'll give them to him."

"They're going to read his mail?" she huffed. "What about his right to privacy?"

"He's in prison, Mrs. Claus. His privacy rights are limited." A nice way of putting it. Other than documents from his lawyer, everything he had—including his own body—was subject to search whenever the COs deemed it warranted.

"But he's innocent!" For the first time, she sounded like a regular mother.

"As long as he's incarcerated, he'll be treated like any other inmate, so when you write to him, remember that someone else will be reading your letter." I assumed she was smart enough not to write anything about the Santa business.

I could almost hear her frowning. "I don't like this," she said, as if it mattered. "Can you speak with Ralph?"

"He's entitled to call his attorney. Once a week, I think."

"And you can visit him?"

"Yes. In fact, I met with him over the weekend."

"Thank you for doing that," she said. "What if I came down? Could I see him?"

"As long as you have a photo ID. Most people use a driver's license, a state identification card, or a passport. Do you have an ID from a country the corrections officers would have heard of?" I could only imagine what would happen if she appeared with a card showing her address as the North Pole.

Another lengthy silence. "Does he have email?"

"Inmates don't get internet access." Such activities were strictly prohibited. Even if they weren't, I'd have told Ralph in no uncertain terms to stay away from any more websites.

"I don't like this," she said again. Apparently, my handling of this case wasn't living up to her standards. Drawing another deep breath, I reminded myself to show compassion. Her son was in prison. Naturally, his mother would be distressed. Before I could dredge up an encouraging platitude, she continued, "You'd think things would be slow after Christmas, but between the clean-up and the planning for next year, it's not. We really need him here."

My sympathy evaporated. She sounded like Cyril Walker complaining about a recalcitrant employee. "I'm sure he'd rather be there, too," I said. "He's in protected custody. It's not pleasant."

"Then we need to get him out." *Release the prisoner! Queen Meredith has spoken!*

"That's not possible. The judge heard argument this morning, and he denied my request for release on bond. There's nothing left to do at this point."

"We'll see," she said. "Thank you for your time."

The commoner is dismissed. "You're welcome," was all I said, and she clicked off. "Can you believe that woman?" I said to Lulu, who flicked an ear at my tone.

"Problem?" Michael stood in my doorway.

"Ralph Claus's mother," I said. "Thank Drew again for setting up the visit. It helped."

"Is he out?"

"Judge Marcos wouldn't budge. What's up?"

"Nothing. Just wanted to see how it went. Drew says your client's a good guy."

"Drew's right. And this whole thing smells funny."

Michael plopped himself into a chair. "What whole thing?"

"This meeting with the kid." I gave him a brief sketch of Ralph's account. "Why would the nanny insist on taking him back to the Leopolds'—the one place everybody should have known he wasn't supposed to be?"

"It sounds weird," Michael agreed. "Have you talked to Russ Carsten?" Russ was our favorite private investigator. Pricier than most, but worth the extra money."

"Not yet. I've been tied up ever since I got back."

My voice must have revealed something, because Michael peered at me. "Everything okay?"

"More or less." At his raised eyebrow, I admitted, "Ed and I broke up."

He contemplated this. Just when I thought he might come up with something supportive, he said, "Does your Santa guy know you're back on the market?"

"Get out of here!" I threw a pen at him and he left the room, chuckling at his own wit. I pulled up Russ's cell number. "Call me as soon as possible," I told his voicemail. "I have a case that needs your special touch." A special touch, and a healthy dose of magic.

Twenty-Eight

I spent the rest of the afternoon trying to think anything other than Ralph sitting in prison. Cyril Walker's case provided decent distraction. My research into recent wrongful termination verdicts dispelled any hope that a settlement could be achieved for less than six figures. I sketched out a memo of my findings for Cyril. He would not be pleased.

It was nearly four o'clock before Russ Carsten called. I explained the facts, including my suspicion that something wasn't quite right. He said he'd get right on it.

At the office the next morning, I'd barely poured my first cup of tea when Russ called. "Victoria Leopold doesn't have a nanny," he said instead of "hello."

"Huh?"

"The girl your guy says was with him and the kid at Lizzie's? She wasn't the nanny. There isn't one. And not for nothing, but the people at Lizzie's say she wasn't there."

"What are you talking about?" A dark gritty cloud of doubt descended into my mind.

"They said he was alone with the kid."

"That's insane!" Or maybe I was. Ralph's unshaven face rose up before me. He was so convincing. I was so stupid. "Who did you talk to?"

"Barb Landon. She's the owner. She also happens to be some sort of cousin to Victoria Leopold. Barb is Hal Zenkman's wife's niece."

I blew out my breath. "Really." So much for *family friend*. "What's the relationship between Zenkman and Victoria?"

"Victoria's stepfather was the brother of Zenkman's first ex-wife."

"How many wives has he had?" I drew a quick family tree to keep track.

"Zenkman? Two or three, I think. I can check."

"Do it." Not that it was likely to matter. These days, serial marriages were commonplace. "Where does Barb Landon come in?"

"Her mother is the sister of the current Mrs. Zenkman." I was adding them to the family tree when he said, "There's more."

"Tell me."

"Barb Landon says the kid kept trying to leave,' but your client wouldn't let him. Bought the kid an extra hot chocolate to keep him there."

"Thereby conveniently accounting for the purchase of three hot chocolates," I said, half to myself. "Let me guess: they saw Trevor get into my client's car and drive away? Even though my guy doesn't have a car?"

"She said she didn't see them leave," Russ said.

"And it never occurred to her how weird it was that her cousin's six-year-old kid was alone with a strange man? She never stopped by the table or called the kid's mother?"

"She says the restaurant was too busy. She saw them, but she didn't have a chance to talk to them." Before I could comment, he said, "It doesn't hold together. I don't think she expected to be questioned, at least not this soon."

"Thank God for bad planning." Maybe Ralph was telling the truth after all. "Ralph said the pseudo-nanny got a call while they were at Lizzie's. The nanny said it was from Victoria Leopold. Can you get phone records for both?"

"Sure thing." He clicked off.

The rest of the day crawled by. Funny how dull everything seemed when there was no chance of Ralph dropping by. I texted Holly to see if she wanted to come over, but Amy had brought her new boyfriend over for dinner. *U can come over,* she texted back. *No thanks,* I responded. Instead, I stayed at the office until everyone else had gone. On the way home, I picked up a bottle of wine and a pizza with mushrooms, roasted garlic, ricotta, and crumbled sausage, and I tried not to think about what prison food was like.

The next morning, the phone woke me. "Hello," I growled.

"Carsten."

"Russ!" I fumbled for the note pad and pen I kept on the night table. "What do you have?"

"The girl is Barb Landon's stepdaughter. Works as a nanny for a family in Avon. Occasionally babysits Trevor. Maybe his mother doesn't think he needs a nanny since she's home all the time."

"She doesn't work?"

"Not since she landed a doctor husband. She used to be a nurse. Hooked up with him when he and his first wife moved to Hartford."

"Figures." It was one of the most common scenarios in family court: nurse gets involved with married doctor, he divorces wife #1 to marry her, she thinks she's set for a life of leisure, and a few years later, he dumps her for the next upgrade. It happened in other professions, but for some reason, the doctor-nurse dynamic was the most common. The sad part was that the successor wives were always so surprised, as if they'd never heard one of the most basic relationship truths: *if he'll cheat with you, he'll cheat on you.*

I hung up the phone and flopped back in bed. "I hate my job," I said aloud. I imagined working in a world where people didn't lie, cheat, or do bad things to each other.

Like the ones who spent their days making toys.

Twenty-Nine

DOC rules allowed inmates to call their lawyers once a week. Ralph didn't call until Friday. He reported that he was trying to get a job in the license plate shop. Just like in old movies, prisoners make Connecticut's license plates. At seventy-five cents per day, the plate shop was one of the best-paying jobs at Foster, its tiny wage enabling inmates to purchase items at the commissary like pens or toiletries—things somebody in the dusty past had decided they shouldn't get for free. Ralph commented, "That guy never shared a cell with someone who'd rather buy cigarettes than deodorant."

But Ralph was in PC, so there would be no job for him. No job meant no income, and no income meant nothing to fund his inmate account. Ordinarily, his family could have deposited money by electronic transfer, but they had no U.S. bank accounts, and recent security protocols barred transfers from foreign banks—yet another facet of the incarceration experience that failed to meet with Meredith Claus's approval. She inquired whether someone could open a U.S. account so she could deposit Ralph's money there. It sounded logical enough, but I didn't know nearly enough about international banking to advise her about an arrangement that wouldn't trigger an investigation into money laundering. Some families arranged funding through private companies, but these companies were tightly regulated. Unless the Clauses wanted to keep sending elves down with cash to buy money orders, it would be a logistical nightmare.

Finally, I said, "Don't worry. I'll take care of it." From the original ten thousand dollars, the firm took the fee that had been earned so far, and when Lucy Jane issued me a check for my share, I deposited some of it into Ralph's account. Maybe it was an ethically questionable move, but as far as I was concerned, the money was mine to do with as I saw fit. I could buy a sweater, pay the mortgage, or give my friend a few bucks so he could purchase a toothbrush.

"I'm paying you back," he said the first time he called after learning of the deposit.

"There's no need. The money came from the retainer you paid." Not directly, but I didn't want him feeling uncomfortable about it.

Winter melted into spring, and the trek to Granby became a familiar one. One day, as I passed the regular visiting room en route to the pro visit room, I saw an older inmate with a gray buzz-cut and a deep red crevice of a scar running down the length of his cheek from his gray-black eyepatch—no Hermy Jacobsen color-coordination for him. He glowered at the woman who sat across the scratched metal table. She might have been my age, but we'd clearly had very different lives. Her long hair was faded crayon-red except for a couple inches of dark brown roots, and her bedraggled green sweater clung to her skinny frame. The inmate raised his voice and started to lean toward her, but before she could react, the CO stepped forward and said something I didn't catch. When the inmate didn't move, the CO barked, "Let's go! Now!" His mouth twisted with resentment, the inmate glared at the woman one more time and shuffled to another door where another CO escorted him away. Shoulders slumped, she murmured, "'Scuse me," as she moved past me and disappeared around the corner to the exit.

"That was Filos and Cara Jo," Ralph said when I described the incident to him. "Believe it or not, he's not a bad guy. Last week, he donated three pens to the writing class. We were all pretty surprised. He could've bought a couple packs of cigarettes with that money."

"A writing class? Like the one that writer did with the women down at Niantic?" A local writer had started a creative writing group at the women's prison. The group's work had even been published.

"Nothing like that," Ralph said. "These guys are learning to write letters and fill out a job application."

"I thought you weren't allowed to mix with the rest of the population." That was what protected custody was supposed to be about—keeping these inmates separate from the others.

"This class is restricted to PC," he said. "The regular population has a few more choices."

"Sounds a little . . . elementary."

"It's that or sit around counting my fingers. Sometimes the guys ask me for help, which is nice."

"You probably have more education than most of them." As I spoke, I realized that I hadn't seen a school at the Pole. Then again, I also hadn't seen Santa, so obviously our tour hadn't been exhaustive.

"You'd be surprised. The number of college graduates in prison is a lot higher than you might think. Filos did a year and a half at community college. Criminal justice."

"And now he's here." Criminal justice from the other side.

Ralph's mouth quirked, acknowledging the irony. "Filos has problems. This is his third time inside. Assault, disorderly, stuff like that."

"Domestic?" I thought back to the woman.

"Uh-huh. This time, their ten-year-old got in the middle of it, and Filos knocked him out. He says it was a mistake and he was aiming for her. In any case, that's why he's in PC. My cellie says last time, Filos did time in ad seg for punching a CO." It was disconcerting how easily the prison slang rolled off his tongue. *Cellie*, for cellmate. *Ad seg*, for administrative segregation, formerly known as solitary confinement. *PC*, for protected custody.

"Is he medicated?" I hoped so, especially if he was anywhere near Ralph.

"Not enough," Ralph said. "They don't do much with psych meds here. Only enough to take the edge off, keep the anger and psychotic episodes under control. They don't deal with things like depression, which is a shame since pretty much everybody here is depressed."

"Including you?"

He looked startled for a second. "A little," he admitted. "But I shouldn't be. I've got it a lot better than most of these guys. My family is in contact all the time—I get mail practically every day. Plus, I know that when we go to trial, I'm getting out of here."

"We hope," I said firmly. There was plenty of work left before trial. I had depositions scheduled for a number of witnesses, including Victoria Leopold. Antonio had already moved for permission for a psychological evaluation of my client. Hal Zenkman was becoming the new face of child protection, making barely-veiled references to the Claus case nearly every time he urged Connecticut residents to keep our children safe from predators.

"It'll be all right," Ralph said with so much conviction that I could almost have believed him. "The truth will come out."

I didn't tell him that was exactly what I was afraid of.

Thirty

When I returned to the office, Marilyn handed me a sheaf of message slips. I flipped through them quickly. Three were from Cyril Walker.

"I was only gone a couple hours," I muttered.

Marilyn smirked. "Mr. Walker does not like to be kept waiting."

"Did he say what was so urgent?"

"I'm lucky he speaks to me enough to ask for you. I offered to put him into your voicemail, but he said he'd already left a message there and you hadn't gotten back to him."

"You're in trouble now," Michael singsonged as he strolled past, coffee in hand.

"Oh, please." I followed Michael up the stairs. "I've already told him. The plaintiff won't do an ultrasound, so paternity can't be confirmed until the baby is born and they do the DNA test. Unless Walker wants to agree to child support for a kid who might not be his, there's nowhere to go at this point."

"Maybe not, but this guy needs handholding," Michael said as we reached the second floor. "And handholding is billable."

"Now you sound someone else we know." I glanced over at Elsa's closed door. He sauntered down the hall to his office, and I went up to the third floor where decisions were made based on urgency and strategy, not some rich client's desire for attention.

I poked my head into Robin's tiny office. "Anything going on?"

"Antonio called," she said. "Wants to set up the psych eval for Claus."

"Did he say who he wants to use?" With any luck, it would be somebody with an obvious bias so I could revive my objection to his motion.

"Ken Solberg."

Damn. I'd used Solberg myself on several occasions. He was thorough, sensible, and well-credentialed. More importantly, judges knew him and routinely found him credible. "Fine, I'll call him." I went back to my office and made tea. While it steeped, I reviewed the specific charges. Then I dialed Antonio's number.

"My paralegal said you called," I said after the usual pleasantries. "What's up?"

"My motion for a psych eval was granted," he said. "We need to set up a meeting for Ken Solberg and your client."

"Or we could save the taxpayers a few bucks and figure out a way to resolve this," I said as though the notion had just occurred to me.

"What do you want?"

"Lose sex four, enticing a minor, and risk of injury, and we work with the other stuff and agree to time served." Sexual assault in the fourth degree, commonly referred to by criminal lawyers as *sex four*, encompassed all sorts of sexual contact between an adult and a minor, including teacher/student and coach/player relationships, consensual or not. An adult who held a kid so the kid was pressed up against the adult's genitals for the adult's sexual gratification would be guilty of sex four.

"Not happening," said Antonio.

"Come on—you don't want to try this case. You want to be the big bad lawyer who put Santa away?"

"I'm not putting *Santa* away. Your guy's like those scary clowns who victimize innocent children."

"He didn't victimize anybody," I snapped.

"First he does the home invasion. Then, the second he's out on bond, he tracks down the kid, cons him into meeting, and plies him with hot chocolate so he can get his hands on him. If the mother hadn't come in, who knows what could have happened?" He sounded smug.

"That's your case? Speculation and innuendo?"

"Fact," he replied. "Do you deny that he met with the kid and had his hands on him?"

"He hugged a little boy who was upset."

"He groped a child," Antonio retorted.

"Oh, come on. There's a world of difference between a hug and a grope. Besides, my client didn't track the kid down. The kid contacted him."

"On your guy's website."

"They met in a public place with another adult present. An adult of the mother's own choosing."

"Agreed on the public place, but the girl denies being present."

"The girl's lying. I have witnesses who saw three people at that table—the boy, my client, and a young woman." Silence. "My client doesn't have a car. How would they have gotten from Lizzie's to the Leopolds' if the girl wasn't driving?"

"How did he get to the house the first time?"

"Seriously? You're asking me for information?" I wasn't about to say *reindeer*. "What does your investigator say?" It was one of the few good things about being on the defendant's side: the prosecutor had to disclose all his evidence.

"Your guy doesn't deny being in the house without permission." In other words, he had nothing on the transportation angle.

"Wrong," I said. "He doesn't deny being in the house. He had permission. Both times."

"The letter he claims to have gotten from the kid?"

"Permission from someone who lives in the house," I corrected him. "Last time I checked, the law didn't set a minimum age for inviting someone in."

"Are you suggesting a six-year-old is competent?"

"To invite someone to his house? Why not? Haven't you heard of play dates?"

"If my kid wants to have a play date, the mothers set it up. The jury's going to have issues with a grown man who shows up at a little kid's house without talking to the parents first."

"I can handle that." Which, of course, was a lie. "Besides, I'm not the one with the burden of proof. You've got to prove he *didn't* have permission."

"I've got the mother—"

"—who was not the only person in the house, or the only person living there for that matter. Even if you don't believe the kid, you're forgetting about Dad." Lawyers routinely referred to the parents in domestic disputes as *Mom* and *Dad*.

"Dad doesn't live there anymore. You can't give permission for someone to enter somebody else's house."

"He may not live there *now*," I said. "But as of the holidays?"

"As of the holidays, he was already out of the house."

"You sure about that? He was a hundred percent out? Not back and forth? You know how these things go. They fight, he stays with the girlfriend for a few nights, he comes home for a while, they fight again, he's with the girlfriend again—some couples do this for years. Did Mrs. Leopold ever get an order of exclusive possession?" I already knew the answer, courtesy of Russ. The good Dr. Leopold had filed for divorce more than a year ago, but as of last week, Victoria Leopold still hadn't asked the court for an order barring her estranged husband from entering the marital home. Jilted wives never did. Not as long as there was a chance the wandering husband might find his way back. "Face it, Antonio. You don't want to put Santa on trial."

"He's not Santa. He's just nuts. You can't have nutjobs showing up in people's homes claiming they were invited by some kid."

Crazy, not evil. I was making progress. "But he's sincere. The jury isn't going to hear that he was a threat. He brought presents, for Pete's sake."

"What do you want?"

Back around at last. I scanned the list of charges as though I didn't already know it by heart. "Drop the home invasion and burglary to simple trespass. Simple's just an infraction. Even if you made criminal, you probably couldn't get as much time as he's already served. Drop the rest, and you'll have a week to spend at the Cape."

"Can't do it. Your guy was seen holding the kid." He said *holding* as if it meant *molesting.*

"It's only risk of injury if there really is a risk of injury," I said. "The kid was in his own house with his babysitter and his mother. Besides, my client wasn't doing anything inappropriate. If he were an uncle or a friend of the family, nobody would have blinked."

"If he were an uncle or a friend of the family and there was a court order requiring him to stay away from the kid and he got caught pressing the kid up against himself, there'd be a whole lot more than blinking going on," Antonio said. "I can drop home invasion and burglary second to criminal trespass second. That's a class B misdemeanor, and it's a gift. Tell Mr. Santa 'Merry Christmas.'"

"There was no pressing! And you can't prove enticing a minor— the website is clean. You sure as hell can't prove endangerment or sex four. The jury's going to think you're out to get him, and they'll feel sorry for him." That would be our best break, and with a client who looked as good as Ralph, it was a real possibility, especially if Antonio overplayed his hand. The state's eternal balancing act: *prosecute, don't persecute.*

"I can't do anything about that. I've got your guy on enticing a minor. I mean, a website that invites a six-year-old to contact him? Class B felony. Minimum five years non-suspendable."

"There's no evidence that my client was trying to do anything sexual." The statute was designed to catch dirtbags who set up websites to suck kids into prostitution or sexual activity. I'd gone through every corner of TheSantaClaus.xyz personally, and it was clean.

"Mom says she walked in to see him holding the kid right against himself."

"Oh, for God's sake! How many times do I have to say it? A hug is not the same as a grope! What kind of sick world do you live in?" *Take it easy. It's nothing personal. Just another negotiation.*

"Mom says it looked like your guy was rubbing up against the kid."

"That's not only sick, it's a flat-out lie!" So much for taking it easy.

Robin poked her head in the doorway and mouthed, *Are you okay?* I waved her away.

"That's for the jury to decide," said Antonio with annoying matter-of-factness. "I can't let it all go. At a minimum, he'd have to plead to risk of injury and sex four."

"Which means five years, plus he'd have to register." For the rest of his life, Ralph would be listed on the state registry of sex offenders as if he were some kind of pervert. Those bastards.

"Considering what he's exposed on, it's worth considering. The powers that be aren't going to let him walk without something on the sex claims."

"Screw the powers that be! You don't have a shred of evidence on any of this crap. Your only witness is a flaky woman whose lying relatives can't even keep their stories straight. Nobody's going to believe these people, especially when they can't answer a simple question like why the babysitter insisted on taking my client back to the Leopolds' house. The jury's going to think he was set up."

"No motive," Antonio said with a touch too much smugness. "Look, I have your guy dead to rights on risk of injury, enticing a minor, sex four, and child endangerment. I might be able to drop enticing and endangerment, but I'm telling the truth here—that's as far as I can go. Mom's got friends in high places. If you make me take this to trial, you know what's going to happen."

Yeah, I knew. He'd go full-bore on the whole list of charges, and something was bound to stick. I sat back and took a long sip of cold tea. "He's not pleading to risk of injury," I said at last. "Certainly not sex four. I might be able to sell burglary, but not second. Third, for time served."

Long pause on the other side. I knew Antonio didn't want to try this case either. He was a dogged opponent, but he was basically decent. Victoria Leopold's friends were about to destroy an innocent man, and I had a feeling Antonio knew it.

"Talk to your client," he said finally. "I'm in court tomorrow morning, but I'll be in after that. In the meantime, I'll set up Solberg unless you have a problem with him."

"Nope, no problem." I hung up and made notes so I'd have an accurate record of the conversation. As if there was any chance I might forget.

The phone beeped. My stomach flipped. I pressed the intercom button. "Yes?"

"Cyril Walker on line one," said Marilyn.

"I can't talk to him right now," I said. "Tell him I'll call him back." Lulu slept peacefully in the corner chair as I paced around my office to avoid making a decision I really, really didn't want to make.

Thirty-One

So instead, I called Russ Carsten and asked him a question. An hour later, he called me with a name and a phone number. The next morning, I headed over to Hooker Memorial Hospital, named after one of Hartford's founding fathers and not, as some public defenders claimed, its leading profession.

A petite young woman in blue scrubs and a white coat breezed across the lobby, her long black ponytail bouncing. I rose and extended my hand. "Dr. Damdar? I'm Attorney Riley."

"Katrina Damdar." Victoria Leopold's replacement gave my outstretched hand a firm, no-nonsense shake. "I only have a few minutes. I have a lobectomy this afternoon."

Low-backed armchairs in groups of four dotted the lobby. I led her to a remote corner. Her phone buzzed as we sat; she glanced at it, then me. "What can I do for you?"

"As I told you on the phone, I represent Ralph Claus," I began.

"The person who broke into her house," *Her*. Clearly, there was no love lost between the current and former paramours of Dr. Robert Leopold.

It wasn't a break-in, I wanted to say, but I doubted Dr. Damdar would respond well to correction. "What I can't figure out is this: why is it so important to Trevor's mom that this man goes to prison?" I was careful not to use Victoria Leopold's name.

The doctor glanced around as if she was about to let me in on a private joke. "If you ask me, I think it all got out of control," she said. "She's been trying to get Rob to leave me for ages. He moved into my place last fall, and she's always calling about stupid things." Her voice slid into a high-pitched whine. "She can't find the number for the oil delivery guy, the kitchen faucet's dripping, the door on the wood stove won't latch right." Her pitch returned to normal. "Just stuff to get him to go over and help her."

"Does he?"

"He did at first, but after a few weeks of that crap, I put my foot down. She's a big girl. If she's so hot to keep that house, she should learn how to fix it. So he told her to figure it out, and that drove her batshit. She even started making up stuff about Trevor—he had a game and really wanted Rob there, he got a bad grade on a test and Rob needed to talk to him, things like that."

"These things weren't true?"

"Who knows? Rob would talk to Trevor, and it was never a big deal. It was just her."

"Do you remember what happened on Christmas Eve?"

"She called him all hysterical in the middle of the night, saying somebody broke in. Rob thinks it was somebody she brought home and then had second thoughts about."

"Does she do that kind of thing?" Anything that impugned a witness's character could be useful.

The young doctor shrugged. "You'd have to ask Rob. He's the one who lived with her. How he put up with her for that long is anybody's guess. Talk about high-maintenance."

Not that Dr. Damdar appeared to be easygoing, but the issue wasn't Robert Leopold's taste for demanding women. "When she called him that night, what did he do?"

"He went over there. The middle of the freakin' night—Christmas Eve, and one night we both actually had off—and he has to get out of bed and go to her house, and all for nothing."

"What do you mean?"

"By the time he got there, the guy was gone—the cops took him. Rob said she tried to get him to stay—said she 'didn't feel safe without him.'" Again the whiny, mincing lilt when she quoted her predecessor. In her own voice, she went on, "What a load of crap. I mean, she's got an alarm system. Rob says she's obsessive about setting it, always has been. That's why he figures she let the guy in. No way was somebody getting in without the code."

I already knew the answer to my next question, but I asked anyway. "Is their divorce final?"

A snort of disgust revealed everything I needed to know about Katrina Damdar. "She keeps dragging it out. She can't let go of him. I swear, she'd do *anything* if she thought it would get him back." Her phone buzzed. She checked the message and rose. "Listen, I've gotta go. I don't know if that helped you, but—"

"Absolutely, thanks," I said. "Just one more thing—I may need to have you come to trial to talk about some of the things we discussed today. Is that something you'd be willing to do?"

Her phone buzzed again. "Whatever," she said. "Maybe once this is over, she'll figure out Rob isn't coming back to her no matter how much drama she whips up."

"Thanks for your time," I said. "Where can I reach you if I have any other questions?

She pulled out a business card. "My cell's on the back." With that, she was gone in a swirl of white coat and disdain for the woman whose marriage was interfering with her life.

*****

"I don't know why I didn't think of it before," I said to Michael two hours later. The tiny round table was barely large enough to hold our paper plates and cans of soda, but Guido's made the best pizza in Hartford. "Ralph said the kid overheard somebody talking about how this wasn't going to make Daddy come home, but it was so ridiculous I didn't think anything of it. I mean, who does this? She's putting an innocent man through the wringer because she thinks that'll get Dr. Screw-Around to come home. The woman's a fruitcake."

Michael wiped his greasy fingers on an inadequate paper napkin. "What did the client say when you told him?" He was always careful not to use names in public.

"I haven't yet. I still need to talk to him about Antonio's offer. I figured it would be good to have something positive to tell him at the same time."

"Somebody using him as a pawn to get her husband back is positive?"

I finished my crust. "I'm not saying it's great, but at least it's a reason. There's logic."

"Sick, twisted logic." Michael drained his soda can. "Ready?"

I crumpled my napkins and paper plate together. "Granted, but that whole setup angle was so weird, it's almost a relief to have an explanation. Why would somebody go to all that trouble to set up a

206 / P. Jo Anne Burgh

perfect stranger? At least I can tell him it's nothing personal."

"What about her uncle? Isn't he in the running for somebody with a motive to screw your guy?"

We edged through the lunch crowd toward the trash bin. "I haven't ruled him out, but I'm thinking he's just opportunistic. Assuming his niece or whatever she is has cooked up this whole conspiracy to woo hubby back, it would be just like—that *charming* man—to spin it for political gain." I dropped my voice. "Did you hear he might be running for governor?"

Michael shoved his trash into the waste bin. "The question is, does he matter to the case?"

"Dunno," I admitted as I did the same. "The setup issue will go to Mom's credibility."

"Assuming the jury doesn't feel sorry for her," Michael warned as we headed out the door. "Her husband dumped her and the kid, and she's desperate for him to leave the tramp and come home so they can be a family—so much that for a minute, her judgment got a little clouded, and she inadvertently exposed her kid to this pervert who poses as Santa Claus and who she caught manhandling the boy."

I shuddered. "I'm glad you're not prosecuting this one." A bus roared past us, threading its way between cars parked on both sides of the street.

"So am I. Getting ordered around by the big boys was never my idea of a good time. Speaking of which, how're things going with Elsa's guy and the paternity claim?"

"I forgot to call him." I took a second to tap a reminder on my phone, looking up just in time to avoid a collision with a texting teenage boy.

Michael whistled. "Somebody's not going to be happy with you."

The fine golden pollen of early spring coated street signs and parking kiosks. A plump pale man standing at the bus stop was having a sneezing fit. Ahead of us, a scrawny woman with light brown skin and long gold braids pushed a stroller with one hand and dragged a red-shirted toddler with the other. We maneuvered past them on the narrow sidewalk as I said, "She's fine. Walker loves her."

"As much as Claus loves you? What is it with the women in this firm, anyway?"

"Don't be stupid. Ralph Claus doesn't love me."

"Bullshit. I talked to him. He's smitten." His voice was casual. Typical lunchtime banter.

"You're nuts." My voice was louder than I intended, and a woman in a dark suit paused in the middle of texting. Lowering my voice with an effort, I said, "Ralph is not smitten with me. He respects me as a lawyer. That's all."

"That's not all," Michael said. "And if you're not seeing that. . . ." He studied me for a second, and then it clicked. He stopped walking, his easy smile gone. "Is there something between you two?"

"Don't be ridiculous." I started to walk again, but he put his hand on my arm and I stopped.

"What the hell—are you involved with this guy?" His voice was low and granite-hard.

"No. No. Absolutely not. Nothing like that." But he didn't speak, didn't move. Didn't believe. He just stared at me until I said, "Okay. There was kind of—at the beginning—some hints that something could happen. But not now. Nothing since New Year's."

"'Hints'? What are you talking about?" But I could hear it in his voice. He knew.

With anyone else, I'd have denied everything and walked away. Sprinted, maybe. But this was Michael. I took a deep breath. "He kissed me."

We faced each other, blocking the sidewalk. A dark-bearded millennial in work boots barked, "Hey, do you mind?" We moved closer to the metal rail surrounding a parking lot. State workers in sneakers hustled past on their way back from lunch. Finally, Michael said, "Did you kiss him back?"

"Yes." My voice was so low I couldn't imagine he heard me, but his eyes darkened.

"How many times?" His tone balanced on the knife-edge between professional detachment and cold fury.

"What does it matter—"

"How. Many. Times."

"—three."

"Three kisses." Gathering information.

"Three—occasions."

"Sweet Jesus, Meg." He waited. When I didn't volunteer, he asked: "Did you sleep with him?"

"No! Of course not!" I snapped as though I had the right to be offended.

"When was the last time you kissed him?"

"Before New Year's. When I left for the weekend. That's the last time. I swear to God."

"No wonder he thought. . . ." His voice trailed off as he started walking.

I hurried to catch up. This time, I grabbed his arm. "You can't tell anybody." At his emotionless stare, I said, "Yes, it was wrong and stupid, but I cut it off before it turned into anything, and it's over. There's nothing now. He's just a client, and I'm just his lawyer. There's no reason to tell anybody."

He looked me up and down, his face grim. Slowly, he shook his head. "I don't know," was all he said. We walked the rest of the way back to the office in silence.

Thirty-Two

"I was just going to text you guys," said Marilyn as I trudged into the office behind Michael. "Partnership meeting at two."

Partnership meetings were always scheduled well in advance to accommodate fluctuating schedules. A last-minute meeting meant something serious was brewing. *They don't know,* I told myself. *They can't.* Even Michael hadn't known until fifteen minutes ago.

"Did Eckert say what it's about?" Michael asked.

"Huh-uh. Guess it's a surprise." She beamed as though she knew a juicy secret.

"Okay, thanks." I went upstairs without waiting to see whether Michael would follow. Alone on the top floor, I picked up Lulu and settled into an armchair. Ten to two. Not enough time to call Cyril Walker. I'd call him after the meeting. *Right after,* I promised.

At two minutes to two, I brushed black cat hair off my tan suit and went back downstairs. Michael and Roy were already in the conference room.

"What's going on?" I asked as I took my place at the conference room table.

Roy shrugged. "Elsa's got big news, that's all I know."

On cue, Elsa and Eckert appeared in the doorway. My scalp prickled. They took their usual seats, and Eckert favored the rest of us with a wide smile.

"Elsa has some news," Eckert said. He indicated Elsa, who smiled graciously. I glanced at Michael. His face was unreadable.

"I received a telephone call a few weeks ago from the CBC," she said. "Connecticut Business Council," she clarified for those of us who weren't in the corporate loop. "I've met with their people several times, and this morning, they made a very exciting proposal." She paused for dramatic effect. I suppressed an urge to give her the bored-teenager look I'd see so often on Ed's daughter. "The CBC wants our firm to serve as its legal advisor in legislative matters." She beamed at us.

"Congratulations!" said Roy.

"Congratulations," I echoed. "That's very exciting." I didn't mean to repeat her words, so I added another "Congratulations."

"Congratulations," said Michael. He didn't sound as enthusiastic as he normally would. Probably still digesting my news. "What exactly would this involve?"

"That's the most exciting part," said Elsa, ignoring the inadequacy of our responses. "As you all know, the CBC's strongest ally in the legislature is Senator Zenkman. We would be working directly with the senator's office to develop new legislation to improve the state's business climate."

"Wait a minute—Senator Zenkman?" I said. "The one who's related to the victim's mother in my Claus case?"

Elsa's smile didn't drop, but a hint of rigidity crept in. "I'm certain that won't be a problem," she said smoothly.

"How can it not be a problem? Zenkman's people have been holding Victoria Leopold's hand the entire way through this case. Every time there's a development, Zenkman's all over the media screaming about keeping children safe from perverts."

"Don't you think we should keep children safe?" Elsa's voice was steely now.

"That's not what I'm saying, and you know it. I just don't think we should be taking on clients who have publicly denounced our other clients—who, by the way, were our clients first because a judge specifically requested that we take the case." Elsa might not care who came first, but even she wasn't about to piss off a judge.

"Calm down," said Eckert. "I appreciate Meg's point. Once this liaison is established, it would obviously be better if the senator refrained from public comment about the Claus case." He turned to Elsa. "Perhaps this is something you'll want to discuss with him."

"The senator has the same free speech rights as anyone else," she replied. "As an elected official, he has both the right and the responsibility to speak out on matters of public concern. Even if he didn't, I don't think we should be muzzling our clients."

"I'm not talking about muzzling a client," I said. "I'm talking about the Rules of Professional Conduct. Conflicts of interest among clients. That sort of thing."

Roy said, "If I understand correctly, Zenkman wouldn't be the client. It would be the CBC."

"Which apparently works directly with Zenkman's office," I retorted. "Sounds like a very thin line to me."

"The senator can say whatever he chooses, and we have no right to interfere," said Elsa. "I know Meg feels strongly about Mr. Claus—"

"I feel strongly about his *case*," I interjected.

"Really." Her eyes were icy.

Fiery defensive anger surged in me, barely controlled. "Really."

"What are you suggesting?" Eckert asked her. She didn't acknowledge him, so he changed his tactic: "Meg? What's going on?"

"Nothing." I bit the word off. Next to me, Michael shifted slightly. We were partners, all five of us. We owed a fiduciary duty to each other. If I didn't speak up, he would have to. With only a slight softening of my tone, I said, "When I first took on Mr. Claus's case, I spent time with him in order to assess his claims. That time included two dinner meetings."

"That's unusual, isn't it?" Eckert mused. "I mean, with a criminal client. I know we do it all the time for marketing, but. . . ." His voice trailed off as if he was trying to figure out an explanation.

"Unusual, but not unheard of," Michael said. "Sometimes defendants let down their guards outside the office, and they reveal information you might not otherwise get." I could have hugged him.

"And that's all there was?" Roy asked. I turned my glare on him, and he drew back, muttering, "Sorry, didn't mean anything."

"We've gotten off the topic," Eckert said. "The issue today is Elsa's new client, which will be a significant source of revenue for the firm. The CBC has been represented by Hogan & Louderman for several years, and I'm told the fees generated have been quite substantial." He didn't lick his lips, but his smile broadened.

"Why are they looking for a new firm?" Michael asked. "Gene Louderman's excellent at this kind of thing. He was in the House for—what was it, three or four terms? He knows his way around a bill better than any of us—nothing personal," he added as Elsa bridled slightly.

"Cyril Walker was our in," she said. "Clients beget clients. Cyril's on the CBC's board. He's been so pleased with our corporate work that he told the CBC they should switch." The reference to *our corporate work* did not pass me unnoticed.

"Well, I think it's a marvelous accomplishment," said Eckert. "And who knows where it may lead? It may be time to think about expanding our focus into more of this kind of legislative work." He smiled at Elsa, who returned the smile with a noncommittal nod.

"Wait a minute. This is a done deal?" I looked from Eckert to Elsa. "Did you already commit to this client?"

"Is there a problem?" Eckert asked.

"Of course, there's a problem," I said. "The whole Zenkman thing. Not to mention this complete shift in the focus of our practice. We should discuss it. You don't just come in here and announce we're adding a whole new practice area. That's not how a partnership works."

"I agree," Michael said. "Also, I'm concerned that the senator's comments about Mr. Claus may constitute a conflict. I know Senator Zenkman wouldn't actually be the new client, but the affiliation is close enough that I think we need to look into it. Taking on representation of an organization that works so closely with someone who has publicly denounced a client of the firm sounds like an ethical gray area to me." He turned to Roy. "What do you think?" Clever maneuver: we all knew Roy was likely to agree with the most recent comment.

"I don't know," Roy said to my surprise. "What I do know is costs are up and revenues aren't. In terms of billing, we're flat. If we want to boost earnings, this sounds like a good way."

"Even if it means compromising our ethical responsibilities?" I interjected.

"No one's suggesting compromising anything," said Eckert, ever the paterfamilias. "Michael raises a good point, though. I suggest we run the issue by Geoff Quinn." Geoff Quinn was one of the bar's leading experts on professional ethics. He was also a friend of the firm: Michael and I had represented two of his nephews in several DUIs over the years.

"Fine," said Elsa. "I'll call him today." Only someone who had worked with her as long as we had would have heard her smoldering anger.

"One other thing," said Eckert. "Don't say anything to the CBC just yet. We don't want them to think we're waffling. If they ask, tell them we're doing a standard conflicts check." He turned to the rest of us. "I think we're done. Thank you, everyone." He and Elsa left the room. Roy glanced at Michael and me and followed.

Michael regarded me. His mouth was set in a grim line. The disappointment in his dark eyes was as intense as my father's on that long-ago night at Steve's. I swallowed hard. "Thanks."

"Don't thank me," he said. "Next time, I won't keep quiet."

"There won't be a next time."

"There'd better not be." He left, and I was alone at the table.

Thirty-Three

May's glorious blooms gave way to the lush green of soggy June. The weather folks chirped that we were heading for a record, with abnormally hot temperatures and rain at least three times a week. Leaving the air-conditioned office felt like stepping into the tropics. On the corner by the capitol, a group of rotund women and lanky men, all with gray-streaked hair and Birkenstocks, held laminated signs demanding, "STILL DON'T BELIEVE IN CLIMATE CHANGE?" Marilyn complained to anyone who passed her desk that her sinuses were dripping and the copier was jamming and the entire office was going to sprout mildew any day.

Cyril Walker's ex-office manager had her child on the first of June. The DNA test confirmed that Cyril was the father. Hermy Jacobsen's demand immediately went through the ceiling. An incensed Cyril called me at least once a day, ordering me to do something to stop this travesty because the DNA test was obviously wrong, and did I know that his wife was drinking again? I mustered as much patience as I could, but by July, I was dodging at least two of his calls for every one I took.

Ken Solberg issued his report. It could have been worse. He opined that Ralph had narcissistic personality disorder and possibly suffered from delusions because—

"You told him you were Santa's son?" I tried not to sound incredulous. "I thought that was a secret."

His unshaven cheeks reddened slightly. "He kept pushing about why I was in the house, why I'd brought gifts to total strangers. Finally, he asked if I thought I was Santa Claus, and I said, 'No, I'm his son.'" He ran his hand through his hair. "I know, I know. But he wouldn't stop. I didn't tell him anything else, though." The report stated that the defendant had refused to answer any more questions.

"Don't worry, I'll figure out something." I didn't care what questions Ralph hadn't answered as long as Solberg testified that Ralph might be nuts, but he was sincere. And harmless.

In mid-July, I deposed Victoria Leopold. Hal Zenkman's prep school roommate represented her at the deposition. The about-to-be-former Mrs. Leopold looked like every woman I'd ever seen on the walking trails at the West Hartford reservoir: silken blond hair, perfect profile, impeccable muscle tone. Every time I saw one of them jogging behind a stroller, not the slightest hint of a bulge or jiggle beneath their spandex workout garb, I felt short and flabby and fuzzy-haired.

Victoria Leopold insisted that she'd set the alarm on Christmas Eve. She testified that a week later, she walked into her living room to see Ralph with his hands on Trevor. When I pressed for details, it turned out she wasn't quite clear about where his hands were or how close their bodies were, but she firmly rejected the notion that what she'd seen was anything other than perverted and sick. She denied any knowledge of the meeting at Lizzie's, suggesting that maybe it had been her cousin Barb's idea, but she was unable to come with a reason for Barb to concoct such a scheme. And yes, she was certain her husband's absence from the marital home was temporary. "Once he gets tired of his little doctor bimbo, he'll be home," she said. "He knows how much his family needs him."

"How long were you engaging in a sexual relationship with Dr. Leopold before he divorced his first wife?" I asked.

Her delicate nostrils flared. "That wasn't the same thing. We were in love. Besides—"

"Nonresponsive. Please answer the question. How long were you and Dr. Leopold engaging in sexual relations before he and the first Mrs. Leopold were divorced?"

She glared at me until her lawyer said, "You have to answer the question."

"Two years," she spat. "But it was different. They didn't have—"

"There's no question pending." Let the little nurse bimbo get a taste now of what trial would be like. Maybe she'd rethink her strategy.

Antonio and I had tried a couple more times to discuss a plea deal, but he wouldn't budge off Ralph pleading guilty to sex four and enticing a minor, so we went to caseflow to pick a trial date. Belinda scheduled us for August, which wasn't ideal, but at least the legislature would be between sessions. With any luck, Hal Zenkman would be vacationing on the Vineyard instead of holding nightly press conferences on the courthouse steps.

At least once a week, I slogged through the rain to Granby. Not that so many visits were strictly necessary, but I told myself that keeping Ralph from becoming depressed was important. The jury needed to see him as a nice, normal guy, not a sad-sack creep. It was a mighty thin argument, though. Rather than explain to either my partners or Ralph's mother, I logged these visits as "practice development" on the firm calendar, and I only billed one visit out of four.

The question that haunted me was how to convince the jury that Ralph truly believed he was Santa's son. Any decent con man could say the right things to the court-appointed psychologist. Even if Solberg believed Ralph was sincere, that testimony would only take us so far.

"Would it help if I testified?" Ralph asked one humid morning in late July. "Obviously, I can't talk about Santa, but I can tell them what happened at Trevor's house and Brittany not driving me home and all that."

"Absolutely not." The notepad I'd brought in from the car was damp, the paper buckling, but in this hermetically sealed concrete world, you'd never guess it was practically tropical outside. The men who lived within these walls knew seasons were passing only because the calendar said so. An hour a day in the rec yard was their sole glimpse into the world where the rest of us moved freely. Ralph said once that even when it poured, the PC guys always took their rec time in the yard, just to see the sky. His voice grew wistful and trailed off, as if he was remembering nights when he and a reindeer-drawn sleigh flew through that very sky, with stars their only light.

I forced my attention back to the conversation. "If you took the stand, Antonio's first question would be, 'Have you ever touched Trevor Leopold?', and as soon as you said 'yes,' that would be the end." Casually, as if it were just occurring to me, I said, "What we really need is someone who's seen where you live and can describe it to the jury. Let's face it—nobody would set up the kind of operation you have if they didn't mean it." When he didn't respond, I spelled it out: "We need to get your family to come down here and testify."

"No." His voice was tight.

"I'm not talking about your father." Only in movies would Santa Claus arrive at court in splendid red-and-white regalia. This was real life. "What about your mother, or one of your brothers? Or even somebody like Anya or Claire?" I couldn't remember the name of the other sister-in-law.

"No way. And no elves either." *No kidding.* The last thing I needed to worry about was explaining an elf. "Nobody's coming down. Nobody's talking about what the Pole looks like or what we do there. We're not revealing the mystery of Santa just to get me out of here."

Noble, but naïve. "If you're convicted on sex four or enticing, you're probably going to be in PC for your entire sentence. That's a minimum of five years." I let that settle before I added, "They don't have to say you're Santa. They just have to say you believe you are, and they don't have to say why." It was our best shot, but it was still dicey. If Antonio asked any of the Clauses if they also believed Ralph to be Santa's son, that would be the end of their credibility.

Ralph shook his head, resolute. "The answer is no."

A knock, and the door opened. "Time," said the CO.

Saved by the bell. Ralph rose and held out his wrists so the CO could unlock the cuffs and relock Ralph's hands behind him. The CO took his arm, and Ralph didn't look back as he was led away.

Thirty-Four

"What are you going to do?" Michael took a swig of his beer. It was well past six. I'd picked up a six-pack on my way back from Granby in the hope that he'd be here.

"I can cross-examine the pseudo-nanny. Mom barely saw anything and her cousin's a liar. Carla can talk about the second letter."

"Which Antonio can claim Ralph created."

"I can trace the ISP of the emails. I already lined up Todd Vincus." Todd was our computer guru. If it weren't for him, I wouldn't even know what an ISP—an internet service provider—was, much less why it mattered.

"Could somebody fake an ISP?"

"Probably." Hackers could do practically anything. Like accessing Santa Claus websites to monitor the email traffic.

"You can't cut a deal?" Michael popped open another beer.

"Antonio's people want blood. Risk of injury, child endangerment, enticement. Sex four. He says he can get home invasion down to criminal trespass second. Like that's going to sell it."

"He's stuck on the sex crimes?" Condensation dripped off his bottle. I tossed him a tissue, but he ignored it.

"Like glue. I'm betting Zenkman's pushing that."

"Ah, yes—our future governor." Michael tipped up his bottle. Elsa sent everyone email reminders about Zenkman campaign events at least once a week. I never went.

"Maybe he wants to help dear Victoria since she's doing so much for him." Practically his only non-business talking points revolved around strengthening laws to protect children from sexual predators.

"Guess she still thinks hubby will come home if his kid's at risk."

Michael rolled his eyes. "So send the kid to live with hubby. Problem solved. I mean, how dumb is this chick?"

"The former Mrs. Doctor Leopold? Let's just say nobody's going to confuse her with a Rhodes Scholar. Never ceases to amaze me, the idiotic things women do to get philandering men to come home." I took a long drink. "Why don't men do stupid things to get women back?"

"Who says they don't?" His tone was heavy with meaning.

"What are you talking about?"

He gestured in a vaguely northern direction. "Your boyfriend Claus."

"He's not my boyfriend!" I snapped.

"So you said. But think about it. If you were in his shoes and you had people who would back up your story, wouldn't you call them? The guy's throwing away his best defense—why? Maybe it's this Secret of Santa crap, but maybe it's something else, like the fact that if he's acquitted, he has to go home to the North Pole or wherever he's really from—which is probably someplace like Jersey. With no real defense, he gets convicted and incarcerated, and he stays in Connecticut and has weekly visits with his lovely lawyer."

I sat upright, and not just because he knew about the Granby visits. "Tell me you're kidding."

"I'm not telling you a thing. I only talked to the guy once. You're the one he's in love with. You're the one who kissed him." *Ouch.* "I'm just saying—guys can do stupid things for love, just like women." He belched as he stood. "I gotta get going. You coming?"

I shook my head. "I need to think about this."

"So think at home. That way, when you fall asleep, you won't be behind the wheel."

He had a point, but then, Michael usually did.

Thirty-Five

So, here was the $64,000 question: when Antonio raised the Santa issue, how could I respond?

Answer #1: Poke holes in it as a ludicrous notion. Which it was. I mean, who the hell were we kidding? Only the nuttiest of nutty defendants would claim to be Santa or any Santa-affiliate. Insinuate that somebody else came up with that theory to make Ralph look skeevy.

Except Ralph admitted it to Ken Solberg. Scratch #1.

Answer #2: Argue that it was true, every inch of it. Ralph really was heir to the Santa throne, the North Pole existed, reindeer could fly, and everything was just as he said.

Sure, and one more thing: have Robin check on whether the Institute of Living—our local high-end loony bin—allowed pets. Because if I tried that approach, my partners would have me committed.

Answer #3: Claim it as evidence of sincerity—Ralph really thought he was Santa (or Santa's son), so he lacked malicious intent. Even if he had a website, its purpose was to make kids happy, not to entice them in a candy-cane-scented hell that would require years of therapy.

It was still our strongest argument. Our only argument, really. He might be nuts, but he truly believed he was Santa ("Santa's son!"). Didn't he bring presents?

Not bad, except for the lack of evidence. Victoria denied the existence of the mitt. No judge would let me put Trevor on the stand. And I couldn't testify about what I saw.

Lulu hopped silently onto my desk. Usually, she stretched out along the edge of my keyboard, but this time, she stepped daintily over it. After a moment of contemplation, she rubbed her cheek along mine, purring. First one side, then the other, until I took her in my arms, holding her close as she snuggled and purred. "I love you, sweet girl," I whispered. As if in response, she lifted her head, her round green-gold eyes glinting light and wisdom. "You are a work of art," I told her.

A work of art.

Like Holly's drawings.

*****

"I don't understand." Holly refilled our wineglasses. "Why do you need my sketches?"

"I can't put Ralph on the stand," I said. "And obviously, I can't testify. But somebody has to tell the jury about the Pole." Which was, after all, the reason I'd taken her along in the first place—to have a witness. "You don't have to say the place really *is* Santa's workshop. All you have to do is say you've been to Ralph's home and this is what it looked like, and show them the drawings. They'll think he's crazy as a bedbug, but that beats pedophile by a mile."

Her face paled. "You promised I wouldn't have to testify."

"I can't just put the drawings in. The rules of evidence say I need a witness to authenticate them, but don't worry, it'll be easy. I'll ask you if you've ever met Ralph. Of course, you'll say yes. I'll ask if you've ever been to his home. You'll say yes. I'll ask you to describe what you saw, and you will. I'll ask if you have any photographs or drawings, and you'll produce the ones you did. That's all. Piece of cake. Then at the end of the trial, I'll argue to the jury about how Ralph truly believes he's Santa, and they can tell because he totally lived the life, and while it's unfortunate that he got caught up in somebody else's marital issues, all he ever wanted to do was deliver presents to this kid on Christmas Eve." I contemplated my own words as I sipped my wine. This would work. I could sell this.

Holly interrupted my satisfied reverie. "But—I wasn't even supposed to make them. You heard them. No pictures."

"You didn't take photos," I pointed out. "These aren't from your Instagram account. You created art. Very, very different."

"You know what they meant. There wasn't supposed to be anything. Nobody down here is supposed to know what it looks like."

"They're not going to know it's really the North Pole," I pointed out. "They'll just know it's where this particular defendant lives. Big difference." She wasn't buying it. I tried a different tack: "If you thought it was so wrong, why did you draw at all?"

"Because . . . the place was so amazing. I felt . . . I can't explain it. It got inside me. Drawing was the only way to release it." Her gaze shifted as though she was seeing something off in the distance, something beautiful and magical.

Ordinarily, I'd have been moved by the way she described the need to create, but right now, I had more pressing issues. "Where are the drawings now?"

"Why?" Her voice was wary.

"Um—I want to see them. I've never seen the finished products." It was partially true. The more pressing point was that I needed to know how far I could rely on her sketches.

She looked dubious, but she led me down the hall to her studio. After her divorce, when we'd finally tracked down her ex and made him pay years of past-due alimony and child support, she'd used part of the money to build a studio. Other than the wall between the house and the new room, every side boasted enormous picture windows with blinds so she could adjust the light to suit her needs. Once the contractors had finished the outside and were working on the inside, she and the kids spent the summer turning the yard into a perennial garden and flagstone patio. One weekend, Holly and I rented a truck and traveled to Vermont for exactly the right type of Giverny-style bench and chairs; now, with the perennials filled in, the view from her studio looked like a Monet.

We stepped down into the studio, and she flicked on the overhead light. The north wall contained a rack of canvases on their ends, topped by a counter. Above the counter were horizontal slots for paper and supplies. From one slot, she drew several large sheets of heavy paper. Silently, she arranged them on the floor and stepped back.

"Oh, Holly. . . ." She'd transferred her pencil drawings to watercolors. Swirls of color captured the movement and energy of the workshop so vividly that I could feel it all again. One painting was a collage of the Margrethe pictures, the joy of her smile vibrant against soft washes of pastel. Another depicted the cafeteria, elves with plates piled high and steaming mugs of cocoa while in one corner, an elf family—husband, wife, and three little ones—was laughing. The finishing room, the wrapping room, the metal shop, the electronics shop—they were all here, populated with elves who focused intently on their tasks. She'd even painted Meredith Claus's office—the inner sanctum itself—with Ralph's mom smiling warmly from her desk at someone who was out of the frame except for one red-clad shoulder and a few white curls.

"These are beautiful," I breathed, the word hopelessly inadequate. I knelt to pore over them, and Holly squatted beside me, pointing out details. It was as though we were back in that world again, where laughter and dedication and joy and love were the order of the day, and the only thing that mattered was making a child happy.

My phone rang, jolting me back to the here and now. Cyril Walker, at seven-thirty on a summer evening. "Go to voicemail," I growled, flicking the button to decline the call. I got to my feet, feeling the distance from the world of the paintings increase as I straightened. "If these don't make the jury believe, nothing will."

Holly rose, her brown eyes somber. "Are you sure this is okay with Ralph?"

"I'll deal with him," I assured her. "Do you still have the drawings you did while we there?" I needed something to show Holly hadn't just created this art out of nothing.

She retrieved the sketches I'd seen her working on in our sitting room. She hadn't turned all of them into paintings. One sketch depicted the sleigh and the reindeer team, just as they'd looked that frigid December night in my office parking lot. Probably better to skip that one.

"Okay," I said. "Just make sure you keep all these safe. Jury selection starts August 6. Probably two or three days, and then we'll start evidence. I'm guessing two days for the prosecution's case, so figure somewhere around the 13th is when I'll need you." *Friday the 13th.*

She slipped the paintings into their slots. "I don't know," she said. "I don't feel right about this."

"It's all we have. If we lose, Ralph is going to spend years in prison—and not just regular prison. Have you ever heard of protected custody?" She shook her head. "That's for prisoners who can't be part of the general population for their own safety. They don't get to talk to the others, eat with them, or even hang out in the rec yard with them. It's not solitary, but it's close."

"But you said Ralph was a good prisoner and they all like him."

"Doesn't matter. Child molesters are the lowest of the low in prison, and if Ralph's convicted of anything that even hints of abusing a kid, he'll have to stay in PC or risk having the shit beaten out of him. Or worse." I met her eyes squarely. "If we don't show those pictures, and you don't testify, Ralph could end up there for years. Is that really what you want?"

"No, of course not, but—isn't that his decision?" She flicked off the light in the studio.

"Don't worry." I followed her down the hall to the kitchen. "He's a smart guy. He'll figure out that this is in his best interests. I'll prep you, and it'll be over before you know it." She carried the empty glasses into the kitchen. As she opened the dishwasher, I said, "You're going to be around, right? You're not leaving the state or anything?"

"I was thinking of going up to Tanglewood." Tanglewood was the summer home of the Boston Symphony Orchestra, nestled in the Berkshires in western Massachusetts. It was one of Holly's favorite places to escape when she needed peace and inspiration.

With any other witness, this comment might have worried me. As a commissioner of the Superior Court, my subpoena authority only reached to the Connecticut borders. As soon as a witness crossed the state line, I was powerless to compel them to appear in court. But I trusted Holly. She might not like what I was doing, but she'd never run out on me.

"Once we finish with your testimony, you can hang out with the BSO all you want. Tell the conductor I said 'hi.'" I kissed her cheek, grabbed my rain jacket, and headed out to plan my examination of my new star witness.

Thirty-Six

Two nights before jury selection began, as Robin and I were organizing my litigation bag, my cellphone rang. "Grab that, will you?" I asked, not looking up from my juror questions.

Robin unearthed it from the pile on my desk. "Hello, Marshal. Everything okay? . . . Really? Let me ask." She held her hand over the mouthpiece. "The marshal says nobody was home at Holly's. He left the subpoena by the front door. Is that okay?"

I usually preferred in-hand service so the witness couldn't deny knowledge of the subpoena, but since it was Holly, abode service was fine. "When did he serve her?"

Robin relayed the question. "An hour ago. He said the house was dark."

"Hmmm." But I wasn't concerned. She could have worked late or gone out for dinner.

"She says it's okay," Robin said into the phone. She listened for a minute, and said, "Hang on." To me, she said, "The marshal ran into a neighbor. She was picking up the mail."

The mail? I held out my hand for the phone. "Hello, Marshal, it's Meg Riley. Someone was picking up Ms. Beardsley's mail? Did you talk to them?"

"Uh-huh. She said she lived next door. I asked where Ms. Beardsley was, but she didn't know. She thought maybe the Berkshires."

A curtain of blood-red fury dropped over my eyes. Barely controlling my voice, I asked, "Did the neighbor say how long Ms. Beardsley would be gone?"

"Nope. Just said she's supposed to take in the mail until she gets home."

"Thanks, Marshal." I jabbed the *off* button so hard I broke a fingernail. "Shit!"

"What's going on?" Robin asked.

"She's dodging me." I grabbed my phone and punched in her number. Voicemail. Ditto with her cell. No surprise there: the Berkshires were infamous for lousy cell service. "I'm gonna kill her," I muttered. "Come on."

"Where?"

"To Holly's."

*****

The house was dark, just as the marshal had said. No matter: Holly and I had had keys to each other's houses as long as I could remember. Cursing under my breath, I unlocked the back door and led Robin into Holly's spotless kitchen, down the hall toward the studio.

"She did pencil drawings, and then she did watercolors from them." But the slot where the drawings had been was empty. Damn her again. I gestured toward the other end of the cubbies. "You start there. I'll start over here."

"But—"

I glared. "But what?"

"Even if we find them, Holly's the only one who can authenticate them."

"I'll figure that out later." If it came to it, I'd have Michael put me on the stand, and I'd say this was what we saw.

Except there was no need for a backup plan, because the drawings weren't in the studio. Neither were the watercolors. With a terse "Stay here!", I left Robin and searched the rest of my best friend's house and garage. I poked around in the back of closets, under beds, down in the basement with the Christmas decorations. Finally, I returned to the studio to face the truth.

The drawings and the watercolors were gone.

"I'll bet she has them with her." I snatched up her phone and called her. Let her see her own number coming up on caller ID. She'd answer that.

Except she didn't.

"Meg, maybe we should go." Robin sounded tentative and soothing, the way you might if you were suggesting to the psych patient that she shouldn't jump out the window because she can't fly.

"This is unbelievable. I cannot believe she did this." As I turned off the studio light, it hit me. "I bet she talked to him. I bet he told her what to do." My best friend and my client, in cahoots. Against me.

*****

The next morning, I was first in line at the prison. As I waited outside the guard shack in record-breaking humidity, my phone rang. Cyril Walker. I sent him to voicemail. I couldn't deal with him now.

I fumed as I waited for Ralph to arrive. He barely glanced at me while the CO unfastened and refastened his cuffs. As soon as the CO left us, I demanded, "Where's Holly?"

"I don't know." Ralph had a three-day growth of stubble and the gaunt look of someone who had spent the past several months living in a six-by-nine cell, but his green eyes glinted with defiance.

"Yes, you do." My voice was even, the ire barely suppressed.

"No, I don't." His tone matched mine.

"But you've talked to her." It wasn't a question.

"She came to see me on Sunday. She was . . . upset."

"She had no right—"

"Of course she did," he cut in. "She asked what I wanted her to do. She said if I wanted, she'd get on the stand and tell the court everything you two saw, heard, felt, smelled, and tasted, and she'd even show them the drawings and the paintings. She said it was up to me."

"Have you seen them?"

"Contraband," he reminded me. "But she told me about them." He regarded me. "You've seen them, haven't you?"

I nodded. "They're beautiful—and accurate."

"I told her I didn't want her testifying and I definitely didn't want her showing any pictures. I couldn't even imagine why there might be a question until she told me about her conversation with you." His voice had a definite edge now.

"The prosecutor is going to raise the issue. Dr. Solberg is on his witness list, which means your statement about Santa will be in evidence. If Antonio can parlay that into something like you stalking Trevor, it's all over. The only way to combat this is to tackle it head-on, tell them you truly believe you're Santa."

"I'm not Santa, I'm his son. And before you suggest it—I forbid you from testifying."

"You *forbid* me?" Of course I wouldn't testify—it was a ridiculous notion. It was the last resort of last resorts. No halfway-intelligent juror would believe a defendant's lawyer on this kind of issue. Actually, *former* lawyer, because I couldn't be both a lawyer and a witness, so if I took the stand, Michael would have to try the case. Since he was already on trial in federal court, we'd have to ask for a last-minute continuance, which, if it was granted—a result by no means guaranteed—would likely leave Ralph sitting in PC for months.

Before I could explain any of this, he said, "Yes. If you try, I'll fire you and represent myself."

"In which case you're looking at a minimum of seven years in PC," I retorted. Pro se defendants always thought they could handle their cases better than lawyers. I'd never heard of one winning.

"Maybe, but that's how it is. You will not testify. I will not testify. Holly will not testify." He sounded exactly like his mother. "I'm the client. I get to decide these things."

"I'm the lawyer," I shot back. "Deciding trial strategy is what you hired me to do—to use my experience and expertise to make decisions about how best to present your case."

"Then you leave me no choice." The sternness faded to disappointment. "Meg, you're fired." *Screw you, you're just my lawyer.* "I'll represent myself." He made the pronouncement as if it were a rational, well-reasoned decision instead of a train wreck waiting to happen.

"You can't do that." Deep breath. Calm, rational, professional.

"I can, and I will. Excuse me. I have to go prepare for trial." He sounded like a lawyer.

"Ralph, wait a minute." This had gone too far too fast. "Seriously, you can't do this. Have you ever even seen a trial?" He said nothing. "There are a thousand things you'd have to be ready for—evidentiary issues, procedural points—believe me, it took me at least my first four or five trials to have a clue what I was doing, and that was after I'd observed half a dozen—and gone to law school. You have too much at stake for this kind of a gamble." Silence. At least he wasn't arguing. "Please—don't make a decision now. Promise me you'll think about it."

He sat silently, glowering. Finally, he said, "All right, you're not fired."

I exhaled silently. I felt as though I'd been holding my breath for hours. If we weren't in a prison, I'd suggest we take a break, order lunch, do something to clear the air and our heads. But those were luxuries for free people. He was entitled to only one attorney visit per day. If either of us left now, I wouldn't see him again until tomorrow, when we met at court for jury selection. On the eve of trial, we couldn't afford to lose that time.

He stood up. "I need to think," he said. Lifting his voice, he called, "Kevin, I'm ready."

"But we're not done. We need to prepare—" The knock on the door silenced me.

"You need to prepare. I need to think." He held out his hands so the CO could remove the cuffs, refastening Ralph's hands behind him. "I'll see you tomorrow."

"Ralph—" I rose, but I couldn't think of anything to say.

The CO led him out of the room. I waited until I could no longer hear their footsteps. Then, I shoved everything back in my briefcase and went to sign out.

Thirty-Seven

"So you're not fired. At least the guy's still got a snowball's chance."

Michael had turned one of the wingback chairs around to watch me at the table. His trial settled just before the jury went out, and he was enjoying a few minutes of unexpected free time. Lulu occupied her regular seat, intent on bathing her glossy fur. Robin was sorting papers into folders with neatly-typed labels. Early evening sunlight highlighted the condensation on the beer bottles remaining in the six-pack. Life as usual for trial lawyers.

"Barely." I tipped my bottle to catch the last drops. "It wasn't a great case before, but now. . . ."

My über-patient partner stretched his legs out in front of him. "If he didn't want people to know about his claim to Santahood, why did he tell the arresting officers he was Ralph Claus? Why didn't he use some other name? You said he wasn't carrying ID, and the prints didn't turn anything up. He could have called himself Ralph Smith—or whatever his real name is."

"He says it never occurred to him to lie. Swears up and down that's his real name. But you're right—the identity thing may be an issue. He doesn't have a social security number—at least, not under Claus. No military record, no credit history. Even the IRS has never heard of him. As far as anybody can tell, until he got arrested, this guy never existed."

"At least not under this name," Michael said. "I assume nothing came up when they ran his prints?"

"Totally clean. Antonio hasn't made a thing of the identity issue other than the Santa part, so I'm letting it lie." Not that it mattered.

If the jury decided that Ralph had groped Trevor Leopold, they wouldn't care whether he was an international con man or a home-grown pedophile.

The phone rang. Robin answered it, then held her hand over the mouthpiece. "Cyril Walker."

I'd dodged him three times since yesterday. I took the receiver. "Good evening, Cyril. I'm so sorry I've missed your calls, but I'm preparing for trial. What can I do for you?"

"That idiot lawyer subpoenaed my wife!"

"He did what?" I gestured to Robin to get me a separate legal pad. Michael snagged one more beer and slipped out of the room.

"He subpoenaed her! He wants to take her deposition!"

Just what I didn't need. I knew why Hermy wanted her. His client claimed her affair with Cyril lasted for more than two years before he fired her, including weekends away, overnights at her apartment, and a week-long trip to Italy for which she produced photographs of the two of them in a variety of romantic locales. Hermy undoubtedly wanted the wife to talk about all the times Cyril hadn't been home. I suspected his investigator had dug up dirt on her stints in rehab, and he intended to link those dates to Cyril's dalliances. Hermy played rough.

I did my best to calm Cyril down. I promised to call Hermy to see if there was some other way to handle the matter. Cyril demanded that I sue him. I explained that Hermy hadn't actually done anything illegal or unethical. The rules of practice allowed him to depose any witness he liked, and it would be difficult, if not impossible, to block or limit the kind of questions I anticipated. "Just say she has health issues," he said. When I said I'd need documentation, he retorted that I'd have a note from her gynecologist in the morning. He hung up before I respond.

Robin waited a few seconds before asking, "Everything okay?"

"Peachy." Deep breath. At moments like this, I envied those who practiced yoga. Serenity seemed impossibly far away.

As far away as the North Pole.

Lulu stood and stretched, arching her back. With enviable lightness, she hopped down from her chair, stretched some more, and sauntered over to her food dish. The reassuring familiarity of crunching kibble soothed my frazzled mind, easing it back toward sanity and calm.

The beep of the intercom pierced my bubble of peace. I reached over and pushed the button so the caller would be on speaker. "Yes?"

"Did Cyril Walker reach you?" Elsa was never one for small talk within the firm. Conversations among partners were not billable.

"Yes," I said in my best *why on earth are you asking* voice. "I didn't expect you to be here this late."

She ignored the jab. "He called me. He's very upset. You haven't returned his calls."

With monumental effort, I maintained a civil tone. "The man calls to rant at least twice a day. I don't have that kind of time to waste."

"I understand completely, but that's how he is. I don't have to tell you how important the Walker business is to the firm."

"And yet, you keep doing it," I snapped. "Look, if you'd rather handle his case, go right ahead." Robin slipped out of the room, closing the door behind her.

"Oh, for heaven's sake." Elsa did not swear. She considered it déclassé. "Listen to me, Meg. The client is not happy. He says you haven't been responsive. I told you at the start, this guy needs to be handled with kid gloves. He's the reason we're getting the CBC. We owe him our best."

"We owe all our clients our best," I retorted. "Regardless of whether they're big-time money makers. I don't prioritize my cases based on which clients generate the most fees."

"Obviously."

"I beg your pardon?"

"I just saw the month-end report for July. Your Claus case has a rather large unpaid balance, and there doesn't seem to be a trial retainer." The receiver fairly vibrated with smugness.

I logged into the firm's internal communication system. Lucy Jane had uploaded the month-end report that morning. A significant portion of Cyril Walker's hefty retainer remained in our clients' funds account, meaning that I could do work on that file and be assured of immediate payment on issuance of the bill.

"Is there anything else? I need to prepare for trial."

"I just wanted to be sure you and Cyril had connected." Her voice was smooth again. She clicked off without saying goodbye.

Thirty-Eight

Five days later. Less than twenty-four hours before evidence began. We had our jury. We were as ready as possible. And nobody was happy.

Ralph sat across from me in lockup, waiting for the judicial marshals to take him back to Foster. His mouth was tense, his eyes downcast.

Holly was still incommunicado. It took all my restraint not to send Russ Carsten to the Berkshires to find her. Carla could testify about the email to Santa, but on cross, she'd have to admit that all she saw was the printout and yes, anybody with minimal word processing skills could have created it—and no, she knew nothing about Ralph's computer expertise. I'd try to get Ken Solberg to say Ralph seemed to be sincere in his delusion, but without Holly, the case hung on whether the jury thought a criminal defendant would lie to the court-appointed psychologist.

At least Ralph had made a good impression on our jurors. Meredith Claus had sent down trial clothes by way of Charles. She'd also sent payment on the outstanding bill, thank God, so I didn't have my partners on my back about our hard-and-fast rule that you never went to trial with an unpaid balance. On the other hand, I still had unbilled trial prep time because I hadn't figured out how to handle all those prison visits, which meant I had no retainer, which meant Elsa and Roy were having conniptions. So I focused on logistics: "Do you need money for razor blades or shaving cream?"

"I'm all set. How long for the trial?"

We'd had this conversation before, but clients always wanted to hear the plan one more time. "With the prosecution's witness list and ours, three or four days. We'll probably rest on Monday."

"And then what?"

"Closing arguments. Jury charges. They'll deliberate, and they'll come back with the verdict, but that's not necessarily the end. We can file post-verdict motions, and if we don't like how those turn out, we can appeal."

"You mean, if we lose." It wasn't a question, but I nodded. "How long would that take?"

"The motions? Not that long. A couple months, maybe. Appeals take a lot longer. It can take a year to get to oral argument, and six months after that for a decision. Then there's always the option of the losing side petitioning to have state supreme court hear it."

I could see him calculating. "So this could take another three years."

"Probably not that long. More like two."

"Would I be inside all that time?"

Another tough question. "Obviously, we'd try to get you released while the appeal was pending, but if the court said 'no'—yeah, you'd be in."

His eyes narrowed as though he was doing math. "So I could be sentenced to five years, and if they give me credit for time already served, by the time we got through all the appeals and got a decision saying I shouldn't have been convicted in the first place, I'd already have served almost all the time for crimes I didn't commit." His voice sounded rough, almost bitter.

"That's one way to look at it, but don't forget—you could be acquitted, and it could all be over soon."

He gave a short, harsh bark of a laugh. "Seriously, Meg. What do you think the odds are? If you were in Vegas, what would you say?"

"With this many charges? I'd say odds of the prosecution hitting on something are better than fifty-fifty." His jaw clenched. "But depending on which charge, it might not mean jail time. If it's one of the original charges, that could mean no time, or time already served."

"But if it's one of the sex charges. . . ." The words were barely audible.

"Then you'd be looking at time." We'd discussed all this *ad nauseum* over the past few months. Clients tended to fixate on one particular aspect of a case, bringing it up over and over even though I always told them the same thing. It was as if they thought asking one more time might cause the answer to change.

But it never did.

*****

The next morning found Robin and me in a near-empty courtroom, unpacking documents and devices while the court marshal fiddled with his phone. As always, I set up my headquarters at the right-hand counsel table, the one closest to the jury; I sat in the left-hand chair, closest to the center of the room, with Robin at the far right and Ralph between us. My peerless paralegal graciously spared me the hassle of crawling under the table to plug in the power strip that enabled us to keep our various electronics functioning, including her laptop, the charger for my tablet, and the chargers for both our smartphones. We arranged the folders containing exhibits on my corner of the table for easy access. The research, deposition transcripts and discovery responses remained neatly organized in the storage boxes parked next to Robin's chair. The relevant pleadings and reports, together with all my notes, were behind color-coded tabs in the trial notebook. We were almost ready.

"Try her again," I muttered as I reviewed my opening statement yet again. I never used notes when I addressed the jury.

Robin picked up my phone and texted Holly for the umpteenth time. Not that I expected a response, of course; the artist formerly known as my best friend had vanished like a wisp of smoke. Neither she nor the drawings had returned to her house, which I knew because I'd hired one of the Michael's motorcycle buddies, Al Denby, to set up a motion-sensitive camera trained on her garage door with a feed to his computer. Al reported in regularly, and all reports were the same: no activity, save for the woman who picked up Holly's mail every evening.

At three minutes after ten, a knock came from the other side of the door behind the bench. "All rise," intoned the courtroom marshal. We rose, and Judge Mwangi entered. She was tall and regal, with short, tight gray curls and sharp brown eyes that missed nothing. The marshal opened court, and the judge asked if there were any preliminary matters before she brought the jury in: in other words, had we reached a deal so that she could send everybody home? *No such luck, Your Honor.*

Judge Mwangi instructed the marshal to bring in the defendant. He left the room, returning moments later with Ralph, who looked damned good. Lucky for us, since jurors are more likely to trust an attractive defendant. His suit was charcoal gray wool, the shirt crisp white, the tie deep green with a tiny pattern. He stood straight and dignified, as impeccably groomed as if he'd come from a barber's chair instead of a holding cell. The marshal escorted him to his chair between us at counsel table. Before he sat, Ralph said, "Good morning, Your Honor." The judge looked slightly startled, but she said only, "Good morning, Mr. Claus." The marshal removed the shackles with a low warning that he'd be right behind us.

"Don't address the judge directly," I whispered. "You're represented." His mouth tensed, but he nodded.

Judge Mwangi said to the clerk, "You may bring in the jury." In accordance with longstanding tradition, everyone rose as the door to the jury room opened and our sixteen chosen ones—twelve jurors, plus four alternates—entered.

The jury didn't look particularly . . . anything. Not bored, excited, annoyed, determined, impatient, energetic, exhausted, or even interested. Jurors rarely were. Occasionally, there might be a civic-minded citizen or a *Law and Order* addict, but most jurors were here only because they'd failed to get out of serving. I hoped their apathy would slide into hostility toward the state since Antonio had the longer list of witnesses, but they might just as easily resent Ralph for committing the crime that was interfering with their beach plans or tee times.

Antonio's opening statement was a blizzard of Santa references and not much else. When it was my turn, I rose. On my instruction, none of us had looked at Antonio during his opening statement. Now, Robin and Ralph turned to watch me as I approached the jury.

"Ladies and gentlemen," I began. "On behalf of Mr. Claus and myself, I thank you for your willingness to serve on this jury." I always said this even though everybody knew willingness had had precious little to do with it. "You've heard the state talk a lot about Santa Claus, as if that's the central issue in this case. I'd like to discuss what you *didn't* hear from the state and what you will hear during this trial. For example, you haven't heard about how the Leopold house has an alarm system that never went off on the night in question. Victoria Leopold is going to tell you that Mr. Claus was in the house without permission, but she won't be able to explain how he could have gotten in without triggering the alarm. Chris Nelson of Triple-A Alarms, who installed and monitors the system, will tell you how he came out on December 26 and inspected the entire house and the alarm system, and he found all the contacts and locks and everything intact and working fine. At the end, after you've heard all this evidence, it will be up to you to decide whether the state has proven beyond a reasonable doubt that Ralph Claus broke into the Leopold house, as opposed to being granted access by someone authorized to allow him to enter."

I paused to let them digest this. Juror #5, a sallow young woman with dirty-blond hair, was ogling Ralph. Juror #2, an elderly Hispanic man, looked skeptical. Juror #11, a red-cheeked older woman who looked like the stereotypical Mrs. Claus, frowned at Antonio as if he'd lied to her.

I highlighted other issues with the state's case, credibility chief among them. I knew better than to promise too much—if I mentioned something that did not come to pass, Antonio would point it out in closing argument, and it would color the jury's assessment of whatever I said. Still, by the time I sat down, I felt reasonably confident that I'd distracted them from the Santa angle for a few minutes. With any luck, the jury would end up seeing the whole case as a big mess of *he said/she said*.

Victoria Leopold testified first. Antonio led her through the "terrifying" experience of being awakened in the middle of the night by her little boy's scream and running downstairs to find a man dressed entirely in black in her living room. "Do you see that man in this room?" Antonio asked.

"Yes." Her voice quavered slightly. *Nice coaching, Antonio.*

"Please identify the man who broke into your house."

"Objection," I said. "There's no evidence that anyone entered the witness's house without permission."

"Sustained," said Judge Mwangi. "Attorney Antonio, please rephrase."

"Of course, Your Honor," said Antonio. "Ms. Leopold, please identify the man you saw in your living room on December 24 of last year."

"He's sitting right there at that table, next to that woman lawyer." She pointed at Ralph.

"Let the record reflect that Ms. Leopold has identified the defendant, Ralph Claus," said Antonio. Juror #4, a middle-aged man in a plaid shirt, nodded with satisfaction that at least one part of this trial comported with his television experience. Antonio continued, "Ms. Leopold, have you ever given this man permission to enter your home?"

"Never!" she gasped in almost-convincing horror.

From there, Antonio went on to the day when Ralph, Trevor, and the pseudo-nanny met at Lizzie's. Over my objections, she testified that she heard voices, walked into the living room, and saw Ralph with his arms around Trevor. She admitted that she couldn't see Trevor's face when Ralph was holding him, but when Trevor turned to her, he had tears on his face. "He was holding my little boy *very* close," she said, shuddering. "Much closer than a normal person would have."

I was on my feet. "Your Honor, I move to strike the last comment. The witness has no way of knowing how a quote-unquote 'normal' person would hug a child who was so upset he was crying. All she can know is how she would do it. Just because she might keep the child at arm's length doesn't mean that's what 'normal' people would do."

"And counsel's assuming facts not in evidence," Antonio retorted. "Ms. Leopold hasn't testified that the child was already upset when the defendant touched him."

"She admits she wasn't in the room," I said. "So she has no way of disputing whether his crying and being upset was the reason Mr. Claus hugged him."

"We're getting off the point," said the judge. "The comment about 'normal people' is stricken. Both counsel are advised to refrain from testifying in their objections. Mr. Antonio, do you have much more? It's eleven-thirty, and unless you're about to wrap up your direct, this would be a good time for our morning break." Antonio indicated that he had a fair bit more, and the judge banged her gavel and declared court in recess.

After the break, Antonio shifted gears, asking Victoria Leopold about her marriage. Suddenly I was on alert. I passed a note to Robin: *get her deposition.* Just as Robin withdrew the transcript from the box, Antonio asked, "Were you hoping that your husband would come over on Christmas Eve?"

"Yes." Her voice was soft.

"Did you do—or maybe refrain from doing—anything to facilitate a visit?"

"Yes."

"What did you do or not do?"

"I—I left a voicemail for Rob, asking if he'd be coming over. He's always been really bad at remembering the alarm code, and I didn't want him waking Trevor up, so—I didn't set it."

Bingo. Robin seized the transcript and flipped through the pages.

Most of the jury was watching Antonio, but two jurors seemed interested in what was going on at our table. With a smidgen of feigned confusion, Antonio said, "But didn't you say earlier in this case that you always set the alarm?"

"Well—yes," she admitted. Antonio moved closer to the jury box so that when she looked at him, the jurors could see her lovely face. Clearly, I'd underestimated Antonio's directorial skills.

"And now you're saying you didn't? I don't understand. Please explain." Such a gentleman.

She bit her lip. "I was embarrassed," she said in a breathy little-girl voice which, in my opinion, was overkill. "I mean—what kind of woman would leave her house open in the hope that her husband would leave his mistress to come back to her? I didn't want to admit I was that pathetic. I mean, it's hard enough that he's been cheating on me and he's breaking up our family for that—*person*." The contempt with which she spat out the reference to Katrina Damdar was so intense that she might as well have used the word we all knew she meant. Then, she caught herself. "I wanted to be the kind of woman who would hold her head high and tell him that if he didn't respect me, he should just get out, but the truth is—I love him. I want our family to be together. So I made it easier for him to come home. I unlocked the side door—that's the one he always used—and I didn't set the alarm." She turned to face the jury squarely for her final statement: "But instead of Rob, I found a total stranger in my living room. I'm just glad that man never had a chance to do anything, like steal anything—or worse."

Robin passed me the police report which included Victoria's statement that all the doors were locked and the alarm was set. I could cross-examine, but if the jury bought her self-serving performance, I'd just lost one of my strongest arguments.

*****

I went for blood. Her performance on direct notwithstanding, Victoria Leopold wasn't a crier. I saw it at her deposition: whenever I confronted or contradicted her, she got angry. It was time to let the jury see how she tried manipulate them.

I started by asking her if she remembered the oath she'd taken that morning. When she conceded this, I turned to the page of her deposition where I asked her about the alarm, and I asked her to read aloud the section I'd marked during the break.

240 / P. Jo Anne Burgh

"Look, I told you—I was embarrassed—"

"Just read it, please."

In a rapid monotone, she read, "'Did you set the alarm before going to bed on Christmas Eve? Yes. Are you certain? Yes. Is there any chance you forgot to set it? No.'" She looked up at me. "See, I didn't think—I meant—"

"There's no question pending, Ms. Leopold." I took the deposition back. "When you were deposed in July, you were certain you set the alarm. Now, a month later, you're certain you didn't. Both times, you were under oath, which means you'd sworn to tell the truth." I went for the ultimate cliché question: "Tell us, Ms. Leopold: were you lying then, or are you lying now?"

"Objection! Argumentative!" Antonio was on his feet almost before the words were out of my mouth.

"Sustained," said the judge. "Counsel, you may rephrase."

"Yes, Your Honor. Ms. Leopold, when you swore to tell the truth at your deposition, and then you testified under oath that you were certain you set the alarm, were you telling the truth?"

"You don't understand—"

"Yes or no, Ms. Leopold."

"No," she snapped. Not a hint of the victim now.

I pushed harder. "I beg your pardon? I didn't hear you, Ms. Leopold. When you testified under oath at your deposition that you'd set the alarm, were you telling the truth?"

"Objection! Asked and answered!" Antonio knew what I was doing.

"Sustained." Judge Mwangi glanced at me.

"To clarify—are you saying no, you weren't telling the truth at your deposition even though you'd sworn to tell the truth?" Out of the corner of my eye, I saw Antonio start to rise, then drop back.

"Yes." The venom was coming out.

"'Yes' as in 'that's correct'?"

"Yes. That's. Correct." She was maintaining control, but barely.

I sauntered back to my table for no reason except to let her stew. I stood still a moment as if thinking. Robin remained appropriately expressionless, but Ralph looked at me as if to say, *Enough.*

Not hardly. I turned back to the stand. "Ms. Leopold, you took exactly the same oath today that you took at your deposition, didn't you?"

"I don't remember the exact words." *You idiot*, her tone implied.

"Well, then, let's review. You swore to tell the truth today, correct?"

"—Yes."

"The truth, the whole truth, and nothing but the truth, so help you God or under penalty of perjury?" Our politically correct oath didn't have the punch of the old one, where you'd land on "God" with a solid thunk and the threat of damnation hanging in the air like a morning fog.

"I believe so."

I turned to the first page of her deposition testimony and handed her the transcript. "Would you please read the first paragraph?"

In a rapid monotone, she read, "Victoria Leopold, called as a witness, having first been duly sworn to tell the truth, the whole truth, and nothing but the truth, so help her God or under penalty of perjury, testified as follows."

I gave her words a moment to resonate before I said, "Isn't it true that you took precisely the same oath at your deposition that you took today, and yet you're now telling us that the testimony you gave at your deposition was false?"

"Yes." She bit off the word. Her cheeks were flushed, her eyes like fire. If we'd been alone, she probably would have bitch-slapped me.

"Thank you." I handed the transcript back to Robin. Juror #3, a thin young black woman with red curls and round purple glasses, was glaring at Victoria. Mission accomplished.

*****

The rest of the day proceeded predictably. Barb Landon testified about Ralph and Trevor at Lizzie's. On cross, she admitted that her stepdaughter had been with them. She had no choice; her own employees were on the witness list, and she didn't pay them enough to commit perjury.

Barb's testimony took so little time that we were able to start with Brittany, who said Victoria had asked her to babysit. When she arrived at the house, Trevor told Brittany they were supposed to meet a friend at the park. Victoria was busy on the computer, and Brittany didn't interrupt her. Victoria's SUV had a child seat in the back, so she used that car to drive to the park. She expected to meet a child Trevor's age. She was surprised that the "friend" was a grown man. Yes, she had Victoria's cell number. No, she didn't call her. No, she didn't know Ralph was the person who'd been arrested at the Leopold house on Christmas Eve.

"What conversation took place while you were at Lizzie's with Trevor and the defendant?" Antonio asked. My objection that this called for a hearsay response was overruled.

"Trevor was upset. He kept talking about how mean his mom was to have Santa Claus arrested. The guy told Trevor not to worry, that everything would be okay. He bought us all hot chocolate."

"Did you know the man you were meeting was the same person Ms. Leopold had had arrested on Christmas Eve?"

"Not until later. He just said his name was Ralph. The only one who was talking about Santa Claus was Trevor."

It was clearly not what Antonio had anticipated. "Did there come a time when you learned how the meeting had been arranged?"

"Yes," Brittany said. "I saw an email from Trevor."

"From Trevor to whom?"

"Objection," I said again. "She's testifying about a document that's not in evidence, and her response is based on hearsay. Also, since the boy was six years old, the chances that he wrote it are pretty slim, so we're talking about a document authored by someone who hasn't even been identified."

The judge said, "Sustained on the first ground." I could tell she wanted to know if he was going to introduce this email. I knew the jury had the same question. Everybody's interest was piqued now.

With a flourish, Antonio produced a piece of paper and asked to approach the witness. "Is this the email you saw?"

"Yes." *As if she'd have said anything else.*

"Are you certain?"

"Yes."

"How can you be so sure?"

She pointed to the paper. "'Cause it has peanut butter on it. When I saw it, it was sitting on the kitchen table, and Trevor was having lunch. He had a peanut butter sandwich."

"Your Honor, I'd like to introduce this document as State's Exhibit 1." He trotted over to my table to show it to me, as per the requirements.

"Objection," I said, rising. "It's hearsay and there's no proper foundation—neither the author nor the recipient has identified it."

"We're not claiming it for the truth of the matters asserted," said Antonio, parroting the standard response to a hearsay objection.

"We're not saying TheSantaClaus.xyz is the defendant's website. We're just saying that this is the email that led to the meeting between Trevor and the defendant."

"I move to strike the reference to the website," I said. Too little, too late. The expression on Antonio's face showed he knew it, too. Creep.

"Overruled," said the judge. "Counsel, approach." We moved close to the bench so the jury couldn't hear us. To Antonio, she said, "Are you planning to bring in the child to testify?"

"We don't need to," said Antonio. "This witness can identify the document by its stain."

"But the contents—" I began.

"Do we need to have full argument?" Judge Mwangi asked. "If so, this should be on the record, and we'll need to send the jury out." She didn't say it in an ominous way, but we both fell silent. Lawyers tried to avoid sending the jury out. Not only was it time-consuming, but jurors resented the notion that they were missing something. Inevitably, when I talked to the jurors after the verdict, they wanted to know about all the juicy things that had been discussed while they were out of the room.

"I've stated the grounds of my objection," I said. "Hearsay and lack of foundation. I don't need to say more."

The ball landed with a plunk in Antonio's court. Gamely, he said, "I've stated the basis for admitting the evidence."

The judge regarded us approvingly. Her Honor liked a brisk trial. "Step back," she said, and we returned to our tables. "Objection overruled. The document may come in as a full exhibit."

"Thank you, Your Honor," Antonio and I said in almost perfect unison. It was a matter of courtroom protocol that you thanked the judge no matter what the ruling turned out to be. Often, it felt hypocritical: *thanks for kicking me in the teeth, Your Honor.*

Antonio pulled out his blow-up of the email, printed on foamcore and big enough for the jurors to read when he propped it on a chair in front of the jury box. The old-school approach still had advantages: that big foamcore exhibit would be sitting in the room when the jurors deliberated. Antonio asked Brittany to read the exhibit aloud, which meant the jury heard and saw how Trevor had written to Santa and asked him to come to his aunt's restaurant, Lizzie's Café. Brittany testified that she always took Trevor there because her stepmother

244 / P. Jo Anne Burgh

would "comp" whatever they ordered. When an order was comped, there was no bill.

"But on this day, there was a bill, wasn't there?" I asked when it was time to cross-examine her.

"Um . . . I don't remember."

I strode over to counsel table and snatched the piece of paper Robin was holding out. "Would it refresh your recollection if I showed you the bill from that afternoon?"

"Objection! Leading!"

Duh. One of the perks of cross-examination was that you got to lead the witness. Antonio knew there wasn't a chance of his objection being sustained; this one was for the jury, so they'd think I was doing something underhanded. Judge Mwangi said, "Overruled," in a slightly bored voice.

I handed the bill to Brittany. "Does this refresh your recollection about whether there was a bill for the refreshments consumed by you, Trevor, and Mr. Claus at Lizzie's?"

"Um . . . yes."

"But this was unusual, wasn't it? I mean, getting a bill when you and Trevor were at your stepmother's restaurant. Didn't you just say she always comped your refreshments?"

"I guess—maybe 'cause none of us knew this guy, so she charged."

"She charged you and Trevor because she didn't know the person you were with? Does she usually charge you if you bring a guest?"

"Um . . . no."

I introduced the bill; Antonio didn't object. I wasn't certain why I wanted it, except to show that the prosecution's witnesses couldn't keep their stories straight. It wasn't much, but this trial wasn't going to be won by a single knock-out blow. It would be more like being nibbled to death by mice.

Thirty-Nine

Ralph was uncharacteristically quiet the next morning. I waited for him to mention how impressed he was at my vigorous defense, but his eyes had a faraway look. Around mid-morning, I turned to see him frowning. I caught his eye and shook my head ever so slightly to let him know he needed to neutralize his expression. At the break, I explained in a low voice, "Look, I know you don't like this, but it's how trial works. We have to discredit the other side. We have to make the jury doubt them, and maybe even dislike them."

"I know," he said. "But—"

"But nothing. Whatever you do, you can't let the jury see you looking upset. In their minds, the only reason for a defendant to be upset is if he's guilty." He bit his lower lip, eyes downcast, and I raised my voice slightly. "I told you before—this is theater. Even though you don't have any lines, you're the star of the show. The jury has to love you. They have to root for you. Which means they have to see Antonio and his bunch as the bad guys."

"I'll behave." His voice was heavy, as though he were doing me a cumbersome favor.

I tamped down a quick flare of anger. All I was asking was that he act in his own best interests. If he didn't want to help me defend him, he could spend another few years in prison.

After the break, Antonio called Dr. Solberg to the stand. The court-appointed psychologist testified that Ralph had said he was the son of Santa Claus and was at the Leopolds' to deliver presents. When Solberg testified that this meant Ralph appeared to suffer from narcissistic personality disorder as well as possible delusional tendencies, Antonio turned to the jury with a Cheshire-cat grin. It was all I could do not to object on the grounds that the smarmy little prosecutor was an asshole with some narcissistic tendencies of his own.

But Antonio wasn't finished. He squinted at the report as if he'd never seen it before, and then he affected a confused expression. "Just so we're clear, Doctor—are you saying the defendant actually believes he's Santa Claus?" One of the jurors tittered. Beside me, Ralph was stone-faced.

"I'm not privy to what any person actually believes," Dr. Solberg said. "I can only make assessments of what's likely, based on what they say and how they say it—are they looking me in the eye, are they shifting or squirming, are their voices higher when they speak of a particular topic. And I'm not saying I can't be duped by a skilled liar. It's happened a few times over the years." He seemed unembarrassed by this confession.

"But you said he has delusions," Antonio said, snatching away my first cross-examination question. "Doesn't that mean he thinks this Santa Claus thing is true?"

"I said he has *possible* delusional tendencies," Dr. Solberg corrected him. "That means it's possible that he might believe what he told me. On the other hand, he could be making it all up. The elements of his story were consistent, which can indicate that he believes it to be true, but it could also be a well-planned scam. What I find more significant is that certain aspects of his story do not comport with the classic myth. His name, for instance. If he were truly invested in the delusion, I would have expected him to say his name was Nicholas as in Saint Nicholas, or Kris as in Kris Kringle. No one's ever heard of Ralph Claus." A juror snickered. Ralph remained motionless. Antonio smirked as his star witness went in for the kill: "Discrepancies like that tend to be red flags indicating that the individual may have delusional tendencies, but he does not actually believe his own delusion."

Never one to leave a dead horse unbeaten, Antonio asked, "What are you saying, Doctor? In layman's terms, please."

"In my professional opinion, this defendant probably doesn't believe he's Santa Claus."

Finally, it was my turn. As Antonio had done with Victoria Leopold, I walked deliberately toward the far end of the jury box. There, I faced the witness so that when he spoke to me, he'd be speaking directly to the jury.

"Dr. Solberg." My voice rang out in the courtroom. "Isn't it true that your assessment and diagnosis of Mr. Claus are based on the fact that you don't believe he could be telling the truth?"

"Objection, vague," said Antonio.

"Sustained," said Judge Mwangi.

Fine. "Dr. Solberg. You testified that you drew certain conclusions about Mr. Claus's psychological condition, correct?"

"Correct."

"Is it fair to say that you don't believe he could be the son of Santa Claus?" The two jurors next to me chuckled slightly, but Juror No. 2 was watching Ralph.

Dr. Solberg maintained a pleasant, detached expression, but the corners of his mouth twitched. "That's a fair statement."

"Is it that you don't believe his statements, or you don't believe his premise?"

His mouth stilled. "I'm not certain I understand."

"Let's break it down. Mr. Claus told you that he is the son of Santa. To accept such a statement, one must accept the existence of Santa Claus as a first premise. In your opinion, is that premise valid?"

"What?" His eyebrows bunched together. He knew what I was asking.

I returned to the table to get my highlighted copy of Solberg's report, avoiding Ralph's gaze. I approached Dr. Solberg, report in hand. "Dr. Solberg, is it fair to say that, in your opinion, Mr. Claus's statement is not factually true? That he is *not* the son of the Santa Claus?"

Dr. Solberg shifted slightly in his seat. He was a veteran of many courtroom skirmishes, but I was willing to bet he'd never before been asked to opine on whether a criminal defendant was of the line and lineage of a purportedly mythical figure.

"In forming my opinions, I relied on a number of things," he said.

"One of which was Mr. Claus's statement that he is the son of Santa Claus?"

"Yes."

"And so my question to you, Doctor, is: do you believe that statement to be accurate?" I didn't have to turn to know that every eye in the room was on me.

"As I said, he has possible delusional tendencies."

"Move to strike," I said to the judge. "Nonresponsive. I ask that the witness be instructed to answer the question he's been asked."

"Granted. Dr. Solberg, please answer the question Attorney Riley is posing."

"I ask that counsel repeat the question," Antonio piped up. I knew he didn't need to hear it again. He wanted the jury to hear it. So did I.

"The question is whether the witness believes Mr. Claus's statement to be accurate. To be clear, Dr. Solberg, I'm not interested for the moment in your opinion of Mr. Claus's sincerity. I'm interested in whether you believe that his statement could reasonably be factually correct."

Dr. Solberg's eyes shifted to the jury. "No."

"And why is that?"

"Because Santa Claus does not exist."

I remained very still, allowing his statement of disbelief to resonate. Just as the judge opened her mouth to tell me to move on, I said, "How do you know that?"

"Objection!" Antonio was on his feet. "Counsel is turning this trial into a circus!"

I turned to the judge. "Your Honor, may I be heard?"

Judge Mwangi regarded me. "Briefly."

I moved toward the bench. Drama was fine during witness interrogation, but not for addressing the judge. "Your Honor, Dr. Solberg comes to this case with a bias. His opinions about Mr. Claus are premised upon his disbelief of Mr. Claus's statement about his parentage. Simply put, he believes it is impossible for that statement to be true. The defense is entitled to examine the basis of that disbelief. If, as I suspect, Dr. Solberg's position is based on hearsay and speculation, rather than on any observable fact or personal experience, this calls his entire opinion about Mr. Claus into question, and the prosecution's reliance on that position is likewise questionable."

"Counsel is making a mockery of these proceedings," Antonio said. "Everybody knows there's no such thing as Santa Claus."

"Your Honor, if the state wishes to undertake the burden of proving the nonexistence of Santa Claus, that is their decision." I could tell Judge Mwangi was itching to ask whether I intended to try to prove that Santa Claus did exist, but she would never inquire about a lawyer's trial strategy.

"Your Honor, are they seriously talking about proving that Santa Claus exists?" Antonio knew no such delicacy.

"The state appears to have forgotten that the defendant doesn't have to prove anything," I retorted. "However, the state is relying on Dr. Solberg's opinions. In so doing, I submit that the state has assumed the burden of proving, at a minimum, that there exists a legitimate factual basis for those opinions—which means the defense is entitled to explore, among other things, whether Dr. Solberg's belief has any basis in objective fact."

The corners of the judge's mouth turned up ever so slightly. "I'll allow it. Objection overruled."

"Thank you, Your Honor." I turned to Dr. Solberg. "Doctor, how do you know there's no Santa Claus? Because you've never seen him?"

"That's only part of it." His voice was smooth and professional, inviting trust. "Mankind has always relied on myths to make sense of the world. The ancients had elaborate mythologies to explain everything from weather events to personal misfortunes. But—" he raised his voice slightly as if to keep me from interrupting "—the difference between a belief and a disorder depends on how one responds to the myth."

"Your Honor, I move to strike this testimony as nonresponsive," I said. "Dr. Solberg has been asked a simple question about his own belief, and he's responding with a speech about ancient history."

"I'll allow it," said Judge Mwangi. "Doctor, please answer the question that's been asked."

He smiled at Judge Mwangi. He'd been in her courtroom at least as many times as I had, and he likely knew exactly how far he could push that particular envelope. "My position about Santa Claus is based on a number of things," he said. "First, I've never seen him. Sec—"

"Do you believe in God?" I interrupted.

"Objection! She has to let the witness answer!" Antonio said. "And she can't ask about his religious beliefs."

"I'm only asking because his first point is that he doesn't believe in Santa because he hasn't seen him, so I need to explore what else he may or may not believe on the basis of what he's seen."

"Sustained as to the interruption. The witness may complete his answer before counsel asks another question."

"Seeing isn't always necessary to believing, at least for me," Dr. Solberg said. "If my only basis for not believing in Santa was that I've never seen him, I doubt I'd take a position one way or the other. But I have other reasons. The myth itself, for example. It's not just about the existence of a person. It's about what that person supposedly does—going down chimneys, riding in a sleigh pulled by flying reindeer, traveling around the entire world in a single night, living at a location where there's no land mass. When all these impossibilities are attributed to a person no one has ever seen, the logical conclusion is that the person probably doesn't exist."

"Isn't it possible for people to create stories and legends about a real person?"

"It's possible, but in the case of Santa, there's no counterbalance. On one hand, you have all the myths and legends, and on the other you have ... nothing. No reliable historical documents, no eyewitness accounts, nothing to substantiate the notion that this person is alive and well today. We know there was once a man named St. Nicholas. Popular lore apparently converted this good, generous individual into some sort of mythological figure who can do impossible tasks, but there's no basis for a conclusion that St. Nicholas was anything other than mortal man possessed of a generous nature. No contemporaneous writings suggest that he had any magical powers. As a psychologist who must employ rational thought and scientific methodology in his assessments, the notion that Santa Claus is not only alive today, but has a son who is sitting in this courtroom, is a premise I cannot accept. To the extent Mr. Claus claims this to be so, I must conclude that he is either deluded or lying."

I scanned Solberg's report. It stated that Ralph had declined to describe his home or provide any information about Santa other than his relationship. But I couldn't end on this note. I squinted at the paper as though seeing something in the report that helped. "Hypothetically, Doctor—if you believed Santa Claus does exist, would that change any of your conclusions?"

He looked startled, as though he hadn't expected the question. I hadn't expected it myself. At least to me, it stank of desperation.

"I'm not sure I understand." Obviously stalling.

"Your assessment of Mr. Claus is based on the premise that he cannot be related to Santa Claus. You classify his statements on this subject as evidencing either delusion or falsehood because in your personal, subjective opinion—" I paused to let the adjectives sink in "—that Santa Claus doesn't exist. What I'm asking is this: if he said he was related to someone who unquestionably does or did exist—if he said he was a descendant of George Washington—would you still consider him to be delusional?"

Solberg looked slightly amused. "That would depend on a number of factors, not the least of which would be whether his claim could be established through historical documents or some scientific method," he said. "But I admit that the likelihood of my finding him to be delusional would be reduced if he were claiming kinship with an actual person."

"Nothing further, Your Honor." I resumed my seat next to Ralph.

Antonio was already on his feet. "Dr. Solberg, when you interviewed the defendant, did he provide you with any objective factual basis that would have enabled you to conclude that he is who he says he is? In other words, when he said he was the son of Santa Claus, did he give you any rational reason to believe his claim to be true?"

"No."

"Nothing further, Your Honor."

*****

Antonio rested just before lunch. Before we broke, the judge asked me if I would be starting with my witnesses immediately after lunch. That was her way of asking if I planned to move for dismissal of the charges on the grounds that the state had failed in its burden of proof. Criminal defendants nearly always moved for dismissal, even when the guilty verdict was so obvious the COs were ready to have the defendant's name laminated over the door to his cell.

The bigger, much bigger, issue was Holly. I'd tried her cell on every break, leaving messages that cajoled, stormed, begged, pled. No response. The second the judge was off the bench, I sent Robin over to her house. "If she won't come, call me," I said. "I'll get a capias and a marshal."

"Are you sure you want to do that?" Robin asked.

"What choice do I have?" A capias was a court order requiring the subpoenaed person to show up. The judge would send a marshal out to escort the person to court. In handcuffs, if necessary. The thought of Holly cuffed in the back of one of the state's black SUVs made my stomach clench.

But she hadn't left me any choice.

My cell rang at 1:44. I snatched it up. "What?"

"She's not here," said Robin. "The neighbor says she's been gone since last week."

"I'm going to wring her neck," I muttered. "Come on back." I disconnected and turned to see Ralph studying his fingernails. "We don't have Holly."

He didn't look up. "I figured as much."

"So we'll start with Carla—"

"Meg." He lifted his head, as solemn as an undertaker.

A shiver raced down my spine. "What?"

"Don't worry about it, okay?" His gaze was intent. There was more to the message than his words, but I wasn't getting it.

"What are you talking about?" He didn't respond, and anger flared in me. I took a deep breath and turned back to my notes. Without looking up from the paper in front of me, I asked as casually as possible, "Is any of your family coming?" If they showed up, I'd put them on the stand and grill them until the jury was convinced that Ralph really believed he was who he said he was.

He shook his head, his lips pressed together.

*****

With no witness to refute Solberg's opinion, I had to shift the focus and shift it hard. So I fell back on the age-old strategy of attacking the victim, encouraging Katrina Damdar to scoff about how Victoria Leopold would do *anything* to get her husband back, including claiming a guy she'd picked up was a break-in. After Victoria's testimony about the alarm, it didn't have quite the same impact as I'd originally planned, but it did make her look desperate enough to lie. Carla talked about how wonderful Ralph was and how she had to practically twist his arm to get him to meet with "that poor little boy, the one who was so sad about what his mama did," but Antonio made her admit she'd known Ralph less than a week when he showed her that letter.

The next morning, three employees from Lizzie's denied seeing anything questionable. They recognized Trevor and Brittany because they came in all the time, and Ralph sat across the table from them. The server who waited on them said Barb insisted on a sending out a bill even though everybody knew she never charged family. Chris Nelson confirmed that the alarm worked. Todd Vincus confirmed that Trevor's letters had been sent from Victoria Leopold's computer, but the response had an international ISP that appeared to originate in Reykjavik.

Just before three o'clock, I told Judge Mwangi that I had one more witness, but I was having difficulty locating her. Antonio immediately piped up that we couldn't keep this trial going indefinitely, and I assured the judge I had no intention of doing so. "With the court's permission, I'd like to hold off until Monday to conclude," I said. "This is an important witness, and I'm still hoping to locate her. I've subpoenaed her, but I have reason to believe she's traveling out of state." I knew from experience that Judge Mwangi hated to stop early. She felt she was wasting the jury's time if they weren't here for a full day. "Even if the witness were here, we wouldn't finish today anyway," I added. "I'll have at least an hour with her, and I'm certain the state will have questions." Which was probably the understatement of the day.

I called and texted Holly every ten minutes from the time we left court until midnight, but she never answered. When I awoke the next morning, I called again. Still nothing. I tried all weekend, to no avail. On Monday, I set Marilyn the task of continuing to try her while Robin and I packed up our files and headed over to court.

The marshal had just unlocked Ralph's handcuffs when the knock came from the door behind the bench. Judge Mwangi took her seat and the marshal opened court. I glanced down at my phone, already on silent. There was no message. Judge Mwangi asked if we had any matters before she brought the jury in.

"No, Your Honor." My voice so low it was a miracle she heard me.

"Very well." The marshal brought in the jury, the judge dispensed the usual greetings, and then she turned to me. "Counsel, you may proceed."

One more glance at my phone revealed nothing. I handed it to Robin. I was out of options. "Your Honor, the defense rests." I could feel Antonio smirking.

Closing arguments and jury instructions consumed most of the morning. At twelve-thirty, the jury began deliberations. We took our lunch break at one; the marshal took Ralph back to lockup, Robin went back to the office to check on non-Claus matters, and Michael showed up with a bag from Sergio and Carla's.

"Walk with me," he said. We strolled down the corridor like an old married couple. When we were out of earshot of any passersby, he said, "Well?"

"We're going down. The only question is how far."

If we'd been at the office, Michael might have slung his arm around my shoulders. Instead, we walked out of the building and ate without speaking on one of the benches next to the block of courthouses where countless souls argued for their idea of justice.

We were nearly back to the courtroom when Robin came rushing down the hall with my phone in her hand. I hadn't even realized she still had it.

"It's Holly," she said, thrusting it at me.

Now she called. Now, when there wasn't a single solitary thing she could do. I snatched the phone and waved Michael into the courtroom with Robin. "Where are you?" I hissed.

"How's it going?" She sounded hesitant. With damned good reason.

"Where the hell are you?" I kept my voice down, but a clerk bearing a sheaf of files turned around anyway.

"Look, I know you're angry—"

"You *think*?" I took a deep breath. "I needed you. Ralph needed you. You dodged a subpoena, for Chrissake! You deliberately left the state so that I couldn't put you on the stand!"

"I know," she mumbled. "I couldn't do it. It was wrong."

"No. 'Wrong' is letting an innocent man go to prison because you won't do what you can to stop it—and, by the way, that's exactly what's about to happen. The jury's out, but they're going to convict. You could have stopped it, and you didn't."

"But he didn't want me to. He said so. He didn't want me to show those drawings."

"He's not a lawyer! He doesn't know what's best!"

"You've always said it's the client's decision—"

"Since when are you his lawyer? You don't get to make decisions here. You do your legal duty, which is to obey a subpoena when it's served on you. If he's convicted, I'm going to move to open, and I'm going to get a capias the second you come back in this state, and I'm going to have a marshal drag you and those drawings into court!"

"You can't." Her voice was barely audible. "I destroyed them."

I couldn't catch my breath. Finally I managed, "You did *what*?"

"I wasn't supposed to make them in the first place. They said no pictures. So I did what was right." Self-righteousness flickered through her nervousness now.

How bloody dare she presume to tell me— "What was *right*? Do you even understand what the word means?" A passing lawyer gestured for me to keep it down. "'Right' does not include dodging a subpoena. It does not include destroying evidence. And it most certainly does not include leaving a man to rot in jail because you're afraid of testifying. Nothing about that is 'right.'"

A long silence. Then her voice was frosty. "You have your opinions, and I understand that. In your world, all that matters is winning. Some of us have bigger goals."

"What the—what the fuck are you talking about? My goal is to keep an innocent man from being locked up in prison for years. I'm sorry if that's not *lofty* enough for you, but that's what I've been hired to do, and I'm doing my best in spite of witnesses who think they're above the law. I'm sorry that working for justice isn't important enough for your exalted tastes. Or maybe you're jealous because I'm defending people's constitutional rights while you're rotting in a cubicle punching in numbers that don't matter to anybody, is that it? Are you trying to sabotage me so you can feel better about your little corporate life? Because if that's what you're doing, I can honestly say I never thought you'd stoop so low. Bad enough you're trying to ruin my career, but this is Ralph's *life* you're—"

Click.

I sat on the unpadded bench in the hallway. I was shaking, but it wasn't from the frigid air conditioning.

*****

I entered the courtroom just as the judge did. Michael sat in the front row behind our table, next to the marshal. The judge brought the jury in to tell them it was time to resume deliberating. They went back out, Michael went back to the office, and we went back to waiting.

At 3:07 p.m., I heard a knock from the other side of the jury room door. It was too early for their break. There were only two possibilities.

They had a question.

Or a verdict.

The clerk opened the door and spoke briefly to the foreperson in a low voice. My heart pounded as he nodded in response. The jury room door closed, and the clerk turned toward the other door, the one that led from the courtroom to the judge's chambers.

"Do they have a question?" I asked. He shook his head, tapped on the judge's door, and slipped inside. He knew. We all did: the faster the jury came back, the more likely they'd found the defendant guilty. I texted Michael. Seconds later, my phone vibrated with a response.

"On my way. Get that look off your face." He knew me so well.

I took a deep breath and sat up straight. Antonio resumed his seat at the other table. The marshal brought in Ralph. As the marshal unlocked the cuffs, I said, "They have a verdict."

"That was fast," Ralph said. "Is that good or bad?"

"No way to know," I lied.

"Whatever happens—it's going to be okay." He sounded like the lawyer, not the client.

The court reporter sat at her desk, put on her headphones, and tapped a few keys to waken her computer. The courtroom marshal resumed his position at the desk at the rear of the courtroom. The clerk walked over to his desk next to the bench, looking straight ahead lest I catch his eye.

A knock sounded from the door behind the bench. "All rise," the marshal intoned, and we rose for Judge Mwangi. Her expression was unreadable as she told us to be seated. The door at the rear of the courtroom creaked. Moments later, I heard the slightest rustle as Michael took a seat behind me.

The judge surveyed us. "Is there anything before we bring in the jury?" In other words, *Have you reached a deal so I can send these people home before they pronounce this man guilty?*

Antonio and I looked at each other. He shook his head slightly. Rising, I said, "No, Your Honor." Antonio lifted his behind off his chair as he echoed my words.

"In that case, Mr. Keeton, please bring in the jury." Was it my imagination, or did the judge sound sad? The clerk walked to the jury room; it was only a dozen steps, but it seemed to take hours. He knocked once and opened the door. The jurors were already lined up. They filed into the jury box, their attention riveted on the task of taking their seats.

Because jurors never look at a defendant they've convicted.

The judge waited until the jurors had settled themselves. I slid my legal pad over so Ralph could see my comments as the verdict was read. The clerk stood poised beside Juror No. 3, who had been elected foreperson. At the judge's nod, the clerk accepted a piece of paper from her and carried it to the judge. Judge Mwangi unfolded it and studied it. Then, she folded it back up, in half and then in half again, just as she'd received it. She handed it back to the clerk, and he carried it back to the foreperson.

"Has the jury reached a verdict?" the judge intoned.

"We have." The foreperson's voice was clear and firm.

"What say you?"

Juror No. 3 unfolded the paper. "On the count of criminal trespass in the second degree, we find the defendant guilty as charged."

Misdemeanor, I wrote.

"On the charge of burglary in the second degree, we find the defendant not guilty."

So far, so good.

"On the charge of enticing a minor, we find the defendant not guilty."

Thank God. But there was still more. . . .

"On the charge of risk of injury to a minor—"

I had to fight not to grab Ralph's hand.

"—we the jury find the defendant guilty as charged."

Fifteen years of experience kept me motionless, expressionless, even as my insides convulsed. Behind me, the courtroom erupted. I hadn't realized so many people were present. The jurors looked uncertain; some flinched as if they thought someone might come at them. The judge's gavel banged. "Order! Order, or I'll have the marshal clear the courtroom! Order!"

"On the charge of child endangerment, we find the defendant guilty as charged."

More chaos. More banging of the gavel. "Settle down, or I'll clear the courtroom!" the judge snapped.

"On the charge of sexual assault in the fourth degree, we find the defendant guilty as charged."

The gallery erupted. Victoria Leopold squealed with delight. Ralph didn't move.

"It doesn't necessarily mean jail time," Michael volunteered from behind us, his voice all but lost in the hubbub. If I could have spoken at that moment, I'd have told him that wasn't the issue—Ralph had proved himself capable of surviving in that environment.

It was the idea that a jury had found him capable of endangering and molesting a child. That was what would break his heart and his spirit.

"On the charge of home invasion, we find the defendant guilty as charged." It was anticlimactic. The spectators who'd been out for blood had already heard what they wanted. Hal Zenkman would have a field day.

The gavel banged as the gallery settled down. The jurors turned their attention back to the bench. I maintained a stony visage as we went through the standard wrap-up. The jury was polled; the verdict was unanimous. Antonio demanded that Ralph be sent back to prison pending sentencing, claiming he was a flight risk since he had no roots in the community. I argued that he'd been a model prisoner and should be released on his own recognizance. Antonio reminded us all that the last time the court had released him, he'd gone after the minor child, resulting in today's verdict. I reassured the court that there would be no question of any contact with any member of the Leopold family and that if any of them tried to contact my client again, I would immediately report such effort to the court. The judge opened her mouth to speak.

"Your Honor, I demand to be heard." Victoria Leopold's voice rang through the courtroom.

"Objection," I said. "This is not an evidentiary hearing. Ms. Leopold is not a party."

"She's the mother of the minor child," Antonio pointed out as though somebody in the room might have forgotten.

"I want that monster kept in jail!" Clearly, Victoria recognized that if she waited for permission, she might not get to speak. "My child deserves to be safe!"

"Your Honor, if Ms. Leopold wants to keep her child safe, she should stop sending emails inviting strangers to meet with her son without her supervision." Maybe it was bitchy, but, I didn't care.

"*He* was the one who was trolling the internet searching for children," she shot back.

"Your Honor, there's no evidence whatsoever to support that accusation," I said.

"I'm aware of that, counselor," the judge said. "Ms. Leopold, sit down." She regarded Ralph, who had not moved since the verdict was read. "Mr. Claus, I recognize that there are a number of issues here. As your lawyer has said, the folks up at Foster have nothing but the highest praise for you. I don't doubt that if I were to release you until sentencing, you would have nothing but the best intentions to comply with every detail of my order." She paused. "The problem is that the last time we let you out, you were back in less than a week because you'd violated the terms of the no-contact order. I know there was evidence that someone contacted you, not the other way around—" Her marble-hard gaze fell on Victoria Leopold, and a flush climbed up the latter's fair cheeks "—but you're the one who made the decision to meet with the boy." Slowly, she shook her head. "I have to put the safety of that child first." Another glance at the child's mother. "So even though I'm certain you'd mean to comply with a no-contact order, I have no choice but to order you back into custody." I closed my eyes. Beside me, Ralph was motionless. On his other side, Robin dabbed at her eyes. "We need to set this down for sentencing. Mr. Keeton, what does my calendar look like?"

The clerk tapped on his keyboard. "First available date is September 2, Your Honor." Judge Mwangi frowned and beckoned for him to come closer. The two engaged in a whispered conversation that included the clerk returning to his computer and then to the judge, shaking his head.

"Counsel, how long do you anticipate you'll need for the hearing?" Judge Mwangi asked.

Antonio and I looked at each other. "I won't be long," he said. "An hour, maybe. I don't expect more than a couple witnesses. The child's mother, mainly."

"Attorney Riley?"

"At least half a day, possibly longer." Depending on whether I could get any of the Clauses down here to testify about Ralph's character. Otherwise, I'd have Carla, Sergio, and maybe Holly—that is, if she didn't dodge another subpoena.

"September 2 it is, then. The court thanks the jury for its service. Court will now stand in recess." She banged the gavel, and the courtroom marshal said, "All rise." We waited as the jury filed out for the last time. The judge exited through the door behind the bench. Then, as Antonio packed up his papers, the marshal approached Ralph with the handcuffs and shackles.

"Wait," I said. Propriety be damned: I reached up and hugged Ralph. "Don't worry," I whispered. "We'll figure something out."

He patted my back. "You did a great job. And don't worry. It really will be okay." I felt his lips in my hair ever so briefly. Then, he stepped back and held out his hands, wrists close together, so that the marshal could put on the cuffs and lead him away.

Book Four

The Fallout

Forty

My office door was open, but Michael knocked anyway. When I pivoted my chair to face the doorway, he gave me a crooked grin.

"What?" My voice was heavy, worn out.

Lulu was curled up in one of the wingback chairs; Michael seated himself in the other one. His voice was uncharacteristically gentle: "It's not your fault."

"I know. It's Holly's. Did I tell you she finally called while the jury was out?"

He reached over to pet Lulu. "She had to surface sometime."

I slammed my hand on the desk; Lulu leapt from the chair and dashed out of the room. "She dodged a subpoena! For chrissake, she left the *state*. I couldn't even get a capias. She totally screwed me over. Did I tell you I called her office? They said she was out because of a 'personal emergency.' I was so tempted to tell them the truth."

"You really think she would have made the difference?" he said with infuriating reasonableness.

"No. Yes. I don't know. Maybe." Arguments and testimony, *should have dones* and *why did Is,* swirled in my mind like a swarm of gnats.

"The victim was a kid," Michael said. "This was always going to be a tough sell, with or without the Santa crap."

For the first time since the jury came back, I smiled. "I'm going to tell him you called it that."

"And what? I'll get coal in my stocking? I'll take my chances."

We sat in commiserating silence for a few minutes. I opened my email to see what other crises were lurking. Three messages from Cyril Walker. Downstairs, I could hear the staff calling good night to each other. "Ruby says, come to dinner," Michael said.

"Since when?"

"Since I talked to her a few minutes ago."

"Does she think I'm going to get drunk on eggnog and binge-watch Christmas movies?" I manufactured a yawn. "Tell her thanks, but no. I'm not up for company."

"Come on. She's making lasagna. She said to tell you she used that sweet Italian sausage you like. Three kinds of cheese on the garlic bread." Ruby came from the tradition that believes the right meal can fix everything. Normally, I agreed.

"Too bad she can't send some up to Foster." I logged off. No more Cyril Walker tonight.

"Don't worry, Drew'll keep an eye out. Make sure everything's okay."

A lump blocked my throat for a second. "Thanks."

He waved his hand: *no problem.* "He says they figure it was political."

"—they—"

"COs, prisoners. Nobody who's met Ralph is buying this verdict."

"Sure, because everybody up there is innocent." It was the oldest refrain in prison: *who, me? I didn't do nothin'!* They blamed the lawyers, the judge, the police, the witnesses, their girlfriends, their victims. Whoever. Incarceration was always somebody else's fault.

Michael rose. "Let's go. Plenty of time for the appeal tomorrow. Tonight, you need food."

"And alcohol." Enough to anesthetize me.

"You're in luck. We've got a very nice chianti. Present from a grateful client."

I clicked off my desk lamp. "Don't waste a good bottle on my defeat. Save it until I win something."

"I don't know if it can age that long," he said.

I couldn't help smiling. Derek might be my brother by blood, but Michael was my brother in every way that counted.

*****

I took a rain check on dinner with the Ruggieros. The prospect of an evening devoted to cheering me up was more than I could face. Instead, I puttered around my kitchen, emptying the dishwasher and refilling it with the plates and bowls that had accumulated in the sink. The clink of glasses, the clatter of silverware. When I opened the refrigerator, the suck of the gasket releasing was amplified in the silence. I filled a pot with water for pasta and set it to boil. Harry and David slurped their food, unconcerned.

It was typical life after trial, I told myself. Except this time, there was no one to hear my laments. No Holly, no Ed. No Ralph.

The landline rang. I grabbed it. "Hello?" The operator asked if I'd accept the charges. I said I would.

"It's me," said Ralph. His voice was low, the way it might be if he'd taken his phone into the bathroom because so his mother wouldn't hear.

"How are you?" I probably sounded more like an anxious girlfriend than a conscientious lawyer, but I didn't care.

"I'm fine. I just wanted to let you know everything's okay, so don't worry."

My antennae perked up. "What's going on? Are you all right?"

"Yeah. I swear." But there was a thread of . . . something.

Reflexively, I shifted into lawyer mode. "Is there a problem? I can come up—"

"There's no problem, I promise." His voice was tight. "I just wanted to say thanks—and don't worry about anything." For a bizarre instant, I felt as if he was breaking up with me.

"What are you talking about? What's happening?"

"Nothing. Everything's okay." The more he said it, the less I believed it.

"Something with another inmate? One of the COs? Because I can call—"

"No, no, nothing like that. You don't need to talk to anybody. It's all under control."

The man couldn't lie worth a damn. I turned off the stove. "I'm coming up there."

"No. Definitely not. Just—goodbye." The phone clicked, and he was gone.

The kitchen clock showed that it was a quarter past seven. I debated calling Michael. Maybe he could call Drew again. I turned on the stove back on. "Relax," I told myself aloud. "He's fine." I dumped too much linguine into the pot and set the timer.

Oh, screw it. I turned off the stove, grabbed my purse and keys, and flicked off the light.

The sky was deepening, the trees more black than green. By the time I got off the exit, fresh dark had fallen, intensified by the trees arching over the familiar road that I barely saw as my mind scrolled through possibilities ranging from benign to sinister.

Movement at the edge of my vision. A doe darted out from the woods. I yanked the wheel hard and slammed on the brakes, my car screeching to a halt at the edge of the road. Gracefully oblivious to the near-disaster, the doe loped off into the darkness as I remained still, my heart pounding. With no approaching headlights in my rearview mirror, I waited to see if any other deer would follow. Finally, I crept around the last curve.

Emerging from the deep shadow of the woods, the harsh floodlights of the prison blinded me for an instant. No energy-saving here; you could have performed neurosurgery under those lights. At the visitor parking lot, a heavy white-painted chain strung from post to post barred entrance. I drove past, peering through the electrified fence for other access points where employees or service people might enter.

Several hundred feet after the visitor lot, I spotted an unmarked road. The razor wire gleamed atop the fence as it turned right, tracking the property edge along the road. I turned right with it. No evidence of life. It was as though the entire facility had been abandoned.

A large black SUV drove straight at me. I veered as far to my side of the narrow road as I could manage to let it pass. The vehicle slowed ominously. Its headlights flashed, and it stopped. I grabbed my phone and dialed 911. Just as I was about to push "call", an unsmiling gray-haired man in a CO uniform got out, the state insignia now clear on the open door.

"Can I help you, ma'am?" he asked.

All at once, the sheer idiocy of my actions overwhelmed me. Even if I found an emergency entrance, I wasn't getting in, because there was no emergency. All I had was a phone call from my client—who'd told me everything was fine.

"Does this road get me to I91?" I asked in my most innocent voice, girlish and breathy.

"No, ma'am," said the CO. "You can turn around right there—" he gestured toward the area ahead of me "—and then go back to the main road and take a left. You'll see signs in about two miles."

"Okay, thanks." I flashed him a smile he did not return. I drove another hundred feet to a gate where the road ended. The SUV didn't move. When I came up behind it, the driver waved me around. Then, he followed me out to the main road, and he remained behind me until I was beyond the glare of the prison lights.

*****

I arrived at the office well past nine the next morning. Lulu crouched on Marilyn's desk, face buried in her dish. "Poor thing was yowling for her food," Marilyn said reproachfully.

"Thanks for feeding her." I rubbed Lulu's head, but she ignored me. "I'm sorry, sweet girl," I crooned. "Is Robin in yet?"

"She's going to be late. Something about Jordy's preschool." Marilyn didn't like arriving first. She never took well to the notion that she was working harder than somebody else.

I trudged up the stairs to my office. Everything seemed vaguely dusty, as if I'd been away for a long time. Discarded papers littered the desk and the work table. I turned on all the lamps, but the room still looked dim.

By the time the electric kettle was boiling, Lulu had forgiven my tardiness enough to saunter back upstairs, followed by Robin. As my intrepid assistant surveyed the post-trial disorder, she asked, "Have you talked to Ralph this morning?"

"Not yet." Which was true.

Robin filled the teapot. After trial, we both needed caffeine. "Where should I start?"

"Exhibits," I said. "I think we've got everything, but cross-check against the clerk's list." Even though parties exchanged exhibits before trial, there were inevitably some we couldn't find afterward.

As Robin created order out of chaos, I sorted through my calendar to see what else was pending. Discovery responses in a slip-and-fall were due by Friday, a motion to compel Sally Howley's financial information needed editing, an objection to a motion to strike a medical malpractice complaint had to be filed by next Wednesday. Nothing urgent.

The intercom beeped. "There's a Major James Otis on three."

"Thanks." I punched the lighted button. "Megan Riley."

"Good morning, Attorney Riley," came a rich baritone. "This is Major James Otis. I'm with the Department of Emergency Services and Public Protection."

"Good morning, Major," I said. "What can I do for you?"

"You represent Ralph Henry Claus, correct?"

268 / P. Jo Anne Burgh

"Yes." My stomach twisted. "Is everything all right?"

"You've also been identified as his contact person in case of an emergency." Not quite a question, but it was news to me.

"Is he all right?" Memories of the previous night's phone call flashed through my mind.

"When was the last time you were in contact with Mr. Claus?"

"Last night. Why? What's going on?"

"Ms. Riley, I need to speak with you about a situation." The velvety voice contained an unmistakable shaft of iron.

"What are you talking about? Is he all right?"

"Please do not leave your office. I'll be there in half an hour." He hung up before I could respond.

I buzzed Michael's assistant. She said he was at a deposition and probably wouldn't be back until after lunch. "Do you have a number for Drew Ferraro?" I asked her. "Michael's nephew."

"Um, let's see. . . . Nope. Michael's probably got it in his phone."

Ah, for the good old days when lawyers ran their lives out of the Rolodexes on their secretaries' desks. "What about his sister?" I hadn't talked with Gwen Ferraro since Michael and Ruby's twentieth anniversary party last year, but it was worth a shot.

"Nope."

"Thanks, Kelly." I punched the "off" button, my mind replaying Ralph's call from last night. *Don't worry. It's all under control.* If I hadn't been so frazzled, I'd have remembered the time-honored maxim: when a client says not to worry, it's time to worry.

Twenty-seven minutes later, I descended the stairs to find two state police officers standing in the waiting area. The door to the conference room was closed. "Is the library free?" I asked Marilyn in a low voice.

She shook her head. "Roy's got a bankruptcy client."

"Any idea how long the conference room will be tied up?"

"Probably a while. Elsa's with the CBC people."

Major James Otis and Lieutenant Kyle Putnam looked like positive and negative of the same person: both tall and well-built, with square jaws, serious eyes, starched gray shirts with black ties. The only difference was their coloring: the major was ebony, and the lieutenant was as pale as milk. I said, "We're a little short on space this morning, but we can talk in my office." They followed me to the third floor. If they were at all put out by either the hike or Lulu's presence on my desk, they gave no sign.

Without being asked, Robin scooped up Lulu and retreated to her own office, closing my door firmly behind her. Trial documents covered the table. To their credit, the officers didn't try to sneak peeks. On the other hand, they also declined my invitation to be seated, so I remained standing as well. "What can I do for you gentlemen?" I inquired.

"As I said, we have a situation." Apparently, only the major was permitted to speak. "When were you last in contact with Ralph Claus?"

"Last night, around quarter after seven. What's going on?"

He ignored my question. "What was the conversation?"

"My conversations with my clients are privileged."

He looked unimpressed. "Did he contact you, or did you contact him?"

"What is this about?"

"Ms. Riley, I'm asking the questions here."

"What's going on? Is my client all right?"

"Please answer the question. Did he contact you, or did you contact him?"

"He's in prison. I can't call him." As they very well knew.

"Did the conversation take place by telephone or in person?"

"Telephone." They knew that, too. The log would have reflected any visitors. A separate log was kept for inmate calls. Major Otis was asking questions he already knew the answers to. The only reason to do this was to test my veracity before getting to the big stuff. But what was the big stuff? So I asked again, "What is this about? Is my client all right?"

"At what number did Mr. Claus telephone you?"

I had to think for a second. Had he called my cell? No. He'd called the landline. My unlisted home number. In a measured tone, I said again, "What is going on?"

"Please answer the question, ma'am." Again, I sensed the iron under the velvet.

"Am I under arrest?" I didn't know where the question came from.

"No, ma'am," Major Otis said.

"Am I under suspicion of something?" The major hesitated, and that was enough for me. "Then I think we should postpone this conversation until I can consult with a lawyer." The words sounded unreal. My voice was steady enough, but everything inside me was trembling.

The lieutenant glanced at the major, but Otis was focused on me.

"Ma'am, you have a right to an attorney if you so desire, but there is a time element involved."

I sensed an advantage. "How so?"

"I'm not at liberty to say."

"Has something happened to my client?"

"I'm not at liberty to say," said the major.

Only one option presented itself. "Excuse me," I said. Leaving them standing there, I went into Robin's office and closed the door. I grabbed her phone and punched in Michael's cell, but I went immediately into his voicemail. "Call me as soon as you get this," I whispered.

"What's going on?" Robin asked.

"I'll be right back. Make sure they don't touch anything." Gamely, Robin went back to my office as I sped down the stairs.

The doors to the conference room and the library were still closed, but fortunately, there was one more partner. I burst into Eckert's office and closed the door behind me. "Quick," I said, still whispering. "I need a lawyer."

A slight crease appeared between his brows. "Is something wrong?"

I handed him his suit jacket as I filled him in. His face impassive, he nodded for me to open the door. We headed up the stairs, I with the nervous energy of a stocky racehorse and he with the calm dignity of an ocean liner. When we reached my office, Robin was shuffling papers on the work table. The officers stood precisely where I'd left them.

"Gentlemen, this is Attorney Eckert Lundstrom," I said. "Attorney Lundstrom, Major Otis and Lieutenant Putnam." Eckert extended his hand, leaving them no choice but to take it.

"Good morning," said Eckert. "I understand you have some questions about Attorney Riley's representation of one of the firm's clients."

"Not exactly," said the major. "At the moment, we're inquiring into her contact with Mr. Claus last evening."

Eckert wasn't a trial lawyer, but he knew enough not to volunteer information. "Where did you leave off?"

"At what number did Mr. Claus telephone you?" the major asked me, disregarding Eckert, who nodded ever so slightly to me.

"My home number," I admitted.

"Is that number published?"

"No."

"Did you give it to him?"

"No. I never give that number to clients."

"How did he get it?"

"I don't know," I said, which was technically true.

"Where were you last night?" Otis asked. His eyes were exactly the same gray as his shirt. Any other time, I'd have been fascinated by his distinctive coloring.

"At home," I said. "Answering the phone when my client called." If a client had said that—especially with the snarky edge—I'd have called a break and taken her out in the hall to deliver a whispered lecture about behaving appropriately with law enforcement. *Whatever you do, don't get snotty,* I'd have hissed. Too bad I couldn't seem to take my own advice.

"Gentlemen," said Eckert with a glance at me. "It's clear that something has transpired involving Mr. Claus. It would be helpful to know what that something is. Obviously, Attorney Riley has been forthcoming, but if we knew what you were looking for, it's possible we could be of much better assistance. Bear in mind, however, our first loyalty must be to the client, and that includes honoring the attorney-client privilege." I opened my mouth to argue the point further, but another glance from Eckert warned me to be quiet.

"I'm not at liberty to say," Otis said yet again.

"In that case, it would appear this conversation is finished," said Eckert with what sounded like real regret.

"Mr. Lundstrom, we can either speak here or at the station," said the major. "We came here as a courtesy."

"Am I under arrest?" I asked again. *Idiot.* Obviously I wasn't: if I were, they'd have said so. Later, I would reflect on how different it was to be the target of questions rather than representing someone in that position.

"No," said the major. He sounded almost grudging as he added, "You're free to stop answering questions if you wish."

"But . . . ?" He hadn't said it, but I'd heard it.

"As I said before, there's a time element involved. If you refuse to cooperate, you may compromise the investigation."

"Investigation? Into what?" Then the light bulb went on. "Has my client been injured? Has there been a problem with one of the inmates—or one of the COs?" Otis started to speak, but I cut him off. "And don't tell me you're not at liberty to say, because I'm the emergency contact person. I'm the one you're supposed to talk to.

I'm the one you're *required* to talk to." He looked ever so slightly uncertain, and I pressed my advantage. "If he's been harmed, I want to know about it, and I want to know now. *And* I want him moved to a hospital, not being treated by some prison doctor." If they were sending out officers to investigate, it had to be bad.

A tap on the door, and Robin opened it without waiting. Before I could say, "Not now," she said, "I'm sorry to interrupt, but I need Attorney Riley immediately." Her eyes fixed on mine. She knew something.

"I'll be right back." Without waiting for permission, I followed Robin into her office and closed the door. She pointed to her monitor.

The video feed was already up, although the news crews had been restricted to the area outside the fencing. Sunlight glinted off the razor wire coils. The grass behind the reporter was as lush as a golf course. She turned up the volume the tiniest bit. My heart pounded as the newscaster intoned, ". . . convicted yesterday in Hartford Superior Court of a variety of charges, including sexual assault of a child." The prison was replaced by Ralph's mug shot as the newscaster continued, "If you see this man, you are asked to call the Department of Emergency Services and—"

I jabbed the mute button on her keyboard. My hands were shaking.

If you see this man. . . .

The only way you might see him, dear viewer, is if he's not in prison any more.

I could feel the concern radiating off Robin like summer heat off a city street. The silenced video played on, alternating between the prison exterior and Ralph. The black turtleneck made him look like a beat poet. A viewer would barely be able to tell how green his eyes were.

"How?" Robin whispered.

"The first question is *whether*," I said. "Did he really escape, or is something else going on?" Girded for battle, I stormed back into my office.

"Were you ever going to tell me he's missing?" I demanded.

Otis's expression didn't change, but the lieutenant looked uncomfortable, as if he'd been caught watching porn on his phone. "As I said—"

"I know, you're not at liberty to say. But as it turns out, the internet is. The local news stations are all over this. So, let's start again. What the hell happened? Where is Ralph Claus?"

"Meg," said Eckert, but it was too little, too late.

The major and I locked eyes. We stood without speaking for a long, long minute. Finally, the major said in a fast monotone, "Mr. Claus went out into the rec yard this morning at seven-twenty. At seven-twenty-six, the CO was unable to verify his presence in the yard. The facility immediately went into lockdown. The investigation is ongoing."

"Who else was in the yard?"

"We're investigating that."

"What do you mean? Don't they keep a list of who goes out to rec or wherever? He'd have been out with the other PC guys, right?"

"We're investigating that." It was apparently his default line.

"So maybe the internet's wrong. Maybe he hasn't escaped. Maybe somebody who doesn't like crimes against kids decided to take justice into his own hands." If that was the case, God only knew where Ralph was. Stuffed in a dryer. Locked in a deep-freeze. Or worse.

"Ms. Riley, we're investigating all possibilities," Otis said. "What I need to know from you is whether you've had any contact whatsoever with Mr. Claus this morning."

"As I told you earlier, the last time I spoke with him was last night." My voice was steady, but my heart skittered like a nervous chipmunk. I shouldn't have listened to him. I should have listened to my gut, the part that said things weren't okay, not even close to okay.

"What kind of car do you drive?" the major asked.

Shit. They'd viewed the security footage from last night, when I drove so slowly around the prison. The CO who told me how to get to I91 had undoubtedly described our meeting. In their eyes, I wasn't just his lawyer or his emergency contact.

I was a possible accomplice.

"This conversation is over." I strode over to the door and opened it pointedly. I'd seen too many clients lock their own cells by trying to be cooperative. I had a constitutional right to remain silent, and it was high time I exercised it, at least until Michael got back. I needed somebody who understood how to stand between the client and the police. In my best dismissive manner, I said, "Let me know when you come up with more information about my client's disappearance."

"Meg—" Eckert began, but I shook my head.

"Eckert, would you be good enough to show these gentlemen out?" Meredith Claus couldn't have been more self-possessed.

Otis studied me for a few seconds. "We'd appreciate it if you didn't leave town in the next few days," he said. "We'll be in touch." It sounded like a threat.

Forty-One

Whoever said work was an effective distraction was full of shit. I tried to draft a legal malpractice complaint against a criminal lawyer who'd screwed up a real estate deal, but all I could think was that one day in the not-too-distant future, someone might be writing allegations about me: *The defendant, Megan Riley, knew or should have known that Ralph Claus was a flight risk, and yet she failed to alert the court and, to the contrary, did by her silence aid and abet. . . .*

When Michael came in, I was grateful for the chance to escape my own dark thoughts. "Nope," I said before he could ask. "Nothing new."

He nodded. I knew that look: he was gathering information. Nothing was good or bad; it just *was*. We played the hand we were dealt, and we didn't waste time wishing for different cards.

It took a moment to register the fact that he hadn't moved from the doorway. "What?"

"We need to talk to the partners. Everybody needs to be on the same page." Sort of like family members being told that one of them has a serious illness. "Can you do it now?"

As I followed Michael downstairs, a flash of memory surfaced: Rick's face as we gathered for the meeting where he begged us not to throw him out. At the bottom of the stairs, I buttoned my blazer, just as I would before addressing a judge.

In a low voice, Michael said, "Be careful." His eyes were somber, as though he too was remembering Rick. He stepped back to let me to enter the room first. Always a gentleman, my friend.

*****

The primary concern was protecting the firm's reputation in view of our client's apparent escape from custody. I reminded them that it was possible he'd been abducted and was still somewhere in the prison. Nobody knew what had happened, I insisted. My vehemence was met with noncommittal hums. Elsa's expression was largely unreadable as we discussed the inevitable publicity that would arise from DESPP's investigation. In the end, we decided that Eckert would address any inquiries from the media with a simple statement that the firm does not comment on matters involving our clients.

As we were about to adjourn, Elsa announced, "I have a question." She waited until all eyes were on her before asking, "Meg, is there anything we should know?"

My heart gave an enormous thump, so hard I could barely believe it wasn't visible. I mustered my best Meredith Claus imitation: "Meaning . . . what, exactly?"

"What are you asking?" Michael said at almost the same time.

Elsa was unfazed by the tag-team approach. "Look, whatever's said here is privileged. To the extent Meg needs representation, she has it from Michael on behalf of the firm. But we're her partners. We're entitled to know if there's a time bomb out there."

The room was very still. In my most incredulous tone, I said, "Are you suggesting that I had anything to do with Ralph Claus's disappearance?"

Roy looked around nervously, but Elsa didn't falter. "I'm asking if there's anything we as your partners need to know about this matter. Anything you would want to know if one of us were in your position."

I sensed Michael ready to jump in. I rested my hand on the table in front of him, the lawyer-to-lawyer version of the hand on the arm. "I had nothing whatsoever to do with Ralph Claus's disappearance," I said, my voice firm and clear. "You can take that to the bank. I knew nothing until the troopers were standing in my office. My only post-verdict contact with the client was the phone call I received last night. I have not heard from him since."

As it turned out, this truth was short-lived. That evening, just as I was setting down the cats' food, the phone rang. Not the landline, but my cell. I snatched it up. The number was blocked. "Hello?"

"It's me."

"Ralph?" I sat down on the nearest chair; my legs wouldn't hold me. "Where are you?"

"It doesn't matter. I wanted to let you know I'm okay."

"What do you mean, it doesn't matter? Where are you?"

"I can't say."

"Are you in the prison? Did you escape? Are you safe? Where are you calling from?"

"I can't tell you," he said. "But don't worry. It's like I said. Everything's under control."

"What happened?"

"I can't tell you that, either. I'm not even supposed to be calling, but I knew you'd be worried. I'll be in touch. Take care." He disconnected the call before I could respond.

I punched the button for the call log and tried to reconnect, but unsurprisingly, the call wouldn't go through. The phone blurred as unexpected hot tears welled up. "Idiot," I muttered. What was there to cry about? Ralph was fine. He'd said so. And he sounded fine—not frightened or tense, as if kidnappers were holding a knife to his throat.

Which left only one option.

The emotional part of my brain argued that if he'd engineered an escape, I should let him go. He shouldn't have been convicted in the first place, so it was only right that he was free. But the rational part pointed out that I'd taken an oath to exercise the office of attorney faithfully, which probably included something about not aiding and abetting a convicted felon's escape.

I paced the room, considering. I had to report the call, but I didn't have to give everything away. I scrolled through my call log. Ralph's call showed as coming from "Unavailable." The log only went back three months, so my early calls to the Pole didn't show. The police would undoubtedly subpoena my phone records, but that couldn't be helped.

I needed perspective. I punched in Michael's number and held my breath until I heard his voice.

Several hours later, Michael and I emerged from the police station. My hand clasped the phone still in my pocket. The officer tried to insist that I should turn it over to him, but Michael refused. "There's confidential client information on it," he said. "She's shown you everything related to Claus. That's all you're getting tonight. If you want anything else, you'll need a warrant."

I'd half-expected to see television vans parked in front of the station—the eleven o'clock news was still in progress—but the street was quiet. A grizzled man shuffled past, hunched over a rusted shopping cart half-full of cans and bottles. I climbed into the passenger seat of Michael's aging Volvo. Not until we pulled out of the parking lot did I finally allow myself to relax.

"Where are you going?" I asked when he drove past the entrance to the highway.

"Sid's," he said. "We need to talk." That was all he said for the ten minutes it took to reach the back lot of a three-family house in the West End. The first floor had been converted into a bar officially called the Brew & Burger, but known to locals as Sid's. Inside, I recognized several criminal defense lawyers and a couple of private investigators at the bar. Michael ordered two beers and led the way to the dark-paneled back room, dimly lit and lined with high-backed wooden booths. In the corner, a wiry bald man with a gray fringe, matching beard, and little round John Lennon-style glasses sat at a battered spinet, playing jazz versions of easy listening standards. The center tables, placed end to end as though to accommodate somebody's softball team, bore empty pitchers and metal pizza trays littered with crumbs and crusts. Nearly every booth was occupied.

We hunkered down in our booth, and Michael slid my beer over to me. "This is just us now. You have to tell me everything. From the beginning." I told, and he did his best not to interrupt, but his eyes grew wide and round when I got to the part about the Pole.

"Hold on," he said. "Are you telling me you went . . . *there*?" It was like he couldn't even bring himself to say it.

"Yep." His mouth was working, but no words came out. "I know what you're thinking. If I hadn't seen it all, I wouldn't believe me, either."

"I'm not saying I don't believe you—" he began.

"I swear to God, if you say, 'I believe you believe it,' you're gonna wear that beer." His fingers tightened on the mug handle. "I know it sounds insane, but I saw it. The workshop, the elves, the whole kit and caboodle. I saw everything—at least, everything except Santa."

He lifted his mug and took the world's slowest drink. When he couldn't stall any more, he said, "You went by sleigh, with flying reindeer and everything."

"Flying reindeer and everything."

Michael shook his head in obvious wonder. "Are you sure it wasn't. . . ?" He couldn't even come up with an idea.

It was my turn to shake my head. "Believe me, I've tried to find another explanation, but nothing else makes sense." *As if this did.* "If it weren't for the reindeer, I could write the whole thing off as some weird-ass fantasy land, but they were real. And when I took those goggles off. . . ." I shuddered again, remembering.

"But even assuming you really went somewhere—and for the moment, let's forget about the reindeer—you never saw anybody dressed up like Santa. So it could be some bizarre—I don't know, high-end destination for elite travelers who want to relive childhood fantasies."

"Holly and I weren't elite anything," I reminded him. "And I didn't see any other outsiders. Just a ton of toys and a bunch of really short people."

"But no Santa. The mother runs the show." The no-Santa part seemed important to him, as though a fat man with a white beard would outweigh flying reindeer on the scales of credibility.

"She thinks she runs the world. If she were secretary of state, we'd have peace in the Middle East by year-end." The elegant Meredith Claus, presiding over a table occupied by dignitaries and terrorists. If anybody could bully them into playing nicely, it was the woman who controlled Christmas.

"Does she know her son's missing?"

The frigid air conditioning wasn't keeping my beer cold. "My guess is, she arranged it."

Michael considered this. "Have you talked to her?"

"I was going to call her this morning, but I didn't know what to say. Until tonight, I didn't know if he was on a beach or rotting in a dumpster." I drummed my fingernails on the scratched glass mug.

Michael drained his glass. When he put it down, his expression was somber. His eyes were riveted on mine. "You knew nothing at all." Except it didn't sound like a statement of fact.

It sounded like a question.

Every defense clicked into place. "What are you asking?"

He didn't waver. "I'm not suggesting you planned it with him or anything like that. But I have to ask—did you know anything? Anything at all? Did he mention anything that sounded like . . . this?"

"No." I summoned courtroom control. "All he ever said was not to worry, that everything was under control."

"You didn't do anything to help? Didn't give him anything—

money, contraband, information, anything? Even if you didn't know you were helping, and you didn't mean to be?"

"You're supposed to be on my side." I could barely get the words out.

"Look, I'm not the last one who's gonna ask this. You already said you put money in his prison account. You went up there a hell of a lot more than the case required, and you didn't bill for all the visits. The cops are gonna look at that as showing more than an attorney-client relationship. So I'm asking: did you do anything, intentionally or not, that might have helped this guy escape?"

All at once, I snapped into fighting mode. "Oh, yeah, I forgot to tell you. I snuck a hacksaw into prison with my legal pad, and I stuck a wad of twenties in his pocket at trial. Oh, and I bribed the CO in the rec yard to look the other way while a couple of elves broke him out." He didn't answer, didn't say I was being ridiculous. He just waited for me to answer my own questions. "Of course not," I spat. "I can't believe you're even asking. If the tables were turned, I would never doubt you. I know who you are, what you are. I know you're not perfect, but I'd never accuse you—"

"—I'm not accusing, I'm telling you how it looks—"

"It's the same thing. If you think—after all these years—my God, Michael, do you even know me at all?" Before he could answer, I slid out of the booth. "Take me home."

"We're not done—"

I snatched up my jacket. "Oh, yes, we are." I slid out of the booth and marched outside, where I stood in the darkness, just out the streetlight's arc, until I heard the crunch of his shoes on the gravel. Wordlessly, we got into the car and slammed the doors, and he drove to my house. At the curb in front of my place, I got out, then leaned back in.

"I shouldn't have to say it," I snarled.

He regarded me, his eyes solemn. I waited for him to apologize, but he turned his attention to the steering wheel. I slammed the door with all my strength and strode up the front walk. Once inside, I leaned against the door and wept.

Forty-Two

I didn't expect to sleep, but I must have, because I was jolted awake by the phone. The number was blocked. I grabbed the handset.

"Where the hell are you?" I snarled.

"I beg your pardon?" I could almost hear the ice queen's raised brow.

"I thought it was your son calling." I turned on the bedside lamp. "Where is he?"

"I can't tell you that."

"But you know." Silence. "The police want all the phone numbers and email addresses I have for the Pole. I'm going to have to turn them over."

"You can't do that." *The monarch hath so decreed.*

Screw the monarch. We were on my turf now. "I don't have a choice."

"What about the attorney-client privilege?" She'd apparently been talking to the Reykjavik contract lawyer.

"You're not my client. Nothing you say to me is privileged." A distinction even a contract lawyer should have known. "Besides, the privilege only protects communications, not facts. A phone number is a fact."

"But you obtained it through communications with your client."

"I have one of them because he used my phone, not because he told me the number."

More silence. Then— "Do you really want to do this?" Her voice was softer now. The boyfriend's mother, trying to persuade the girlfriend to protect the boy they both loved. What unspeakable nerve.

"What choices do I have? The police view me as a possible accomplice."

"I'm sorry to hear that." She actually sounded regretful. "If there had been another way, we'd have used it."

The import of her words sank in. I was right: she was the mastermind. I began to pace around my bedroom. "Why did you do it?"

Long pause. "There were a number of considerations."

"Such as?" My words fairly dripped with fury and contempt.

"I can't discuss those with you."

"Are you kidding? Those 'considerations' are the reason you're flushing my career down the toilet. That gives me every right to know what in hell is going on. You can tell me now, or you can wait for a phone call from the Connecticut state police. Your choice."

"I'm sorry, but there are factors that don't involve you." Her voice was cooler.

"What are you talking about? You used me—I'll bet you even knew I was the one who was going to be appointed to represent your son!"

"Of course we didn't," she chided. "There was no grand plan. Ralph getting arrested was an accident. His decision to meet with the boy was—well, not something on which I was consulted. And the fact that he fell in love with you—I had nothing to do with that." *The fact that he fell in love with you.* "My son is an adult. He is responsible for his own actions and relationships. The only time I get involved is if the organization may be compromised."

"Santa Claus is an organization now?"

"You've seen how we operate. Santa is one person, but enabling the work of Santa to go forward requires a massive effort by literally thousands of people, many of whom are located up here. Having Ralph in prison compromised that work."

"We were going to appeal—"

"A process which would take months, if not years, with no guarantee of success. Realistically, even with the best result, he'd miss Christmas this year and next. And in view of certain other developments—well, you can see why this would be unacceptable."

"'Unacceptable'?" This bitch really did think she ran the world. "The judicial system doesn't have the slightest interest in whether you approve of the way it works. There is a process, and nobody is exempt from that process, not even the heir to the Santa throne." Granted, that was more than a little bit idealistic. Even I couldn't argue with a straight face that nobody ever bent the rules to accommodate somebody's wishes. Ralph probably wouldn't have been in prison in the first place if Victoria Leopold hadn't been so tight with Hal Zenkman.

"Attorney Riley, I think it's clear that you and I are not going to agree about this situation." Meredith Claus sounded utterly unperturbed. "I didn't call to argue with you. Ralph is concerned that his earlier telephone call to you may have put you in jeopardy."

"It would have been nice if he'd thought of that sooner."

"I mentioned that to him," she said. "In any event, my question is this: is there anything we can do, short of producing Ralph, to remedy whatever difficulties have been caused by his disappearance?"

I stared at the phone. Her chutzpah was unbelievable. "Short of producing him? No. Short of you producing him, the police have only one link to this escaped convict: me. Short of you producing him, I'm going to have to work very hard to avoid indictment. Short of you producing him, it's entirely possible that I could be disbarred. Short of you producing him, my career is most likely over."

Another long pause. "Obviously, it was never our intent to harm you," she said finally. "I'm very sorry we have caused you so much difficulty."

"Then produce him. The longer he stays away, the worse it will be when he's caught."

"He won't be caught." A simple fact, like *snow is cold*. Or *reindeer can fly*.

"Nobody ever thinks they'll be caught," I said. "He didn't think he'd be caught at the Leopolds'. He didn't think he'd be caught seeing Trevor Leopold again."

"True," she conceded. "But he won't be in Connecticut again."

"It doesn't matter. He's an escaped convict. Wherever he's found, they'll extradite him." I knew practically nothing about extradition, but I was pretty sure I was right.

"We'll sort that out as we need to," she said, unflapped. "Now. Am I correct that there is an outstanding balance on your bill?"

"Are you kidding me?" Was that really what she thought I was concerned about?

"Not at all. You're entitled to be paid for your work."

"Nice thought, it's too late," I said. "If you try to send me money now, I'm going to be up to my ass in federal prosecutors freezing my assets and wiretapping my phones." The Claus trial bill, which was substantial, would now languish until I could sit down with my partners to discuss whether to write off thousands of dollars of work or try to figure out a way to collect without triggering a federal investigation, because it was a pretty safe bet that the police weren't going to spend a couple days on this, shrug their shoulders, and saunter away without their man.

"In any event, please send us the bill," said Meredith Claus. She sounded calm and businesslike, as if this were a minor snag in an otherwise smooth venture. "If you prefer to have us hold the payment for the time being, that's fine. Just let us know when you'd like us to pay." One more Claus dagger twisting in my back. "Please believe me when I say that we are all terribly sorry the matter became so complicated. Good night, counselor." The phone clicked softly before I could respond.

Forty-Three

Shortly after I arrived at the office, Major Otis called to arrange another meeting, but he didn't offer to come to me this time. I texted Michael, and we arranged to go to DESPP at three. I told Robin to move the deposition of Cyril Walker's wife from this afternoon to next week.

"Cyril's not going to like that," she warned.

"Too bad. Apologize to Hermy and tell him an emergency came up."

"And what should I say to Mr. Walker?"

"Same thing. I'll call him later if he wants." Which he undoubtedly would. Because if there was one thing I would really look forward to after being grilled by the police, it was explaining to a high-maintenance client why his wife's deposition had to take a backseat to an investigation into my possible involvement with an escaped convict.

To add to the joy of my day, Zenkman appeared on all on the morning shows, whipping everybody up into a frenzy about the convicted pedophile who was running around loose. Never ones to tone down a panic, newscasters urged viewers to keep their doors locked and refrain from taking their kids to see Santa. Forget the fact that it wasn't even Labor Day, and there wasn't a red suit for miles around—danger boosted ratings, and Santa was dangerous.

"This is great," I muttered over my turkey on whole wheat. Lulu stood on my desk, sniffing at the other side of my sandwich. "I've turned a revered mythical figure into a pariah."

"You didn't do it." Michael's meatball sub was dripping onto my table. "Your client did."

It probably would have seemed odd to the typical onlooker that after the night at Sid's, Michael and I could sit around with sandwiches like nothing ever happened, but that was our way. We'd had plenty of fights over the years, but we knit ourselves back together by doing normal things and making the smallest of small talk. Now, it was better to focus on Ralph, or maybe the police, or his mother. Anything, as long as it was us against the world.

Moments later, the world came crashing in. Marilyn buzzed us, and we left our lunch to Lulu's delight. Downstairs, we found Roy perusing a piece of paper as four strapping officers frowned. "Let me see that," Michael said, reaching for it.

We all stood silently as Michael read. "No," he said at last to the closest officer. "You're not getting client files." They all towered over him, but he was undaunted. He turned to me. "See if caseflow can squeeze us in this afternoon. Tell the clerk it's an emergency."

An hour later, we were standing before Judge Binchy, a diminutive woman with white hair and a sharp tongue. She listened as we explained why we had to retain possession of my Claus file, and she pursed her pale lips as DESPP's lawyer, a long-time state employee named Carl Lawrence, argued that the file might generate information about Ralph's whereabouts.

Finally, she turned to me. "Counselor, what's in that file?"

"Materials I used to defend Mr. Claus. Pleadings, notes, reports."

"Is there anything that was created after the trial?"

"I doubt it, Your Honor. Since I had conversations with him and with his mother, it's possible I wrote something down. I usually document phone conversations, but these came outside the office, so I may not have—I don't recall. Other than that, there's nothing except my outline of potential appealable issues." Michael nudged my foot to let me know I was babbling, and I shut up.

She peered first at me, then at Carl. Her gaze came to rest on Michael. "Where's the file?"

"Right here, Your Honor." Michael gestured to the half-dozen storage boxes piled beside him. No way were we letting them out of our sight.

"Very well," she said. "Materials as to which you're claiming privilege will be segregated for *in camera* review. I want a privilege log with that." In other words, Judge Binchy would review anything we said was protected from disclosure, and she wanted a list detailing what it was and why we shouldn't have to hand it over. "Attorney Lawrence will examine the non-privileged materials in the presence of Attorney Riley or her designee, and he will identify any documents of which he needs copies. Attorney Riley will be responsible for providing those copies."

"Timeframe, Your Honor?" Lawrence piped up. "I know I don't need to explain that time is of the essence." *And yet you did,* I retorted silently.

"We're meeting with Major Otis this afternoon," Michael said. "That may narrow the scope of the request."

"Or broaden it," Carl said.

The judge regarded the boxes. "I want the privileged materials and the log by noon tomorrow. "I'll have a ruling by the end of the day." She banged the gavel, and that was that.

That evening, I sat in my living room with my laptop and tried to concentrate on work. Luckily, the media had found our document production issue too dull, and we received less than thirty seconds on the news. Video of Carl Lawrence and me leaving the courthouse revealed only that both of us needed haircuts. I flicked off the television, saved a half-written objection, and checked my office email one more time before calling it a night.

There was a new message. From the Pole.

Damn. Don't these people know by now not to put things in writing?

The police would want to see it. So would Michael. They'd all give me hell for opening it. Defiantly, I clicked on the subject line, and the box opened to reveal this message:

Dear Attorney Riley: Please contact Meredith Claus at your earliest opportunity. Thank you, Matilda J. Hansen

At least Tillie had the sense not to include a phone number. On the other hand, anyone reading this would probably figure, quite correctly, that I already had it.

I'd had all the conversations I intended to have with Meredith Claus. I clicked *reply* and sent the following response:

Ms. Hansen: In view of the ongoing investigation into Ralph's disappearance, it would not be appropriate for me to contact Mrs. Claus. Please advise her that local law enforcement is eager to speak with her. Thank you, Meg Riley

Guaranteed to piss the ice queen off, but right then, I couldn't have cared less. "Maybe now she'll leave us alone," I said to Harry, who was curled up next to me. The only indication the cat might be listening was the quick flick of his ear.

His pointed ear.

Pointed. Almost like an elf's.

I sprang from the sofa and snatched up my briefcase, digging in all the pockets. Nothing. I raced up the stairs and flung open the closet door. The dark brown purse? The black patent leather? I yanked them all down, plopped myself on the floor among them, and began the search. Every pocket, every side pouch, every zippered compartment. Finally, I found it. Smushed into the corner of the phone pocket in my black shoulder bag was the small piece of yellow paper I'd received the day I met Ralph.

"You have any trouble with him, call me. My number's in there." He pointed to the non-cash papers that had fallen out of the envelope. *"And make them put you through to me personally. Don't take any crap from anybody."*

It was time to call Charles.

And not take crap from anybody.

Forty-Four

I dialed on my client phone. The first ring was interrupted with "North Pole, Ivy speaking."

"Hi, Ivy, it's Meg Riley. I need to speak to Charles."

"Um—let me get Mrs.—"

"No," I said. "Charles said you should put me through to him personally. Nobody else."

I could almost feel how much she wanted to ask, but all she said was, "One moment, please." A click, and silence so long I wondered if we'd been cut off. Then I heard another click, and a gravelly voice said, "Counselor."

"Hey, Charles. How are you?"

He ignored my pleasantry. "I figured you'd call sooner or later."

"You figured right."

"I can't send him back."

"I know. That's not why I called." Years of experience ferreting out information with subtle, carefully-framed questions fell away. "What the hell happened?"

"I can't give out information."

"Come on, Charles. I can't talk to Ralph—I'd have to tell the cops if I did. You're all I've got." I was supposed to disclose communications with any Claus, but Charles wasn't a Claus. It hadn't occurred to the police to demand that I tell them about conversations with elves.

Long silence. Everything in me wanted to badger him into talking, but I forced myself to wait. Just when I thought he was going to hang up, he said, "He had to do it."

"Meaning?"

"Look, counselor. You know who he is." It wasn't the moment to argue. I murmured noncommittal assent. "So you know what comes with that, the stuff he can do."

"Not really." But I was starting to see a glimmer. Copperfield and Houdini be damned. Ralph Claus was the master of illusion and escape.

"It wasn't easy. That place is nothing like a house. I wasn't sure we'd pull it off."

"What are you saying? You broke him out?" I sank down on the bed.

"You think I'd let anybody else handle something like that? I been looking out for him ever since he was a kid. I ain't about to stop now." *Thank God.* Charles was beyond the state's jurisdiction. Beyond anybody's. "He got himself out of there. I got him home."

"How did you manage without being seen?" That huge flood-lit expanse, like a series of football fields, surrounding the buildings, stretching to the edge of the property with the razor-wire fences. There was plenty of room on the grass to land a sleigh, but no place to hide it.

Rough chuckle. "I've been getting Clauses in and out of places without being seen for a long time."

A memory tickled. Something Fred had said. . . . "Do you go along when they deliver the toys?"

"Every sleigh has a second on board. Especially city deliveries. Not a lot of places to land, too many people watching. Somebody's gotta take care of things while the Claus is making the deliveries."

Then, it clicked. "You were with him at the Leopolds'." He grunted. "And you left him there."

"Had to. I had to get the sleigh out of there. We got protocols."

That sounded like something Meredith Claus would have come up with. "Does one of those protocols involve breaking him out of prison?"

"Listen, counselor. Maybe it don't seem like much to you, but what we do affects millions of kids. If it means we gotta bend a rule here or there, we bend. The important thing isn't him or me or you or some jail. It's Santa, and it's the kids. We do whatever we have to do to keep Santa flying. Maybe sometimes it makes a hassle for somebody. When it does, we're sorry, but that's the way it goes." I could almost hear him shrug.

"A hassle? A *hassle*? Do you have any idea what you've done? Forget violating the law, because that doesn't seem to matter to you people. I've got cops digging through my client files. They're going to find your phone numbers and your email addresses, and I can't stop that. I'm already cancelling matters for other clients to deal with this mess. The police think I'm involved. If they decide I aided and abetted—even though *you* know better—I could be disbarred. I could even go to jail. What happens then? Are you going to come and get me out the way you did for him?" Tears filled my eyes.

Another long silence. "That's why he didn't want to break out. Because of you."

"Then why did he?" I swiped my eyes with a tissue.

"I'm not supposed to—"

"Come *on!*" I punched my pillow, again and again. Damned Clauses. Damned elves. Damned everybody associated with this misbegotten mess.

"Fine! You wanna know why he came back? And you can't tell this to a living soul."

"Like I'm going to tell the police some elf was giving me classified information about the North Pole?" If they didn't lock me up for interfering with a police investigation, they'd do it for being a flaming lunatic.

"I don't know what you lawyers do. All I'm saying is, what I'm gonna tell you is for one reason—so you know he didn't just up and go without—well, you know."

I took a deep breath. "Okay. I'm listening."

"His pop had a stroke."

"*What?*" A thousand questions crowded my head—how bad, when did it happen, how did Ralph find out, why didn't he tell me— but Charles was still talking.

"Not a big one, but enough. He has a hard time coming up with words sometimes now. Not so steady on his feet. The missus is going nuts 'cause he won't use a cane. The workshop made him a real nice one. He says he don't need it, but he does."

"But he's okay? I mean, he's not going to die, right?" Suddenly it was enormously important to me that Ralph's father—Santa—be okay.

I could almost hear Charles shrug. "Who knows? He's getting up there. That's why the boys do so much of the deliveries. Santa used to do most of it, but last year, he only did the specials."

"The specials?"

"The specials. Like, there was this one kid who wrote us from someplace in England. I don't remember the town. Anyway, his little sister was sick. He didn't want nothing for himself, but he wanted us to give her a real soft, warm pink blanket because she got so cold, and pink was her favorite color. We did a little digging and found out what hospital she was in. Six years old and all wasted away from the treatments—they said she was so tiny and bald you'd have thought she was three or four—and she was pretty close to the end. So that one—her name was Jennie—she was a special. Santa wore the dress suit and everything. He said she wasn't awake much by the time he got there, but when he tucked that pink blanket around her, her eyes opened and she smiled and whispered, 'I love you, Santa.' He did a little 'ho, ho, ho!' and kissed her on the forehead, and he told her she'd been a real good girl and now it was time to rest. She closed her eyes, and he sat beside her bed and held her hand until she was gone." I heard something like a sniffle. He continued, "He said she had the most beautiful smile, like she was dreaming of something real nice. Then the monitors went off and he slipped out of there, and nobody ever knew Santa Claus himself was with her at the end."

Tears blurred my vision. "So that's what Santa does?"

"That's what Santa does. 'Course, we don't know what he'll be able to do this year. He might have to sit Christmas out."

"And that's why Ralph went back," I said slowly.

"There's decisions to make."

"Like what?" An image of the Clauses seated around a table in the dining hall, engaged in intense discussion over cookies and cocoa, rose up in my mind.

"That's confidential." His tone was not unkind, but the words had all the finality of a prison door, slammed and locked.

"Okay." In a weird way, it was.

"Sorry we can't do anything for you. You sure you don't want me to have Ralph call? The missus doesn't have to know."

I shook my head as if he could see me. "Tell him to stay there and do his job. I'll get through this mess somehow." I was about to hang up when something occurred to me. "Listen—sooner or later, the authorities are going to trace my phone records if they haven't already. I don't know what numbers are going to show up on calls to and from the Pole, but—"

"Already taken care of."

I didn't know if he meant they'd changed the numbers or were screening calls, or something else entirely. Something magical. It didn't matter. What mattered was protecting Santa. "They're going to find this call, too—I'm really sorry—I didn't think—"

"Don't worry about it."

"And the emails." I couldn't tell him to destroy them, but the grunt at the other end let me know the message had been received. "Thanks, Charles. I hope Santa does okay. And tell Ralph—" Sudden hot tears rolled down my face, and I couldn't say it.

"I'll tell him."

I clicked off, sobs shaking my body. The cats plunked down next to me, their furry warmth pressed against my side. When I finally fell asleep, the last image in my mind was of Santa Claus sitting next to a hospital bed, his red suit and white beard vivid in the dim light as a tiny figure under a soft pink blanket smiled in perfect peace.

Forty-Five

Angry pounding downstairs ripped me from fitful sleep. In the muted light, the crimson clock display proclaimed that it was 6:57. "What the—" I rolled out of bed, displacing a displeased David, and jammed my arms into the sleeves of the blue-striped bathrobe left behind by a long-ago boyfriend. If this was another idiotic journalist, I would call the police. Enough was enough. Tying the belt firmly, I pulled the curtain aside just enough to see the commotion below.

Men in dark suits swarmed the front yard like ants. I couldn't quite make out the insignia on the dark van by the curb. These weren't journalists. If anything, they looked like—

Shit. I lunged across the bed, grabbed the phone, and punched Michael's number. "They're here," I breathed as soon as he picked up.

"Claus?"

"Feds." The word stuck in my throat.

"You say anything?"

"Haven't even gone downstairs." The doorbell sounded. Harry darted under the bed. I squelched an urge to join him.

"Then how can you be sure?"

Michael was using the calm voice lawyers employ with hysterical clients, and it pissed me off. A horde of lawful intruders was about to pry into every corner of my home, shred my privacy, tear my life apart. I was entitled to some hysteria. "There's a mob of suits on my front walk. This isn't Starbucks delivering."

"Okay, okay. Don't let them in. Don't say anything. I'm on my way." He clicked off.

"Ms. Riley!" An indistinct male voice was shouting now.

"I'm coming!" My voice skidded up into the high register. I dropped the phone into my pocket and took my time getting down the stairs, digging deep for a shred of composure. Adjusting the robe's neckline for maximum coverage, I summoned up my best Katharine Hepburn as I opened the inside door just enough poke my head around. Two more suits, one tall and one shorter, glared through the screen. Before they could speak, I said, "Please keep it down. You're going to wake the neighbors."

"Federal marshals," the taller one snapped, holding his badge up against the screen. It looked like every badge I'd ever seen on television, right down to the black flipcase.

"Would you please wait a minute?" I closed the inside door. If a client called with this problem, what would I say? *Don't talk. Don't piss them off. Wait for your lawyer. Don't give anything away. Be polite. Don't talk.* I opened the inside door again. "What can I do for you?"

"We have a warrant to search the premises," Tall Fed informed me.

"What? Why?" My voice squeaked in a distinctly un-Hepburn manner.

He held out a piece of paper. I hated to unlatch the screen door—what if he forced his way in? But there was no choice. I opened the door barely enough to snatch the paper from his hand, and I snapped it shut and locked as if the tiny well-meaning latch would stop them.

The warrant authorized them to search my entire home, including my computer, bills, bank statements, and tax returns, as well as anything else they might want to peruse. My underwear drawer, maybe. Old diaries. The far back corner of the top shelf in my closet, behind the sweaters, where I kept a few books with titles like *The Woman's Sure-Fire Guide to Achieving Orgasm.* I could feel the agent's eyes on me as I studied the warrant and prayed for Michael to hurry the hell up.

The phone in my pocket rang. "Call from The Lundstrom Law," caller ID intoned.

Shit. "Excuse me." I closed the inside door and punched *talk.* "I can't talk now," I hissed.

"There are federal officers here with a warrant!" Roy screeched.

Double shit. I should have known they'd pull something like this. Harder to defend on two fronts. "They're here, too. Michael's on his way over. Don't let them in the door." He didn't say anything. *Triple shit.* "You already did."

"What was I supposed to do? They're federal marshals!"

At last, my brain clicked into lawyer-mode. "Take it easy. Where are they?"

"In the waiting area."

"Tell them your lawyer is on his way, and they have to go back outside. Whatever you do, don't let them touch *anything*."

"What if the staff shows up?"

In spite of myself, I almost laughed. "At this hour? But call Elsa. Head her off." If anybody would show up at the crack of dawn, it was Elsa. "Have her call everybody else. *Nobody* comes in until you hear from us." Advising somebody else was a thousand times easier than advising myself.

"But—"

"I've got to go." I disconnected the call and drew a deep breath. Smoothing out my robe, I opened the door again. "Sorry about that. Seems your friends are also at my office." None of them looked surprised, or even interested. "My lawyer is on his way. As soon as he gets here, we can discuss this." I indicated the warrant I still clutched.

"Ma'am, we're federal agents—"

"Which is why we will talk about this when my lawyer arrives." I closed the door again, locked it, and sank against it, my heart pounding.

By the time Michael's faded Volvo slid into the spot behind the van, I'd dressed in my black suit. Whatever was happening, serious and professional was my best bet. I splashed water on my face and gathered my slept-on curls into a large barrette at the base of my neck. In the mirror, I looked ghostly-pale except for red stress blotches on my cheeks and neck. Before I could decide whether to put on makeup, I heard a familiar voice outside. My cavalry had arrived. I sped down the stairs, peered through the peephole, and unlocked the door to admit my lawyer.

"Wait here," Michael said to the agents as he slipped inside. I closed and locked the door, and we moved into the living room, out of earshot. I thrust the warrant at him. He read it over. When he looked up, his face was grim.

"I assume the office got the same thing," I said. His eyebrows raised a fraction. "Didn't Roy call you? They're there, too."

He muttered an expletive and punched numbers into his phone. "Roy, it's me. Have you seen the warrant? . . . Get it and send it to me pronto." He clicked off, and we stood in the middle of the room, not speaking, until a quick two-note chime indicated he had an incoming text. Two taps and a swipe later, he was comparing the office warrant to the one in his hand.

"Well?" I asked when he didn't speak.

"This is bullshit. Your home is one thing, but. . . ." He studied the warrants again. Then, he entered another number, waited a moment, and said, "Slim. It's me. Got a situation, and I'm hoping you folks can help. My client's client escaped from prison. . . . Yeah, that's the one. . . . No idea. . . . I'm at her house. Feds are outside. . . . Warrants for her home and our law firm. . . . Yeah, she's my partner. . . . Computers, client files, phone taps, the works. Fishing expedition if I ever saw one. Any chance His Honor has some time? . . . Whenever you say. We can be there in twenty. . . . I owe you." He disconnected. "Judge Rickert will hear us at nine. He has a trial, but Tony says they can push it back a few minutes." Tony Marchietti, a/k/a Michael's law school buddy Slim, had been the court services officer—CSO—for Judge Rickert for fifteen years. If Tony said the judge would hear us, the judge would hear us.

"You're the best," I whispered.

Michael was already back on the phone. "Roy, it's me. Tell the agents we're in front of Judge Rickert at nine. Nobody enters the office until we're done with the judge. . . . She's going to have to move the meeting. I don't care about the CBC right now. Nobody goes in. . . . Tell her to call me. . . . Just stay put. I'll call you when we clear court." He clicked off. "Let me go talk to those guys," he said, indicating the front walk. "Close all the windows. Make sure every access point is locked and set the alarm. I don't think they'd try anything, but you can't be too careful." He folded the warrant and tucked it into his inside pocket. "See you at the car."

*****

An hour later, our little group—Michael, me, two of the agents, and their lawyer—stood in front of Judge Rickert. Not a single hair graced His Honor's enormous head. His liver-spotted scalp gleamed in the fluorescent light.

The government's lawyer was a perky blonde who looked young enough to be heading back to cheerleading practice after the hearing. "Good morning, Your Honor," she chirped. "We have reason to believe that Attorney Riley either knows where Mr. Claus is or can provide us with information that will lead us to him."

"What Attorney Riley does or doesn't know is irrelevant, because the federal government has no jurisdiction," Michael said, rising. His voice was merely smooth, not forceful. He had to walk a fine line: be strong and persuasive without appearing to beat up the little girl. "Mr. Claus was tried in state court, he was convicted of violations of the state penal code, and he was incarcerated in a state facility at the time of his disappearance. The state police have already obtained a warrant for the firm's files as they relate to Mr. Claus. We argued the scope of that warrant yesterday before Judge Binchy, and we're in the process of complying with her order. Everything's being handled at the state level. There's no basis for federal involvement."

"There's also no reason to believe Mr. Claus is still in the state," the blonde replied. "He said he was from the North Pole, and regardless of whether Your Honor buys that, he most definitely was *not* claiming to be from here. There's no reason to believe that, after breaking out of a prison located ten miles from the state line, he decided to stick around Connecticut, where he absolutely could count on being caught and re-incarcerated."

"Judge, the government's claim is based entirely on speculation," said Michael. "Mr. Claus may be in the state, or he may not. Nobody knows for certain." I remained expressionless, my eyes on the judge, as I scribbled "NO" on the legal pad in front of me and slid it over toward Michael. He glanced down, and his mouth tightened.

"Why was he here in the first place?" asked the judge.

"To deliver Christmas presents," said Michael with a completely straight face.

The judge scowled. "Mr. Ruggiero, I pushed back a trial for this. I'm not playing games."

"Neither am I, Your Honor," said Michael. "Mr. Claus told the psychologist who conducted the court-ordered evaluation that he was the son of Santa. The prosecution never proved otherwise."

"But what are the chances he's still in-state?" the blonde piped up. "Everybody knows he called Attorney Riley after he broke out, and if he'd already crossed the state line, that's federal jurisdiction." She gave a little head-bounce as if to add, *So there!*

Judge Rickert glanced at Tony, who shook his head slightly. "Ms. Fitzgerald," he said to the blonde. "I appreciate your argument, but you haven't provided me with any evidence." He glanced at me.

A more experienced lawyer would have taken the hint and called me to the stand to ask point-blank what I knew, but she said nothing. Sighing, he continued, "Your entire argument is supposition. Get me evidence that he's calling here from out of state, and we'll talk."

"Just using the phone lines—" she began.

"—isn't enough," the judge concluded. "There has to be some basis in federal law for the agency's intervention, and you haven't shown me what it is." He perused the warrant, shaking his head. "That said, Mr. Ruggiero, if I were you, I'd suggest your client give some very serious thought to cooperating with these people. Nobody's saying you have to violate client confidentiality, but there's a convicted child molester on the loose, and the only person he seems interested in talking to is Ms. Riley. You two are officers of the court. In the interests of returning him to the facility where the state says he belongs, it would behoove you to make law enforcement's job easier." He banged his gavel. "The motion to quash is granted, and the government's motion to compel is denied without prejudice to renewal if they ever come up with any evidence." A victory, at least for today.

Out in the hall, the taller federal agent said to Michael, "Will you at least consent to having her phone tapped? Just until we track him down."

"Are you insane?" I demanded. "Haven't you heard of the Fourth Amendment? Unreasonable searches? What phones are you talking about? Home? Cell? The office?"

"Well, sure," shrugged the shorter agent.

"No way," said Michael. "You're talking about privileged communications between attorneys and clients. If I consented to this, I'd be grieved by every client the firm has."

"We'd agree not to listen to calls that weren't from, to, or about Mr. Claus," Ms. Fitzgerald said.

"How would you know whether the calls were to, from, or about Mr. Claus without listening to them?" Michael asked.

She seemed stumped by this one. With people like this representing the government, it was a miracle they ever accomplished anything.

"You should think about it," said Tall Fed. "If we get a wiretap order from the court, we're going for everything. What we're offering now is a lot narrower."

"Forget it," I said. "Let's go," I added to Michael. As we walked down the hall, I muttered, "Can you believe those clowns?"

Michael didn't say anything until we were safely outside the building. Then, without pausing or looking directly at me, he said, "Let me talk to them."

"About what? We can't let them tap the firm's calls!"

"No, but we can let them tap yours."

I stopped. "Are you serious?"

"Listen to me. We pulled this off today because their lawyer's an idiot. What she should have done was put you on the stand and ask if you knew whether he was in the state." He let that sink in for a moment. "All they need is one shred of evidence that he's been calling you from out of state, and it won't just be phone taps anymore. It'll be phone records and receipts and everything you can think of, yours and everybody else's. They'll go through every piece of paper in the office. We'll be lucky if they let us keep any of the computers. It'll be a frigging nightmare, and we have a duty to our clients to keep that from happening if at all possible."

I considered his words as we walked to his car. "I can't even think how we could structure something they'd buy," I said.

He unlocked the door. "That's my job."

Forty-Six

Life acquired a nightmarish patina. The evening news showed officers in SWAT gear traipsing through the woods along the state border as news anchors warned viewers about the convicted child molester posing as Santa Claus. Michael told me Drew was being questioned about whether he'd ever done any special favors for Ralph. Lucy Jane's monthly account of receivables showed a five-figure unpaid balance on the Claus account.

The first search of Ralph's file revealed nothing useful, so the police went back for another warrant. This time, they got what they wanted: they tapped my personal landline, confiscated all my cellphones, and subpoenaed two years of phone records. Only Michael's most valiant efforts kept the court from allowing taps on the office phones. He tried to block a request to produce the firm's phone records, but the best he could get was permission to redact client phone numbers other than the Clauses', a task that took Lucy Jane and two assistants three full days and ultimately bore no fruit: I overheard one officer telling another that he'd called all the Claus numbers, but not one worked.

"You called one of these numbers on August 18 and talked for half an hour," Major Otis said in yet another of our near-daily meetings. "Now, when our guys call—even using your phone—we get a message that the number is out of service. Can you explain that?"

"The number must be out of service," I said. Michael kicked me under the table.

"Do you have any other contact information for anyone who knows where Mr. Claus is?"

"No."

"Have you been in communication with Mr. Claus or his family since August 18?"

"No."

"Emails? Texts?"

"No."

"When you called that number on August 18, who did you talk to?"

I could feel Michael not looking at me. "A family friend. Charles. I don't know his last name."

The shark smelled blood in the water. "Does this family friend know where Ralph Claus is?"

"I didn't ask." Which was true, but it didn't stop the barrage of questions. I admitted asking if Ralph was all right, but when Otis said, "And that took half an hour? Come on, Ms. Riley—what did you really talk about?", it was all I could do not to tell him about Santa Claus and little Jennie and a world of beauty and kindness and joy. When we finally staggered out of the state police barracks, dark had fallen, but floodlights blinded us as reporters shouted unintelligible questions, ignoring Michael's repeated, "No comment! No comment!"

That night, as I clicked on the television—the police had confiscated my laptop—the first face I saw was Victoria Leopold's. "Hal Zenkman helped me get justice for my little boy after he was assaulted in our own home," she said to the camera, her eyes earnest. The scene shifted to Victoria outside the courthouse as Zenkman's voiceover intoned, "As governor, I will strengthen laws protecting the precious children of our state from predators." The vulnerable, hurting population—abused children, crime victims, single parents—had always been out of his privileged white reach. Ralph and I handed him an otherwise unattainable demographic. I refilled my wineglass as the sun glinted off the senator's expensive haircut and he assured us that he approved this message. *No shit.* The bastard owed me a thank-you note.

While Otis focused on tearing my life apart, his cohorts sought yet another warrant. This time, it was scary-ugly. They wanted the files of all our clients, apparently suspecting we'd intentionally misfiled something to hide it. I fought the battle from my office, juggling deadlines on Michael's cases and my own as Michael returned to court to wage war over our clients' right to privacy in their dealings with counsel. I offered to go along, but he said, "I'll take Eckert."

They returned just before five o'clock, dark and silent. The judge authorized the police to search the firm's files and computers, with the only restrictions being that they had to do it during normal business hours and they couldn't remove anything from the premises except by specific order. Two hours later, we huddled in Elsa's living room for an emergency partnership meeting to debate whether ethical obligations to our clients entitled—or required—us to refuse the police entry when they descended upon us eight-thirty the next morning.

"It's a legitimate order," Eckert said for the fiftieth time. "We can't disobey the court."

"It's completely unreasonable," Elsa said. "How is combing through the CBC's file going to help them figure out if Claus has been in touch with Meg?"

"Not to mention our financials," Roy said. "It's nobody's business who's paying us. Besides, everything we got on Claus came in as cash. What good will it do them to see that?"

"It's going to look suspicious." Elsa sipped her wine, a red so elite I'd never heard of it. We didn't usually drink at partnership meetings, but if anyone was surveilling us—more likely, me—wine and crudités made us look more like a book club and less like lawyers plotting to break the law.

"Criminal clients routinely pay cash," Michael reminded her.

"Except we have no idea where the money came from," said Elsa.

"That's true of all our clients," I said. "Just because they write a check doesn't mean the money wasn't laundered six times over."

"We're getting off the topic," Eckert said. "The question is whether we comply with the court's order." Any decision meant risk: if we disobeyed the order, we could be held in contempt and fined—or even incarcerated—but if we complied, we could be grieved and sued.

"Can't we appeal?" Roy asked. "Doesn't that freeze the order?"

"It's not a final judgment," I said. "You can't appeal from a ruling that's not a final judgment." I could tell he didn't understand, but before I could launch into a primer on appellate law, Michael said, "First thing in the morning, we're filing a petition in the state supreme court for permission to take an immediate appeal. That'll stay the order for now."

"How much time does it buy us?" Eckert asked.

"Not a lot," said Michael. "The chief justice has to rule within seven days. If he denies it, the stay is lifted, and we're right back here." He looked around the group. "These petitions are almost never granted. We need to decide what we're going to do when the Supremes say 'no.'"

Elsa poured more wine into her glass and Eckert's. Mine remained empty. "I move that if we're going to disobey the order, it has to be unanimous," she said. "If we're opening the firm up to contempt charges, we should all agree to undertake that risk."

"Second," said Roy.

"All in favor, raise your hand," said Eckert. He, Roy, and Elsa raised their hands.

"Very well," said Eckert. "I suggest we wait to see what the supreme court does. If they deny the petition, we'll decide then how to respond."

"Can I just say something?" I interjected. "If we comply with the court's order, our clients are going to jump ship. If we refuse, that lets them know we're willing to fight for them even when it costs us." I met Elsa's gaze. "In other words, it's good business."

"You're leaving out the part about damage to our reputations," she retorted. "Besides, if the court finds we willfully disobeyed the order, the fallout won't be covered by our insurance." She must have spent the afternoon reviewing our malpractice policy. "Our professional ratings will drop, our premiums will go up, and A-list clients won't come anywhere near us."

"If they have any sense, they'll be impressed by our dedication to protecting client privacy," I shot back, but the rejoinder sounded weak even to me.

"In a year, no one will remember why we were disciplined, just that we were," she said. "This heroism you seem to think is so compelling will fade, but the black marks on our professional reputations will be permanent. I'm not saying I like the notion of disclosing client information, but if we do it because a court orders us to, how can the clients complain? Isn't that what you tell them all the time—there's nothing you can do because the court ordered this or that?" Her eyes burned into mine. "Isn't that what you told Cyril Walker? That his wife had to do that deposition because the court said so? How can you tell him that and then turn around and say the court's orders don't apply to you?"

"To *us*," I said in my iciest tone. "And that's entirely different.

We're ethically required to keep our clients' information private. Walker just didn't want anybody asking his wife about his cheating."

"All right, all right," said Eckert. "I think it's clear that the thing to do right now is wait for the ruling on the petition. We don't have to make any decisions until then." He started to rise.

"There's one other choice," said Roy. Eckert sat back down. His eyes on his wineglass, Roy said, "Meg could resign. For the good of the firm."

"What?" I could barely get the word out.

"Don't be an idiot!" Michael snapped as Elsa said, "That's not a bad—"

"Enough!" Papa Eckert's booming bass cut through. "No one's resigning. That is not an issue before us." He glared from one to the next. "Besides, it wouldn't help," he said, his voice relaxing. "The question is about what's happened up to now. Changing Meg's future status won't alter her past contacts with Claus." He rose, this time with deliberation. "I hereby move to adjourn this meeting."

"Second," said Michael. He and Eckert voted to adjourn, and I chimed in. A minute later, Michael and I were on Elsa's pristine brick walk.

"Don't worry," he said before I could speak. "You're not going anywhere."

Roy and Eckert still hadn't come out of Elsa's house. It didn't take a wiretap to know what they were discussing. All the way home, Roy's words echoed in my head: *Meg could resign. For the good of the firm.* And Michael's declaration: *You're not going anywhere.*

I wished I were as certain as he was.

Forty-Seven

By dawn, the media vultures were camped in front of our building. They weren't allowed on the property, but that didn't stop them from racing to the edge of the driveway and shouting questions every time a shaken client tried to drive in or out. An escaped convict was already big news in our little state; combined with the notion that his female lawyer might have helped him escape, it was a great big juicy slobberfest of innuendo. They didn't come right out and say I'd been sleeping with Ralph, but they slithered up to that door and banged on it with all their might.

Inside the office, things were no better. Roy's words still rang in my ears, competing with a full voicemail box and dozens of emails from anxious clients. Several clients appeared unannounced in our waiting area, braving the media circus for the privilege of venting their ire in person. Janine Lane, the collaborative divorce client who'd thought Ralph's advice so wise, shrieked about how reckless I'd been in allowing him to be alone with her, how lucky she was that this felon hadn't attacked her, and how truly, utterly fired I was. "And don't think you're going to see another penny from me!" she shouted, storming out of the conference room and through the waiting area where a clutch of nervous-looking clients stared in horror.

Most of them were terrified about what the police might see in their files. The concern was understandable: client files routinely contain compromising information about activities from drug deals to embezzlement to infidelity. We did our best to reassure them, but by Labor Day, nearly a quarter of our clients had demanded their files. When we said we couldn't just hand them over—which was true, and not just because of the warrants—the clients screeched that they would sue us or grieve us, or both.

The morning after the holiday weekend, Robin slipped into my office. "Elsa lost CBC."

"They're here?" I hadn't seen any custom-tailored suits in the waiting area.

Robin shook her head. "Dawn says she got the call last night."

Elsa must be spitting blood. "Cyril called her?"

"Not Cyril," Robin said. "Gene Louderman." CBC's former lawyer, now back in the fold. "Elsa's been on the phone for hours trying to reach somebody over at CBC. All she got was an email confirming they've gone back to Louderman and asking for a final bill."

"Thanks for the heads up." I flicked through my calendar. The deposition of Cyril Walker's assistant was scheduled for next week. "Have we heard anything?"

Robin shook her head. "Not yet."

Twenty minutes later, an email flashed on my screen. "Partnership meeting at two," it said. Nothing about the content, but I could guess.

The police occupied the conference room, so we assembled in Eckert's office. "We've lost CBC." Elsa bit off the words, barely containing her rage. "Because of all *this*." She swept her hand around to indicate the current chaos. "They said the firm's reputation was not what they'd been led to believe, and they couldn't afford to be affiliated with us."

"I don't suppose you pointed out to them that the reason for all this uproar is their good friend, Hal Zenkman," I said.

"I didn't," she snapped. "Because it isn't true. The reason for this—uproar—is your handling of the Claus matter."

"I had nothing to do with his escape!" She raised her well-manicured brows: *Really, now.*

"That's enough!" said Eckert.

"And we may lose Walker Industries," Elsa added. "Cyril has not been pleased with the way you've handled his case, even before he had to worry about the police reading his file."

"What are you talking about? I've handled his case just fine." I might not have swooned over the client, but I'd represented him ably. I'd stake my malpractice policy on it.

"I told you from the beginning, he's an important client. Instead of making his case your number one priority, you've been wasting time on Claus—and you see where that's gotten us."

"Wasting time? Claus was coming up for trial. Cyril Walker's is still in discovery, so it doesn't need as much attention right now. Pardon me if I haven't churned the file enough for your tastes." *Churning the file* meant doing unnecessary tasks to create the illusion that the lawyer was working on the matter. In fact, the only reason to churn a file was to run up bills.

"I beg your pardon." Fury blazed beneath her icy exterior. "There's a difference between taking care of a valued client and churning a file. If you don't know that, maybe you're not equipped to be handling high-end matters."

"I said, that's enough!" Eckert sounded like my father had when my brother and I argued at the dinner table. "The purpose of this meeting was to apprise you of the fact that we've lost a significant source of revenue, and we're at risk of losing more."

"We knew that," Roy said. "Fourteen of my clients have fired the firm. It's a nightmare." He turned to Elsa. "Is there anything we can do to keep Walker from pulling his business?"

Elsa afforded me a long look. "Not as things stand."

"What does that mean?" Michael asked.

"It means the firm's reputation has been compromised." Eckert's voice was heavy. "The question is whether we can come back from it."

I felt as though I were drowning. "What are you saying?"

"Nothing," Michael cut in. "No one's saying anything. The feeding frenzy will die down when the police see that there's nothing here. In a few days, everything will be back to normal." His voice was clear and strong, but no one looked convinced.

Eventually, because there was nothing else to say, we all trudged back to our offices. Robin, the Bearer of Bad News, stood at the top of the stairs as I ascended.

"What?" I asked. As if I couldn't guess.

"We're off *Howley versus Walker*." She handed me the printout of an appearance, the document a lawyer files with the court to let them know who represents a party. This appearance had been filed by McGooley, Rose & Swarthorn. Our old firm. I didn't recognize the name of the lawyer who'd signed it, but he'd checked the box that said MR&S's appearance was in lieu of mine. In other words, they were in, and we were out.

"Everybody who's surprised, raise your hand," I muttered. "Did we at least get an email officially firing us?"

"Nothing," Robin said. "The appearance is stamped as e-filed about an hour ago."

I scrolled through my contact list and punched in Cyril's cell, only to be sent immediately to voicemail. I called Walker Industries and asked to speak with Mr. Walker. "It's very important," I said, but I was already on hold. After easy-listening renditions of half a dozen songs I'd known in high school, a female voice purred, "Mr. Walker's office."

"This is Attorney Megan Riley. I need to speak with Mr. Walker, please."

"I'm sorry," she said, not sounding at all apologetic. "Mr. Walker is unavailable."

"Will you please ask him to call me?" I spelled my name and recited my phone number.

"I'll give him the message." She clicked off without saying "goodbye."

"You're not going to get him," Robin said from the doorway. "Dawn said he's been ignoring Elsa's calls all day. Landline *and* cell, and he always answers his cell when she calls."

"Maybe he's out," I said.

"Out hiring new lawyers," she replied. I glared at her, and she shrugged.

My emails included a message from one Jonathan Digruel, an associate at MR&S, requesting that I prepare the file on *Howley v. Walker* for transfer. He offered to have someone pick it up in the morning. I responded that there would be a delay in preparing the file and reminded him that he could access all pleadings on the judicial branch website. I wasn't about to tell this little twit that I couldn't hand over the file until the police had finished combing through it. Instead, I emailed Lucy Jane to let her know we would be closing the file and that I'd prepare a final bill by morning. I forwarded the message to Robin with a note to get me all her unbilled time in the next hour. Then, I sat back and listened to the silence.

Forty-Eight

At first, it seemed as though Michael might be right. Once the police finished wasting taxpayer money scrutinizing our files, the media largely ignored us. DESPP folks would only say that the investigation was ongoing. We remained steadfast in our refusal to comment. Eventually, television vans disappeared from the street in front of our building.

The flood of clients out the door had slowed; that was one good thing. The ones who had fired us still called, demanding their files or complaining about their bills, but we handled them.

Michael had an off-the-record chat with Evan York, a former prosecutor who now handled white-collar criminal defense cases. Evan opined that the police might keep digging, but it didn't sound to him as if there were grounds for indicting me. "Sounds like she was stupid, but she didn't break the law," was his conclusion, which Michael repeated to me verbatim.

Just when I thought the worst might be behind us, the intercom buzzed. Marilyn's voice sounded strained: "Meg, can you come down here?"

"For what?" I was in the midst of drafting a demand letter for LaVonda Esposito, who broke her wrist when she slipped on the icy walk in front of her apartment building. LaVonda's landlord, who claimed to be a very religious man, subscribed to the notion that when it came to snow and ice, God put it there and God would take it away.

"Just come down." She clicked off.

Possibilities raced through my mind. The television crews were gone. The police were gone. The flood of client complaints had slowed to a trickle. Who else? An elf. Or Meredith Claus, regal as ever. Or even Ralph, coming to give himself up. My heart pounded as I descended the last flight of stairs, braced for an ambassador from the North Pole.

Stan Liebjak, a marshal we routinely used for serving process, stood by Marilyn's desk. I squared my shoulders and approached with a neutral expression. "Morning, Stan."

"Morning, Attorney Riley," he said. He usually called me "Meg."

I tried to sound casual, businesslike. "What's up?"

He handed me a large brown envelope. The upper left corner bore the imprint of the Statewide Grievance Committee. I knew he knew what it contained, because any time a marshal served papers, he had to file a return that identified in detail exactly what documents he'd served and on whom. I wasn't about to ask, though. Not here. Not now. I thanked him and took the envelope back upstairs. Later, I couldn't remember if I said "goodbye."

I closed the door to my office and spilled the contents of the envelope onto the table. The committee was summoning me to a hearing, but it wasn't about a grievance filed by a client. I was being summoned to appear and show cause why I shouldn't be subjected to professional discipline for my improper relationship with one Ralph Claus and my role in assisting, facilitating, or otherwise aiding and abetting in his disappearance from the custody of the state of Connecticut. Clipped to the summons was a complaint containing vague and overly broad statements about my supposed wrongful acts, as well as very specific and chilling descriptions of the possible consequences—including disbarment and referral for criminal charges.

I sank into a chair. Lulu hopped up onto the table, nosed the documents, and peered at me. I knew I should call Michael and Geoff Quinn—though maybe not in that order—but I couldn't make myself move. For the first time, I truly understood all those clients who kept insisting that they shouldn't be in jail, they hadn't done anything wrong, they were completely innocent. Because *I* was completely innocent. I truly had no idea Ralph was planning to escape. I didn't even know he was gone until the prison called. And God knew, I never asked him to call me after he escaped.

For that matter, I never asked for any involvement in this case. It was dumped on me by a guy I drank beer with in law school. I certainly never asked to haul my ass up to the Pole. I never asked Ralph to meet Trevor Leopold while I was away. And I sure as hell wasn't the one who told Ken Solberg that Ralph was Santa's son, all but guaranteeing that we'd go down in flames and he'd end up in the very prison he managed to escape from. That was all Ralph, every last bit of it.

Lulu rubbed her whiskers against my face. That was when I lost it.

Kate Hepburn would have done the same.

*****

"I don't understand," I said the next morning in Geoff Quinn's picturesque conference room. Like the other firms in our neighborhood, Quinn Law, LLC was ensconced in a renovated Victorian. With the same understated elegance as the Lundstrom Law Firm, it should have felt familiar, but being on the other side of the file changed everything. "They've already gone through everything. They've tapped my phones, searched my house, scoured my office—they know there's nothing there!"

Geoff's face was unreadable. After twenty-seven years of defending lawyers, there was little he hadn't heard. Still, I was probably the first of his clients to be implicated in a prison break by Santa Claus's son.

I hadn't been to confession since my junior year in high school—specifically, the day after I celebrated my acceptance into the National Honor Society by surrendering my virginity to Tom Motten. Father Verona absolved me, but he warned that I couldn't do it again until I was married. Since I didn't want to lie to a priest, and I really didn't want to stop having sex with Tom, the only choice was to stop going to confession.

Now, with Geoff's unblinking eyes on me, I admitted almost everything. Putting money in Ralph's prison account. Unbilled visits disguised as attorney visits so we could have the pro room. Traveling to his family's toymaking facility, although I didn't mention the reindeer. I just said the family lived way up north and I wasn't quite certain where—which was true, because after all, I only had their word that it was the North Pole. It could have been Canada, or Greenland, or some other icy place. Dinners at the diner and the sushi place.

"Did you have a sexual relationship with him?" Geoff's tone was neutral. He might have been inquiring what year I was admitted to practice.

"No." He said nothing. "No," I repeated. "I never had sex with him." He kept waiting, expressionless. "We kissed," I said finally. "But that's all." No comment. "Really, that's all." When he didn't respond, I said, "Break it to me gently. How bad is this?"

He leaned back in his chair. "Not good, but not as bad as it could be. You've definitely deviated from acceptable attorney behavior, but it doesn't appear that you've violated the Rules of Professional Conduct." Before I could enjoy a moment of relief, he went on, "That said, I can certainly see why they want to squeeze you for information. Since the investigation is ongoing, the police won't give me a copy of your statement. Did you tell them all this?"

"Some of it. The prison visits. The money. The dinners." He waited. "I told them I'd never seen him anywhere outside of Connecticut." When he said nothing, I pointed out, "It's true. He wasn't there when I went to see his family. And yes, they asked if I'd ever slept with him, and I told them the truth, too." Not that they'd appeared to believe me, but in my darkest moments, I couldn't fault their skepticism. If I'd been questioning me, I wouldn't have believed it. "What's going to happen?"

"It depends. From a legal standpoint, I don't see a basis for disbarment, but that doesn't mean they won't try. The bigger the threat, the more likely you are to reveal information."

"But I didn't do anything wrong!" For an insane instant, I felt like crying.

"I wouldn't go that far. Your conduct was far from exemplary. With an escaped felon involved, the committee is likely to put pressure on you in the hope that you'll reveal something more." He eyed me as if expecting me to volunteer more information, but I remained silent. "Very well, then. I'll let you know when I receive notice of the hearing. In the meantime, make a list of any witnesses who will support your position." He closed his folio and subtly pressed the button on his thin gold watch that had timed our meeting.

The crisp autumn air usually energized me. As I trudged back to my office, I tried to think of witnesses to support my position. Michael had no first-hand knowledge—other than his one conversation with Ralph, he only knew what I'd told him, and the committee's lawyer could argue that I used him to establish my story. As for Holly—even if she was willing to cooperate, her testimony would hurt more than help. She knew about the Pole, but she also knew my feelings for Ralph.

By the time I reached our front porch, I had to face the facts.

I was on my own.

Forty-Nine

At the beginning of October, the grievance committee issued notice of the hearing for the first of November. Geoff said this was speedier than usual. I asked if that was good or bad, and he said, "I imagine someone's running out of patience. It's been several weeks, and there's no sign of your client. If pressuring you this way doesn't work, they may be out of options."

"And the election's coming up," I reminded him. Geoff had never said whether he subscribed to my theory that Hal Zenkman was pushing this whole matter, but no one could ignore Zenkman's nightly commercials proclaiming that he was a friend of business and our state's children. Pictures of Victoria and Trevor Leopold featured prominently in those ads.

The news people lost interest after an initial tidbit about how I might be disbarred for an unethical relationship with an escaped convict. The news didn't say we'd been having an affair, but internet trolls knew no such delicacy: multiple times each day, people clicked the "contact us" link on the firm website to send vulgar messages about what I'd supposedly done with Santa. We couldn't disconnect the link lest we miss a real client, so our IT guy set up a filter to screen out a variety of obscenities, as well as some of the more colorful terms used to describe sex acts.

It was the loneliest time I could recall. Geoff had cautioned against speaking to anyone about the case, saying, "You don't want to create witnesses."

I'd only heard from Holly once since the day of the verdict. After Ralph's disappearance, when the news was full of clips of me walking out of the state police barracks, she texted me. Not a visit. Not a phone call. Not even an email. Just a lousy text asking, *Are u ok?* When I responded *no*, she asked, *Anything I can do?* Another *no*, and the conversation ended.

"Do you know if she's been questioned?" I asked Geoff.

"I imagine so. You haven't been in touch, have you?"

"Barely," I said. I told him about the texts, and all he said was, "Good. Keep it that way."

On the surface, my relationship with my partners looked normal enough. Elsa was more formal since Cyril, Walker Industries, and CBC decamped, but Eckert and Roy behaved as they had before, neither hostile nor solicitous. They made no unnecessary visits to the third floor, leaving me in solitude with Robin and Lulu. Even Michael was around less now that he was spending more time soliciting business. When I suggested that I do the same, he said, "I don't think that's a good idea right now."

*****

When I was in middle school, kids in a group would taunt one who was alone: "You're NF! You have No Friends!" It was the worst thing we could say about a person.

Lawyers were subtler. When I entered Courtroom 102 for short calendar, no one turned his back, but neither did anyone meet my eyes. Maybe they really were engrossed in their papers, but as I walked to the front to check in with the clerk, I felt at once conspicuous and invisible.

"Good morning, Irene," I said a shade too loudly. "I'm here on number 6. *Raffles v. Akhtar*. Motion to dismiss. Megan Riley."

"Good morning, Attorney Riley." She didn't look up from the screen. "You're all set. Next?"

"Thanks." I turned around to see a number of heads ducking slightly. Gripping the handle of my briefcase, I returned to the gallery and took a seat at the aisle end on the front bench. As nine-thirty drew near, I heard and felt movement behind me, lawyers settling into their seats, but no one sat on my bench.

Just as the knock on the chambers door announced the judge's entry, Hermy Jacobsen squeezed past me. "Got your own spot here," he whispered as I rose. When the judge told us to be seated, I expected him to move down a bit before sitting, but he remained by my side. I wasn't certain whether to be irritated at his disregard of my personal space or relieved that someone didn't consider me a leper.

My case was the second one called. If the judge knew about my recent travails, he didn't let on. It didn't matter. I lost anyway.

On the way out of the courthouse, eyes on my phone, I nearly collided with a blue-suited figure. "Oh, I'm sorry," I said, looking up.

"Meg! How are you?" It was my ex-partner, Rick. His capped teeth gleamed, his hair gel shone, and his suit probably cost as much as my mortgage payment.

"Hey, Rick," I said, trying to muster some enthusiasm. "How are you?"

"Great! I'm just great!" He sounded slightly manic. I was tempted to look around for a television camera to see who he was performing for, but in truth, Rick had always been like this. Why dignified Eckert thought Rick was a good fit for our firm would forever remain a mystery.

"Glad to hear it," I said. "How's—" I couldn't remember her name.

"Trisha," he supplied. "Oh, she's great. Did you know we had another kid? That's three now!" He whipped out his phone and started thumbing through pictures— "That's Ricky on his fourth birthday, and there's Taylor with his fire truck, and see, here's Trisha with Bristol—she looks just like her, doesn't she?" I made appropriate murmurs, but he didn't seem to notice any lack of enthusiasm. Just when I was about to escape, he looked up. "How're things with you?"

"Good. Busy. You know the drill." No way would I mention the Claus mess.

I didn't have to. He leaned closer. "Don't worry, Meg. You'll be okay."

"I beg your pardon?" I tried to sound frosty.

"Look, I understand," Rick said, his tone disconcertingly intimate. "Everybody's criticizing you, and you think you're never going to get out from under it, but you do. I mean, look at me. Back when I got kicked out of the firm, I thought I was all washed up, but now, I'm in with Carter Fitzhugh—you know Carter, right?" Carter and Rick had a series of commercials that aired during late-night talk shows: *Is your marriage over? We can help! Make sure you get what you're entitled to! Call Fitzhugh & McGee at . . .* whatever the number was. 1-800-SHYSTERS, probably. Rick bubbled on: "So many people are splitting up, we're *cleaning* up. Sometimes I barely get to see my own wife, I'm so busy helping other guys get rid of theirs!" He chuckled at his own wit. "Listen, if you need anything, let me know. I can send you some cases. I'm up to my eyeballs these days. I could use the help."

I forced a smile. "Thanks, Rick, but I'm good. As it happens, I'm pretty busy myself." Managing my own catastrophes was time-consuming.

The Dalai Lama of Disgraced Lawyers nodded. I half-expected him to stroke his beardless chin. "I know how you feel," he said, lowering his voice to a confidential level. "Remember how everybody judged me when I got together with Trisha?" Apparently, he'd forgotten that I judged him right out of the firm. "But the thing is, you can't choose who you love." He winked and patted my shoulder.

"It's not the same," I said, stepping back. "Ralph Claus is my client, not my opponent, and I'm not involved with him."

"Sure, whatever." He waved his hand in placid disbelief. His nails were clear and shiny. I'd bet anything he got manicures. "Just remember, it's not practicing law that matters. It's love. If you've got that, nothing else is important," said the divorce lawyer in the four-figure suit.

"Good to know," I said. "I have to run. Take care!" I ducked past him and was out on the street before he could do more than turn around.

Fifty

The days ran together as the hearing drew nearer. Nausea and headaches were my constant companions; I tried to convince myself it was the flu. My waistbands squeezed tighter as extra glasses of wine and boxes of cookies took their toll. While I brushed my teeth or walked through the supermarket, I argued with a phantom attorney about whether I'd been zealous or unethical. In my dreams, vengeful ex-boyfriends told a courtroom full of my colleagues how they weren't surprised I'd been banging my client since I was always kind of slutty, and did anyone want to hear about the time. . . ?

Efforts to focus on work were fruitless. Alone in my too-quiet office, I dredged my memory for any professional misjudgment that the grievance committee's lawyer would wave around like a bloody shirt as proof that I was unfit to practice law.

I spent hours calculating the bare minimum I'd need to earn if they disbarred me. What marketable skills did I have? A fondness for sushi, a better-than-average knowledge of movie trivia, a passion for cats, wine, and David Copperfield—these did not add up to a paycheck. With no particular interest in children, teaching wasn't a viable option. I could write legal briefs, but who would hire a disgraced attorney to craft their message?

"You could do Mrs. C.'s job. Wouldn't that be your role anyway when Santa retired and Ralph got promoted?"

I shook my head to rid myself of Holly's words. I loved my home, my practice, my world. I didn't want to leave the life I'd built here. I just wanted everything to go back to normal.

I didn't tell Michael any of this, because he'd have said not to worry until it was time. I didn't tell the other partners, because I didn't want to give them any more reasons to doubt me. I didn't tell my mother when she called, because there was no point in worrying her. I didn't tell my brother, because he had enough on his plate—he was struggling to save for college for three kids, and his company was downsizing. I didn't tell Geoff, because I already owed him a substantial sum and it didn't seem prudent to announce that I might not be able to pay him if we lost. I didn't tell Holly, because I hadn't heard from her since those texts.

And I didn't tell Ralph, because I couldn't.

*****

The low-ceilinged hearing room was humble, to put it nicely. Soundproofing tiles hung on the left wall, presumably to reduce the echo from the worn linoleum floor. Blond paneling circa 1976 ran along the opposite wall. More soundproof tiles, some with brown-edged water stains, covered the ceiling. The hearing officer's table sat on a platform that barely elevated his padded metal chair above the witness chair to its left. The two counsel tables were just large enough for two chairs each. A court reporter sat at a tiny desk to the right of the hearing officer. Three pairs of scraped-up wooden benches afforded seating for a couple dozen spectators.

From my seat next to Geoff at counsel table, I looked around. Eckert, Elsa, and Roy sat in the front row of the gallery. Michael was in New London, picking a jury for a case that used to be mine. No sign of Holly. A few people I didn't recognize were scattered throughout the room. No media organization had requested permission to bring in a camera; even Zenkman's thirst for publicity didn't reach this low.

More people trickled in. "Are we the only case?" I whispered to Geoff, who nodded. Everybody was here to find out what I had to say.

Victoria Leopold swept in, a well-dressed young man by her side. I'd have bet anything he was one of Zenkman's aides. They seated themselves in the front row on the other side, behind the committee's lawyer. When she saw me, she lifted her nose as though smelling something distasteful. Robin, who'd been tracking the progress of the Leopolds' divorce case, had told me Friday that judgment had entered, meaning the couple was officially divorced and so Victoria's presence today was pure *schadenfreude*.

The hearing officer, a New Orleans transplant named Jacques

St. Pierre, was tall and broad with a gray ponytail that curled halfway down his back. His drawl made condescending New Englanders think he was a clueless good-ol'-boy. In fact, before he joined the SGC, he'd made a name for himself representing executives accused of high-level white-collar crimes.

By the time he called for order, the room was packed. He explained the procedure: there would be no opening or closing statements. The Statewide Grievance Committee would call its witnesses; then Geoff would call ours. Post-hearing briefs were optional. Simple, straightforward. Nowhere to hide.

The SGC lawyer, Scott Frazier, called me to the stand. I raised my right hand and swore to tell the truth, the whole truth, and nothing but the truth, so help me God or penalty of perjury. I stated my name and addresses, home and business. I testified about my education, how long I'd been in practice, what kind of cases I handled, how long I'd been with the firm, and how I'd never had the slightest blemish on my record.

Then, Frazier moved on to Ralph Claus. He noted for the record that I wasn't being asked to reveal anything that was protected by the attorney-client privilege; St. Pierre nodded his approval. I testified about Judge Pearce's request, emphasizing that I'd never met this client before. I described the arraignment, adding, "I've done a number of arraignments before Judge Marcos, and I've never seen him set such a low bail. It suggested to me that the judge did not see Mr. Claus as a threat." In the gallery, Victoria Leopold glowered.

Frazier inquired about the initial charges. Then, he caught me by surprise, asking, "Was there anything about this case that was any different from a typical breaking-and-entering case?"

I didn't know how to answer. I wasn't about to tell the world about my trip to the North Pole, or my dinners with Ralph, or how it had become clear early on that Ralph had a crush on me and vice versa. I glanced over at Geoff, willing him to object, but he remained seated. "I'm not certain I understand the question," I said, more to buy time than anything else.

"You said Mr. Claus was released on bond. How long was he out before he was arrested again?"

Thank heaven. I explained how I'd been out of town for New Year's—no specifics about where or why—and my partner called to tell me the client was back in jail. Citing the trial testimony, I explained that according to Victoria Leopold's niece, Trevor had sent an email to Santa, asking to meet, and Ralph had gone, only to have the niece drive him to the Leopolds' home where he was arrested again. I did my best to make it sound as if they'd deliberately set him up. Victoria Leopold's handler whispered something to her.

"At what point did you become aware that Mr. Claus intended to escape from prison?" Frazier asked.

The abrupt shift startled me. "After the state police came to my office to investigate his disappearance. It was on the internet." Geoff frowned slightly, a cue to tone it down.

"You didn't know anything at all before then?" Frazier's skepticism was plain.

"Not a thing." Geoff had said not to be too emphatic—*just answer the questions*—but I couldn't afford any quibbling.

"During the pretrial period, how often were you in contact with Mr. Claus?"

"Fairly often. If memory serves, he was permitted one phone call a week to his attorney and one attorney visit a month."

A flicker of annoyance darted across Geoff's face. *We're not hiding anything*, he'd cautioned. Strictly speaking, I wasn't. But we both knew my answer was misleading, and the visitor logs would reveal the truth. So I added, "During his pretrial incarceration, I saw him approximately once a week." Out of the corner of my eye, I saw the hearing officer make a note on his yellow legal pad.

"Is that your typical practice with an incarcerated client?"

"No, but Mr. Claus had no local friends or contacts. So much of the case was going to depend on his state of mind that I felt it was important to support him, to keep him from becoming depressed, especially since he was in protected custody." Geoff fixed his eyes on me. I was talking too much. That was how witnesses got themselves into trouble.

"And yet, you didn't bill for many of these visits, did you?"

"Some yes, some no." But it was too late. Frazier introduced my bills, my internal time sheets, and the Granby visitor logs to show that I'd hadn't billed for most of my visits to Ralph. In the front row, my partners were stone-faced.

Frazier moved on to the verdict, Ralph's call that night, my trip to Foster, and the events of the next day. "Why did you go up to the prison on the night of August 16?" he asked.

"I was concerned for Mr. Claus's safety. He'd been convicted of sexual assault on a young child. I knew he was in protected custody, but I had no idea how well-protected he was."

"And yet, you didn't contact the prison," Frazier pointed out. "You thought he might be in danger, but when you were stopped by a security officer, your response was to turn around and leave."

"I felt I might have overreacted," I said as evenly as possible. "Mr. Claus had said he was fine. In retrospect, I was probably worn out and not thinking clearly. It was a difficult trial."

"It wasn't unusually long, was it?"

"No."

"The legal issues weren't particularly sophisticated, were they?"

"Application of the law to specific facts always involves sophisticated analysis," I said. "My client was charged with violation of several different statutes. I had to research each one."

Frazier perused my bills. "Is that what you discussed with Mr. Claus when you went to visit him every week of his incarceration?"

"Objection. Attorney-client privilege." Geoff didn't even bother rising.

"Sustained," St. Pierre drawled.

"She's already talked about what he said," Frazier protested. "She opened the door."

"Only as to one specific conversation which occurred after the trial ended," Geoff said. "Anything before that point is part of the communications between attorney and client in connection with her representation of him at trial. Also, it's not relevant to the issue of whether Attorney Riley violated the rules of conduct, and that's what we're here about."

The hearing officer regarded the lawyers. "You gentlemen know we don't go strictly by the rules of evidence here." It was true: hearing officers had a tendency to let practically any evidence in. "Just because it was a conversation between lawyer and client doesn't make it privileged. I'm ruling that any communications after the end of trial are admissible unless they pertain specifically and directly to what Attorney Riley was going to do next in the case—whether she was going to file motions, take an appeal, that sort of thing."

"What about pretrial communications that don't involve the representation?" Frazier asked.

"There's no evidence of such communications," Geoff responded.

"The evidence is clear. Attorney Riley never met Mr. Claus before Judge Pearce asked her to represent him. Within a week of that meeting, he was back in prison, and he remained there until August seventeenth, when the corrections officer reported him missing."

"Then what were they talking about in all those weekly meetings?" Frazier asked. "You're not going to tell me a busy lawyer takes time out of her schedule every single week to go up to Foster to discuss a fairly straightforward case with the client. And if she did, why wasn't she billing? Does she routinely work for free? This wasn't pro bono. They have billing records and a ledger sheet showing payments. She was going up there to see this guy, but she wasn't charging him, and that smells an awful lot like something other than a lawyer representing a client." I was half-afraid St. Pierre would agree, but he just told Frazier to continue his examination.

The remainder of the morning was a grueling, picayune examination of my bills and time sheets, as well as everything I'd done that wasn't reflected in those documents. By the time we broke for lunch, I was drained.

"I thought it went well," Roy offered across a scratched Formica table at a diner near the committee's offices.

"Please don't discuss the case," Geoff said.

My appetite had uncharacteristically taken flight, but Elsa ordered a chef's salad for me. "You'll need protein," she said. Without consulting me, she selected low-fat balsamic vinaigrette dressing. Given a choice, I'd have chosen creamy Italian, full of fat and comfort, but I just thanked her.

With the primary topic on our minds off-limits, conversation dragged. Eckert solicited everyone's opinions about the current crop of judicial nominees. Elsa described Desirée's latest interior design job in a new office building down in Greenwich. Michael texted that he had three more jurors, but he'd be stuck in New London until at least mid-afternoon. When he asked how it was going, I responded, *Can't say*.

When we reconvened, Frazier launched into my conversations with Ralph's family. My time sheets included several entries over the past year for "telephone conference with M. Claus." Luckily, I'd never made entries for "meeting with elf" or "travel to North Pole."

"To the best of your knowledge, where is Meredith Claus?"

It took a mighty effort not to shrug. "I have no idea."

"Is she in this room?"

I looked around. "No."

"So you'd know her if you saw her?"

Damn. I walked right into that one. "Yes."

"You've met her? In person, I mean?"

"—Yes."

"When did this meeting take place?"

"At the beginning of my representation of Mr. Claus. Before his second arrest."

"Was he present at the meeting?"

"No."

Frazier looked slightly disappointed. He was clearly hoping that I'd had a conversation with Ralph in the presence of a third party so that he could argue we'd blown the privilege. *Sorry, Scotty, I'm not that stupid.* "Where did this meeting take place?"

I shot Geoff a *help* look, and he was on his feet. "Objection! Where Attorney Riley met her client's mother has nothing to do with these proceedings."

"Mr. St. Pierre, this goes to the question of where Ralph Claus may be," Frazier began, but Geoff interrupted.

"This is not an investigation into Mr. Claus's whereabouts," my lawyer said. "The committee's allegations are about the propriety of Attorney Riley's conduct. If Mr. Claus believes that his attorney acted improperly in meeting with his mother, he has the right to file a grievance saying so. Short of that, there's no reason to go down this road—unless, of course, Mr. Frazier claims that during this meeting, that Mr. Claus's mother disclosed his plans to escape from prison if he was convicted. Mr. St. Pierre, the committee has made very serious allegations against Attorney Riley. I ask that you instruct the committee to stop wasting everyone's time with this wild-goose chase into where Meredith Claus was last December and focus on a line of inquiry that has actual bearing on these allegations."

It was the most worked-up I'd ever known Geoff to get. Even the hearing officer appeared taken aback. Later, when I described the scene to Michael, he said, "Never knew he had it in him. He must have suspected you were holding back something pretty bad."

If Frazier hadn't smelled blood in the water before, Geoff's outburst did the trick. He launched into a tirade about how everything was intertwined and I was obviously hiding something, at

326 / P. Jo Anne Burgh

which point the hearing officer fixed him with a steely glare.

"The witness has already testified that she does not know where Meredith Claus is," St. Pierre said. "Even if we assume that to be relevant to this matter—and I haven't made a decision on that—why should I care about the location of a meeting that happened ten months ago and didn't involve the missing gentleman?"

"Because for all we know, that's where he is now," said Frazier.

"Then ask her that," said St. Pierre.

"Mr. St. Pierre, relevance—" Geoff began.

"Overruled," said St. Pierre.

With a gleam of triumph, Frazier approached me. "To the best of your knowledge, where is Ralph Claus?"

"I don't know." Being Ralph, he could quite literally be anywhere in the world.

"Is he with his mother?"

"Asked and answered," said Geoff.

"Overruled," said St. Pierre. "The witness will answer."

"I don't know," I repeated. "I don't know where he is, and I don't know where she is." Technically, I was telling the truth: at that moment, I did not know where either Ralph or Meredith was. Meredith might have been in her office, or in the cafeteria. She might have been by Santa's bedside as he recuperated from his stroke. Ralph had to learn the geography, so who knew where he might be? I wasn't lying. At worst, I was misleading, but I told myself that if Frazier were better at framing his questions, this wouldn't be an issue.

"What is Ralph Claus's address?" Frazier asked.

"I was never provided with a mailing address," I said. Before Frazier could follow up, I volunteered, "According to Dr. Solberg's psychological evaluation, Mr. Claus claimed to live at the North Pole." I smiled as if to say, *The North Pole. How silly.* A few appreciative chuckles from the gallery let me know my message was clear. In an attempt to steer the examination, I added, "On his instruction, I emailed all bills to his mother."

"What was her address?" Frazier asked.

"I don't remember. I communicated with her through my old email address. I haven't had access to that since the police locked it." More of the myriad inconveniences Ralph had wrought: the need to close my firm email address, create a new one, notify everyone of the change, jump through technological hoops to retrieve materials sent to the old address, and hear the constant whine of, "But I sent you an email!"

By the end of the day, I was completely wrung out. Trying a case as the lawyer was a thousand times easier than being the defendant. Fifteen years of experience making snap assessments of opposing counsel's questions fell away. With each inquiry, my brain raced through the same litany: *Why is he asking this? What does he know? Where is he going? If I say X, am I admitting something? What if I say Y? Or Z? What if I'm wrong? What if I say the wrong thing and it all blows up?*

For years, I counseled clients with Mark Twain's famous line: "If you tell the truth, you don't have to remember anything." It sounded so simple, so sensible, but the harsh light of the hearing room exposed its flippancy. What was the truth? Ralph Claus living at the North Pole—was that the truth? A royal family with hosts of elves making toys? Did the North Pole even exist? Had I really been there? Was that whole trip a masterpiece of deception and illusion?

And what about the reindeer?

Fifty-One

On the way home, I stopped at the supermarket for a rotisserie chicken, a container of macaroni and cheese, and a marked-down bag of Halloween candy. I wasn't in the mood to cook, but I was very much in the mood to eat.

The pungent aroma of herbs and poultry filled the car, momentarily lightening my mood. When I walked into the house, the cats swarmed around my legs, rubbing and purring. Priorities being what they were, I poured wine for myself and pulled off pieces of chicken for them. I microwaved the macaroni and polished it off standing at the counter. I nibbled briefly on a piece of chicken before dividing it between the cats, stowing the rest in the refrigerator and ripping open the candy.

At least I had time to catch my breath. Administrative hearings rarely ran on consecutive days; the next session was two weeks away. I forced myself to stash the remaining chocolate in the freezer before I unearthed the remote from beneath a stack of newspapers. Harry hopped up on the back of the sofa; David curled up in my lap. "You're such good boys," I crooned as I flicked through dozens of channels to no avail.

The ping of the doorbell sent the cats scurrying from the room. Startled, I checked the clock. Nine-forty. Nobody dropped in this late. Only one possibility: reporters. "Bastards," I muttered. Geoff probably would have counseled against answering. Screw that. I wasn't hiding from anybody. I stomped to the door and peered out the peephole, but whoever was out there was standing clear of it. "Who's there?" I demanded.

"Meg?"

My stomach lurched. It couldn't be. But I yanked the door open. "I said, who's there?"

"It's me." The voice came from the shadow of the Alberta spruce beside the step.

"Show me." I wasn't ready to trust.

Ralph Claus, State of Connecticut Department of Corrections Prisoner #16085478, stepped into the light. He spread his hands slightly as if to say, *This is all I've got.*

"Get in here!" I hissed. He slipped inside, and I slammed and locked the storm door and the inside door. For good measure, I turned off the porch light.

"What are you doing here?" I swiveled to ensure all the drapes were drawn.

"This has gone on long enough," he said. "I'm putting an end to it."

It took a second for his meaning to register. "You mean—?" I couldn't say it, but he nodded, resigned and resolute. A thousand thoughts crowded into my head. The one I blurted out was the last one I expected: "Does your mother know where you are?"

A short bark of laughter escaped him. "I've missed you so much," he said, folding me into his long arms. I inhaled the faint, biscuity scent that was his alone.

"I missed you, too," I murmured. We stood like that for several minutes before it occurred to me to ask, "Do you want to take your coat off?"

"Huh? Oh, sure." He released me and shrugged out of his coat, hanging it on the cast iron coat stand by the door. Then he wrapped his arms around me again, and my cheek rested against his scratchy wool sweater.

"We can sit down if you want," I said without moving. "Do you want something to drink? Or I could make you a sandwich."

"Sounds good. It was a long trip." He followed me to the kitchen where the cats paced. "This must be Harry and David," he said, stroking their backs. "Which is which?"

"Harry is the long-haired one, and David is the tabby." I poked in the nearly-empty bread drawer. Thank God for the chicken. I assembled a sandwich while he retrieved wine and glasses. To anyone watching, we looked like a regular couple in our familiar domestic routine. We carried our picnic into the living room. Without discussion, we sat on the sofa, barely touching.

I waited until he'd had a chance to finish half the sandwich and a glass of wine before I asked, "What are you doing here?"

"This whole mess has gotten way out of control," he said. "I finally put my foot down. I'm sorry it took this long. I was hoping I could get the family to go along with this."

My mind was racing. "What's 'this', exactly?"

"I'm turning myself in."

I caught my breath. *Calm. Professional. Control.* "Are you sure?"

"It's the only fair way. None of this is your fault. You got stuck in the middle because you were trying to help me." His words were calm enough, but I heard the passion underneath. My mind's eye could see him pounding on Meredith Claus's glossy desk as she shook her head.

Without thinking, I took a piece of chicken that had fallen out of his sandwich. "I appreciate the sentiment more than you know, but at this point, turning yourself in won't solve anything. You'll be back in prison, but they'll still want to know what I knew about your first escape."

He flinched at *first*. "I wouldn't leave again."

"Which means five more years in protected custody, plus time for the new charges. Escaping is its own crime, with its own penalty. Three, four more years. Maybe longer." My stomach clutched as I thought of just how not-happy the COs were going to be. Ralph's escape had made them look bad. Small deviations from protocol had been unearthed—nothing dramatic, but enough to upset a lot of people. Two COs had been suspended pending further investigation into allegations that they'd been smuggling contraband to inmates. One way or another, Ralph would pay for that. "It's a lovely thought, you going back and owning up, and as your lawyer, it's what I have to recommend," I said, holding my voice as steady as I could. "But as your friend, I think you're insane."

"You sound like my brother."

"Phil?" He'd always sounded like the most sensible one.

"Mitch."

"What do the rest of them think?"

Instead of answering, he took a bite of his sandwich. I waited. He chewed slowly, deliberately. I said nothing. Finally, he swallowed. "They're worried. About me, about operations. About you."

"Me? What do they think I'm going to do? Spill the beans?"

"It's not like that. They're concerned about you." I must have looked skeptical, because he set down his sandwich. "They're not a cold-hearted group. Not even my mother," he added before I could say anything. "They just look at the whole thing from a different angle."

"Which is?"

"First priority is to deliver the toys on Christmas Eve. Everything else comes after that."

"Including me."

"It's not that they don't care about you."

They? What about . . . ? But this wasn't that conversation. It was Claus 101, and the light was finally dawning. "But my life isn't their first priority," I said slowly. In a peculiar way, I understood their position. His position, because he was one of them.

"They appreciate what you've done. They feel bad about this." His eyes were clear and urgent.

Another *they.* "Nice to hear."

He leaned over and kissed me. "Level with me. Will it help you if I go back in?"

My first impulse was to say *no.* Protect the client. Don't tell him how his wrongdoing is affecting the lawyer. That's not his concern.

But he wasn't just my client now. He had a lot on the line. We both did. He deserved the truth.

"Probably," I said. "I'm not saying it would end everything, but the police and the grievance committee—everybody—would have a lot less reason to hound me. My lawyer says the reason they went after me was because they thought I could lead them to you."

"That's what I figured."

"But—and this is a big 'but'—whether you're back or not, Geoff says the chances of my actually being disbarred me are very, very slim." Not a direct quote. What he'd actually said was that disbarments were rare. Then again, so were prison escapes. "Either way, I'm going to be fine," I said with as much conviction as I could manage.

He laid his hand on mine. "How would you earn a living if you lost your license?"

"I'd manage." I withdrew my hand and refilled his glass. "Eat."

"What would you do? Mop the floor at Carla and Sergio's place? You've been a lawyer for a long time. Can you honestly tell me it wouldn't matter if you couldn't practice anymore?"

"I'd figure something out." I refilled my own glass and took an unsteady sip. The law was all I knew, all I'd ever wanted to know. The practice might be aggravating, the practitioners obnoxious and petty, but the end was something higher and better. The law resolved disputes in a civilized manner, without bloodshed. It organized society, relationships, interactions. Without a system of laws, who would know when someone was right or wrong? If a person did something wrong, what recourse would there be without the law? As much as clients and colleagues and judges might drive me batshit crazy, I wouldn't walk away. The law might leave me, but I wouldn't leave the law.

Even if it came down to a choice between the law and Ralph?

I tried to swat the thought away. He reclaimed my hand and said, "I can't let you go down in flames out of loyalty to your client."

"I'm telling you, I'll be fine." The cynic in my head roared with laughter. Wasn't Ralph in prison for crimes he didn't commit? What if the same thing happened again—this time to me?

"You don't know that." It was almost as though he was tracking my thoughts. "I'll tell them the truth—I escaped all on my own and you don't know anything about it."

"Except now I do." When I testified this morning, I could say honestly that I didn't know where he was. By showing up now, he'd taken away the only defense I still had.

His eyes widened with understanding. "I keep screwing things up for you. Listen, I'll go now, and I won't tell you where. That should help." He started to rise, but I grabbed his arm.

"Don't go. Just—let me think for a minute." He settled back on the sofa, his eyes fixed on me, his hand stroking my hair.

Which way to jump? If he walked out the door, I still had a chance to keep my license, my profession, my life. But if he vanished, and I never saw him again. . . . Tears threatened, and I looked away. He was just a man. A fascinating, attractive, well-meaning, very good man who admittedly had a penchant for bumbling into unwise situations, but could he be enough? What would my life become if I threw my lot in with him? Could I really leave everything I knew and loved? Pack up the cats and move to the North Pole? I'd spent my entire adult life carving out an identity, a profession, a family who, though not all biologically connected, were still my people, my world. If I put all that on one side of the scales of justice and Ralph Claus on the other, which would prevail?

"I know." His voice was quiet. My head snapped around, and he chuckled, a *ho-ho-ho* I'd never heard from him. "I don't know how you manage to practice law. You have the worst poker-face I've ever seen." He kissed the tip of my nose.

"I'm actually very good," I said primly. "Most of the time."

"You're amazing. All of the time." His hand caressed my cheek. "I'm sorry. I shouldn't have come. I wanted to try to fix what we did."

"And I thank you for that." Feelings swirled like dry leaves in a windstorm as his fingers tangled in my curls and his lips met mine. Amid the uncertainties, one thing was certain. "Don't go," I murmured. "Not tonight."

He pulled back slightly. His eyes held a question. I nodded, and his smile broadened. He kissed me, long and deeply. The world spun with delicious intensity as I felt his warmth, the slight stubble on his face, his hands in my hair, his tongue exploring my mouth. I lay back, pulling him on top of me, my heart swelling, my body heating up. His lips moved down my neck, my hands down his back.

Just as his hand reached under my sweater, my concentration was broken by rustling and a loud thump. Ahead of conscious thought, a wave of panic broke. *State police. Federal agents. Lawyers. Cameras. Media. OhmyGodohmyGodohmyGod.*

My eyes flew open. On the slate hearth in front of the fireplace stood Mitch, brushing soot off his clothes.

Ralph twisted, his elbow digging into my side. I yelped. "Sorry," he said, sitting up. To his brother, he snapped, "What are you doing here? And don't get anything on the rug."

"What am *I* doing here? More like, what are *you* doing here? Hey, Meg." Mitch gave me a half-wave.

Ralph sat up; I felt cold without his warmth. He began, "Look, I already had this discussion with Mom and—"

"Yeah, I know. She's freaking out. Everybody is."

"Oh, for the love of—she sent you, didn't she?"

Mitch shook his head. "I figured I'd try to bring you back before she got here."

"No. No way. She's not coming down here." It sounded less like a statement of fact than a pronouncement.

"Not right now, but only because Pop's not feeling well."

"Wait—how did you guys get here?" It suddenly occurred to me that there might be a pair of reindeer-drawn sleighs in the visitor spots.

"I got dropped off," said Ralph. "What do you mean, Pop's not feeling well? What's going on?"

Mitch glanced at me. "Nothing much. He's got a headache, that's all."

"You're sure?" Ralph was on his feet, alert, poised to go.

"Does it make a difference?" Mitch shrugged.

"Don't be a jackass." Ralph approached him with quiet menace. "Is he okay?"

Ralph had at least six inches on Mitch, but Mitch didn't appear daunted. For a long moment, the brothers glared at each other. Then, Mitch relaxed slightly. "Yeah. He's okay."

"All right, then. Get out. There's no reason for you to stay here."

"Isn't there?" Mitch eyed me.

"This is between Meg and me. It's none of your business."

"Hate to disagree, but it's absolutely my business," said Mitch. "You need to get back to work. Do your job, and let Meg do hers."

"We've already been through this." Ralph's voice was heated now. "I'm not hanging her out to dry anymore. I'm done with that. What we did—what *I* did—it's not right. I'm not going to fly away and leave her to take the consequences."

"You're a noble soul, Ralphie. Throw over an entire legacy to rescue the damsel in distress. Sounds like one of those stupid romance books: *How Santa Saved His Lawyer Girlfriend*."

"I'm warning you—"

"She doesn't need you. She can do this just fine by herself."

"She shouldn't have to. It's not fair for me to hide at the Pole and leave her here to clean up the mess I—*we*—made!"

"Meg's gonna be fine. All you're doing is screwing everything up."

"All I'm doing is the right thing!" Ralph began to pace. "All I'm doing is taking responsibility for my actions. It's too bad nobody else can seem to see it that way."

"This isn't just about you. There are a lot of people—I mean, a *lot*—who are counting on you to go home and do your job."

"Maybe this is more important than my job." The words sounded like a challenge.

"Are you out of your mind?" Mitch was pacing now, the two men weaving around each other like tomcats staking out their territory. "You can't just walk out!"

"Why not? I'm not essential. I spent most of the year down here, and you got along fine."

"But it wasn't Christmas. And Pop wasn't—I mean, he was—" His eyes cut to me.

"Don't worry, I already know," I said. "Charles told me."

Mitch didn't look surprised. "So you know why he has to go home."

"I don't know anything," I said. "I didn't even know he was coming here tonight. All I know is that your brother and I need to talk about a lot of things, and one is whether he's going back in."

"Yeah, I saw how much talking you were doing," Mitch said.

Ralph grabbed the front of Mitch's jacket. "Watch your manners, little boy," he said in a low voice. "Or I'll stuff you right back up that chimney." He released Mitch with a shove that sent him stumbling. "The fact is, whether I was there didn't end up making a difference. The work got done, didn't it? You're not saying there are kids whose stuff isn't won't be ready?"

"Of course not, but—"

"Exactly. It doesn't matter if it's me or not. Santa will still fly. The toys will still get delivered. The world will still spin."

Mitch ran a hand through his thick hair. A dusting of soot fell to the rug like black snow flurries. "I can't believe you're saying this. Are you seriously thinking of—" He stopped as though the word was too awful to say aloud.

"Maybe." Ralph's voice was quiet now.

"Do Mom and Pop know?"

"We haven't talked about it. I needed to talk to Meg first." He resumed his seat next to me, and I rested my hand on his.

Mitch flopped into my recliner. "This is unbelievable. You're really thinking of—staying here? For good?"

"What?" I blurted.

"I haven't made up my mind." His fingers wrapped around mine.

Mitch gave us a long, probing look. "Haven't you?"

"I'm just saying—I haven't ruled anything out." His thumb rubbed the back of my hand. I couldn't tell if he was expressing affection or telling me to calm down.

"Well, you better rule something out. It's less than two months 'til The Day. You know what happens if you're not there."

"Shut up!" Ralph hissed.

"What? If she's gonna be the reason you walk out, she should know what's going on." Mitch faced me squarely. "Brother Ralph here is apparently thinking of throwing over the whole Santa gig and sticking around here for good."

"What are you talking about?" I looked from brother to brother.

"I said, shut up!" Ralph snapped.

Mitch ignored him. "Is this really what you want? Do you want him in prison for the next five years, just so he can come home to you afterward?"

"We're not there yet," Ralph said. Thank God; I felt as if Mitch had kicked the breath right out of me. "We're just talking about me going back to prison. That's as far as we've gotten." He squeezed my hand: *really, that's all we're talking about.* "Besides, you'd manage without me. If I died instead of being locked up, Santa wouldn't end."

"You're not dead," Mitch said. "This is different. You're—oh, crap, what do they call it? There was some king who gave up the throne for some woman. What was that?"

"King Edward the Sixth," I said. "He abdicated the throne for Wallis Simpson." Amazing what inconsequential trivia the mind could retrieve under stress.

"Yeah, that one," Mitch said. He turned to his brother. "Is that what you think you're doing? You're gonna—what was it?"

"Abdicate," I supplied.

"You're gonna abdicate being Santa for—?" He waved his hand to indicate me, the room, the life Ralph would have here.

Ralph rested his arm around my shoulders. "What would be so wrong about that?" His hand rubbed my shoulder. I didn't know whether to sink into his embrace or bolt from the room.

"Everything!" Mitch sprang to his feet, pacing again. "You can't just walk away. This isn't some summer job at a burger joint. What do you affects millions of kids."

"And the rest of you will handle it just fine," Ralph said evenly, his gaze locked on Mitch's.

For a second, I thought Mitch might cry. His jaw hardened. "Yeah. We will," he said. "Don't worry about us." He strode to the chimney, then turned for his parting shot. "But don't think you're gonna come waltzing back into the job when you're done here."

"That's enough!" For the first time, Ralph sounded slightly shaky.

Mitch narrowed his eyes. "You know how it works. You wanna step aside, that's up to you, but there's no in-and-out. If you give it up, you give it up for good." Neither of us moved. Mitch's words rang in the silence. "Make your choice, Big Brother. You can be Santa. Or you can stay here. Not both." He ducked as if he was about to go back up the chimney, but then he straightened. "Force of habit," he said with a half-smile. He sauntered to the front door and stood with his hand on the handle. "Pick a side, Ralphie." With a nod to me, he walked out the door, and Ralph watched him go.

Fifty-Two

After Mitch left, Ralph stood motionless, focused on the door as though he expected it to reopen. Tentatively, I asked, "Are you okay?"

"Huh?" For a second, he looked dazed. Then he smiled. "Oh, sure. Kid doesn't know what he's talking about."

"Neither do I," I said. "Care to enlighten me?"

Instead of answering, he wrapped his arms around me and kissed me. At first, his kiss was light, almost teasing. Then, he stopped, and I opened my eyes to see him gazing at me. The corners of his eyes crinkled as he smiled. "I love you," he whispered. Before I could speak, he was kissing my mouth, my neck, my earlobes. "I love you," he whispered again, his breath tingling in my ear. His hands roamed down my back, cupping my bottom and pulling me close against his delicious hardness.

With the two or three brain cells that were still functioning, I managed, "Wait." His tongue paused in the act of teasing my ear. I forced myself to say, "We need to talk."

"No," he said. "No more talking. I'm about to go to prison for a long time. This might be our only chance. I don't want to waste it."

My heart pounded. His moist breath steamed my skin. Forget tingling—everything in me was afire. Rules of professional conduct be damned. I pulled his shirttail from his pants and ran my fingernails lightly down his long, smooth back, relishing his groan. When his hands slid under my sweater, I shivered. "Let's go upstairs," I whispered.

"Oh, yeah," he breathed. He picked me up—literally swept me off my feet in the classic, corny, fabulous tradition of all those old movies—to carry me up the stairs. It could have been an incredibly romantic moment, but movie sets have wider staircases. The whole way up, he kept twisting one way or the other, trying not to hit my head on the wall or my feet on the railing, until we were both laughing so hard he nearly dropped me.

I won't go into detail about what came next. Suffice to say that Santa knows what a woman wants, and he delivers.

If only he hadn't been heading to prison in the morning, it would have been perfect.

If only.

*****

Here's a little tidbit nobody ever tells you about Santa.

He snores.

I don't mean a few little snuffles. I mean, he *snores*. They could use that snore to call the reindeer in from the far reaches of the tundra.

After the second round, I contemplated a lifetime of sleeping next to a foghorn. I was trying to remember if Ed snored when Ralph emitted a thundering, gurgling snorfle.

"Okay, that's it," I said. "Come on, sweetie. Roll over." I wedged my hands under his left shoulder and attempted to shove him onto his right side. His mellifluous snoring continued unabated. "Let's go. Work with me." Maybe pulling, rather than pushing, was the answer. I reached across him to lift his right shoulder. Nope. Now I was just holding him as he snored in my face. I slid on top of him with the true and genuine intention of sliding off the other side of him and pulling him onto his side, but as soon as I was lying on him, he woke with a start.

His face broke into a drowsy, contented grin. "Hi, there," he said, sliding his hands down my body. And it was time for Round Three—which, in case anyone was wondering, is an excellent way to stop your beloved from snoring.

*****

The next time I woke, I was alone in the bed. In the netherworld between fully asleep and fully awake, where inhibitions vanish and feelings run wild, a tsunami of grief and fear flooded my being. *He's gone. He changed his mind. He went back to the Pole. Or he was never here. It was all a dream.*

The bridge of my nose burned as tears began to build. Dreams exposed truth in a way rational thought never could. And the truth was that I wanted him. God help me, I loved him. I squinched my eyes shut, desperate to return to my dream, to his caress, his kiss. To him.

The toilet flushed.

I flicked on the bedside light to see Ralph walking out of the bathroom. He squinted in the brightness. "Sorry," he said. "I didn't mean to wake you."

"You didn't." My voice cracked slightly.

"Are you okay?" He peered at me. I tried to nod, but his large hand held my face, his thumb brushing away a tear. "What's the matter?"

"Nothing. It's just—I thought you left, or that I dreamed you."

His face relaxed. He kissed me gently, tenderly. "You didn't dream me. And I'm not leaving."

I finger-combed his tousled hair. "What about what Mitch said?"

"You mean about abdicating?"

"Is he right? If you stay, is it all over?"

He plumped the pillows and lay back. Not looking at me now, he said, "If I go back to prison, I give up my place in the succession."

"That's not fair." I turned on my side, my hand on the sprinkling of dark hair on his chest. "You didn't ask to be convicted."

"It's not the conviction. It's making the choice to be here. To miss Christmas."

"So if you stay here—even if it's just for your sentence, not forever—you'll never be Santa?"

He flinched at my words, but his voice was casual, as though we were discussing someone else's life. "That's how it goes. Phil would inherit the job."

"Can't he say 'No, I won't do it, you have to wait for Ralph'?"

"Doesn't work like that. If Phil declines—which might be the best thing, because nobody else can do what he does—next in line would be Fred. He'd definitely do it."

"Yeah, but he has a wife and kids up there. That makes a difference."

"Maybe." Ralph sounded unconvinced.

"This doesn't make any sense," I said. "The people in charge are your parents. Why can't they say, 'Look, we're not thrilled about your choice, but you're the heir and we'll hold your spot until you get back'?" Maybe by that time, I'd have figured something out. Not that years of waiting and conjugal visits were an ideal solution, but if there was another way to fix everything—get through the hearings, keep my license and my practice, buy time—I couldn't think what it might be.

"That's not how it's done. Some of the reasons are obvious, like— well, what if something happened to Pop while I was still inside? If I left again, you'd be right back where you are now, except you couldn't say you didn't know anything about it because you'd know everything."

"Don't worry about me." I didn't mean to sound testy. "I just don't get why you can't take a break and then go back."

"It's the lineage," Ralph said. "What Mitch said before, about that king—that really is what it's like. You're in or you're out." He adjusted his pillow. "Pop had some great-great—I don't know many greats— uncle who walked away from the job. His brother took his place. That shifted the whole line of succession."

"Hold on. You mean you're not really in line to be Santa?" A curious sensation—half disappointment, half relief—swept through me.

"Sure I am. Because once the brother became Santa, it was his heirs who succeeded him."

"What happened to the heirs of Great Uncle Whoever?"

"They're regular people. They live down here somewhere— Europe, maybe. I don't know if any of them even realize what their bloodlines are."

"Did Great Uncle Whoever—"

"—Robert, I think—"

"Did he have to leave the Pole?"

"He made the choice. He met somebody who didn't want to live the life, so he moved to Finland for her." His expression was grave. "We're not under lock and key. I can leave. I can even go back. I'd just be out of the line of succession. I could be there, but I couldn't be Santa."

I lay back, considering. Then, something occurred to me. "If you had the ability to get out of prison all along, why did you stay? Why didn't you leave that first night?"

The corner of his mouth quirked. "Truth? At first, I was embarrassed. I mean, getting caught like that—rookie mistake. Even Mitch wouldn't screw up like that. I figured I'd earned a penalty. Then I started talking to the guys who were in, and it was a real eye-opener. We breeze through when we're learning the geography or delivering the gifts, but we don't spend a lot of time down here. Besides, we're focused on the kids. Talking with some of these guys made me realize I had no idea how they live. Have you ever been down in the Hartford lockup?"

"I don't think so."

"That's one grisly place. Did you know there's a padded cell down there? Except almost all the padding has been clawed off the walls. There were guys in with me who were real casual about being there—I guess it happens all the time for them—but some guys were drunk or high or coming down off whatever. One great big guy sat in the corner, crying. I tried to talk to him, but all he kept saying was how, if she'd let him put the tree by the window, he wouldn't have done it. Never did say what happened." Ralph's voice faded. I touched his hand, and it seemed to bring him back to the moment. "Plus, I knew I could always leave. That makes a huge difference. My original plan was to go back as soon as they released me. But then I met you." He squeezed my hand. "You should have heard my mother when I told her I had to stay here."

"Did she believe you? I mean, that you *had* to stay." Difficult to picture Meredith Claus falling for that one.

"Pop worked on her. He suspected what was really going on. I mean, that's how he met Mom."

"He got arrested?" I tried to remember if I'd ever heard of any other cases where Santa Claus was a criminal defendant.

"Just caught. Mom was home from university—her family lived in Vancouver—and he was delivering presents for her youngest sister. The delivery team didn't wear black in those days—that was actually her idea, later on—so when she saw him, he was pretty obvious."

"And that was it? She believed him?" I couldn't imagine Meredith Claus signing on that easily.

"Hardly. Pop says she was a tough sell. He kept coming back to see her, but she thought he was some kind of kook. Even threatened to call the police if he didn't leave her alone."

That sounded more like the woman I'd met. "How did he finally convince her?"

"He took her up there. I think he made her a bet on whether it was all real—if she wasn't totally convinced, he'd leave her alone forever. So he pulled out all the stops—the best sleigh, eight reindeer, the works. She saw the compound, met the family, met the elves—that was it. Guess there's something about those flying reindeer."

I tried to picture Mrs. Claus as a young bride, a sleigh loaded with her earthly possessions landing at the North Pole. Was she scared? Nervous? Wondering what she'd gotten herself into? What did she tell her family? Did they ever come to visit? Did she visit them?

"What about you?" Ralph's tone was deliberately casual. "Would you ever consider moving north?"

"I don't know." It was a question I'd been pondering for months. There were a thousand reasons to stay, and only one reason to go. "I don't know," I said again.

"That's what I thought." I couldn't tell whether he was disappointed or just resigned.

"I'm not saying 'never.' I just—it's a big decision."

"I know." He kissed the tip of my nose. "It's your whole life. I get it."

"Does this make me a selfish bitch?"

He laid his hand on my cheek. "Impossible. You're being honest. Which is one of the things I love about you."

"Will you still feel that way in prison?"

"Yes," he said with absolute certainty.

"You're a better man than I am, Gunga Din." I kissed him. He was an incredible man. Selfless and good. I was a fool to hesitate.

If we'd been in a low-budget romantic comedy, this would have been the moment. I'd say *yes*, the violins would swell, and the audience would be teary-eyed as we packed the cat carriers into the sleigh—including Lulu, who would miraculously get along with the boys—and flew off into the night while Michael and Holly stood in the parking lot, waving goodbye.

But this was real life, and in real life, people didn't just give up their lives, their identities, their entire worlds, without a lot of thought.

Double that for lawyers.

Tears filled my eyes. "Don't do it. Not now, anyway. Not until we've talked more."

"Do which?"

"Both. Going to prison. Giving up Santa. I love that you're willing to do this, but I can't let you."

"You're not 'letting' me do anything. I make my own decisions. I've had a lot of time to think about this. I won't lie and say it's going to be easy, but it's what has to happen. . . ." *If we're going to be together.*

I could hear the last words as clearly as if he'd said them.

"I still don't understand why your folks won't let you finish your sentence and then come back," I said. "Don't they trust you?

"It's not about trust." He sounded slightly irritated now. "It's about an orderly succession. When King Edward abdicated, he handed off the throne permanently."

"He was ruling an empire, not delivering toys. He had people's lives in his hands."

Ralph was silent for so long that I thought he'd fallen asleep. Finally, he said, "I know we're not ruling a country, but what we do *is* important. Important, and much more complicated than you know."

"I saw what it was like."

"You saw the tip of the iceberg. You could be there six months and not see everything. Plus—when you ask people to commit their lives, you have to commit your own. Everybody up there has devoted their entire lives to Santa. The ones who've come in from down below, like Claire and Anya—they made a lifetime commitment not only to their husbands, but to the work. If I can bounce in and out at will, it cheapens what they've sacrificed—and don't kid yourself, it's a sacrifice. There isn't one of us who doesn't occasionally wish for a different life, someplace with sunshine in winter or movie theaters or pro football games." He fell silent for so long I thought again that he'd dozed off. Then, he asked, "Do you know what I've always wanted to do?"

"Go to the beach?" It seemed a reasonable dream for someone who spent his life surrounded by snow and ice.

"I've been there," he said. "One of the perks of having to learn all the geography. Kids in the Caribbean celebrate Christmas. I even got sunburned," he added proudly.

"Um—play tennis?"

"Done it. I was lousy."

I thought of other summertime pleasures. "Seen the Red Sox at Fenway?"

"No, but I've been to Shea Stadium. Seen the Mets."

"No comparison," I said. "I give up. What do you want to do?" I walked my fingers down his torso, slowing as I reached his navel.

"Oh, that, too," he said, guiding my hand lower. "But I've always wanted to mow a lawn. Did you ever see that movie, *Forrest Gump*? Remember how he rides around on that little tractor thing in the sunshine? That's what I want to do someday."

Growing up, my brother and I argued about whose turn it was to mow the lawn. Hot summer afternoons, with dust and shreds of grass sticking to our sweaty skin as we pushed the mower back and forth across the front lawn. The scent of fresh-cut grass. The blare of the mower's engine. The sudden silence when we shoved the switch to "off". The stripes of lighter and darker green, dappled with late-afternoon sun and shadows. I pictured Ralph riding a mower as I brought a pitcher of iced tea out onto our porch. A sweet, normal life.

"I don't have a lawn, but maybe I can figure out a consolation prize." I slipped under the covers, my head moving to where my hand had been, and there was no more discussion of yardwork.

Afterward, as the deep dark of night began to lighten, a thought popped into my head. "What if you turn yourself in, and then you change your mind? Will you still have your Houdini powers?" It would be the best of both worlds: he could stay just long enough to get me through this rough patch, and then he could slip back out and return to being Santa while we sorted out our future.

"Huh?" His voice was foggy with the beginning of sleep. I repeated my question. "Probably not. If I go back in, I'm there for the duration."

The duration. His original sentence, plus more as punishment for escaping. Seven or eight years, or more—for me. I kissed his earlobe. "How sure are you about this? Staying, I mean."

He turned on his side. I could barely make out his features. "Don't you want me to?"

"Don't be stupid," I said more harshly than I intended. "I love you. If this were a normal situation, I'd want nothing more than to have you here with me, but. . . ." Dark turned to gray as we lay without speaking, without touching. Finally, I said, "Nobody knows you're here. You could go home. We could talk about the whole thing after Christmas. See what other options there might be."

"There aren't any," said Ralph. "At least, not for me. I love you, and I want to be with you. That means being down here."

"Not necessarily. I mean, I haven't really thought about the idea of moving, but it's not like I couldn't consider it. We have choices. We could wait until after you finish dealing with Christmas, and then we could try to figure it all out."

"By that time, you might be disbarred," he said.

"Maybe." My voice was slightly breathless as my heart thumped in panic. I forced myself to sound casual as I added, "In which case I'd have less reason to stay here, wouldn't I?"

"That's not what I'm saying," he protested, but a sound like jingling bells cut him off. "What the—" He sprang from the bed and dug through his clothes for his phone. He flicked the screen and muttered, "Oh, no," as he sat down on the end of the bed.

"What's wrong?" I asked.

He ignored me, punching in numbers. "It's me. What's going on? . . . Is he okay? . . . Shit. . . . Yeah, I know." His voice was heavy with resignation. "Set it up. . . . What's the ETA? . . . Done." He clicked off. Without looking at me, he said, "I have to go."

My heart clutched. "What's going on?"

Even in the dimmest of early dawn light, I could see grief creasing his face. "Pop had another stroke."

"Oh, my God. Is he—"

"No, but—" I could hear it in his voice: *it's bad.*

I kissed his shoulder. "I'm so sorry." I put on my robe, turned on the lights, and said, "Let me call the office. I have a hearing this morning, but Robin can reschedule it."

"Huh? What are you talking about?" He blinked in the light, as perplexed as if he'd never seen me before.

"I'm coming with you." I opened the closet to see what I had that would be adequate for a trip to sub-zero temperatures. My winter clothes were still in storage, but if I layered, some of the fall sweaters might work.

"No." He began to dress. "You deal with your stuff here, and I'll deal with mine."

"Don't be ridiculous—"

"Look, Meg, it's different now." He wasn't snapping, but he was close. "I have to focus. It's only a few weeks 'til Christmas. I can't be worrying about anything else."

"Like us," I said slowly.

"Like anything," he said. He zipped his jeans and reached for his shirt. "I'm sorry, but that's the way it is. That's life at the North Pole. Especially at Christmas."

Talk about a quick turnaround. One minute, I was the beloved maybe-wife for whom he would sacrifice everything, including Santahood. The next minute, I was a distraction that kept him from focusing on what was really important. "How will you—?"

"They're making arrangements. I'll be gone soon." It sounded as if he was being deployed.

I wanted to ask when *soon* would be, but that probably wasn't something a Claus disclosed to a mere distraction. "I'll make you some coffee for the trip."

"Meg." Normally when he said my name, I could hear his delight. Now, it sounded leaden. His face was grim. "I'm sorry. I'd never have come down last night if I'd had any idea—"

"It's not your fault. And for what it's worth—I wouldn't have missed last night for anything." I opened the drapes. The sun was peeking through the branches of the Japanese maple. "People are going to be able to see you."

"No, they won't. We have our ways." He finished buttoning his shirt and pulled his sweater over his head. As he bent down to put on his socks, I went downstairs to dust off my rarely-used coffee maker. By the time Ralph came down, coffee was dripping into the pot.

"I hope it's okay," I said. "I keep it in the freezer so it won't go rancid."

"It'll be fine." His eyes, so rich with love last night, were dull with sadness and grief.

It seemed as if there should be something to say, but I couldn't think of anything. We waited in silence until the coffee had finished brewing, and I poured it into my insulated thermos. "Milk? Sugar?"

"This is perfect." His phone jingled again, and he pulled it out as I screwed the lid on the thermos. He tapped on the screen. "They're ready for me."

I followed him into the living room. He zipped his jacket and kissed me. "I love you," he said. "Remember that. No matter what happens." It sounded ominous. Like *goodbye*.

"And I love you." I kissed him one last time and handed him the thermos. "Keep me posted about your dad."

"I'll try. And thanks," he said, holding up the thermos. He opened the front door and stepped outside. When I reached out to close it, he was already gone.

Fifty-Three

For the first two days, I floated in a Ralph-induced fog. He loved me. He came back to do the right thing. My career and my world were safe. All was well.

But two days turned into three, five, seven, and more, and still no word from him. The fog began to dissipate. In its place came cold, clear reality. He came, we screwed, and he left. All his big talk about turning himself in, and he was out of here at the first opportunity. If he truly intended to abdicate, that would have been the moment: *Tell Phil he owns it. I'm staying in Connecticut.* Okay, it was understandable that he'd want to see his father, to nurse him through this crisis, but if he really meant to come back, wouldn't I have heard from him by now?

Not a call, not an email, not so much as a lousy text. He walked out my front door and off to God only knew where, and that was the last I heard of Ralph Claus. The more I thought, the angrier I grew. He couldn't even be bothered to let me know he was okay, or how his father was doing, or to tell me again that he loved me and he'd be back soon.

"Look, Meg, it's different now."

Like hell it was. It was Steve all over. The scene with my father had spelled the end of our relationship. Not that Steve officially broke up with me. Instead, he ignored me. He didn't call, he didn't pass me notes in class, he didn't sit with me at lunch. When I tried to talk to him, he turned red and ducked away, mumbling something about being late for practice. I even attempted to talk to his best friend, but all Brad said was that, well, y'know, Steve was real busy.

I wanted to pour my heart out to my best friend, but that door was closed and bolted. I hadn't heard from Holly in weeks. Maybe one of us needed to make the first move, but with my career in shambles and my heart in shreds, I couldn't. Not now.

I couldn't even talk to Michael. If he knew I'd had Ralph in my home and hadn't called the police, he'd be irate. I could almost hear him: *You did what? You <u>slept</u> with him? And then you let him walk out? Why? Because there was still a snowball's chance in hell you might <u>not</u> lose your license? And you might <u>not</u> torpedo the firm in the bargain? What were you thinking? Don't you know a con man when you see one?* I told the Michael in my head that Ralph wasn't a con man, but as days passed and my phone didn't ring, I started to wonder.

As the next hearing drew nearer, my life felt like a courtroom in a bad movie where everyone I'd ever wronged was lined up to testify about all the awful things I'd done, how I was stupid and careless and slutty and monumentally self-centered. In sleepless nights or nightmares, they took the witness stand, one after another, telling how I'd forgotten birthdays or missed deadlines or bounced checks or broken hearts. My father recounted finding me at Steve's. My mother told how I hadn't shed a tear at my father's funeral. *Like a stone*, she said, and the jury smirked its agreement. My first boyfriend claimed I'd dumped him for his best friend. Ed said I was good in bed, but when it came to his children, I was utterly cold-hearted.

Then, the shit got serious. Elsa testified that I'd ruined the firm, and she put Cyril Walker on the stand to say that he'd pulled all his business because I was incompetent and obsessed with my boyfriend, that Claus fellow. Holly told how she'd always thought I was a friend, but I dragged her to the Pole and forced her to make the drawings, and then, when Ralph didn't want her to testify, she had to flee the state to get away from me. Even Michael shook his head and said he used to think I was trustworthy, but it turned out I was foolhardy and didn't care about anybody but myself.

Meredith Claus took the imaginary stand. Calm and elegant, she spoke of how I'd mismanaged her son's case, taken advantage of him, and placed him in an untenable position, my silly crush placing the entire Santa Claus empire in jeopardy. Anya testified that she knew I wasn't serious about Ralph, that I took advantage of his isolation to amuse myself. Charles admitted he'd been worried all along that I'd use my power to manipulate Ralph into walking out of the job. Mitch talked about how I exploited his big brother's feelings, how I was willing to let poor Ralph go back to prison so I could have my nice, tidy life, and how, even when their father had a stroke, all I could focus on was why he hadn't called, and that was proof positive that I wasn't the right woman for Ralph, because I was the most selfish bitch in history and thank God they'd gotten Ralph away from me. By the way, he added, their father hadn't actually had a stroke at all; it was just a story they'd concocted because while I was sleeping, Ralph had texted Mitch that he needed an escape hatch.

In the silence of my solitary bedroom, my resolve hardened. Screw them all. Screw everything. I had to look out for Number One, because nobody was going to do it for me. Maybe I'd been an idiot, believing Ralph had come to town for something more than a quickie. Well, no more. Nobody needed to know about that tiny lapse in judgment. It would be my secret. To hell with the law and the oath and all the rest. If I had to lie my fool head off, so be it. The only one I could count on was me.

*****

The second day of the hearing on my fitness to practice law began thirteen days, two hours, and seven minutes after Ralph left my home that November morning. In all that time, I'd heard nothing from the North Pole. Not from him, not from any other Claus, not from an elf. It was embarrassing to admit how much his silence hurt, so I didn't. Instead, I squeezed into the black suit that used to fit before stress-eating became my daily routine, fastened my grandmother's silver brooch to the lapel, and went off to do battle for what was left of my life.

"You recall that you're still under oath," Jacques St. Pierre told me as I resumed my place on the witness stand.

"Yes, sir." And I fully intended to abide by that oath—unless somebody started asking questions about the last time I'd been in touch with Ralph Claus.

Naturally, that was Scott Frazier's first question: "Have you had any contact with Ralph Claus since this hearing recessed on November 1?"

I looked him squarely in the eye. "No."

"Have you had any contact with any member of his family in that time?"

"No."

"As you sit here today, do you know where Ralph Claus is?"

"No."

Three *nos*, and you're out. Frazier shuffled through papers. I could feel Geoff's eyes on me, but I never looked away from Frazier. I was through being jerked around. Maybe I couldn't control Ralph and his little Clausdom, but I could sure as hell control this hearing.

St. Pierre had another matter at one o'clock, so we were to stop at noon. For ninety-three minutes, right up to the morning break, Frazier probed and pried and tried to get me to admit what I would never, ever admit. When we resumed, his first question was whether I'd had any contact with Ralph Claus during the break. I could smell his desperation, and I started to relax.

The clock on the back wall read eleven fifty-three when I saw him. In the back row, barely arm's-length from a reporter for the local legal news rag, sat Mitch. He wore Claus-black. His face was expressionless.

"Attorney Riley?"

"What? I'm sorry—I didn't—would you please repeat the question?" I dragged my attention back to Scott Frazier, who was holding out a piece of paper.

"Have you ever seen this before?"

I took the document and pretended to study it. It was the Claus bill covering work done in July, when I was in the thick of trial preparation. Lucy Jane must have prepared a draft bill. "I don't recall," I said finally. It felt like the first honest answer I'd given all day.

"This seems like a good time to stop," said St. Pierre. I knew I should be looking at him, but I was watching Mitch, silently urging him to stay where he was. The rest of the gallery was beginning to gather up coats and purses and briefcases. Victoria Leopold frowned with obvious displeasure; her handler was stoic. St. Pierre recessed the hearing, and I darted off the stand.

"I'll be right back," I whispered to Geoff. Before he could tell me to stay, I made my way through the cluster of spectators and out the back door.

"Mitch!" I called. He was halfway down the long hall, and he didn't stop walking. "Mitch!"

He was nearly out the door when I caught his arm. "I didn't expect you here."

"No kidding." His voice was brittle.

"How's your dad?"

"I can't talk about that." This time, he met my eyes with a searing glare. "I have to go."

"Wait—" I dropped my voice. "Is he here?"

"No." He bit the word off.

My heart plummeted. "Why did you come? To see if I was going to give away Santa secrets?"

He snorted with what sounded like pity. "I have to go." He yanked his arm out of my hand and shoved the door open.

"Wait!" I hurried after him, heedless of the November wind. "What are you pissed off about? This is my license. My life. I'm the one who has to save it, and I'll do whatever I have to."

He stopped walking then. "So you lied. He was willing to give up everything for you—and you couldn't trust him enough to tell the truth."

"What are you talking about? It's not the same thing. Not even close. He had a choice—and he made it." I tried to keep my voice from rising. People were walking past us. Someone bumped against me. "I did what I had to do. Because I *don't* have a choice."

He snorted again. "Whatever."

All at once, a memory surfaced: Mitch sounded exactly like Ed's obnoxious children. It was the last straw. "Oh, for the love of—tell me, Mitch. What do you think I should have done in there? Should I have told the hearing officer that Ralph came to my house and offered to turn himself in, and I let him leave? Is that what you think I should have said? I had an escaped convict in my house, but I didn't call the police. I didn't call my lawyer, or my partners, or anybody. Instead—"

"—Meg—"

"—I took him upstairs, and I fucked him. I fucked him good. Is that what you think I should have said? Santa Claus came to my house, and instead of calling the authorities, I fucked his brains out?"

"Shut up!" he hissed.

"Nice talk, lady!" somebody shouted. "You kiss your kids with that mouth?"

"Get out of here!" Mitch barked to him. He took my arm, but it was my turn to pull away.

"I have to go." Gradually, I became aware of people around us, staring. "I have to go," I repeated. I whirled and froze.

Victoria Leopold stood less than five feet away. Her face broke into a satisfied smirk. She whispered something to her handler. Without another word, they went back inside.

"Come with me," Mitch urged.

I shook my head. "I have to go." I pushed my way through the crowd. By the time I reached my car, I was running. I yanked the door open, slammed it behind me, and locked it before I dropped my head to the steering wheel and the tears began to fall.

*****

I spent the rest of the day alternating between rage and terror. How dare Mitch lecture me? How dare one of the perpetrators of the biggest myth in the world get testy about telling the truth? Why in hell was he even there? His mother probably sent him to make sure I didn't spill the beans. If that was it, he should have been proud of me, because I protected their secret. Even though it meant lying under oath—committing perjury—I hadn't revealed anything.

I called Geoff and told his assistant it was an emergency. By four o'clock, I was sitting in his conference room. I confessed the events of the past few weeks, probably more than he wanted to know. I admitted I'd dropped the f-bomb a few times. "For the first time since high school," I added, as if my language were the damning part of the story. When I told him about Victoria Leopold, his mouth tightened, but he didn't interrupt.

"What happens now?" I asked at last.

He consulted his pad. *Sex with a client. Harboring a fugitive. Lying under oath.* "I'll try to catch Scott Frazier tonight. Maybe there's a way to resolve this before the hearing resumes."

"When's that?" By the time the lawyers and the hearing officer were discussing schedules, I was on the sidewalk yelling at Mitch.

"Jacques wants to issue a decision by year-end," Geoff said. "We're on for the thirtieth."

"Just so you know, I never actually admitted anything," I offered. "It was all, 'Is that what you think I should have said?' I never said I did any of it." After fifteen years of practice, I knew how to spin a bad fact.

Geoff was unimpressed. "Scott's going to ask about it all. You have to tell the truth."

I sank back. "What happens then? Am I going to be charged with something?"

"I don't know," he said. "But considering that the whole point of these proceedings was to flush this guy out of the bushes, and you had him and didn't call the police—I can't say it's impossible."

"So I need to tell my partners before I get arrested." My voice broke.

"One thing at a time," Geoff said. "As you said, it wasn't an admission. We'll start there." He laid down his pen, a signal that our time was up. I closed my folder, and he rose. "I'll let you know when I've spoken to Scott." He stepped back to allow me to exit the room first. I bade him good night, and he replied, "Have a good evening."

The line was so obviously automatic that I didn't bother telling him a good evening was out of the question. That reindeer had already taken off.

Fifty-Four

The six o'clock news opened with a sunny young woman describing the scene in front of the office of the Statewide Grievance Committee, when a Hartford attorney who was accused of harboring a fugitive had essentially admitted to doing just that. "Get your facts straight!" I snarled as the news cut to footage of the same reporter interviewing Victoria Leopold, identified as the mother of the fugitive's victim. Victoria, who had apparently found time to get her hair done since that morning, exuded innocence and dismay as she recounted how I'd screamed terrible obscenities. "She said she—well, I won't repeat the word she used—that she'd been intimate with him," said Little Miss Pure-As-The-Driven-Snow. "She used the f-word. Several times. It was very disturbing." It wasn't clear whether Victoria was claiming to be more disturbed by the facts or my language.

They cut to Governor-elect Hal Zenkman, still glowing from his recent victory, who vowed to enact stronger laws to protect children from predators. Zenkman's name hadn't been mentioned in our office since the election. The segment ended with footage of Geoff striding past a reporter with his hand out, saying, "No comment" in a loud, firm voice. Maybe we'd pulled it off.

As it turned out, all we'd done was bait the media. When I awoke the next morning, three news vans were lined up in front of my house, and a cluster of reporters and camera men milled around out front. I left the blinds closed as I got ready for work. Blessings on my attached garage, and more blessings on the inventor of the automatic garage door opener. I backed my car out, narrowly missing a gangly young man with a microphone, and sped off as reporters yelled questions at my closed windows.

Even though I was early, our parking lot was nearly full. I let myself in the back door and stood for a moment, perplexed by the lack of sound. I walked down the short hall to the waiting area, where every chair held a client. At my appearance, they all looked up. Then, as one, they looked away.

"Good morning," I said to Marilyn, whose eyes were fixed on her computer monitor.

"Morning," she said without looking up.

I gestured to the conference room. "Who's in there?"

"The door was closed when I got here." She kept typing.

"Thanks." I headed down the hall to Eckert's office. Empty. Up to the second floor, where the other offices were also unoccupied. Which wouldn't have meant anything, except that I'd seen my partners' cars in the parking lot.

How dare they hold a secret meeting? Who authorized them to decide my fate without giving me a chance to defend myself? I marched downstairs and flung open the conference room door. Four heads swiveled to face me.

"Sorry I'm late," I said. "I didn't receive notice of this meeting."

"We were just going to call you," said Eckert. "We were discussing your . . . situation."

"Really." I didn't believe for a minute they'd been about to call me, but I had no doubt the rest was true. I closed the door. "Exactly what were you discussing?"

"The latest round of negative publicity." Elsa appeared calm, but I could sense the smoldering anger beneath the glacial surface. "Is it true?"

No wonder she wasn't a litigator—she couldn't frame a decent question. "Absolutely. There is indeed negative publicity."

"I'm talking about the substance," she said as if to one who was slow.

"Are you asking if I said what's being attributed to me?"

"No," said Eckert. "We're not asking if you said it. We're asking if you did it."

It was that night on Steve's front steps all over again. "I can't answer that."

"We're your partners," Roy said. "We're entitled to the truth."

"And we still represent you," Elsa said. "Anything you say here is privileged."

"That only means a prosecutor can't use it against me," I said. "It doesn't mean you can't. Or won't." I looked from face to face, letting my gaze linger long enough to make each uncomfortable. But none looked away. "There's no point in my saying anything—you've made up your minds. Forget due process. Forget the presumption of innocence. I'm guilty. So much for the Constitution."

"This isn't about the Constitution," said Elsa. "It's about what your reckless behavior has done to this firm. You've exposed us to all sorts of negative publicity. There could be charges brought against us. We've lost so many clients already—"

"That's the real issue, isn't it? That you've lost money." I glared at her. She didn't look away.

"What's wrong with that?" Roy asked. "We're a business. We need to make money to stay afloat. We can't do that if we have a partner who's openly breaking the law."

"Breaking the law? Because I represented my client?" My voice didn't squeak, but it was close.

"Sleeping with a client is not representing him," Elsa said. "Neither is having an escaped convict in your home and letting him go instead of turning him in."

She was right, but I was damned if I'd admit it. "It's like I said. I'm already guilty in your eyes. There's no point in my saying anything."

Eckert said slowly, "If you didn't do it, this is the time to say so." He sounded so sad, so resigned, that I wanted to be able to deny it all.

It was tempting. I wasn't under oath now. I could have kept the lie going. Victoria Leopold misunderstood. She twisted my words, turned my questions to Mitch into confessions, because her plan to lure her husband away from Katrina Damdar failed, and the Woman Scorned wanted revenge. I opened my mouth, ready to sell this theory with everything I had.

Except Michael was watching me. In his eyes, I saw the grief that comes with knowing.

The only way out was, literally, out. "I'm not having this conversation," I said. "You've already made your decision."

Eckert began, "Meg—"

A knock on the door interrupted him. Marilyn slipped inside and closed the door. "The police are here," she said, clearly shaken.

Michael was on his feet. "What do they want?"

She looked as if she was about to cry. I reached out to stop her from speaking. "It's okay. Tell them I'll be right out." She darted out of the room, closing the door behind her. I regarded my partners. "I guess this is it."

"Not yet," said Michael. He strode past Roy's chair and stood beside me. Relief and gratitude rushed through me like a river. "Come on," he said. "Let's get this over with."

Fifty-Five

The police didn't arrest me, but only because they didn't have enough evidence. I was a person of interest, which meant that instead of putting me in handcuffs in front of a waiting room full of clients, they asked me to come to the station "to answer a few questions." Michael accompanied me, and I spent the most of the day saying "I don't know" and "I have no idea." The lack of substance in my responses didn't slow them down one iota. They pelted me with questions until I wanted to make something up, because maybe then they'd stop.

Outside the station, we blinked in the setting sun. Reporters shouted questions at us and shoved microphones in our faces. Michael's "No comment!" was firm and loud. I didn't duck my head or hide my face, but only because he reminded me not to before we opened the door: "Hiding is for lowlifes. You're an officer of the court. Act like it." So I stood tall and walked beside him, grateful that once more, he stood between the world and me.

That night, my brother called. "Megs, what's going on?" Derek asked. He didn't sound terribly worried, but he'd seen the news and thought he ought to check in. I assured him it was no big deal—as usual, the media had everything ass-backward. It was all about a client who was missing, I told him. No worries, but he shouldn't mention it to Mom, because she'd get upset over nothing.

"No problem," he said. "What are you doing for Thanksgiving? We're going to Boston if you want to come." With that, the topic of my troubles was closed. I felt a pang even though Derek and I had never been close. He had his life, and I had mine. As I hung up, I found myself thinking about the Claus brothers. Ralph and Mitch were obviously capable of aggravating each other, but I knew that each would do anything for the other. As I poured chardonnay, I thought of Meredith Claus presiding over her brood of boys. No wonder she could rule the Pole. Anyone who could raise five sons without losing her mind knew how to manage.

What about Santa? Where was the father in all this? He definitely existed, even if he was in questionable health now. But his stroke hadn't come until the summer, months after my visit. Or had it? Maybe the reason I hadn't seen him was that he was bedridden, an invalid. Maybe that was why Ralph was delivering toys that night.

Or maybe there was no Santa—just a big family who lived up in a remote place and ran an enormous toy distribution facility. Maybe there wasn't even any magic.

But what about the reindeer?

*****

My professional life continued to deteriorate. Most of my clients had fled, seeking less notorious counsel. The legal newspaper's "Verdicts and Settlements" column reflected that *Howley v. Walker* settled for an undisclosed amount and confidential terms.

Janine Lane, my erstwhile collaborative divorce client, hired Rick to file motions so she could get exclusive custody of the twins. Gary hired fireball Louie Pasternak to file motions of his own for alimony, custody, and child support. Less than a year ago, they'd been co-parenting in relative peace. Now, they were in court every week fighting about this or that, with Rick and Louie egging them on. What they needed, in my opinion, was a mediator who could get them to see sense. Somebody like Ralph, who'd gotten through to Janine better in ten minutes than I'd managed in six months.

Last year, I spent most of Thanksgiving weekend in the office. This year, I took Wednesday off and didn't set foot in the office until Monday, and nobody noticed. I declined invitations to Thanksgiving from Michael and Ruby, and Carla and Sergio. Instead, I ordered sushi and watched a *Bonanza* marathon even though the ranch scenes reminded me of Holly's ex, which reminded me of Holly, which reminded me that I hadn't heard from her even though it was Thanksgiving. I played computer solitaire and made desultory lists of Christmas card recipients. I'd brought Lulu home in the hope that she and the boys might be able to make their peace, but she spent the entire time huddling under the bed in the guest room while Harry and David glared at me from the foot of the stairs.

On Monday morning, Robin came into my office. "I have to talk to you." I gestured for her to take a chair. She said, "I'm leaving. This is my two weeks' notice."

It was an unexpected punch in the gut. "What are you talking about?"

"I got a job with the state. I'm going to be a paralegal in the appellate clerk's office."

"When did this happen?" I tried to focus on the past few months as she might have seen them. "I don't understand. Why didn't you talk to me?"

She gave me the same kind of sweet, sad look I'd seen her give Jordy when he said something especially naïve. "I need something more stable. More regular hours." *Less chance of her boss being fired.*

I stirred my cooling tea. "You never said anything."

"I wanted to wait until I was sure. You have enough on your plate."

"But why didn't you tell me? We could have figured something out."

"Like what?" Her voice was gentle.

"You can't work in a catless office," I said.

She smiled for real then. "I'm going to miss both of you."

"We'll miss you. I don't know what we'll do without you." Her dark eyes glistened. "I'm sorry. I don't mean to make you feel bad. You have to do what's best for you and Jordy."

"I know." We sat in silence. Lulu hopped up into her lap, pushing her small black head against Robin's hand, and that was when we both started to cry.

I walked around the desk to hug her. "You're going to do great," I whispered.

"So will you," she whispered back. "That's the one thing I feel bad about—leaving before you're through all this."

"Don't worry about me. I'll be okay." I gave her another squeeze. "Now, get back to work. You only have two weeks to put my files in perfect order."

Tear tracks glistened on her cheeks, but she smiled tremulously. "I'd need a whole lot more than two weeks for that." She bent to kiss the cat in her lap. "You're going to have to take of her now, Little One," she said. Then, she handed Lulu to me, and she returned to her office.

*****

The November 30 hearing was postponed when Scott Frazier ended up with food poisoning after his mother-in-law's holiday weekend open house. Geoff said Frazier suspected the crab puffs. The next date everyone was available was the thirteenth. "There's nothing sooner?" I asked when Geoff called. Waiting was torture. One way or another, I needed resolution. Because the writing was on the wall: if I didn't come out of this hearing with flying colors, I'd be finished at the Lundstrom Law Firm.

The firm had been my family for nine years. Now, I felt like the estranged wife of a favored son. I barely saw Michael because he was working nonstop, handling nearly all the firm's litigation matters. My other partners were polite, but no more. When Eckert sent around the annual email detailing holiday functions at which the firm needed a representative, I offered to attend the same ones I'd handled last year; he responded an hour later that those functions were already covered. I ate lunch in my office with Lulu. The staff edged away when I approached. Robin tried to be supportive, but she was busy organizing everything for her successor—assuming, of course, I was there to need one. When I broached the subject of hiring a replacement with Michael, he said, "You may want to hold off."

The door was opening wider each day. Unless something changed, I would be shoved out.

And still, not a word from Ralph.

"So you lied. He was willing to give up everything for you—and you couldn't trust him enough to tell the truth."

Mitch's words rang in my ears at odd moments. I had no idea what he'd meant. What did trusting Ralph have to do with telling the truth?

Once Scott Frazier recovered from his crab puff debacle, Geoff tried to negotiate, but Frazier figured he had me dead to rights. Geoff and I spent an afternoon preparing for the hearing. I didn't mention the reindeer. He had enough to deal with.

But late at night, when practically every channel showed *The Santa Clause* and *Rudolph the Red-Nosed Reindeer*, I compared Hollywood's depiction to the North Pole I'd seen. Ralph's version wasn't anything like the movies, but strangely, I liked it better. Elves in sparkly red and green might be cute, but the elves I saw were doing jobs, and their sensible work clothes reflected that. The décor wasn't elaborate with high ceilings and gilt and glitter; it was more like a

Scandinavian manufacturing plant, clean and pleasant, low-ceilinged and energy-efficient. Resources and supplies didn't appear from nowhere; they were procured by a dedicated team headed up by a slender, elegant woman with silver hair. No plump white-haired grandma smelling of freshly-baked cookies here—this Mrs. Claus was an executive who never lost sight of the ultimate goal, even when her single-mindedness meant chaos for bystanders and lawyers.

The Pole wasn't sparkles and candy canes, garland and carols. It was logical, functional, practical. Real people working at real jobs to support the mission of a great and generous man.

But it was also elves. Family. Cocoa and cookies. Caring. Commitment. Joy. Love.

There were still a thousand unanswered questions: *Why don't more people believe? Haven't other Santas gotten caught? How do parents explain the presents they know they didn't buy? How can anybody live in a place with no land mass? What about kids who ask for impossible things, like ponies or a million dollars or a new daddy? Where do the Clauses get the money to buy supplies so they can make toys and feed elves and live in such a strange place?*

Time was when even one unanswered question would have been a deal breaker, proof that the Pole wasn't real. Because I lived in the world of the law, of reason and logic and evidence. Of things that could be seen and touched, read and studied, analyzed and dissected, measured and evaluated. Even David Copperfield could be explained. No room in my mind, in my heart, for the unknown. The unimaginable. The inexplicable.

Until that December night when I took off my goggles to find myself surrounded by the night sky.

It was like Father Verona said in catechism all those years ago, about faith being confidence in things hoped for, evidence of things not seen. Faith was a mystery, he said. But it was also a decision. To believe was to make a choice.

I saw what was there, in that sleigh and at the Pole. Heard it. Smelled, tasted, touched. Felt the essence of that world. Marveled at its joyfulness. Admired its beauty. Reveled in its spirit. I still didn't know everything—far from it—but what I did know, I couldn't explain away, and I was tired of trying. Somewhere along the way, the rigid clay vessel of conviction had cracked, and certainty was seeping out, leaving room for light and air, delight and surprise and wonder—and magic.

There was no other explanation. Only a choice to be made.

In the quiet of my home and the tumult of my heart, I finally admitted the truth I'd struggled against for nearly a year.

The North Pole I'd seen was real. So was Ralph. And so were the reindeer.

Which could mean only one thing.

So was Santa.

Fifty-Six

On the morning of the third hearing, I woke to a gentle snowfall. Overnight, my condo complex had been transformed into a Christmas card. Soft, moist white clung to evergreen branches. Birds darted to and from the suet feeder hanging from the post on the deck rail. Harry and David sat by the window watching, their tails swishing fiercely.

I might have seen the picturesque precipitation as a good sign if it hadn't been the first snowfall of the year. It is a little-known fact that the summer sun melts the lobe of the Connecticut brain where winter driving skills are stored. As a result, traveling our roads during a December snowstorm takes twice as long as in February. This morning was no exception, especially once the lovely snow began to change to a nasty wintry mix of snow and sleet. At seven-thirty, Geoff texted that the hearing was pushed back to ten o'clock due to the weather. I left anyway, and I barely arrived on time, my already-frayed nerves jangling.

Any hopes that the storm would keep people away were dashed when I pulled into the parking lot. I tried to tell myself all those cars couldn't possibly be there for me, but when I walked into the hearing room, the gallery was nearly full.

No sign of any Claus. I didn't know if this was good or bad.

Scott Frazier started precisely as I'd expected, pelting me with questions with the force of the sleet that had rattled against my windshield. "When was the last time you saw Ralph Claus?"

"November 2."

"When you were here on November 15, you denied having seen

him since before the November 1 hearing, isn't that correct?"

My stomach twisted, but I kept my voice steady. "Yes."

"So you weren't truthful, were you?"

"No." It wasn't a whisper, but it wasn't a shout, either.

"I'm sorry, I couldn't hear you," said Frazier even though we all knew he could. He was playing to the gallery. "Did you say that when you were here last time and you testified that you hadn't seen Ralph Claus since before the first hearing, that testimony—which was given under oath—was false?

"Yes." I had to fight to keep my voice up.

"Even though you'd taken an oath to tell the truth, the whole truth, and nothing but the truth?"

"That's correct." Out of the corner of my eye, I saw Geoff square his shoulders, a cue to me to do likewise. I sat up straighter and faced my accuser.

"You're an officer of the court, aren't you?"

"Yes."

"And yet you came into this proceeding and lied under oath, isn't that true?"

Geoff objected to the question—asked and answered, argumentative, badgering the witness—but it didn't matter. He was trying to protect me, but I was beyond protecting.

Frazier shifted his focus. "Have you communicated with Ralph Claus since November 2?"

"No."

"Do you know where he is?"

I hesitated. "I haven't been in contact with him since November 2, so I can't be certain." With a few short weeks until Christmas, I assumed he was at the Pole, but who knew? He could be in China picking up computer chips.

Frazier moved closer to the witness stand. "Do you have a reasonable belief as to where he is?"

"Yes." His closeness felt oppressive.

He took another step. He was barely arm's-length from the witness stand. I could smell his Old Spice. His face filled my visual field as he leaned closer and asked, "To the best of your knowledge and belief, where is Ralph Claus?"

I offered up a mental apology to Geoff. He said to tell the truth, but there was no way he was expecting this truth. I drew a deep breath and said, loudly and clearly, "The North Pole."

The room erupted. "Order!" called Jacques St. Pierre. Hearing officers didn't have gavels, but Jacques could bellow when he needed to. "Order!"

The crowd settled down to a murmur. Frazier glared at me. "Are you trying to make a mockery of these proceedings?"

"No, sir," I said. "You asked for the truth."

"Why should we believe such a ridiculous answer? You've already said that the last time you were here, you lied even under oath. Why should we believe you're telling the truth now?"

"Because she is."

The words came from the back of the room. All heads turned. Frazier moved slightly, and I saw the lithe young man in Claus-black striding up the aisle. When he reached the front, Mitch winked at me. His message was clear: *I'll take it from here.*

"Young man, sit down," said St. Pierre. "Do not disrupt these proceedings."

"Too late," said Mitch. "Do you want the truth, or don't you?"

"Mitch, don't," I said. Visions of Mitch being led off in handcuffs filled my mind. I didn't know whether he had Houdini powers.

Mitch shrugged ever so slightly. "I've got orders."

St. Pierre turned to me. "What's going on here? Do you know this person?"

"Yes, sir," I said. "His name is Mitch Claus."

Geoff rose. "May I have a word with my client?" At St. Pierre's nod, Geoff approached my chair, waiting for Frazier to step back out of earshot before he whispered, "Who is this kid?"

"Ralph's brother," I whispered back. "I didn't know he'd be here again."

"What's he going to say?"

"No idea." Mitch was still standing between the counsel tables. His stature reminded me of a soldier ready for battle. "Call him," I said suddenly. Geoff's eyes widened, and I repeated, "Call him."

Geoff stepped back. "Mr. St. Pierre, at this time, I respectfully ask that we take this witness out of order. I believe his testimony may serve to speed the matter along."

"Considering this is day three, that's a worthy reason," said St. Pierre. Over Frazier's objection, I left the witness stand, and Mitch stood by the chair. He raised his right hand and swore to tell the truth, the whole truth, and nothing but the truth.

"State your name and address for the record, please," said St. Pierre.

"Mitch Claus. The North Pole." His face was serious now.

"Mr. St. Pierre, he's already mocking the tribunal," protested Frazier.

"No, I'm not," said Mitch. "You wanted the truth. That's the truth."

"Are you Santa Claus?" Geoff asked.

Mitch snorted. "Don't you think I'm a little young to be Santa?"

"Answer the question," said St. Pierre. He sounded stern, but Mitch appeared unflapped. I tried to catch his eye to remind him Geoff was on my side.

"No. I'm not Santa," Mitch said.

"But you said your name was Claus, and you live at the North Pole."

"That doesn't automatically make somebody Santa," Mitch said. "There are a lot of us Clauses up there, but there's only one Santa."

Geoff tried a different tack. "What is your relationship to Ralph Claus?"

"He's my brother."

"Do you know where he is now?"

Mitch looked as if he wanted to roll his eyes. "At the Pole. I don't know if you noticed, but Christmas is next weekend. That's not much time. It's a big world, and there are lots of kids. We've got to finish getting ready. By the way," he added, gesturing to Frazier, "if you keep this up, you're getting coal in your stocking. I'll see to it personally."

"Mr. St. Pierre!" Frazier was nearly apoplectic. "They're turning this hearing into a circus!"

Geoff interjected, "I don't have any control over this witness. All I can do is ask the questions. The witness will answer as he chooses, and it will be up to Mr. St. Pierre to decide whether he finds the witness's testimony credible." As if there were a chance of that. St. Pierre might be from New Orleans, with its reputation for myth and mysticism, but he wasn't crazy.

Frazier sat down in a huff. Geoff continued, "Do you know the respondent, Attorney Megan Riley?"

"Yes."

"When did you last see her?"

"You mean, before right now? A few weeks ago. I was at the last hearing."

On cross, Frazier picked up this line of questioning. "Why have you been attending these hearings? To make sure Attorney Riley didn't say anything about your brother's whereabouts?"

Mitch shook his head as if to suggest Frazier couldn't possibly have understood. "I was sent here in case she needed help—which, now that I see how you do things, was a good idea."

Frazier crossed his arms. "You were sent here? By whom? Santa Claus?"

"Yes."

Mitch's voice was quiet with authority. Frazier seemed taken aback. The room was silent. The usual movement in the gallery ceased. Frazier approached Mitch the same way he'd done with me. As he opened his mouth to speak, a gravelly voice called, "Hey, Mitch! We gotta go!"

We all turned around. There in the center aisle stood Charles. His black parka was dripping. "Sorry to interrupt, folks, but the weather's getting bad. C'mon, Mitch. We gotta get moving. Hey, counselor," he added as he spotted me.

Mitch started to rise, but Frazier wasn't that easily defeated. "Mr. St. Pierre, I ask that the witness be taken into custody."

"What!" I blurted out.

"What are you talking about, Mr. Frazier?" asked St. Pierre.

"He knows where Ralph Claus is," said Frazier. "For all we know, that's who sent him here. He could be harboring an escaped convict." A murmur began in the gallery.

"Order!" St. Pierre called, and the murmur subsided.

Mitch regarded St. Pierre. "Look, I hate to cut this short when we're having such a good time, but I have work to finish."

"The witness can and should be detained for questioning," Frazier insisted.

"Absolutely not," I said, rising. Geoff placed his hand on my arm, the universal signal from attorney to client for *shut up*. Like practically every client I'd ever known, I ignored it. "Mr. Claus is not under subpoena. He came here voluntarily, and he can leave if he wants to."

"And if he stays, he's going to invoke his right against self-incrimination, and he won't be giving any more testimony," added Geoff, eyeing Mitch meaningfully. The youngest Claus brother looked to me for direction. When I nodded, Mitch said, "Yeah, that's right. I'm doing what he said."

St. Pierre regarded Frazier. "You can't require a witness to incriminate himself," the hearing officer said. "Especially when you're talking about possible criminal charges."

"Look, I don't know what you're talking about, but he's gotta come back," Charles said. "There's a glitch with a bunch of tablets that're going to Spain. Mitch is the only guy who can get them fixed in time. We need him in the workshop now."

Mitch rose from the stand. Frazier snapped, "I didn't dismiss you."

Mitch shrugged. "Whatever. I've told you everything." To St. Pierre, he said, "She was protecting my brother. That's all. She didn't do anything wrong." He started toward the gallery, and Frazier grabbed him by the arm. Mitch froze. In a low, menacing voice, he said, "Take. Your. Hand. Off. Me." I couldn't see his face, but it must have been impressive, because Frazier turned pale and wide-eyed. He released his grip on Mitch and stepped back, mumbling what sounded like an apology.

"See you, Meg. Merry Christmas!" Mitch headed up the aisle. "Let's go," he said to Charles, and the two were out the door before anyone could gather the presence of mind to stop them.

"Wait!" Frazier sprang to life, sprinting up the aisle and bursting through the door into the hallway. Moments later, he returned looking perplexed. "They're not out there."

"Beg pardon?" St. Pierre asked. "You sure?" But he looked more amused than surprised.

"They're not there. They're not in the hall." Frazier sounded dazed.

Most of the crowd scrambled to their feet and stampeded the hall. Victoria Leopold and her handler whispered furiously. St. Pierre sat back, a smile playing on his lips. Geoff peered at me as we listened to people thundering up and down the long hallway as if they might find Mitch and Charles in an alcove—except that there weren't any alcoves. No nooks, no crannies. When you left the hearing room, you walked at least ten feet before coming to the next doorway, and if no one was in that room, the door would be locked. Realistically, a person leaving this hearing room would travel at least thirty feet before reaching the first opportunity to turn a corner. Frazier had been out of the room too fast for Mitch and Charles to reach that corner, even if they'd been running—which they weren't.

Spectators began to trickle back. St. Pierre called for order. Frazier took his seat and snuck worried sidewise looks at me, as if I were a witch or a space alien. St. Pierre directed me to resume the stand. As I rose, Geoff asked me in a low voice, "Do you know where they went?"

"The North Pole. You heard Charles. Those tablets aren't going to fix themselves." With that, I returned to the stand so a pony-tailed hearing officer from New Orleans could determine my fate.

*****

Afterward, I couldn't remember how the hearing ended. In the hallway, the crush of reporters was hot and thick, their shouted questions hammering my sensibilities. Geoff steered me through the jungle of microphones to the front doors. We negotiated the slippery steps down to the sidewalk, huddling under Geoff's umbrella as we made our way across the slick parking lot to my car. As I fumbled for my keys, Geoff spoke for the first time since we'd left the building: "Well. You don't see that every day."

"Mitch was really something." My gloved fingers located the key fob in the bottom of my purse.

"Not him—you. You basically testified that you believe in Santa Claus," said Geoff. He glanced over his shoulder. The media leeches were climbing into their vans. Even so, he lowered his voice. "Just between us—were you telling the truth?"

"I was under oath." The door lock released. I tossed my briefcase and purse into the car.

"That's not what I asked."

I turned to face him squarely. "Yes. I was telling the truth."

The corner of his mouth tipped up. All he said was, "Drive safely." Before I could thank him for everything, he was making his way across the ice-crusted pavement to his Jaguar. I ducked into my car and slammed the door shut. Sleet pelted the windshield. I turned the defroster to high. As I waited for the windshield to clear, I checked my phone; the top news item was that all non-essential state employees were being sent home due to the weather. I sat in my slowly-warming car, wipers squeaking against the glass, as the parking lot emptied around me. Then, I went home to wait.

Fifty-Seven

If the world had felt compelled to weigh in after my last hearing, that was nothing compared to the emails and letters and phone calls that flooded my home and office this time. Strangers reviled me for lying under oath, making a mockery of the hearings, screwing my client, and generally being the worst person since Hitler. Reporters accused me hiring an actor to say he was from the North Pole. People posing as new clients came in to ask questions about Santa Claus. A cluster of crazies wanted me to speak at their pro-Santa rally on Christmas Eve. Our tech guys had to shut down my office e-mail address after somebody sent me an infected attachment.

My brother called again, but the distance between us was too well-entrenched for him to provide any real comfort or support. I felt like a mourner when a distant friend of the deceased sends a sympathy card: *Thanks for the thought.*

Holly didn't call. She didn't email. She didn't text. She didn't show up at my door with a bottle of wine or a plate of brownies. It was as though she'd died, only worse, because at least if she'd died, her silence would have been involuntary. As I sprawled on the sofa with the cats night after night, the silence was deafening. More than once, I punched the phone's "talk" key, just to see if there was a dial tone. There always was.

Nothing from Ralph. I told myself they were Christmas-busy, but surely Mitch had told him what happened. After everything I'd been through, couldn't he have carved out a minute to get in touch? Still, not a word.

Eckert had words, though. Plenty of them. So did Elsa, and even

Roy. It boiled down to this: I'd disgraced the firm. My outrageous conduct could not be tolerated any longer. I'd compromised the firm's reputation, possibly beyond repair. If they were going to rebuild, they needed to demonstrate that they were serious about fixing the damage I'd inflicted. It was in everyone's best interests to make a change. They took a vote. Three to one, and I knew who'd stuck up for me. Roy would run the numbers to see what I was owed, but I was out, effective December 31.

"Including that cat," Elsa said.

I fought, but my heart wasn't in it. I negotiated a return of my buy-in, which gave me some ready cash for setting up my new office since the chance of being hired by an established firm was pretty much nonexistent. If Rick could resurrect his career, so could I.

Assuming the Statewide Grievance Committee said I still had one.

I should have gone to the Pole. It wasn't as though I had much left to lose here.

Except that as ragged as my world had become, I still wanted it. I wanted the career and the life I'd worked so long and hard to build. Maybe I'd just spent too long in the Land of Steady Habits. Maybe I'd forgotten how to take a chance.

Even my efforts to escape into Jane Austen were futile. Fluffy-headed Emma Woodhouse mused, "Wickedness is always wickedness, but folly is not always folly.—It depends upon the character of those who handle it." As I read the line, Holly's words echoed: *Everybody is entitled to one breathtaking piece of folly in their lives. But you have to choose well, because it will need to last you your entire life.*

No two ways about it—I'd had my folly. Whether I'd chosen well, whether I had the character to handle it . . .that remained to be seen.

In the guest room, I lay down on the braided rug. Lulu peered at me from under the bed. "You have to come out sometime," I said. "I know the guys can be scary, but they're really good boys. You'd like them if you just gave them a chance. Besides, you're going to choke on all that dust." But Lulu wasn't one for change, either.

I finished cleaning out my office on the twenty-third. Drew and a couple of his buddies moved my furniture and law books to my basement; I took the tea set and Holly's watercolor in my car. When the guys were done, I offered them beer and cash. They took the beer and tried to refuse the money, but I insisted. When they were gone, I went back to the office and climbed the stairs.

The room where I'd spent so much of my life echoed. No phones rang, no messages beeped. Dust bunnies softened the corners. The faint odor of cat litter wafted from the bathroom. My footsteps clacked on the bare floor as I walked over to Robin's former office. That furniture and computer belonged to the firm, but with no boxes or files—not so much as a pad and pen—it was stark and lifeless, as though someone had died there.

"I thought I'd find you up here," said a familiar cherished voice.

For anybody but Michael, I'd have tried to manufacture a smile. "Yeah."

"Drew and the guys do okay?"

"They were great." I wanted to be stoic, but the words came out in spite of my best intentions: "You ever think it would come to this?"

"Never." Anyone else would have said something like, *But you've got great things ahead of you.* Michael knew better than to bullshit me.

"What brings you up here?" I asked finally.

"Ruby says, come to supper." The familiar *fix-Meg* response.

"No, thanks. I'm not feeling real social." An understatement if ever there was one.

"So don't talk. She wants to feed you, that's all. She'll do all the talking." Which would undoubtedly avoid even a breath of verboten topics—Christmas, the law, and the future.

"Tell her thanks, but really—no. I don't have it in me right now. Maybe after Christmas."

"What are you doing for Christmas?" he asked, as casually as if his coming up here wasn't a set-up for this very question.

"Derek called. They're going to Boston. Invited me to go along."

"And you said 'no'." I never could fool Michael.

"I'm tired. I just want to sleep for a week and wake up to find this was all a dream."

"Want to go for a beer first?"

I shook my head. "Not tonight. I'm going to go home and crash. Try and get Lulu to come out from under the bed. Figure out what I want to be when I grow up."

"You can be a lawyer. I have a hunch you'd be good at it."

"From your lips to Jacques St. Pierre's ears," I said. "It's so weird to think my entire profession is in one man's hands. If he decides the lying was too big a deal. . . ." Tears welled up, and I turned away so Michael wouldn't see.

"Come here," he said, turning me back. He hugged me, and the dam broke. I clung to him as storms of weeping wracked my body. When I finally quieted, I rested my wet, snotty face on his shoulder as he stroked my hair.

The early winter sunset accented the bare branches outside the window. Incredible to think I'd never stand here again, never swivel in my chair to watch the sun set over the rooftops. "You should move up here," I said suddenly.

"Hadn't thought about it," he said, clearly uncomfortable. The body was barely cold.

"You should. The penthouse is the best. Besides, I'd hate to think of Elsa up here. God only knows what Desirée would do to the place."

"Elsa would never move," Michael said. "She likes being in the middle of things. But she's not your problem anymore."

"True. I've got a shitload of problems, but at least she's not one of them." The room was growing darker. "I think I could use that drink after all. Just promise me one thing."

"Anything."

"I want to go someplace that doesn't have Christmas decorations."

Michael slung his arm around my shoulders. "Deal." He led me out to the landing. I looked back once to see the setting sun peeking through the black branches. Then, I walked down the stairs for the last time.

Now

The young man in Claus black rises from beside my fireplace, favoring me with that familiar crooked half-smile. "Don't tell Ralphie," Mitch says. "He'd never let me hear the end of this."

"He's not with you?"

Mitch shakes his head. "It's Christmas Eve. He has a job to do."

"So do you, and you're here." A tear trickles down my cheek. "Damn," I mutter. More tears follow, and he hands me the tissue box from the coffee table. "Do you know where he is?"

"Norway, maybe. Ted did the flight plans." But Mitch looks past me, and his grin broadens. "I should have known. By the way, this stop wasn't on the list of specials."

"It's my list. I get to put on any stops I want." I whirl, and there he stands, resplendent in deep red velvet and white fur. The dress uniform, just as Charles said. The suit for the "specials."

It's only been a few weeks, but there's something different about Ralph now. It's not just the clothes. There's a glow in his eyes I've never seen before. The air around him shimmers, almost as though he's surrounded by tiny sparkling snowflakes. His hair is still dark, and he's still trim, but there's no mistaking who he is. Who he was always meant to be.

I reach up to touch Ralph's face. "You grew a beard." Unlike all the pictures, his beard is closely trimmed and mainly dark, with just a few gray hairs.

"It's a tradition. Pop shaves his off right after Christmas, but I might keep it."

"When does it turn white?"

"I imagine that depends," he says. "On how much grief I get from a certain lawyer." He leans down to kiss me, and his facial hair tickles. In his ear, I murmur, "I think I'm going to like this beard." To my delight, he blushes. Behind me, Mitch hoots, "Oh, man! He's turning all red! What did you say?" He starts singing, "I Saw Mommy Kissing Santa Claus."

"Shut up, you punk Claus!" Ralph says, but he's laughing, too. "You're supposed to be in Pennsylvania by now. Move it!"

"Yes, sir! Anything you say, sir!" Mitch salutes, still laughing. He jerks his thumb toward the hearth. "Your gift's over there. Merry Christmas!" He plants a kiss on my cheek, and an instant later, he's gone.

"I'm sorry I couldn't get in touch sooner," Ralph says. "With everything so hectic with Pop, and I didn't want to mess anything else up for you. . . ."

"How's your dad doing?" I ask with some hesitation. If the answer is bad, I don't want to make him say it now.

"He's better now, but his speech is affected, and he has a harder time getting around. So—" Ralph holds out his arms to display his suit.

"—you're Santa Claus," I say slowly. The decision has been made.

"Pop says 'hi.' He really liked you and Holly. He wants you two to come back for more cocoa and cookies."

"Huh?" I wonder if Ralph's father's stroke has affected his mind.

"When you were up at the Pole. You guys met him, remember?"

"I never met Santa Claus. Nobody would tell me where he was."

"Sure you did. Remember when you and Holly went to get cocoa and you ran into him?"

I think back to that night. We'd been wandering around, and we'd encountered— "Julian? That's your father?"

"That's Pop," says Ralph.

"But—I had no idea." I feel as dazed as when I first arrived at the Pole all those months ago. "I turned that place upside down looking for Santa. Why didn't he tell us who he was?"

"It wouldn't have mattered. If you'd believed, you'd have known when you saw him." He searches my face. "What about now? Do you believe now?"

"Yes." It's strange and fantastic, utterly devoid of logic or reason, but I do. Maybe it was the reindeer after all.

He kisses me. "Listen, I have to run, but we need to talk." His eyes are serious. "I love you, but coming back here—it's not an option anymore."

"I know." I knew from the moment I saw the suit. It was made for him, or vice versa.

"Once Christmas is over, maybe you can come up for a visit," he ventures.

"I could do with some time away from here." The events of the past few months rush through my mind like a swarm of hornets, and I burrow my head against his luxurious red suit.

"That reminds me," he says. "I have a special gift for you, but technically, you're not supposed to have it yet, so you can't tell anybody I gave it to you now."

"Who would I tell?" Who could I possibly call and say, *Gee, look at this great gift Santa Claus brought for me*? Holly, maybe. She'd appreciate it. But I won't, because Santa Claus said not to.

He reaches into his suit pocket and draws out an envelope. My heart thumps when I see the return address: *Statewide Grievance Committee.* "Don't worry," he says. "We didn't steal it out of the mail or anything like that."

"Then how—?" I turn the envelope over in my hands.

"It's like I told you a long time ago. Believers are everywhere." He kisses my forehead. "Go ahead. Open it."

My hands are trembling. I tear open the envelope and unfold the document. I skim the beginning, and then turn to the second page for the findings, conclusion, and order.

"A reprimand," I breathe. "For lying under oath. And that's all."

"You can go back to practicing law any time. Tonight, if you want." Later, when I read the decision more closely, I'll see that although St. Pierre disapproved of some of my actions, he did not find that they rose to the level of warranting professional discipline. He's not saying I was right, but I can live with that. The important part is that I'm still a lawyer. I have real options. If I decide to go to the Pole now, it will be a choice made of my own free will, not something I did because all else failed. I can stay, or I can go. It's up to me.

I kiss Ralph—Santa—again, long and deep. When we come up for air, I whisper, "This is the best Christmas present I ever got."

He gestures over my shoulder. "Better than that?"

I turn around to see Harry and David sitting on the hearth, watching us—with Lulu in the middle. I catch my breath as Harry licks her head and she allows it. "Well, look at you three," I say. "The lions and the lamb." I start toward the fireplace.

"I've really got to get going," Ralph says. "Merry Christmas. I'll call you."

"Wait," I say, turning back. "Did you—"

But he's already gone, leaving only a few sparkling snowflakes drifting in the Christmas night.

ACKNOWLEDGMENTS

Nowadays, we hear that it takes a village to do practically anything. I can't speak for other writers, but I can assure you that without my village, this book would never have made the transition from idea to reality.

First, many thanks to all those who shared their knowledge and experience about a wide variety of subjects: Kathleen Morrison Grover, Esq.; my friend, Dan; John Dzen, Jr.; Andrew J. Cates, Esq.; Vincent A. Balardi, Esq.; Marjorie Drake, Esq.; Chuck 2.0 Landau; the public relations folks at the Connecticut Department of Corrections. Any inconsistencies between my book and reality are my doing, not theirs.

Also, many thanks to Susan Schoenberger and my classmates at the Mark Twain House and Museum, who were the first to see any part of this book and encouraged me to keep going; and Rosemary James of the Faulkner Society, who took time from her myriad other responsibilities to read this book and tell me she loved it.

Enormous thanks to those generous souls who read and commented on this work at divers times during the process: Dawn Campisi Hoffman, Pat Grubb, Jill Fletcher, Kathleen Morrison Grover, Carol Huss, Lois Lake Church, David Handler. Thanks and hugs to everyone who advised, encouraged, educated, and cheered me on throughout my writing journey, including (but not limited to): Joan Trautman, Sue Miske, Cathy Zenka, Eliz Davoli, Will Clark, Graham Drake, Karen Downey, Kay Roseen, Mary Tuomey, Matthew I. Bishop, Donna Seeley Ulloa, Alex Ulloa, Joan Schlottenmeier, Nancy Bell, Jennifer Moss, Debbie Stock, Debbie Peacock, Clare Lucrece, Brian Lewis, and Sarah Hayes Gilligan. To my beloved aunt, Betty Bernett, and my dear friend, Charles Daehnke, both of whom have gone on ahead, my eternal gratitude for your love and support.

Special thanks to the generous and talented Christine Penney and Kayla Martel for helping me to look like a real author; to the artists at Design for Writers and Polgarus Studios for helping this volume to look like a real book; and Meghan, Ernio, and everyone at River Bend Bookshop in Glastonbury, Connecticut, who champion writers and readers alike.

To my parents, David and Shirley Burgh, who have loved, supported, and encouraged me even when they weren't quite certain what I was doing or why, I can only offer unending thanks and love, always.

Finally, to Olivia, Ned, Rosie, Danny, and Charlotte: Mama loves you, and she thanks you for inspiring her and for your patience. Now, stop fussing. Dinner's nearly ready.

ABOUT THE AUTHOR

P. Jo Anne Burgh is an author, lawyer, musician, and cat lover. Her short stories have appeared in a variety of anthologies and journals. She lives in Connecticut.

You are welcome to visit her at pjburgh.com, as well as on Facebook (P. Jo Anne Burgh, Author), Twitter (@PJoAnneBurgh), and Instagram (@pjoanneburgh).

Printed by Amazon Italia Logistica S.r.l.
Torrazza Piemonte (TO), Italy

16466205R00223